The Dragons
of
Wyvern Hall

The Dragons
of
Wyvern Hall

NANCY WOLFF

Cover design by Bernard Pearson,
using elements from
Solomandra © Dreamstime.com

ACKNOWLEDGEMENTS

I want to thank a number of friends, who have read the chapters in all their versions— you know who you are. These especially include Nicole, who introduced me to self-publishing; Laurie and Deborah and Joy, who read very fast and begged me to get a move on; my cousins Robin and Sandra, and my friends Tish, Clare, Helen and José.

And Sir Terry Pratchett, who made me laugh and think deeply and whose Discworld universe has given me amazing friends and a safe harbour in which to incubate this novel.

Special thanks go to my friend Roger Marston, who did the donkey work of proofreading, and who, to my surprise (he'd never heard of Young Adult Fantasy) then turned out to like the book.

Huge thanks also to Bernard Pearson, who designed the wonderful cover.

Prologue

The Dragon King is old—dragons live a very long time, centuries as children and adolescents, but thousands, even millions, of years as adults. Chen Shi doesn't remember how old he is, even though now, playing the part of central heating furnace for a large fake-gothic castle, he has all the time in the world to think. He remembers…oh yes, he remembers. The beauty of young dragons, lithe and dainty as fairies or butterflies (if a fairy or butterfly could be some 60 feet long). He remembers spring nights when this world was young, so young that it was spring all year long. Where swamp gases were luminous and the things with huge teeth that lurked in the rippled waters were something you teased and taunted to excite the girls. A big dragon, an important dragon, had little to fear on this ancient earth. He could stride through swamp and plain, leaving deep footprints, and trailing his wings through the grasses as he spread them to subdue and delight in equal measure his fawning subjects. T. rex bowed before him, the great Brontosaurus stepped nimbly aside when he swept by. Youth and strength and hubris. He could dive as deep in the oceans as a blue whale, spring from the waves into the air and span whole countries with a single wing beat. Or so it seemed to him now peering back through the mists of time.

Such are the dreams of an old dragon, tethered within a cavernous cellar on a bed of old iron and rusting garden furniture by evil magic. Such is the way he passes the long warm months as the world turns and he grows weak without food. Because they live for centuries, even eons—so much longer than the thoughts of a mere mortal could even begin to encompass—like the life of a star or a planet, so far beyond anything we could imagine, dragons are very good at entertaining themselves when circumstances decree they be still. Chen Shi had once, more than once, off and on through many, many long times, dwelt in great caverns hung with stalactites of impossible richness of colour, lying, not on rusty bedsprings and old wheelbarrows, but on great collections of gold and jewels, just as dragons were always thought to do.

Dragons as a species are not prone to anger. Oh, they can get angry, and when they do it is wise to be somewhere else, far far away. If possible several continents away actually. But as a rule a dragon is a patient, though never a docile, creature. Living for eons, patience is more than a virtue, it is a necessity.

Chapter 1

Lying face down in the grass, Kate was flicking her tongue in and out as fast as she could. Which wasn't very fast, and quickly became very tiring. *How do you do it?* she demanded silently of the little lizard a few inches from her nose. Not that it was flicking its tongue, rather it was basking, just as she was, silent and drowsy in the unexpected warmth of the spring sun.

The lizard with its golden-brown skin and bright eye was one of the first things she'd really noticed since setting foot in England some two weeks ago. Before that had been the dreadful time when they told her that her grandmother Lucinda was dead and that she was to be uprooted once more. She had heard Lucinda use that term, and ever since in her imagination she could see, could even seem to feel, her tender white roots being torn up from the soil. *No wonder I droop*, she thought, remembering the nurses and teachers who deplored her posture. *I'm always being transplanted. I'm always in shock.* (She wasn't above playing it for dramatic effect).

In shock, she thought, but also thought of the tough, brown bigger roots that even then she knew she had. As lost as she sometimes felt, as real as the pain and confusion were, those roots were also real, and she knew that with any kind of reasonable care she was a survivor. But plants do die if they are put in the wrong kind of soil, she might have said, and some of the places her mother had left her were certainly wrong for her. And so she had drooped, and defied and refused.

I was the bane of Mrs. Thorp's existence, she now thought with some satisfaction. "I have had thirty-five years' experience in dealing with children," Mrs. Thorp had said. "But Katherine is beyond me, quite beyond me…she has become the bane of my existence." And Mrs. Thorp had left "in a snit" as Kate's mother Amanda described it. Which made Kate, who envisioned a Snit as a small car something like a Volkswagen Beetle, giggle.

She giggled now, which startled the lizard who… who spread a collar, or, or wings, jewelled wings? and flew up into the air, then dived, disappearing under the ferns. *What the hell? Did I just see it fly? I must be seeing things*, thought Kate. *But it flew! Or maybe it just has one of those neck things, collars that inflate, and it jumped. It must have jumped…and I'm just tired.*

"Wait! Oh, damn! Sorry, please come back, I'll be quiet." she said. An only child, with her head full of fantasies and her nose always in a book, even at the age of sixteen Kate was good at being quiet. "Sullen, that's what she is," Amanda had said. "Well, at least she's quiet," the latest lover replied. "But children — teenagers — aren't supposed to be that quiet," objected her mother. "Girls Kate's age should be, oh, I don't know, active, lively." "Be thankful for small blessings," said the lover.

Am I a blessing? thought Kate now. On reflection, she knew she was not. She rolled onto her back and surveyed the expanse of herself that she could see. A rather small, skinny teenager in faded jeans and tee-shirt with a griffin on it (she loved mythical creatures), her skin was very pale. Fish-belly white, with spots (by which she meant freckles), she thought with disgust. Her hair which fell in waves to her shoulders was the colour of a new copper penny and truly beautiful, but since it had been the occasion of her being called "carrot-top", "ginger-snap" and teased for her redhead's temper, she wasn't very fond of it. And it accounted for her colouring and sensitivity to

4

the sun, which she hated. Her eyes were green, which was promising, but her lashes were pale and "rabbity" which seemed hopeless.

And my posture is bad, I'm sway-backed and potbellied, and my feet had to be fixed, assessed the pitiless Kate. Actualy she had the unconsciously arrogant posture of a young ballerina when she was unobserved. She was growing up to be a beauty, but nothing could have convinced her of this. Kate, alone in the woods near the summer cottage they had rented last year, was an elf, a sprite, a fairy princess, moving with natural grace, her skin touched with apricot by the sun, her hair a gold and copper cloud, her face alight with the gladness of being alive and free. But let someone else come on the scene, and she wilted and drew in on herself as quickly as a sea anemone at a foreign touch, leaving a sullen lump as the only reminder of what had been a shimmering flower.

"You'd be pretty if you'd just smile," her mother would say. But Kate wouldn't smile for Amanda. *I can't*, she pleaded inside herself, *it wouldn't work anyway*. But she couldn't explain and, "You see, she's just *sullen*!" Amanda would cry in exasperation. "I don't know why, she's had every advantage."

Every advantage. Her mother was beautiful, her father a handsome, intelligent, fairly wealthy man, her antecedents, as Grandmother had told her, were amongst the best and brightest. There had been nursemaids, governesses and good schools...several of them, because "Katherine doesn't get along with her peers," and "Katherine doesn't live up to her potential," and "We are sorry that we haven't been able to do more for Katherine" and also "We recommend that Katherine be enrolled in a remedial reading program."

"Well, if you won't read for them, dear child, they are going to assume you can't read," said Grandmother reasonably, when Kate cursed bitterly at the injustice of having to go in after school for reading lessons. "But I do read. I read faster and better than anyone," she might have said, and it was true, she had been reading since she was three. But it was also true that she wouldn't read aloud after a humiliating experience when she mispronounced several words and the teacher, a dried-up woman who really didn't like children and was just putting in the time to retirement, ridiculed her attempts in front of the class. So remedial reading it was, and perhaps it hadn't been so bad, because she did learn how to pronounce many of the words which until then had perforce been only in her reading, not her speaking, vocabulary. She still wasn't sure she felt comfortable calling the Banks boy in Mary Poppins "Michael" rather than her original guess at "Mitchell" (well, in a right-thinking world it would be Mich-ael, surely?). "It's a difficult language, Pumpkin," her father said, giving her a hug. "When I was small I taught myself to read too, and I was extremely surprised to find that Egypt was pronounced E-gypt and not Egg-wiped!" That made it all better somehow. She wished she could have stayed with her father, but he was always travelling and couldn't provide a properly stable home for a little girl.

Every advantage, except that her mother drank and partied too much and kept leaving for faraway places with a series of lovers that seemed to change as often as the colour of her hair. Kate had seen her father only four times since her parents divorced when she was eight, and somehow she simply hadn't got the hang of living in the world. She felt odd, and it seemed she was odd, so most people left her alone.

The last three years had been better, since she had gone to live with her Grandmother Lucinda. Lucinda seemed to understand and to offer hope. "Sweetheart, you're like a foal or a fawn, all legs and awkward bits, darling, while you find your feet. But I promise you this too shall pass, and you'll have a wonderful future before you. And your blazing intelligence that gets you teased and misunderstood now, is going to be a great source of pleasure in future. It's just right now that the world seems a strange and unpleasant place, but it will become a source of as much magic and happiness as you presently find in books. I promise you this, I do."

Grandmother (the other grandchildren called her Baba, but Kate still preferred to say Grandmother) loved gardens and gardening, even though she lived in New York City, and would take Kate with her to visit the botanical gardens, naming the plants and talking about what suited them best. It had given Kate the notion that she, too, would be all right if she were suited. I would thrive then, thought Kate. And to shut out New York City, the girls who teased and the teachers who scolded, the strange inability to please her mother or win her love, and the grief for her father, Kate would bury herself deeper in the books she loved best. Here Kate spent her days in a waking dream, in a halcyon country misted with a golden haze by day and pleasantly eerie by night. Her friends were Ratty and Mole and Toad, Mary Lennox and Colin in *The Secret Garden*, Nancy and Peggy and the Swallows. She was enamoured of the more modern fantasy novels, too, especially Terry Pratchett's Discworld series. And with Grandmother she read her all-time favourite book, *The Sword in the Stone*, about the boy Wart who became England's legendary King Arthur — and that Merlin had told the Wart "the best thing for being sad is to learn something". In fact Kate was obsessed with all things English, and loved to have Grandmother tell her about her own childhood in England. From such dreams Kate would be dragged reluctantly and somewhat crankily back to reality.

"I bet if I could get to England," she told Lucinda, "I'd fit in, I'd live up to my potential, like Miss Roberts said." And Grandmother had promised that they would go to England together to visit her brother-in-law, Admiral Sir Hugh Mallory at Ashley Manor. Kate found that repeating over and over, "We are going to stay with Sir Hugh Mallory, Ashley Manor, Devon, England, was a potent charm against the great sins of fear and despair.

"Fear limits you and despair paralyses you altogether," Lucinda would say. "They are the great sins, because they keep us from joy —and the gods meant us to be joyful."

"I will be joyful when I'm in England," Kate would reply, "When I get to Ashley Manor."

But now she was at Ashley, and so far she had felt only numbness, confusion and the exhaustion that comes with grief. "Grandmother," she cried to the sky, "You were supposed to come too!" And a tear crept out of her eye, across her cheek and into her ear, to be followed by another and another, until there was a torrent of tears, and she turned onto her stomach and cried her heart out into the ferns.

She cried for all the times in the last months that she hadn't cried. "The girl is unnatural," said the aunts, "not one tear." "Well she never loved her like we did," said the oldest cousin, "she wouldn't even call her Baba."

"But I did, oh, I did...I do... love you so much," sobbed Kate into the ferns. "Oh Grandmother, how could you do this? You weren't supposed to die! How will I go on without you?"

And like a clear little bell, she seemed to hear Lucinda's dry, amused voice. "Kate, sweetheart, I know how much you love me, as I love you. But think, darling, before when you didn't have England, it was England that was going to make living possible. Now you have England, but you don't have me, so living is still not possible. My little love, I know you must grieve, but you must also learn that the secret of living isn't in other people

8

or places, however beloved or longed for. It's inside you, Kate darling, it's all there waiting for you."

"What's inside me is a black void, and it's empty and it aches," whispered Kate.

"The secret, my love, is to take the void and sprinkle it with stars," said Lucinda gently. "But you're tired. Go to sleep, dear child."

And that was how Sir Hugh found her sometime later, a small figure asleep among the ferns in the wild garden. He had been looking for her, but coming on her unexpectedly like this, he was taken unaware, and he saw her as a young nymph or dryad, with the shimmering copper of her hair and the grace of a young fawn curled in sleep. He caught a glimpse of the beauty that was becoming hers, and the power…and something else. She looked like Lucinda. It caught at his throat and clutched at his heart. The soft groan he gave woke Kate, who was instantly again just a teenage girl, sleepy-eyed and bewildered with a tear-stained face.

"Uncle Hugh?" she faltered. "Where am I?"

"You fell asleep, Kate, here in the wild garden. Get up now, it's nearly time for tea." And he held out his hand to help her up. "Are you all right?"

"No, I'm not," she said. "But I will be." And she took his hand.

When they were gone a voice from among the trees said quietly, "Well — who would have thought it would be her?"

Chapter 2

As they came round the bend in the path, Kate was transfixed by an almost blinding radiance from across the valley. It was like a great fire, but all silvery gold with no orange flames or smoke.

"Uncle Hugh," she said in awed tones, "what is that?"

At her side, Hugh shared her wonder though he'd seen the sight before and knew what it was. "It's the Manor. Every now and again, when the sun is going down it will strike the windows at just the right angle and, if you're up here, you'll see the whole place come alight this way. It always reminds me of the sparklers and fireworks we used to have for Guy Fawkes or the Queen's birthday." And indeed the windows catching the setting sun reflected the light back prismatically, breaking it into a cascade, a veritable firework of diamond sparkles. Kate just stood, stunned at the dramatic sight of her beloved house turned into a diadem, all diamonds and gold.

But even as they watched the sun slid lower and the blinding blaze of light from the many-windowed west front of the house faded away. In its place the Manor reappeared, glowing golden now in the last rays of the sun. From up here you could see the lovely classical lines of the late 17th Century house, made of mellow golden limestone. Stone that was golden in the sun and shades of grey and beige in the rain or under cloudy skies. The slate tiles of the roof, encrusted as they were with lichen and moss in hues of gold and green and grey, blended now, after almost three centuries, with the walls in an harmonious way that couldn't have been the case when the house was new.

"It's like a precious cup in a green saucer...or a jewel on green velvet," said Kate. "Or a thrush in a nest of moss." Her look of happiness caught at his heart. He was aware that she was not a young woman who easily shared her imagination, rich as it was, with anyone. She had been too often embarrassed and ridiculed to wish to expose these private thoughts where she did not trust. That she was beginning to trust Hugh was a great joy to him.

"I have imagined," she continued, "the Manor all lit up for Christmas. Every window would be sparkling with lights, not like just now, but lights against the dark of the night, warm and glinting. And the ground would be covered with snow and the air crisp and biting, so your nose would feel crackly when you breathe."

§ § §

It is in Elizabeth's time that the Manor looks like that. Elizabeth is twenty and newly married the Christmas of 1860. It is her first Christmas as lady of the manor, and she rises to the occasion with enthusiasm. Every window sparkles with candle light, providing a warm welcome to the relatives and friends coming up the long avenue between the ancient lime trees on Christmas Eve. They come in carriages and on horseback, and a few come in sleighs riding through the new-fallen snow. As they enter the Hall, they see the Grinling Gibbons staircase wound with greenery, boxwood and pine, and set with candles and fruits, with a pineapple on the newel post to signify the hospitality of the season. In the great fire place logs the length of a man are blazing, giving off the comforting smells of apple wood and pine, and over the mantel are more arrangements of evergreen and fruit. All over the house, on mantels and walls and tables and consoles, gleam candles in tall candlesticks and elaborate wall sconces of silver and brass and bronze and silver gilt. Big

11

flower arrangements add the bracing scent of chrysanthemums and the sweetness of roses to the Christmas smell of pine and balsam and spruce, oranges and cinnamon. Under this is the smell of the house itself, the smell of wood fires, beeswax, furniture polish, baking bread, damp boots and dogs …that indefinable smell that distinguishes one family, one house from another as surely as fingerprints identify a man.

Having checked that all is well with the house, Elizabeth goes to find her sister-in-law, the irrepressible Maude. Elizabeth knocks on Maude's door. "Dearest, are you ready?"

"Elizabeth, come in. Jesse's just finishing my hair. What do you think of my dress?" Maude makes a little twirl. The iridescent greens, blues and purples and golds of her dress rustle with the sound only silk taffeta can make. "I ordered it from Worth of Paris. Isn't it the most fabulous creation?"

The bodice is embroidered with a pattern of tiny overlapping feathers in deep royal blue, pinned at the shoulders with enamelled peacock eyes. The underskirt spread over the big hoop is in shades of green and blue iridescent taffeta, the overskirt of gold tulle embroidered like the entire circular fan of a peacock's tail feathers. The effect is exotic and stunning with Maude's dark hair pulled up into a knot and ringlets with a jewelled comb in gold and emeralds.

"Oh, Maude, darling, it is, you are, exquisite. But, dearest, peacocks are supposed to be such bad luck, and it's not really the dress for someone who isn't yet married. I wish you'd asked my advice before you ordered this."

"And if I had you'd have had me in pink or peach or maybe powder blue! Elizabeth, you know you would. With roses or lilacs. And I couldn't bear it."

Elizabeth looked sadly at her sister-in-law, "Sebastian won't be pleased, and he counts on me to make sure you don't become talked about for the wrong reasons."

"Oh, cheer up, darling! I'm already being talked about for the wrong reasons! But you know I'm quite as pure as the driven snow, and I do intend to stay that way until I marry. So do stop worrying. And look at my muff — in case I get invited out onto the terrace. Isn't it just the most cunning thing?"

Elizabeth, who is in a sparkling silk and satin creation in pale blue embroidered with snowflakes and scattered with pearls, with a tiara of snowflake shapes in pearls and diamonds and small sapphires, hugs Maude and smiles because it is quite impossible to stay cross with her. Maude, with her dark hair and startling blue eyes, is herself like a bright sparkling creation from a fairy tale, so full of life and mischief that no one could help but smile. Arm in arm they proceed down the great staircase to take their places beside Sebastian and greet the arriving guests.

In the hall a footman waits to take their wraps and Morgan, the butler, announces each arrival as he ushers them into the big sitting room where an enormous spruce reaches almost to the ceiling. Among the guests that first Christmas is Sir Ivor Wyvern, newly made baronet, newly moved into his incredible Gothic Revival mansion designed in part by William Burges and in part by Sir Ivor himself. Wyvern Hall is some three miles up the valley from Ashley Manor, situated upon a pinnacle of land overlooking the river. Sir Ivor immediately has his eye on Maude, said to be the inspiration for Tennyson's poem.

"May I present my sister, Miss Maude Mallory. Maude, this is Sir Ivor Wyvern. He's built a new mansion up the valley in the Gothic Revival style I understand." Ivor bows low over Maude's hand, and she felt a tiny electric thrill as his lips just brushed her finger tips. When he straightens up she has to look up into his face. A long face with upswept eyebrows that echo the arch of his cheekbones and hazel eyes with a dark ring around the iris and a pupil that for a second was a cat-like slit. He looks like he'd been carved, not quite flesh and blood at all. But then he smiles and she was dazzled by it. Although he is dark, it is like he sparkled.

At eighteen Maude is quite taken with how his saturnine countenance and dark hair and eyes give an air of mystery and danger to this new neighbour. Elizabeth on the other hand is repelled by him, but on this night all are made welcome and she smiles warmly as Sir Ivor bends over her hand as she stands framed by candlelight like a Madonna in a Renaissance painting.

The tree too is sparkling with light and hung with hundreds of fragile hand-blown glass balls from Germany and Bohemia in the shape of Santas, pinecones, fruits, birds, angels and plain balls of green and blue and red and gold and silver. Popcorn, cranberry and tinsel garlands drape the branches and silk flowers, angels with lacy wings and carollers made of fabric scraps peep from blue-green caves among the branches. There are candles on every bough, and three servants replace them as they burn down and keep a constant vigil against fire. At the very top, Sebastian has affixed the angel. It's a wonderful angel in flowing robes of jewel-like green and gold and soft peach, its androgynous face a picture of wisdom and peace, its hair long and golden and its wings are real feathers dipped in shimmering gold. In its hands it holds a scroll. Sebastian and Elizabeth found it in Italy on their wedding trip in May.

The angel continues to grace each tree down through the years, becoming for Hugh and James and Alice and Victoria, and then for Lucinda when she marries James, a family tradition, the last thing each year to be placed on the tree. In its Renaissance splendour, it gazes down on the passage of years, on new servants, different presents, different dogs, watches Elizabeth's hair turn grey,

14

then white, sees her children grow up and marry, sees her great-grandchildren James and Hugh in school uniforms and then in Naval uniform, accepts the Christmas in 1963 when Hugh's wife Daphne decorates the tree all in white and pink. Daphne does not want the angel on this tree, but Hugh, who rarely challenges her, insists on his way in this, and the angel tops the tree, "spoiling it" says Daphne. Then Daphne is gone and Hugh and his mother have smaller trees, but the angel still graces each one. Then Hugh is alone and a tree seems a mockery for one lonely late-middle-aged man, so he stops having them, though for a year or two more he brings out the angel. The he forgets her, too, and there is no more Christmas at Ashley.

§ § §

Now, listening to Kate, Hugh remembers the angel. "We haven't kept Christmas at Ashley for years," he said, "but that could change now. By god, Kate, we will have a splendid Christmas. The kind my parents used to have…oh, they were glorious, you'd have loved them. We'll do that this year, Kate." And stopped, both of them together struck by the thought that possibly they wouldn't be at Ashley come Christmas. Their mutual dismay would have been comic if the awfulness of the situation hadn't been so real. This reality was the law suits and legal entanglements that had Ashley mortgaged to the hilt and fighting for its life against the estate of Ivor Wyvern, the same Ivor that Maude had found so compelling and Elizabeth had found repulsive. It appears that Elizabeth had the better instincts, because due to various complications, including the elopement of Maude with Ivor, he had sued first Sebastian and later his heirs, and once Ivor was dead, his own estate continued to harass Ashley, right down to the present day.

It was Kate who recovered herself first. "We will be here to keep Christmas, Uncle Hugh," she said fiercely. "I don't know how yet, but I can't believe I came this far only to be sent away again. I believe there's a good spirit in the world, and I don't think it meant me to get here, where I have always wanted to be, only to send me away so soon. The trouble is, I don't know what it does mean. It's very scary, but Grandmother always said that fear makes us blind to the new doors that are opening and our job when we are uncertain is not to give in to fear, so we can see the doors that open for us. Then it all works out for the best. I believe that if we don't get so scared that we can't see, some power greater than ourselves will show us the way to save the Manor."

"And do you know, Bates," said Hugh later as the two elderly men sat by the kitchen fire with cups of tea (an unheard of situation between master and man just a few years ago, but very comforting to Sir Hugh now), "do you know, she makes me almost believe that she, or an angel, or something, will find a way out of our difficulty. I too almost believe that she can't have come here only to have to go away. There's amazing strength in that child. Amazing grace perhaps."

"She do have the look of her grandmother about her, that she does," said Bates.

"Do you think so? Do you remember Miss Lucinda that well?"

"Oh, aye, I do that, she be a hard one to forget, that one. I remember her right well, and she were a wonder…prideful and high spirited as that chestnut hunter she loved so, for all she could seem so quiet. But you can be certain, sir, that Miss Lucinda wouldn't have let the Manor go."

"Well I hardly think even she would have been able to stop the Inland Revenue and that godawful law suit that just rolls on and on, Bates," Hugh said with some asperity. "Do you think I haven't done all that is possible?"

"Oh, no, sir, I didn't mean that," said Bates. "You've done all in your power, we none of us doubts that. But Miss Lucinda, and now Miss Kate, they believes even when there's nothing left to believe in. They are in touch with the magic, sir, and there's no accounting for what can happen then. Lookee, sir, you said yourself, the little 'un has got you believing that something will turn up."

Placated, Hugh's thoughts turned again to Lucinda. "I remember that chestnut hunter, Bates. Foxfire, Lucinda called her. Egad, it was the same colour as Lucinda's hair, and how magnificently they took the fences together."

"Yes, sir, like one sleek animal they was. I used to tell the Missus, weren't none could hold a candle to Miss Lucinda on a horse." And to himself Bates thought, what a pity it was that you let her get away. She only married James to spit in your eye because you'd been taken in by that scheming minx, Daphne. And just see how badly that turned out. Like any good servant, Bates thought a great deal that he never said but, being Bates, he said a great deal as well.

"We'll have to get Kate a horse," said Hugh, his thoughts leaping ahead over the enormous hurdle of lawsuits and back taxes, "She can ride with me this season, by God, and the County will see something they haven't seen for fifty years."

"It would be a right treat, sir, so it would," agreed Bates, knowing that this would never happen as the estate could hardly keep them and would never cover the expense of horses or hunting, even drag hunting as it was now.

And as they retired for the night neither of the old men admitted that they were comforted by the fantasy of Kate on a beautiful chestnut horse riding hell for leather through the autumn leaves, while knowing full well that

17

such a thing was well-nigh impossible. Hugh fell asleep planning to start the search for a chestnut mare, and dreamed of Lucinda on Foxfire, Lucinda in a skin-tight forest-green riding habit, looking as the cottagers said for all the world as if she'd been melted and poured into it.

Chapter 3

Having gone to sleep with a beautiful dream of times past, Hugh woke up remembering that he was having what was bound to be a stressful meeting this morning with Maggie Spenser, who had arrived back in her home town trailing degrees and tales of adventures in faraway places and a child who had surely been an infant the last time Hugh saw him (and that was only a bit ago, wasn't it?), but the kid was a teenager now, and one with plenty of attitude. Just like his mother has, thought Hugh who knew that the appointment, made against his will by Maggie herself, would be difficult and deal in subjects that he usually simply tried to put out of his mind entirely.

Sir Hugh knew Maggie Spenser from her childhood in the village and when, after university, she came back on occasional visits with a baby but no husband 'to speak of' as the village gossips said, he was pleased he could recommend her for a job at an auction house where many items of worth from Ashley had found their way into other hands.

Maggie was blond and dreamy-eyed but this was deceiving because she was brilliant and decisive. The village gossips were quickly put in their place as she made a point of showing them her infant son with his dark curly hair and gold-flecked brown eyes. "And look," she'd say, brushing his hair away from his ears "his ears are pointed, see, like one of the Fae, like Oberon in *A Midsummer Night's Dream*. That's because his father is a faerie prince and this little fellow takes after him quite a lot."

That she could claim an alliance or dalliance with a faerie prince didn't actually make them scoff, because their part of the world still held the belief in such beings —but such things were never spoken of. So she frightened them (as she'd meant to). No woman should be so bold in speaking of these things, and besides the child did have brown eyes with gold flecks and somewhat pointed ears. And as far as the rest of the world was concerned, "there's nothing like telling the truth to make them believe you are just teasing them," Maggie would say. "Who in their right mind would believe in faeries? Except in Devon, of course."

Robin Spenser therefore grew up knowing he was different, and, although he wasn't bullied or spoken of behind his back, he seemed to have a sense that he was unique in ways that were wonderful but also difficult. It sat comfortably with him in childhood but as adolescence took hold (when everyone becomes uncomfortable in their own skin for a while at least), he began to be less charming and more difficult. When his mother became aware that he was spending more and more time in the parks and gardens of the city, hanging out with what might be gangs, and that he had a pinched look and seemed to become pale somehow under his swarthy complexion, she decided it was time to move them back to Devon, back to the Combes and hills, the wildness of Dartmoor and the hidden places where the 21st century couldn't penetrate. They moved into the house Robin's father offered them.

Maggie herself was a sort of woman of all work — and a witch. Witchcraft and magic were in her blood, and she practiced the ancient arts of healing and good nutrition. But she also used it to help in her studies and all her other work. After all, she said, if you've got unusual talents, use 'em. She had a degree in the fine arts, had progressed to second to the head of old master paintings at the prestigious auction house, had run an antique shop, and she was also an amazing cook and — most unexpected — had a really good head for finance which had led her to take a degree in accountancy. Becoming aware, despite every effort on Sir Hugh's part, of the rundown state of the Manor and the skeleton staff that told its own story (and the postman occasionally commented on the letters and documents from London solicitors that he delivered), Maggie took it upon herself to beard Sir Hugh in his den where, she later told Robin, he behaved like a bear with a sore head.

"Woman!" he barked, 'I tell you none of this is your business, and I'll thank you to take yourself and your ideas away. There's nothing wrong here that I can't handle as I have always done."

"And it looks like what you've always done is refuse to acknowledge anything is wrong, and by burying your head in the sand, have let things go from bad to worse," snapped Maggie. "Don't think no one knows, because everyone does. Everyone knows there is trouble here, financial trouble, and everyone would help if they could, but your damnable pride won't let anyone near enough."

"I have not *let* anything go bad — I have done everything my solicitors advise, and things have still got worse. I am not a goddamn ostrich, madam! My head is up and my eyes see what is happening. But it's like some damn great ocean liner, or one of those awful cruise boats — it's loomed up on the horizon and is coming ever closer, and when it gets here poor old Ashley will be swamped. And now you, just a chit of a girl, want to tell me how to fix it? " You haven't the slightest idea of what we are facing here." He'd run himself to a standstill and stood now breathing heavily.

"So tell me," said Maggie, taking his hand and leading him to the big easy chair in front of the fire. "Sit down, Sir Hugh, and let me know what Ashley is facing. Because if there are things I am expert in it is art and architecture and finance. You might find someone with these talents who also happens to live nearby — and who has your best interests at heart — to be useful. So tell me, Sir Hugh, what has gone wrong."

Hugh sat with his head in his hands. "It started with my great-great-aunt Maude. She fell in love with a monster. My great-grand parents tried to forbid her to marry him, so she ran away to be with him anyway. He was furious that they didn't approve the match and vowed to ruin them. And it happened that as he got richer, Ashley Manor fell into decline. He brought lawsuits against us that continue to this day. My parents and I have had to spend fortunes fighting in the courts over boundary lines and inheritances. None of it makes good sense, but he often appears to have the law on his side. I swear I believe he buys judges y'know. And we don't even know what happened to Maude, she went to him and seemed just to disappear. There are no records of a marriage or children or of her death. For that matter there is no record of his death either, and he must be dead by now, because if he isn't he would be nearly 200 years old. Yet the solicitors continue to harass our estate just as if his malignant spirit is still pulling the strings."

"And the name of this man, or his heirs?" asked Maggie.

"Ivor Wyvern, builder of Wyvern Hall, that godawful Gothic monstrosity up the valley, only no-one can see it these days because of the walls and the woods."

Maggie felt the hairs on her body stand up. She knew the name, she did indeed. "He's the one who started Wyvern Consolidated Heating, yes?" Oh, yes, she knew of him. Her lover, who as it happened was indeed one of the Fae, had told her what he and his tribe believed about the furnaces and heating appliances Wyvern manufactured. They believed they were not furnaces in the shape of dragons, but actual dragons under an enchantment that enslaved them. It was a sickening thought, to take a beautiful being that would live for eons and force it into a state of permanent paralysis where it would breathe fire into a central heating system. Of course they were terribly

22

expensive, but as a piece of one-upmanship over the neighbours having a Wyvern Furnace was hard to beat. She knew too that he had built the enormous Victorian Gothic castle on the rocky outcrop overlooking the river that then coursed further south to run through Ashley land. She had once seen Wyvern Hall from a distance in winter and was shocked that its soaring towers were not the local limestone but a mix of red and black stones that made it sit against the setting sun like a bad nightmare. Such a man would indeed be capable of anything she thought. But these were thoughts she couldn't share with Sir Hugh.

What she did say was "Lawyers! They are like carrion crows, feasting on the bones of their clients. There aren't many truly good ones, and by the sound of it your family are in the hands of dreadful incompetents, or worse, those that are competent in fleecing their own clients."

Hugh shook his head like a wounded bear. "I can't abide them either, my dear, and can't make head nor tail of their bloody paperwork. It simply piles up like mountains. I'm not a stupid man, but those papers have me feeling like my head is on fire. So I fear I've just let them get on with it, because when once I tried to fire them I was handed such a huge bill for work and long 'explanations' of what would happen if I dropped the case that I gave in once more and just let them go on. I am nearly at the end of my rope with it all."

"Well," said Maggie, "this is where I can certainly give you a hand. I'm not fond of solicitors, but I'm very good at reading those impenetrable papers they generate — there's a trick to it, and I know the trick. Plus it's about time you got to grips with the realities of your estate in the 21st century — you've got to slim down and modernise and I've got a million ideas of how to get Ashley on a sound footing if you'll allow me to have a go."

"Maggie, I had no idea you would come home disguised as a guardian angel." And Sir Hugh smiled properly for the first time in days. "I can't pay you much, m'dear, but I'll do what I can."

"Leave all the financial stuff, including my salary, to me, Sir Hugh. Anyway there are two things you can do for me that would otherwise cost *me* a lot of money. Let my son Robin come to be educated with your great-niece Kate. He was so utterly miserable at the public school his father found that he 'arranged' to be expelled. It wasn't right for him from the beginning, but would Kailen listen? No, he wanted his son to be totally integrated into the upper echelons of the British system."

"Just reassure me that his expulsion isn't a sign that he's actually a criminal and of course he can come and study with Perry and Kate. And the other thing?"

"I believe you got sent down from the same school, Sir Hugh! The other thing is a lease in my name on the land around the old bridge built over the stream coming down the valley from the river. I'd like to live there."

"Anything you fancy, dear woman, if you can help me get Ashley out of the rapacious claws of Wyvern's solicitors. But there's no house there — where will you live? "

"Leave that to me and Robin's father, Sir Hugh. Kailen will make all the necessary arrangements, he's very good at things like that." What she wasn't saying was that she and Robin already lived there, and that what looked like a crumbling bridge was in fact a glamour that protected the building that ran along and over the stream and provided a unique and wonderful home. What she wanted to make sure of was, that should the worst happen, should it be impossible to save Ashley from the claws of the rapacious lawyers and their invisible clients, that her own home would be safely and legally in her hands and not just part of the goods and chattels that would be disbursed.

24

Chapter 4

Robin was lobbing stones at a beer can in a desultory manner—not caring much if he hit or missed. That was the trouble, he was a hit or miss sort of kid. Neither here nor there, not quite this or that, and—most importantly— neither witch nor Fae.

The beer can was the one whose contents he'd just finished drinking. There were five others lying beside it, or possibly ten, since he was definitely seeing double at this point.

Neither a witch nor a faerie. And unwilling, unable, to tell anyone, anyone at all, that he wasn't quite human. The boys in this crap public school his dad (the Faerie Prince—oh, yeah, he was a Prince too, or a half-a-prince—a prince-ling? a witch-ling? His bloody, bloody parents, may they rot in whatever hells their species had). Yeah, where was he ...oh, his 'Yes, Your Grace, Bloody Faerie Prince' father had decided Robin should 'explore his humanity' by joining this group of wealthy and/or high-born human kids at this so-called progressive public school. The kind where they didn't thrash you and where it was forbidden for older boys to make fags of younger boys. As if—they might not be entitled to make younger boys their servants (the meaning of 'fag' here—not the other meaning, i.e. gay or queer—although that went on too), but they sure as hell knew how to make the life of anyone different into a very special hell. It was indeed a 'real world' experience; Robin knew that. What he didn't quite understand at that age (he was sixteen) was that his experience of being the only person in the world going through this was in fact a very common one. The millions of "only people in the world" being so alone was certainly a very human experience. Welcome to bloody humanity.

At around that point in his muddled thinking, Robin threw up. And that was another thing. His may-they-rot-in-hells parents were magical. They could do magic. Robin couldn't. His half-ling collection of genes and chromosomes apparently had left out, or cancelled each other out of, the magical bits. He could see magic, see magical beings, but he couldn't do magic. This really pissed him off. He couldn't even get drunk and avoid a hangover with a small spell. He couldn't even hit a crappy beer can with a stone. He couldn't … he couldn't … he passed out.

This is Robin: more than average height, but fine-boned, black hair and deep brown eyes with so many gold flecks that they looked gold from some angles, long fingers that look made for playing an instrument, only he doesn't. He's a beautiful young man, and that is no advantage at the age of sixteen. He wears his hair a bit long, just so it covers his ears. Because his ears are pointed. But communal showers and compulsory swimming have revealed these ears to the rest of the school. It's not impossible for a human child to have pointed ears so they don't twig that he really is part faerie. After all, there are no such things. But they call him Elf-Spawn (among the kinder nicknames) anyway and make a ward-off-evil crossed finger sign sometimes when they see him. He hates them, he hates them all; and if, along with all the horrible things his wretched parents bestowed upon him, they'd only seen fit to add some real magic, he'd have been hurling fireballs at those teenage goons or turning them into toads.

What he does instead is launch himself at these bigger, stronger boys intent upon turning them into garden mulch, but the laws of nature see to it that mostly he is the one who gets soundly thrashed.

The saving grace for him is discovering the unarmed combat courses available, and in these he finds solace and even a kind of salvation. A way of using the weight and height of your opponent against them. A fearfully beautiful way of destroying the enemy with only your own body as the weapon.

He loves it. He excels at it. And, unlike what his teacher admonishes, he uses it outside the gymnasium to waylay and lay out his main tormentors. Soon there are multiple letters from an assortment of parents complaining that their sons are being injured by another boy. These sons of minor aristocracy and mega-rich bankers are breaking the unwritten rules of the school — you don't tell on your classmates—but they never considered Robin as really one of them anyway, so it's not quite the same.

Therefore it is at this point that Robin's father, at the insistence of both Robin's mother and the headmaster, takes Robin out of this upper-crust hellhole and sends him back to Maggie. Where Robin, far from being properly grateful, is temperamental, bored and angry that, just as he was getting the better of his tormentors, he is deported. Only to be shortly installed as the second pupil in the very exclusive 'school' that until then consisted solely of Kate and her tutor.

Chapter 5

April gave way to May. Like the trees in the orchard, Kate grew and blossomed, but in many ways quite differently than she had thought might be the case. Any notions she'd had about how life in England would be were changing every day.

A stray puppy found starving in a shed was brought to her and it made a huge difference to have something that needed her love and protection.

"I was planned on getting her a Cavalier King Charles Spaniel," grumbled Sir Hugh.

"With a pedigree as long as your arm I suppose" laughed his butler, valet, chauffeur and odd-job man, but mostly now his close friend, Bates.

"Umph, well, naturally," said Sir Hugh, but he smiled. "But I mean, look at that thing!"

Thing was cavorting madly around Kate, who was whirling one of those dog toys just out of its reach. Thing was black and white and tan in spots and splashes, gangly and large, with paws that promised it would get even bigger. A great long black tail went on and on and just when it seemed it would end, there was another eight inches of plummy white like a flag waving madly. And Thing now had a name, most unsuitable for something that might have auditioned for the Hound of the Baskervilles—she was called Poppet. "Because she's my Poppet," Kate had said on the day the puppy was rescued, cuddling the then small animal and letting it suck on her thumb. No one told her that, along with the endearment qualities, the name could also be applied to a witch's familiar. Perhaps she knew it anyway.

What she also knew was that she was happier with her tutor, Peregrine Sinclair, who Sir Hugh had found for her (through Maggie's recommendation) than she had been at any of the schools in New York. Peregrine was only in his early twenties, so tried very hard at first to establish an old-fashioned student-teacher relationship out of nervousness. But within a short time he and Kate had established a more equitable relationship where, although he taught and she learned, they became friends, and sometimes she even taught him, since her knowledge of plants and rock music far outstripped his.

A few weeks later Perry also took on Maggie Spencer's son Robin when he was, according to Sir Hugh, 'rusticated' (an old-fashioned, very English word for being sent down, or in US parlance, expelled). Maggie was Hugh's one-woman office staff and general know-it-all who had volunteered her services when she moved back to the area and took in (apparently by osmosis or some occult sense according to Sir Hugh) the state of Ashley's finances.

Robin and Kate started out like chalk and cheese, glaring across the library that had been commandeered as a school room. Kate was loathe to share her teacher, and saw Robin as disruptive to the good time she'd begun to have. Robin was angry at being expelled and generally pissed off at the world. But Peregrine was patient and Kate, remembering her own unhappiness in new, unwanted, situations, wasn't going to make it very hard on him. So after some days the relationship that developed was one of slightly wary acceptance and some appreciation of each other's lonely pasts.

"I want an essay on anything that takes your fancy for Monday," said Peregrine at the end of the second week they were sharing the class. "Five-hundred words and special attention to grammar and spelling." Kate thought that should be an easy assignment until she realised she didn't have much of a handle yet on English spelling or for that matter English vocabulary. "Two countries separated by a single language," stage-whispered Robin as he passed her on his way out. "Yeah, about that…" said Kate. "How about a little help with the English?"

"What, you need help with your English? I thought that's where you excelled."

"I excel in American English, and just like you said, it isn't the same." Kate held her head in her hands, mocking the difficulty of getting her head around the differences.

"What'll you give me if I help you?" It wasn't that he didn't want to help, but Robin believed in a quid pro quo.

"Well, what do you need help with?"

"Biology," said Robin making a 'yuck' face.

"I can do that," said Kate. "Perry isn't going to make us dissect formaldehyde frogs or stuff like that. We're going to do field work."

"As in out dissecting cow pats?"

"No, as in doing butterfly, bird, bee and amphibian counts to add to the national data base. So we need to know or be able to find out what it is we see. Take photos and make lists. And if we do find anything dead that isn't too decayed, we could dissect that. And wild flowers — we can dissect wild flowers — they've got male and female parts you know, they're hermaphrodites."

Robin was looking at her like she'd grown two heads, but also with greater respect — this was a girl who talked about dissecting roadkill. They agreed to meet up later that evening, "Because I have another sort of class first" said Robin.

"What kind of class?"

"Self-defence. Mainly oriental but with boxing elements."

"Oh, wow! Can I come?"

"You're a girl."

"So what? They don't take girls?" Robin looked away to hide his grin.

"Aw, they do take girls! You're messing with me."

"Yeah, okay, they take girls, but you'll have to have the right clothes and shoes. And not be afraid to get hurt."

"I thought the idea was not to get hurt."

"It is, yes, but while you're learning, believe me, sometimes it hurts."

"I need to learn," said Kate flatly.

"Why? You're the bloomin' lady of the manor — who's gonna mess with you?"

"Maybe that's true here, but when I was in New York everybody was messing with me, and I really, really would've liked to know how to knock them flat. Where can I get the right clothes?"

"They'll probably have something you can borrow and there's a catalogue for ordering. Meet me at Stolen Moments for coffee at five and then we'll go to the Dojo, it's just down the street over the old cinema. Don't bring Poppet — she might want to protect you, and that could get crazy."

A few hours later, sitting at a table outside Stolen Moments, Kate stirred her coffee and poked at it as if she could somehow make it a better beverage.

"So what's the matter now?" muttered Robin.

"No one around here can make a decent cup of coffee — this is so weak and watery. Coffee should be, oh, I don't know, rich, and really give you a wallop when you drink it. This is dishwater. Sorry, I know the English love tea."

"Not me, not big on tea. I like, well, beer."

"You what? You're not old enough."

"Yeah, well that didn't stop me. It's why they threw me out."

"You got expelled for drinking beer?"

"No, I got expelled for getting caught drinking beer underage. Oh, and also for beating up some of the kids who had been beating on me." His grin was lopsided and infectious.

"Well, I think I'll stick with coffee for the time being, but getting a good cuppa is not happening around here."

"We could go out to one of the service areas on a motorway, they've got Costa Coffee and Starbucks now."

"Small problem, neither of us is old enough to drive."

"There is that. Well, we can go adventuring down the valley. But for now we can go to the Dojo and kick the crap out of something, or maybe each other."

And so began Kate's education in the fine art of self-defence, with a side order of imagining kicking the crap out of all the people who had bullied her or let her down over the years. It was just what she needed. Because spring was casting an unsettling spell that made her both irritable and bemused, full of restless energy but also dreaming magic dreams.

Chapter 6

Kate woke with the startling suddenness that usually meant that she'd been having a bad dream. Her heart was pounding but she couldn't remember the dream, if there had been one. It took a moment for her to orient herself and for her eyes to adjust to the pale, unearthly moonlight flooding through the windows.

Pale moonlight…there was no warm dim yellowy-orangey glow from her nightlight that kept the moonlight and demon shadows at bay. The nightlight was out and she was left in the livid dark watching the twisting, pulsing shadows of trees and curtains outlined in gelid bands of moon light along the ceiling and the walls. Kate actually felt the hairs on the back of her neck and her arms grow erect, a shiver ran through her and she drew the covers up to her chin and lay as if frozen, afraid to move since movement might draw unwanted attention to herself.

She closed her eyes against the dancing phantoms and tried not to imagine what might be lurking in the far corner where the dark seemed to be piled up, darker than the surrounding darkness, or in the wardrobe or (here her mind recoiled from visions of skeletal hands reaching up) under the bed. Dammit! She was too old to be this frightened of the dark! But frightened she was.

It was useless. Lying with her eyes closed simply multiplied the imagined terrors, and she could all but feel icy breath fanning her cheek as *something* loomed over the bed ready to pounce. She opened her eyes. Just night, and moon light and dancing shapes. No more but unfortunately no less. She remained rigid under the covers, breathing in a shallow kind of way designed to make her as motionless and soundless as possible. Her heart at last had slowed and the blood in her ears no longer pounded, drowning out other sounds. She began to distinguish the sounds of the night.

She could hear voices. Not crickets or cicadas or even the hoo-roo of an owl, but voices. It sounded like a party, laughter and chatter, rising up through the leaves and drifting in her window on the bands of moonlight. A clear voice like a bell. A robust laugh. A distant, but distinct, screeching cackle. And splashing, as if someone or several someones were disporting themselves in the lily pond.

Her curiosity began to get the better of her fear, and warmth stole back into her along with a flickering courage. She knew that the voices were an oddity definitely more outrageous than shapes in the moonlight, but somehow they didn't inspire the same irrational terror. Besides, they were clearly having a whale of a good time. Kate got cautiously out of bed and, avoiding the bands of moonlight, crept to the window overlooking the gardens.

As if on cue music, light and thin and clear, drifted up toward her. It sounded like a flute, or...Pan-pipes, thought Kate with a thrill. Now the voices began to fall in with the tune, singing now high, now low. It was an old song, a love song and a pastoral. A song such as shepherds sing to their sheep out on the lonely hills, a melody that was of the fields and streams. She seemed to hear a stream running through a flower-studded meadow, see sheep like fleecy clouds, hear the wind sighing in the willows. And the man and his maid. Did they sing all that, or did the music itself tell her? Try as she would the words wouldn't come clear, yet the story told itself. How I love this land, it sang, how I love the fields and streams, the animals and the flowers, the trees and birds and butterflies. Love, it sang, love. I love you. I will come back, I will not forsake you, I will come back and all will be as it was before. How I love this land, how I love my home.

And Kate felt a tear, and then another as the sadness and wonder of the music overwhelmed her. And the dying fall of the pipes was overlaid with a splashing from the fountain (had the wind changed that she could hear it so clearly?) that made it sound as if the land itself wept too.

Now the music was done and now too a cloud and then another moved to cover the moon, so true darkness descended at last. Kate was left with a feeling of wonder and loss, but strangely at peace. She realised she was very tired, and made her way back to her bed, stopping to turn on the nightlight. It obediently lit. What, she wondered sleepily, had caused it to go out? But even as she thought this, sleep overcame her, and she sank rapidly through the layers of false sleep, so like the false dawn (when we think we see, but cannot), into real sleep, burrowing down as an animal does through the warm earth, deeper and deeper through the warmth and darkness. So Kate slept and dreamt confused dreams of creatures gambolling in the garden and she was dancing and singing the old songs with them, until these too departed and she slept and did not dream.

The next morning was fair, and warm breezes filled with the scents of early summer ruffled the curtains and stole across her pillow to tease her hair. She woke with a pleasant sense of anticipation. Poppet, seeing that her mistress was awake, leapt from her basket and onto the bed to stand over Kate, her plumed tail waving slowly and her merry brown eyes alight with anticipation.

"Oh, Poppet," sighed Kate, stretching luxuriously. "I had such a strange dream. There were -- well, beings -- in the garden, and I played with them. And there was a song... But, oh damn, it's going now." And in the way of dreams it escaped her, leaving only the feeling. Anyway, she thought, if it wasn't a dream then Poppet would have been awake and joining in or chasing things away, and it seemed like she hadn't been there at all.

Poppet, ever the pragmatist, thought this was enough foolishness for one morning and with a bound she flattened Kate back on the pillows. A roughhouse with giggles and mock growls followed during which you might have seen (had you been rude enough to spy) Kate play-bite Poppet on the paw and lick Poppet's nose. That she wasn't supposed to do such things she well knew, but like all intelligent young people with good manners she understood that manners were for when people were watching, and what was done in private was one's own business. Kindness of course was for everywhere at all times, but manners — not so much.

If you said that Poppet's nose or paws were dirty, she might have explained in a patronising tone that the human mouth was far dirtier than any part of a nice dog, as proven by the really nasty infections resulting from human bites. Since Kate usually had her facts straight, and could undoubtedly have found the reference for you as well, perhaps you would have been routed. But in Kate's experience adults often flew in the face of the facts and enforced senseless dictums anyway (such as "I don't care what you say, you will not lick that dog's nose, and that's final."). This she understood to be simply one of the many unfairnesses involved with being a child. Explaining that she was a teenager, not a child, hadn't cut any ice in the past and she didn't expect it would now. Old enough to do all the boring unpleasant things, not old enough to do the crazy fun things...the story of her life, she thought. In this, had she but known it, she was remarkably like her great-great aunt Maude.

It was Poppet who, at the tender age of five months, already saw herself as the champion, protector and to some extent nursemaid of her adored mistress, who called a halt to the rough-and-tumble by leaping off the

36

bed and going to stand by the door with the classic 'I want to go out' expression. Kate, recalled to her responsibilities and to the lure of the sunny morning outside, dressed quickly and she and Poppet let themselves out her door, down the long corridor and quickly down the great stair. Kate paused as always to caress the intricate curves of that magnificent example of the woodcarver's art, passing her hand over the wood smoothed by generations of hands, until the wood glowed like amber and flowed under the hand like silk. Then she and Poppet padded over the marble tiles of the great hall toward the stairs down to the kitchen, where she grabbed a roll left over from last night's dinner, and up again into the corridor leading to the big drawing room and the French doors that opened onto the terrace.

Achieving the terrace, its stone flags interplanted with low growing plants that spread a multi-coloured carpet of leaf, flower and fragrance, Poppet and Kate paused a moment in homage to the new day. It was still only a little past dawn. The sun rising behind them threw long shadows of the house and the trees, but its rays caught the dew on lawn and tree and shrub and caused them all to sparkle like diamonds. Birds were singing 'loud enough to deafen a body' as Mrs Sykes would say and flowers just kissed by the sun were giving off an ecstasy of perfume. The freshness and mingling of both the lingering cool of the night and the warmth to come gave the whole a magical newborn quality as if it were the first morning of creation.

The moment was broken by Poppet, bounding loose from the spell and racing madly about first the terrace, then down the three steps to the first level of the garden where she tore in circles, leaping and turning for the sheer joy of being alive on such a morning. She quickly stopped to puddle, then continued her mad career. Kate, who — though not religious — had been murmuring 'the world is alive with the glory of God' because she liked the sound of it, and it suited the jewel-like quality of the morning, laughed aloud and ran to join the puppy, each of them running in circles then straightening to tear down through the long borders as fast as they could run.

Panting, her heart beating madly, Kate pulled up, coming to rest against the statue of a harpy that lurked here amongst a planting of azaleas and rhododendrons. A harpy is a fearsome creature, but this one, though her sharp talons gripping the plinth of her pedestal as if she would tear it to shreds, had wings half-spread protectively like those of a swan or an angel, and her woman's face was beautiful. The sculptor had been quite up on his legends: this harpy had the face of a maiden, the icy beauty of classical mythology, but with none of the fury harpies were known for. Now, as Kate leaned companionably against the statue, for - as with all the others - she had befriended it, her hand stroking the moss on the plinth, a bit tore away and her eye was caught by letters. Intrigued, she pulled away more moss and found they were a few lines of poetry.

> *Come into the garden, Maud,*
> *For the black bat, night, has flown*
> *Come into the garden, Maud,*
> *I am here at the gate alone.*

"How strange," thought Kate, "how mystical and sad." It reminded her of her dream, and she thought perhaps this was what the creatures were singing. "I'll look it up after breakfast." She said to Poppet, 'I'm sure I've seen it before."

Just then her eye was caught by a flash of turquoise in the undergrowth at the other side of the path where another harpy perched on its plinth. This harpy was definitely of the more terrifying variety, its face contorted in a furious grimace, but holding its bat wings folded against itself in a protective way. Its hands, complete with talons, were also folded as if in prayer. Making her way around the base by bending very low under the rhododendrons, she found a string bag containing knitting. Pulling it out she saw that whoever had left it here had been knitting a sweater, but such a sweater! It was a travesty of a sweater...a symphony of dropped stitches, with one arm considerably wider but shorter than the other. *It's what I would do if I tried to knit*, thought Kate, *all any which way*. It was far from finished and there was evidence in the piles of crinkly yarn that a lot of it had been pulled out to be done again. Nor was it any too clean.

"Now this is very strange," said Kate. "It can't be Binny's because she couldn't knit if her life depended on it, and she wouldn't want to be bothered. And I'll bet Mrs Sykes wouldn't be caught dead doing anything this sloppy." The thought of some stranger coming here to sit under the shrubbery to knit wouldn't wash either. A vision of Bates trying to knit a sweater for his rheumatism brought on a fit of giggles. So perhaps it belonged to some village girl, who waited here to meet...who? Her boyfriend? But there were plenty of deserted spots more amiable than this, closer to town and not so close to habitation. More mysteries — the poem and now the knitting. *And mysteries need solving, so I'll start with the poem,* said Kate to herself.

Chapter 7

Peregrine was determined on algebra for that morning, and Robin was making 'yuck' faces behind his back as Perry wrote an equation on the board. Kate, screening out his voice and Robin's facial contortions, was typing 'Come into the garden Maude' into her laptop, which quickly brought her the entire poem by Tennyson.

Come into the garden, Maud,
For the black bat, night, has flown,
Come into the garden, Maud,
I am here at the gate alone;

And the woodbine spices are wafted abroad,
And the musk of the rose is blown.

For a breeze of morning moves,
And the planet of Love is on high,
Beginning to faint in the light that she loves
On a bed of daffodil sky,
The faint in the light of the sun she loves,
To faint in his light, and to die.

All night have the roses heard
The flute, violin, bassoon;
All night has the casement jessamine stirred
To the dancers dancing in tune;
Till silence fell with the waking bird,
And a hush with the setting moon

I said to the lily, "There is but one
With whom she has heart to be gay.
When will the dancers leave her alone?

She is weary of dance and play."

Now half to the setting moon are gone,
And half to the rising day;
Low on the sand and loud on the stone
The last wheel echoes away.

I said to the rose, "the brief night goes
In babble and revel and wine.
Oh, young lord-lover, what sighs are those,
For one who will never be thine?
But mine, but mine," I swear to the rose,
"For ever and ever, mine."

But that's very like the song last night, she thought. *How can that be? And why put this on the pedestal of the statue of a harpy? Is Maude a harpy?*

"The last time I looked, Alfred Lord Tennyson was not solving algebraic equations in that poem, Kate." Perry was looming over her shoulder looking at the poem on her screen.

"Oh, Perry, I'm sorry, but I found a bit of this poem on a statue this morning and wanted to find out about it. Besides," she said truthfully, "I hate algebra. Equations are a mystery to me, but this is a real mystery and I want to solve it."

Peregrine wasn't that fond of algebra either, and any excuse to follow up on something else was welcome. Not that he'd tell Robin and Kate that. "Which statue?"

"That's what's so mysterious. This is a love poem, and the quote, the first four lines, is on the pedestal of the harpy in the garden. Who'd be in love with a harpy?"

"Another harpy?" came from Robin.

"Not likely, they are all female if I've got my mythology right and they don't even like each other." said

41

Perry. "It is strange. Unless the plinth belonged to a different statue to begin with, one of a beautiful young woman."

"I don't think so," said Kate. "The ornamentation on the plinth and around the feet, or claws, of the Harpy is identical."

"One of the Mallorys was named Maude — she'd be your many times great aunt or maybe a cousin, back in the 1860s."

"How do you know that, Perry?" asked Kate.

"Because I was curious about Ashley Manor and the Mallory family so I looked it up in the Bible."

"Ha, the Mallorys aren't that old," said Robin.

"Don't be silly," snapped Kate, "he means the family bible, there's a family tree at the beginning and every time a child is born they add it in. Perry, let's go look."

"Do this equation, guys, and we can go."

Grumbling, Robin and Kate settled into graphing the equation. "Which is the Y axis?" whispered Kate. "I always forget."

"The vertical one" hissed Robin.

A short time later they were all hovering over the big Bible on its lectern stand. The stand itself was beautifully carved with medieval animals peeking out of foliage and flowers, the Bible itself bound in dark red leather with gilded lettering and an intricate lock. But it was open now at a very lovely illuminated illustration of a castle on a rock with medieval lords and ladies in a garden in the foreground with a fountain that brought a gasp of recognition from Kate. "It's so much like the garden here, the fountain is so much like..."

"I think you'll find that the Mallory who built Ashley Manor did incorporate elements of these wonderful illustrations into the design of the gardens." Uncle Hugh had appeared behind them and was also enjoying the

42

illumination. "Perry, are you doing bible study or medieval manuscript art?"

"Oh! Good morning, Sir Hugh. No, we're doing some ancestor hunting. Kate found a bit of Tennyson's *Come into the garden Maud* on a statue in the garden and I told her one of your ancestors was named Maude so we've come to find out the relationship. The Bible just happened to be open to this page."

"Shouldn't be," grumbled Hugh, "light's bad for the colours. Shouldn't be left open on a page like this. But I'm glad you've seen it, Kate, it's all part of our history and the influences that have shaped Ashley."

Perry gently turned the pages back to the front of the Bible and found the family tree. It started in the mid-1600s and went on down to the present, where Kate saw someone had lightly pencilled in her name with her birthday in October 2001.

Uncle Hugh put a hand on her shoulder, "That was me, Kate, I can't do the script so I've just pencilled it in. Look, you can see where a few of the other names are only in pencil too. It doesn't mean they are somehow less-than or in disgrace, it's just that whoever did it meant to get the proper inked script done later, but didn't for some reason."

"Thanks, Uncle Hugh, it means a lot to be there somehow. Look, there she is — there's Maude!"
And there she was, Maude Mallory, younger sister of Sebastian Mallory. But there was a strange wavy broken line connecting her to her husband, Sir Ivor Wyvern.

"Why is that line all distorted, Uncle Hugh?" asked Kate, pointing.

"That's a long, bitter story," said Hugh, sighing. "Maude was always head-strong and she wouldn't pay attention to her brother or his wife Elizabeth when they tried to tell her they felt there was something very wrong about Ivor Wyvern, that what she took to be an 'interesting' and very attractive hint of darkness in his

43

character could be real evil. She fell in love. Apparently he did too. Sebastian refused permission for them to marry, so…well she simply ran away and moved in with him. It's said Ivor cursed the family and we've been having bad luck ever since — crop failures, fires, stock market crashes, law suits. One of the latter, long-running and damnably expensive, was between Ivor and Sebastian over boundary rights, and after Ivor died, his estate carried it on, down through the generations. Apparently Ivor's instructions were to carry on the suit "in perpetuity" and when there is any chance of a reasonable settlement, his estate lawyers find some reason for it to be unacceptable to them. Still in court occasionally."

"So it wasn't a curse" said Robin, "just angry neighbours and a lawsuit."

"Some people would say lawyers are a curse," said Sir Hugh wryly.

"*Bleak House*," murmured Perry.

"Exactly," Hugh sighed.

"Dickens," added Kate. "But what happened to Maude? She would have been scorned by Society wouldn't she?"

"Exactly right," said Hugh. "But it seemed she didn't care. Elizabeth and Sebastian wrote to her regularly, and she answered at first, saying she was happy, and would marry as soon as she was twenty-one and secured her part of the inheritance that their father had settled upon her. Then at just around that time she stopped writing and their letters were returned unopened. The family never saw her again. There is a record that they married, which my lawyers say is fake, and that Ivor claimed her inheritance or what would have been, and I suppose was, her dowry if they married. But we know nothing else. There is no record of her death or of children, nothing. It's as if she disappeared off the face of the earth.

"In fact, although occasionally it would appear that there are people at Wyvern Hall, it seems that Ivor must have died without issue, as again there is no record of children, but what is very strange is that there is no record of his death or any will providing for inheritance of the Hall. Yet down the generations a law firm continues to harass us over the boundary and Maude's dowry, and the legal costs continue to mount up. It is like his ghost is slowly strangling our income, stripping away our means of support bit by bit. We've tried some countermeasures, like suing for the part of the estate which would have rightfully belonged to Maude once women were allowed to inherit. Since there is no record of her death for legal purposes she can be said to be alive and able to inherit, at least that's what the lawyers told my father. But that's only got us deeper into the financial pit. *Bleak House* indeed."

"What are you talking about — what's Bleak House?" Robin looked distinctly pissed off to be out of the information loop.

Perry put a comforting hand on his shoulder, "*Bleak House* is a novel by Charles Dickens exploring how a prolonged lawsuit, continuing for generations, ruined many people financially and drove some to suicide or madness. In the end there was no money left at all, and the only people who profited were the lawyers. Dickens hated lawyers."

"Holy crap," said Robin, "so if you fight it you lose and if you don't fight you lose too? Bloody ingenious and really, really evil."

"That's rather how we've felt, that it's a trap we're caught in, and that the man who set that trap was indeed evil." Hugh was shaking his head sadly. "What makes it even more upsetting is that Ivor was also an incredibly talented artist and architect. Do you know he sculpted the statues in the garden? We're still being sued for the price of those too. That someone who could create such beauty should also be so wilfully wicked is hard to imagine."

"Then he made the harpies?" asked Kate. "So if he sculpted the harpies he made one of them Maude and did the inscription! Her face is very beautiful. But he must have come to hate her. Maybe he killed her."

"Elizabeth thought he could have killed her, she never trusted him at all. It was her influence that made Sebastian forbid the marriage. Because at first Sebastian thought Ivor was rather wonderful, it's why he contracted him to make the statues, and was even planning to have him do some work on the house, but over the years he too suspected and then was sure that Ivor was wicked." Sir Hugh sounded exhausted.

"But, Robin, your mother is as good as promising me that she can actually do something about Ashley's finances and maybe even battle the lawyers. She's helped me with auctioning antiques in the past, but now she has decided to take on our big financial problems. She's a real wizard when it comes to finance. I'm very relieved, although not counting any chickens just yet."

"Yeah, that's Mum — a wizard for sure," Robin was grinning.

Chapter 8

1840

Ivor was bored, he was often bored, and when he was bored he tended to find trouble. At the age of ten he had shown no emotion when told his parents were killed when their coach lost a wheel and ran off the road into a river in flood. Ellie later found him playing with a piece of cast iron that looked suspiciously like a lynchpin — the pin that passes though the axle-end to keep the wheel in position. She was horrified that she could even entertain the thought that Ivor, her little brother Ivy, could somehow (but how?) have been involved in the accident that killed their parents. Still the thought took root, and from then on she tended to watch him more closely and take nothing for granted.

Indeed, she was now required by circumstances to watch him more closely because with their father's death it was revealed that he did not possess the wealth they had taken for granted, but was actually nearly bankrupt. The fancy townhouse and the country mansion were both sold to pay the debts and the two children were shortly re-established in a pokey three-bedroom brick row house in an unfashionable part of town. Their governess was let go and a second cousin they were told to call Aunt Thompson moved in to provide an adult presence. She liked her gin, and the care of Ivor fell more and more to the fourteen-year-old Ellie. She was of a naturally motherly disposition and, if Ivor had been an easier child, they might have thrived even in these inhospitable circumstances.

But Ivor, thin and pale with black hair and deep-set unnerving hazel eyes, was secretive, and often disappeared for hours at a time. When questioned by his exasperated sister he would only say he'd been playing with a friend in the woods that ran down to the river. On another occasion she heard him chatting away in his room, and there seemed to be another, much lower voice responding, but when she went in only Ivor was there. "Ivy, who were you talking with?"

"No one," he sulked. "And I don't like it that you can just come into my room when you want — you should knock."

Like most of the rooms in the row house, Ivor's room was small and stuffed with shabby, hand-me-down furniture, a narrow bed in the corner, an out-size desk with a blotter and a cracked mug holding pens and pencils, some text books and an oil lamp. A set of cheap deal bookshelves displayed a miscellaneous collection of things he had found on long walks by the river: mostly rocks and a few crystals, but also a few small animal skulls and some other bones and a very small shoe. The shelves also contained a prized collection of books including Mary Shelley's *Frankenstein*, Dickens' *Oliver Twist*. There were American authors too: *The Fall of the House of Usher and Other Stories* by Edgar Allen Poe and *Tales of the Alhambra* by Washington Irving. There was a copy of *Faust* in the original German with bookmarks, and Coleridge's collected verse, also with bookmarks. Hidden behind the others was a dog-eared copy of *On Murder Considered as One of the Fine Arts* by the opium eater Thomas de Quincey. In pride of place, however, were some texts on architecture and sculpture.

Ellie smiled: he was growing up. "You're right. I will knock from now on. But I'm sure I heard you talking and there seemed to be another voice…?" She raised her eyebrows and smiled at him again, hoping to make him feel safe to confide in her.

"I was practicing for a school play," he said glibly. "I've got the part of a huntsman, and we've found a wild boar, that other voice was the boar."

"A talking boar?" She laughed. "It's a fairy tale where beasts can talk? How novel."

Not nearly as novel as what is really going on, he thought. But he smiled and nodded.

And what was really going on? Ivor was deeply involved in the relationship with his imaginary friend with whom he talked constantly. And he was learning much more than he did at school.

"I didn't know they would actually die."

But you wished that they would die.

"That's because Father beat me when he discovered I'd cut off the cat's tail. And Mother refused to speak to me or have me in the same room."

And it got infected and the cat died.

"Yes, well, I didn't intend that part to happen."

Actions have consequences, wishes have consequences too.

"I don't believe that — not that wishes can make things happen. I didn't make my parents die. And if wishes worked, well, I wouldn't be living here, would I? I hate it here."

No, but your wish is my command. See, I brought you the lynchpin that sheared away and caused the coach to crash.

"But that wasn't what I really meant…look, now we've lost the house and the money and have to live in this horrible house with horrible Aunt Thompson who stinks!"

Wishes and actions have consequences, consequences beyond our original intentions. Wanting to punish your parents you have instead punished yourself.

"So what should I do?"

I'm sure your sister would tell you not to take the selfish action in the first place, but we know better, don't we?

"We do? What do we know?"

That before you decide on a course of action you need to look ahead at all the possible outcomes and make contingency plans, plans that will avoid unforeseen consequences.

"Well, if I can't foresee them, how can I make con-tin-see plans?"

Contingency - a contingency is something that might happen in the future, usually with a bad effect. Contingency plans are those that take into account all possible outcomes, or as many outcomes as possible, and have things in place to deal with them.

"I can't do all that! I can't!"

But that's why you have me, because together we can.

Eleanor was disturbed to discover, on enquiring, that the school wasn't putting on a play. On and off she did hear Ivor seemingly chatting with what she decided was an invisible friend, something she had read was not uncommon with children who were mostly alone. And for whatever reason Ivor didn't make friends at school. Queried about this, he very nearly snarled that they were common and not worth befriending. Indeed he had been sullen and withdrawn more than usual ever since he was taken from the prestigious public school he had attended for the previous three years. But it seemed that this new imaginary friend was filling more of his time and seemed to be cheering him up somewhat. Ellie decided that she wouldn't interfere in what seemed to be a positive relationship.

She felt vindicated in her hands-off policy when Ivor won a scholarship to a more prestigious school that had a speciality in arts and architecture. A place where Ivor did extremely well and won a series of prizes for his drawing and sculpting. His inability to make friends or suffer fools (and Ivor thought most of the human race were fools) however did still cause her concern — out in the world it would be hard to get and keep clients for his talents if he couldn't cultivate a pleasant manner

Chapter 9

October 1849

Ivor was restless, he kept picking at the frayed edges of the upholstery on the arm of his chair, which drove his sister crazy. "Ivy, will you stop that! I spend half my life mending and you make more work whenever you're bored or upset. Just for heaven's sake stop it!"

He looked at her with a mix of annoyance and contempt, "You're not my mother, Ellie, and if you don't want to mend things, well, don't! No one gives a damn about this place anyway." His gaze took in the middle-sized, middle-class, middle-middleness of the room that made him want to scream.

"I don't belong here, I'm going out!" And he rose so quickly that the book he'd been pretending to read fell off onto the floor, bending the pages back and spilling the glass by the chair. This so enraged him he grabbed the glass and threw it hard at the fake-Gothic fire surround, where it shattered. "And don't call me Ivy!"

The door slammed behind him, and Ellie bowed her head into her hands as usual when she felt she'd provoked him. "Ivy Wyvie" she muttered under her breath, as if he could still hear her, the hated nickname bestowed upon him at the public school his father had sent him to, using the last of the family money. It was the only way she had of getting back at him, for his ferocious temper kept her from facing him down more directly. Then she sighed and went for the dustpan and brush to sweep up the glass.

Ivy Wyvie was indeed in his mind as he strode down the street of shabby semi-detached houses where his parent's intemperate spending had ended them up. Well, Ivy Wyvie would show them, show them all! At 19 he didn't know how, but he had no doubts that some combination of circumstance and cleverness would win him everything he desired. He would make it so, and anyone who even remembered that Ivor Wyvern had once been the snivelling Ivy Wyvie would have cause to regret it. Really, really regret it. The black look on his face made several passersby move quickly aside. That was more like it.

Sitting in the corner of his favourite pub, Ivor was using a newspaper to screen himself from any possible interruption as he steadily imbibed his pint and chewed in a desultory manner on a pork pie. So it was several moments before he noticed the small voice coming from near his elbow. "'Ere," it said, "if you ain't eatin' all of that, give us a bite, ok?" He looked up but saw no-one. 'Down 'ere," said the voice. He looked down — there by his elbow was a small … animal? It was not much bigger than a large cockroach, but seemed to have a mane and a tail and to be wearing a waistcoat. "'At's the ticket,' said the apparition. "I could do you a bit of good, I could. If I had a mind to, if you was to be a generous sort of bloke, don'tcha know."

"I doubt it" hissed Ivor, holding his newspaper so no one could see he was talking to the table. "Go away."

"Nar, don't be like that," said the thing. "You need help, you know you do, you ain't been gettin' anywhere by yourself, see. We was close once, and we could do great things if you'd just listen."

"You're no bigger than an anaemic mouse" muttered Ivor, "What could you possibly do for me?"

"Oh, if it's size you wants…." said the thing, "I CAN BE AS BIG AS YOU CAN POSSIBLY IMAGINE." The walls, the floor, the ceiling, all seemed to shatter silently outward as the being expanded as swiftly as an explosion, filling all the available space and then expanding further until, although it was also seemingly transparent and insubstantial, it pushed and squashed Ivor back against the wood of his seat until his ribs screamed with pain and he could no longer breathe.

"Sssstop". He managed to exhale. In the flick of an eye the being was once more no larger than his thumb.

"Well," it said, "are you interested?"

"What _are_ you?" murmured Ivor when he'd got his breath back and ascertained that his ribs were after all whole and unbroken.

"I'm your classical chimaera sort of fing." said the beast.

"Oh, mythology," sneered Ivor, trying to regain the upper hand.

"Since when did myfology do what I just did?" The Chimaera laughed, a laugh with deeper, rougher undertone, as if the huge beast of moments before were still somehow present.

It shut Ivor up. From being scared senseless with only his bravado between him and total meltdown, he finally began to think once more. "What is it you want to give me?"

"Power," said the Chimaera. "Power and wealth and influence, creativity, effectiveness — all beyond your wildest dreams. Oh, and immortality, of course."

"Why?" snapped Ivor, too used to being put upon to believe this easily.

"Why not?" parried the beast.

"Why me?" said Ivor more carefully, "what's special about me?"

"You," said the creature carefully, "are full of spite and malice and energy, but also of untapped talents and undreamed of resources. You could be great. I could make you great."

"And I'm supposed to believe that you go around London making offers like this to angry young men?"

"Aaah, not to just anyone, not to anyone at all akchully. Just you. I've come just for you."

"Because I'm so special?"

" 'At's the ticket, because you're so special, yeah. Remember, I've known you for a long, long time."

"Remember you? I don't. Never seen you before."

"Not seen me, no. But we talked, we played, we made up stories and you were always the hero, and I always helped you. You called me Mr Dream. And I said I'd make your dreams come true. Remember?"

And suddenly he did. The imaginary friend that gave him amazing ideas and promised him that he would do fantastic things. After all that's what he'd been preaching at his older sister, Ellie, for years, how he was special, so much better than… so much more talented than… so totally incomprehensibly, immeasurably superior than…. He had dreams, dreams of creating great things, an empire… and of making art as well. Dreams of subduing the world that laughed at him. And then showing them, showing them all that it wasn't just strength and anger, it was creativity of the highest order, the ability to make worlds, to make things better. But better in his own special way.

The Chimaera seemed to hear all this and smiled secretly. He'd hooked his fish, now to reel him in. "Come on then," he said, "we gotta get outa here."

'Why? Where?" Ivor came up out of his dream of world domination and stared at the tiny being that was promising to make his every dream come true.

"Put me in your pocket," demanded the creature, "and we'll go home."

"To my house? My sister…"

"Nah, ya daft bugger, to your real house, to get these things started."

"I don't have a house, just this rented thing…"

"Yeah, yeah, well you won't need it anymore now you've got me. We're goin' places and we'll start with a better place to live. Anyway, we need privacy."

"Privacy? For what?"

"Contracts, selling your soul, you know, in return for the power and immortality and all that sort of fing. Oh and you have to consume me."

"Okay, enough is enough, joke's over. You can go — poof!— back where you came from. Go on — poof!" Ivor waved his hands in a sweeping away motion.

But the Chimaera had already jumped into his jacket pocket from where his muffled voice came in irritable tones. "Poof! Shoo! I ain't no friggin' fly, son, I am your chosen destiny." And there was a distinct feeling of heat, a needle of heat coming through Ivor's coat and trousers and poking him altogether too near his private parts. He stood up gingerly, and looked around to see that no one in the pub seemed to have noticed anything at all. He walked out carefully, aware that the creature deep in his pocket had powers he could only speculate upon. Immortality coupled with power and wealth! The opportunity to become a great artist! To shape men's lives! He figured selling his soul [which he wasn't sure existed in any case] would be worth it, but the idea of eating the thing turned his stomach. Still, it would effectively dispose of it. Or would it? Perhaps it meant to dispose of him. Well, he'd just have to see that that didn't happen.

And off into the evening fog went the not-so-ill-assorted pair.

Chapter 10

Carrying the Chimaera, Ivor walked for what seemed a long time through neighbourhoods with which he was unfamiliar. Finally they turned into a street he knew well, the street where he'd often stood across from a grand house that he knew should have been his, watching people who shouldn't have been there, because he should have been. The hideous nickname 'Ivy Wyvie' would never have been if he had only lived where he belonged. The stone wyverns flanking the door would have silenced any such impertinence.

Now the house was shuttered and still as it appeared out of the fog. Whoever had lived there wasn't there now. But the door stood partly open.

"In there," said the voice from his pocket. Up the stone stairs past the stone wyverns and under the coat of arms carved into the stone lintel they went. "It belonged to my grandfather, before my imbecile parent got his hands on his inheritance."

"Well, it's yours now."

"Won't people notice?"

"People see what they want to see."

"No" said Ivor. "They have sharp eyes and sharper tongues when it comes to sudden wealth and elevation of station. They won't accept this. There will be too many questions."

"Well, let's just say there will be a slight adjustment to the timeline. You've always been here, sort of fing. You'll get used to it very quickly once we've done the contract and all that stuff."

They continued on up to the first floor and into a large study where a welcoming fire was already burning with two large wing chairs and matching footstools in front of it. A large intricately carved partner's desk sat within the curve of the bow window and was spread with a variety of papers, pens, and boxes. There was also a small tray of deep red Chinese lacquer with a crystal goblet, an ancient-looking flask and a small dagger set upon it.

The Chimaera scrambled easily out of Ivor's pocket and settled himself into the chair opposite the desk. Ivor blinked. The thumb-sized thing that had accompanied him was now a full-sized man, or man-like being. The only recognisable feature from before was his mane of reddish-blond hair, longer than fashionable. He was dressed in a tailcoat and high collar with a cravat that Count d'Orsay would have approved. His eyes slanted slightly and glinted yellow in the firelight, with a pupil like a cat's and it was just possible to see slight knobs or small horns peeking through the mane of hair.

And now the voice was no longer that of a cheeky cockney but a deeper more resonate baritone with faultless upper-class vowels that seemed to have undertones that went on and on. He was a formidable presence.

Ivor felt underdressed, undernourished and generally a bit overwhelmed. But he wasn't a Wyvern for nothing, and this being had chosen him particularly to gift with amazing powers. He strode first to the fireplace and leant there with one casual elbow on the mantel, then moved to pour a drink from the decanter of port beside the armchairs and pick up a cigar. He was, after all, the owner of Wyvern Place.

Look now at Ivor Wyvern, about to become one of the most formidable presences on the planet. He is tall, with hair so dark it shines with blue highlights where the firelight hits it. His face is as angular as his body is lean, with cheek bones sharp enough to cut glass, a slightly Roman nose with flaring nostrils and — unexpectedly — light hazel eyes under thick dark eye brows. His eyelashes would make a maiden swoon. But his mouth is a thin slash across his face and when he smiles it is predatory and hungry. In fact he is hungry, he is usually hungry, but not for food. He is hungry for praise, for recognition, for the ability to make his will into reality. He has no belief in love, for he has never known love. Or rather, his sister does love him, but he is not equipped to recognise that emotion, and simply thinks her weak and malleable.

The Chimaera looks upon this man with something akin to delight. Finally, finally here is the vessel that will fashion his own purpose into a reality. For the Chimaera is no mere messenger from either the gods or the demons. He is here entirely at his own behest, with an agenda that he has been shaping for a very long time indeed. By joining forces with this feckless and irritating young man he will be able to achieve finally what he alone has been unable to accomplish — the vanquishing of dragons.

Ivor feels the approval radiating from the Chimaera and relaxes somewhat more into this role he has imagined for himself for most of his life. The Chimaera nods toward the desk. "There's work to be done," he remarks mildly. "If this is how you want your life to be, there are certain things we must do now."

He made his way to the partner's desk and sat down, gesturing Ivor to the chair on the other side. "We will start with the paperwork. Here is a standard form for a company merger, only somewhat amended to allow for our particular needs. Ivor picked up the heavy vellum page and saw that C M Proteus and I Wyvern were to merge "for the mutual benefit of both parties to the contract" and to "further the interests of both parties as set out in a separate list." He stared around for another paper, to see only blank pages with a place for each signature at the bottom. "Proteus? That's you?"

"It's a name I often use, yes."

"C M stands for?"

"Chimaera Mutabilis of course."

"And our interests? There's nothing written here at all. I'm not signing anything I don't understand, you could add anything here at all."

"As could you. What would you put?"

Ivor thought — there was power, of course, but that was too vague. Immortality — did he really want immortality? That was an awfully long time, would he get bored or sick of life? Or what about wars and famines, would he be caught in those? Not, he thought, if he had enough money and power to live exactly as he pleased and have whatever he wanted. But what did he want? To move in society? Maybe, so long as he received nothing but the treatment due to someone rich, powerful, and famous. Or did he want fame? No, need to be careful here. Fame included the possibility of being bothered by all sorts of people he had no use for at all. So, not fame. Reclusive then? Well, privacy certainly. Trusted servants — how do you make sure people can be trusted? A house or houses of his own design so large and exciting that it would entertain him for years in the design, building and then furnishing.

So, endless wealth, privacy, trustworthy underlings, women — there should be women available for pleasure. He couldn't envision a wife or family, but nor did he want to rule them out entirely. So, a wife and family should he want them. Could that be made a condition? Work — he didn't want to 'work' as such, not sit at a desk and run an empire, not be troubled with hundreds of decisions every day, not even the bother of signing his name on things. So again trustworthy underlings were necessary, totally a necessity. But what guaranteed trustworthiness? Money, he thought, money and fear. Okay, he could supply both. Oh, and health, of course, what use would all this be if he was crippled with

60

in a debilitating illness. And aging — he didn't want to spend his life being nineteen, but nor did he want to live on for centuries becoming older and older. No, a reasonable age must be acquired and stuck to. And creativity, he had always absolutely known he could be a really fine artist if he had the time, money and - yes - training. Somehow he felt that although a good extra dose of talent was a prerequisite, being able to turn out masterpieces without any real work would be cheating. He wanted his art to matter, so work would be involved. Besides it would give him something to concentrate on and perfect over many, many years. Perhaps he could sell them under a pseudonym or otherwise guard his privacy while enjoying a measure of fame. The money wouldn't be unwelcome either. Maybe a separate special fund for special things...

He should be making notes, it would be very inconvenient if he were to make a list and leave out something crucial. He opened his eyes to find that the blank sheet in front of him was filling up with notations of all these thoughts.

"What the hell?" said Ivor pushing back from the desk as though the paper might bite him.

"Nicely done" said Proteus with a grin. "Is that all?"

"No," said Ivor, "It's just my thoughts, I can't be bound by just my thoughts. This needs to be organised and simplified and, above all, be watertight so I'm not left in a pickle. I've read about these contracts, they always work out badly for the human being."

"Oh, well, that's all right then," said Proteus, "because shortly you will no longer be entirely a human being. You will in fact be something akin to a god, or what your species thinks of as a god. No problem with a few stray adjectives or something left out by accident. Us Creatures aren't tripped up by such petty stuff. But I think you have left out something that is actually of great importance to you."

Ivor stared at the list and then up at Proteus. "I don't see... What is it that you think I want so much and haven't put down?"

"Revenge."

In the end they each made a short list..

Chapter 11

"And now for the important part," Proteus' smile was that of a hyena just before it bit into the neck of a quivering antelope. "We merge."

Ivor found himself drawing back in his chair. "I've, erm, been giving some thought to that," he managed to put a tone of superiority into a voice that really, really wanted to squeak with fear. "Accepting that this is necessary, surely in this modern world exchanging a bit of blood would more than suffice."

"More than suffice," mimicked Proteus, his face taking on a disgusted grimace. "Don't be a fool, do you think if there were an easier way I wouldn't have thought of it long ago. If you think I relish being consumed you're a bigger fool than you look, and appearances aside, you are no fool."

"Well, it was one thing when you were the size of a bug, now here you are, and I have no desire to add cannibalism to a growing list of sins."

"Eat me? I was wrong—you're an idiot! You aren't going to eat me! I said consume, as in absorb, take in, use up. Although, come to think of it, you won't use me up, we will just conjoin. We will be one person—you—but with all the elements of me, as well as of yourself. You, then, will become the next, and a true, chimaera. A vast improvement on anything you might have become I can assure you."

"And we'll share the same head? You'll be in here with me? I really don't care for that, y'know. Not even to possess all that is on offer here. What if we argue all the time? I mean, I can see us arguing a lot."

"Ah, a palpable hit," said Proteus. "And you're correct, that would never do. No, I will be the silent partner, so to speak. I will exist, but you will never know it. Only in moments of difficulty or crisis would any portion of my, erm, personality come to the fore. But you would find yourself perhaps with some desires and some powers to enact those desires that you hadn't had before. They will however seem quite natural to you. In a word, you will still be entirely you—just, err, rather more you than before. And, of course, should you be in need of a nice chat—well you can always call on me."

"Then how, if not by exchanging blood, do we accomplish this merger?" asked Ivor, much relieved by Proteus' assurances.

"We use that knife." Proteus gestured to the small instrument lying beside the ancient bottle on the red lacquer tray. It was quite plain except for the face incised into the handle, which appeared to be bone. Ivor squinted to make out the face but it eluded his eye, one moment an eagle or falcon, next possibly a lion, then a man but with curled horns. It changed without changing. It made his eyes water—clearly it didn't intend to be looked at closely.

"And do what? Saw ourselves in half and stitch us back together?"

"Bravado is understandable, foolishness is not. It is a simple thing, and not very painful."

Ivor shuddered at the mention of pain anyway.

"You will make an incision into your vein and I will, well, climb into it."

"Impossible!" roared Ivor. "I mean, look at you, you weigh half again as much as I do. It would kill us both if we even attempted such nonsense."

"I wish you would shut up when you don't know what you're talking about. I, of course, will be extremely small once more, and, err, something more suited to manoeuvring in liquid. Speaking of liquid, once this is done, you will quickly burn these contracts and then drink the contents of the bottle here. You will then pass out quite pleasantly and when you wake we will, as it were, be as one. Should you fail to do either of these things, all will be lost. Or, actually, you will be lost. I rather think I myself will survive to search for another who would suit my purpose. So you see you have both everything to gain and everything to lose. I suggest you follow the programme. Should you need my advice or counsel, you will find all you need within yourself. Oh, and put a bandage on your arm, we don't want to end up with blood poisoning."

And with these words Proteus disappeared. Ivor looked around, but until he felt a slight tickling of the hairs on his forearm he saw nothing. But there, beside the large vein running along his forearm was a—oh, ugh—a small slug or possibly a leech. "Cut now!" came a small voice. He picked up the knife with its inscrutable carving and clenching his teeth against the pain, he sliced down along the vein. The knife was incredibly sharp, the cut was quick and clean and didn't even sting to begin with. The thing that he had to trust was Proteus slid over the slick of blood and into the cut as easily as an otter off a riverbank. And was gone, except for a slight feeling of something sliding up his arm.

Into my heart or my head, thought Ivor. *Well, too late now.* He picked up the signed contracts and scanned them quickly—but as he did the words seemed, like the carving on the knife, to rearrange themselves into other things. He couldn't read them, so he did as instructed and threw them onto the fire. He tightly bandaged his arm with linen strips laid out for that purpose. *Where had those come from?* he thought fuzzily—he hadn't noticed them before. He picked up the bottle, sat down in the big wing chair and, disdaining a glass, downed the contents of the bottle in one long swig.

And it was done, irrevocably and forever, done.

Chapter 12

1855

Ivor got older, he wished to get older, he had no interest in being nineteen forever. He also found that his brain was considerably enlarged as to both knowledge and interests. His previous desire to sculpt and paint and design had now become a passion, and his talent proved to be prodigious. Other interests, previously undiscovered, now made themselves apparent. Rather than expose his amazing doubleness to a university, where possible slips of the tongue after a few pints in a local pub could make him either an object of fun or, worse, the object of careful scrutiny, he hired tutors and amassed a huge library whose subjects ranged from architecture to zoology and included every possible book on magic and the occult. There was also a large section on dragons and other mythological beasts, as demanded by the 'other side' of his brain.

One evening after a few brandies he was discussing the vexed question of ageing with the entity that he now called Proteus. "After all being and looking twenty-five is very fine, and a few more years to add gravitas and authority will be even better" he mused. "But there will come a time at around thirty-five when I would choose to stop the ageing of this body and keep that age into my immortality. It wasn't part of my understanding that my body would become decrepit and deformed by age while I continued through the centuries. So now you must enlighten me as to how this will occur, don't you think?"

Proteus made himself felt within his skull, sharing the use of his eyes and even apparently the appreciation of the fine brandy. "It is certainly time, and the key lies in your name and your heritage" said the voice in his skull.

"As I told you, I have a particular loathing for dragons. This is why your studies have included learning as much as has been written about such monsters."

"I assume you are not including me, as a Wyvern, in this loathing. After all you chose to make yourself a part of me."

"Your being a Wyvern is indeed an integral part of my plan, but not as someone to loathe, but someone to cherish. Your name reflects your heritage going back over the centuries into a prehistory, or should I say a hidden history, because the powers that be are not happy to admit that such creatures are not in fact myths, but quite real and with important powers. Your ancestors were given the name Wyvern in the misty past because they were in fact dragon-slayers. I have searched through the centuries and only the Wyverns appear to be capable of enslaving or possibly destroying dragons. Certainly my kind were unable to, and we suffered greatly and our numbers were reduced to only a few hidden and careful chimaeras, using our shape-changing ability to conceal ourselves. I have lived for the day when this awful inequity can be changed. And you will be able to do that."

"That's all well and good, Proteus, but what does it have to do with keeping my body young and healthy during my immortality?"

"Dragons are immortal, one of the few living beings—possibly the only being other than chimaeras—that are so naturally. They can be captured and kept in slavery, they can possibly be slain as your ancestors did, but they will never die by becoming old, they just go on and on. Now, think, please. What is the way in which another so-called mythical beast attains and keeps immortality?"

"Well, you Proteus, are you not immortal, and didn't you confer this upon me by joining with me?"

"Ah, yes that is what I said wasn't it? True in most ways, you will not be able to die in the ordinary way, just as I do not. But you will continue to age and go on ageing. I can change my shape or become part of another being and thus avoid this unpleasantness. So tell me what being can be immortal and forever young?"

"Ah, are you speaking of vampires? But are they not considered 'undead' as opposed to immortal?"

"An ugly name given them by envious humans. They are not 'undead', they are to all intents and purposes alive and immortal—and they do not age. How?"

"Both folk wisdom and fiction say it is by drinking blood, first being turned by drinking the blood of a vampire and then drinking the blood of human beings. But, Proteus, I am not a vampire, and it has been my understanding that that option was not part of our contract."

"Exactly. You are not, nor will you be, a vampire. But your ancestors were known to extend their lives and not visibly age by drinking the blood of dragons. You must find and subdue dragons, keeping them chained or enchanted and drink their blood regularly, that is the recipe for never growing older."

"Oh hell and damnation, Proteus. You say there are dragons, but where? And I'm no bloody knight on a great steel-shod horse with a lance! I'm an artist and a scholar."

"You are also a magician, a practitioner of magic. Magic will subdue a dragon, the right magic at the right time."

"And we'll keep them in the cellars here, shall we? Whatever will the neighbours say?"

"You have been designing a castle, a wonderful Gothic Revival castle, have you not?" breathed Proteus. "Miles of corridors, miles of cellars, great towers, immense dungeons, more than enough space, and you can afford to have miles and miles of land, privacy to do as you will."

"And my will requires dragons? More like your will! I remember you know, I remember that night we joined—you were absolutely incandescent with the idea that you could get your own back on dragons. Vanquish them, I think you said."

"And if I did? Have I ever for one moment led you to believe I am in this from the goodness of my heart? We are joined in a great work here, our power is immense, and it is only right that the great wrong done to me and my kind be avenged. As for you, you require dragons' blood or your bones will bend and break and your skin will wrinkle and go yellow, your eyes will be rheumy and your teeth will blacken and fall out. Yet you will live. Is that what you want? Joined as we are, is it not a fine thing that our needs coincide so beautifully?"

Ivor took a large gulp of brandy and laughed. "You are, as usual, right my friend. Our needs do indeed coincide. And I have a strong feeling that this wonderful castle of mine will be just the place for dragons, wyverns and their ilk. It will, of course, be called Wyvern Hall."

Chapter 13

As spring moved toward summer England was a torrent of bloom and at Ashley it seemed that every tree, bush and bulb was determined to outdo its neighbour. Wood hyacinths, snowdrops and early anemones had given way to the trumpet blare of legions of yellow, cream and pink daffodils and the musky-scented pheasant-eye narcissus. Modest grape hyacinths withered and tall Dutch hyacinths with flower spikes in pink and mauve, deep purple and apricot made a riot of colour at the ends of the borders. Tulip beds cut swathes of colour through the formal lawns. The fruit trees were a glory of tossing pink and white blossom and the buds of the rhododendrons looked swollen and potent with glory to come. Birds were making a riot of song as they challenged each other over territory and mates, and where the swallows and martins were building nests amongst the beams of barns and sheds there were piles of mud, straw and bird droppings building up underneath as well.

Altogether it was not a comfortable time of year. There was something fierce about this general burgeoning, as if only the thinnest of boundaries kept nature from overrunning everything. To Kate, who used to try to surround herself with order and moderation to combat the chaos of her family life, this Bacchanalian excess was both exhilarating and frightening simultaneously.

She was consumed with nervous energy that demanded that she frolic among the flowers, running and leaping until she and Poppet collapsed in an idiotic heap. Or she went to the Dojo and kicked the heavy bolster until she couldn't raise her leg that high any more. Mrs. Sykes, correctly diagnosing spring fever, prescribed afternoon naps. Kate, who in New York would have snapped a refusal, to her own amazement complied without a murmur of rebellion. True, she intended to simply spend the time in her room reading, but found that lying down shortly produced deep and restful sleep. This was a very good thing, as the excesses of late spring-early summer had had the effect of profoundly disturbing her sleep at night.

After dark it seemed her sleep was restless and prone to many sudden awakenings. Though there was no repetition of the strange dream (as she thought of it now), yet she continued to wake suddenly, filled not with fear but with excitement and a vague longing. Sometimes it seemed that she had been dreaming, but these dreams always escaped entirely at the moment of waking, leaving only the sense of loss, almost as if she had waked to find herself on the wrong side of a door, while on the other side was paradise. She found this troubling because as a rule her memory for dreams was good, and her sleep that of a healthy young person, only occasionally disturbed by a real nightmare.

The daily naps, however, improved her disposition and general health to the extent that Mrs. Sykes, who had been on the point of dispensing vinegar and molasses, decided the crisis was past and returned her attention to the many things a very small staff on a large estate must attend to when spring pounces.

Kate, left to herself, continued to have strange nights and blissful days. Blissful because she and Poppet were welcomed everywhere by the working men and women and she was allowed to watch or help with all the myriad chores and wonders of spring on a working estate. And because she enjoyed learning as it was dished up by Peregrine, with the added fun of having Robin to tease.

At other times she would wander off on long walks among the gardens and out into the woods. She saw a water rat supervising the first frolic of its young on the grassy riverbank, the smooth brown mother looking very grave as the youngsters, minute balls of brown fur, rolled and tumbled. She watched as the swans (such gorgeous birds with such rotten tempers and the nasty habit of trying to bite the hand that fed them) came out with their cygnets for family swims in the ornamental lake. First came a vision of perfection in white with its wings held just so as it glided through the water, then six perfectly daft looking fuzzy grey cygnets, then another vision in white, noticeable because her wings were held a demure few inches lower than her lord's. Kate watched the lambs, older now but still darling, play 'I'm the king of the castle' on any small hillock or even the top of the feed rack, butting off the competition, then leaping down themselves just for the fun of it.

Yet much of this real life still had a sense of slight unreality about it, as if the strange feelings of the nights had hung a veil between her and the busy bustling world about her. She moved sometimes like she was still dreaming, not always completely aware of her surroundings. She would seem to hear a plaintive call in her inner ear, and that sense of longing and loss would wash over her.

"Why do you go out alone if it only makes you lonely?" asked Robin.

"Because I might see a unicorn, and if you were there it wouldn't come out," said Kate with a shrug to show she was just being cynical. But she wasn't feeling cynical. She was feeling like just around the next corner something very marvellous indeed might appear.

"Are you kidding? All unicorns just love me!" Robin spread his arms to embrace a herd of invisible unicorns and made Kate smile in spite of herself.

In the midst of this time of busy burgeoning spring, Maggie Spenser had to go to London for a few nights, and Robin asked if he could stay at home as he hated spending time in grimy old London while spring was alive in the hills and valleys. So Maggie asked Sir Hugh if Robin could stay at Ashley, because, as she told Robin, "You may think you're old enough to stay alone here, but I'm your mother, and just happen to think differently." Although a bit offended by this insult to his maturity, Robin liked this plan better than staying alone.

It was the night of the full moon. The air was fresh and soft. Nighttime scents, more subtle than those of the day, wafted on gentle breezes almost as if the spirits of beautiful women were moving by, leaving behind hints of their delicious fragrances. The fountain in the garden made soft plashing water music. In the woods the nightingale sang so beautifully that Kate's heart ached with the sound. She fell asleep listening to birdsong and the gentle fall of water playing about the nymphs and dolphins on the fountain to dream of iridescent singing fish that raised their scaly heads above the ripples to serenade the moon. It seemed then that she was riding a dolphin from the fountain, now a beautiful sea, and they bounded through the gentle swells for the sheer joy of being alive. Then they dived and explored the coral caves, the opalescent shells and brilliant fish, watched starfish and anemones waving their arms lazily amidst the corals. And then Kate nosed deeper into the sea. Passing gold and red octopuses, she reached out to stroke a passing tentacle, marvelled at squid with rippling neon patterns running along their bodies and jellyfish whose colours put even the squid in the shade, finally burrowing down into darkness and deep and dreamless sleep.

A bell rang, soft, hollow, deep. A single sustained note. From deep in the warm dark caves of sleep Kate heard its summons and swam towards the surface. She opened her eyes with the note still ringing in her ears. The breeze had dropped and the night was still. Once again, her nightlight had gone out. But this time Kate did not lie frozen in terror, because it seemed to her she was being called. Getting swiftly out of bed she pulled her light cotton robe over her pyjamas and left the room. Her bedroom curtains had been drawn against the moonlight, but the upstairs hall with its great windows along one side was full of its brightness.

She made her way down the great stair, as always trailing her hand along the carved fruits and flowers, and into the big drawing room with its French doors out onto the terrace. Here she moved from shadow to shadow toward the French doors and when she got there she crouched down in the shelter of the large swagged drapery and carefully looked out. Music was playing now, pan pipes and a violin and just possibly an oboe. Just as her eyes were adjusting to the moonlight, she felt a hand on her bare ankle and jumped, squeaking with fright.

"Shush!" said Robin, clapping his hand across her mouth. "I heard it too. I was coming to find out what's going on."

Kate bit him. "Oy, demon!" whispered Robin. "Cut that out! Come on, we'll get found out."

"Yeah, well, don't creep up on me, you scared the crap out of me."

"Okay, sorry, but…" Robin's voice trailed off.

Thud! Thud! Thud! Like someone was dropping huge stones. Getting louder, coming closer…

A shadow moved across the path of the moonlight. And they both froze because something big, something *really* big was stomping its way across the terrace, making the very ground tremble. Kate felt for and held onto Robin's hand. Hers was shaking slightly.

They remained as motionless as possible, holding their breath as an enormous creature came into view, stalking slowly past the window. It was easily the size of an elephant, but it was a monster. It had the head of an eagle, a lion's body with four huge feet, and enormous wings that were held slightly aloft. The body ended in a long tail with an arrow-head shaped end.

"Oh my god, what the hell is that?" breathed Robin into Kate's ear.

"I can't believe it… It's a griffin, a winged one." whispered Kate. "It's so *big*."

"And it's grey all over," said Robin. "Are they supposed to be grey?"

"It looks like the statue down by the gates. There's two, but one is missing its head. But it can't be the statue—it's moving."

"Oh, it's moving all right," said Robin as the beast statue swung its beaked head from side to side as if trying to scent something. "Quick, move back, it's looking in here."

They moved back further behind the drapes where they couldn't see but could hear the monster snuffling near the doors. Stiff with fright, Kate tried not to breathe. Then the great thudding footsteps moved away.

"This can't be happening," breathed Kate.

"Oh, I don't know," said Robin. "There's a lot around here that 'can't be happening' but—err—it's happening."

"Like what? What are you talking about?" hissed Kate. "Two-ton statues stomping around—that's not possible. What else is going on?"

"That, for one." Robin pointed out the window where now several smaller statues were parading past. The two harpies seemed to be in friendly conversation, one of them holding some knitting, and the statue of Shakespeare was in some kind of heated argument with Socrates. Kate began to shake slightly. Robin was distressed, and put his arms around her "Hush, now, it's okay, don't be scared, they're not after us."

"I'm not scared," Kate managed to gasp, "I'm laughing and trying to be quiet at the same time. See that knitting? Now I know who does the knitting." He looked at her like she'd lost her senses.

"The harpy, look—the older one, she's knitting, see?"

"Is that what that is? How did you know about that?"

"I found it in the shrubbery behind her plinth and I couldn't figure out who could possibly be doing it and have left it there. Now I know."

Their voices had now attracted attention, and a nymph or dryad from the plinth by the ornamental pool was peering in at them. She hissed loudly, making Kate jump and squeak once more. "We've seen!" called the nymph. And with a sound like a shriek a wind seemed to come from nowhere and swept through the garden making the trees and shrubs bend and leaves fly across the windows. Kate and Robin both cowered behind the heavy drapes as even small branches and what could have been pebbles were swept against the French windows with a dreadful clattering like bones. When it died down the moon was behind a cloud and there was no movement or sound in the garden.

Chapter 14

As the clatter and banging of branches, leaves and small stones against the windows and French doors died away, Robin and Kate risked moving to stare at each other. Fear and wonder warred in their eyes and they became aware they were still clutching each other and moved back a pace and dropped their eyes. By unspoken consent, they began to move slowly across the expanse of the drawing room floor, edging from patch of darkness to patch of darkness, avoiding the moonlit areas.

Suddenly a searingly bright light arced across the room and a voice boomed, "Who goes there? Come out now or you'll feel this poker up your jacksie!" Bates materialised in a patch of moonlight, a brilliant torch in one hand, his other hand wielding the fire poker like a sword.

Kate, pulling the reluctant Robin behind her, stepped forward. "It's only us, Bates. We heard all the banging and clattering and came to see if anything was broken or the doors were open. There isn't anybody else here."

Bates lowered the poker carefully and used the torch to check the windows and doors for signs of damage. "Well, Miss Kate, it seems to be as you say. But you two shouldn't be wandering around in the dark all alone—it could have been dangerous."

You have no idea, thought Robin, heaving a sigh of relief.

"Did it wake Uncle Hugh?" asked Kate.

"Nay, lass, him don't wake even for the crack of doom, he's well away with the fairies after a good snifter of brandy."

Fairies, ha! Robin kept this to himself as well, but he and Kate both breathed easier knowing that only Bates had discovered their midnight rambles.

"Please don't tell him we came down alone, you know he worries about me and he wouldn't like to think Robin and I were hanging out together after midnight. But we just met up in the hall because of the noise, and came in to check it out."

"Don't worry, lass, I makes it a rule not to bother Sir Hugh except when it's absolutely necessary. Now you two get on with you, back to bed and we can all go help sweep up that litter in the morning. But it was a strange thing an' all, so it was, the moon full and the sky clear and air all soft—then suddenly there's like a little hurricane and everything blown all over the place." And with that Bates and his light disappeared back through the door leading toward the kitchens.

"Come with me," said Kate. "I've got an electric kettle in my room and we can make hot chocolate and talk about this. No way can I just go back to sleep now. We really need to talk."

Kate's room was spacious and beautiful but very cosy. She lit the small fire laid in the fireplace and some candles and an oil lamp—"because the big electric lights might show someone we are up at this hour"—and filled the kettle from the basin in the adjoining bathroom and plugged it in.

The soft flickering lights showed the big cream-painted four-poster decorated with garlands of flowers and fruit and ribbons, painted in shades of soft greens, blues and golds, with touches of pinks and reds in the fruits and flowers. The same theme was carved into the wood of the fire surround and repeated in the Aubusson rug before it, which had a central oval containing a pastoral scene of an unlikely shepherd and shepherdess in 18th century court costumes of knee britches and lots of ribbons and flounces.

One impossibly clean sheep laid its head on the shepherd's knee while he presented a floral tribute to the princess/shepherdess standing before him. This pastoral idyll was repeated in the plaster central oval of the ceiling, all cream with gold touches. The ceiling also featured cherubs in the corners, mostly obscured by cobwebs, but charming nonetheless. The walls were papered in a wide stripe in faded greens and blues, with again a border of fruit and flower garlands where the wall met the ceiling. The heavy drapes that concealed the big sash windows and kept their lights from being seen outside were woven in silvery-gold and cream.

Poppet, who had spent some weeks sleeping in Kate's bedroom, was now banished to the kitchen after chewing a chair leg and making a puddle on the rug. The kitchen was warm and the garden was only a step away and there were occasional scraps to beg or steal, so Poppet was not pining, although Kate missed her.

Handing Robin a mug of cocoa she had made from a packet, Kate settled down on the carpet before the fire with her own and took a deep breath. "What we saw—that wasn't the first time I've had some sort of—ahh— 'experience' in the garden. I woke up on the last full moon also, and I went down and—I think—danced with creatures, all kinds of creatures, and swam in the pool, but it became the sea and I dived down and down. But I can't remember it clearly any longer and when I woke up the next morning I thought it was just a dream. It was the music that drew me to begin with that time as well. So now I don't know if it was a dream. Now I think it could have been real, a real enchantment. Am I nuts?"

Robin was turning his mug and staring into it like he might find some answers there. "You know how my mother told everybody in the village that my father is a faerie prince?"

"No! I never heard that. But why would she say such a crazy thing?"

"Maybe because it's true?" Robin raised eyes that twinkled and dared her.

"Oh, come on, don't tease me now. Besides fairies are little things with wings that sip dew and flower nectar...." She faltered to stop as Robin grinned and pulled back his hair to reveal his pointed ears. "Oh, they're not, are they? And you're a fairy?"

"Half a faerie and my mother is a witch. And before you say, what! broomsticks and black hats? No, she's a white witch, an earth witch, with excellent powers, and the possibility of harnessing the power of the earth in extreme need. But it means I'm magical." Robin simply left out the bit where, although he could see magical creatures, he himself had not yet been able to do any magic—that wasn't, he felt, any of Kate's business. He continued, "Only I've never seen magic like we saw tonight. I don't know if those statues are enchanted from without or within, if they are real spirits or only very good mechanical engines with some small magic running them. We need to speak to my mother, and maybe to my dad too."

"So there is magic? Real magic? And you and your parents 'have' it? And here at Ashley, are there magic people too?"

"No, definitely not, your uncle and Bates and the rest—they aren't magical, they don't do magic. And most important, they don't see magic. If Sir Hugh or Bates had been with us and if the statues had gone strolling around, well, they wouldn't have seen anything at all."

"But, but...I saw it all. I saw it. And I'm just like my uncle, magic never happened to me."

"Exactly. Never before, but it's happened now. And, trust me on this, it means you're magical. And if you never knew it, well, that means we have to find out about it, and get you some help to use it and not let it use you. Magic can be dangerous, just like electricity. Or it can be useful, like electricity. So we need to talk to my mother and find out how you can learn to use it."

"So I don't get electrocuted by it, is that it?"

"That's one way of putting it, but don't worry. That 'dream' you had last full moon—that sounds like the magic here is on your side, at least most of it is. They let you in. They made you a part of something very special. That wouldn't happen if you were a threat. But there are other powers, who won't be so welcoming. Like tonight, that big stone mythical beast didn't seem friendly at all, and the bloody pixie or whatever that 'shopped' us— definitely not friendly. And the huge wind that blew everything, that was saying 'keep out' in no uncertain terms. So I'm thinking that what you will need is at least some defences in place."

Kate took a steadying breath, "Well, the dojo has taught me to harness my physical core strength and I can now kick the legs out from under a grown man, so it seems to me we now need to find out who can help me discover and use these powers you say I have. Because if there's magic out there and I can sense it, I would hate to be caught without any defence. Do I learn spells? I'm not sacrificing small animals!"

"Oh, you might be willing to sacrifice a very small animal if it meant keeping out of the clutches of goblins! They're tall and slinky and green and they drool and smell horrible." Robin curled his hands into claws and distorted his face.

"What! Oh, ugh, yeech. Really?"

"No, not really, I made those up!" He was laughing almost too hard to speak. "You should see your face!"

"I am going to murder you!" cried Kate, lunging at him, but he dodged and flipped her on her back, holding her down with his hands on her shoulders. For a long moment they remained there, looking at each other suddenly very differently. Then Robin blinked and the moment passed.

"Well," he said, rolling away, "I think we'd better see my mum as soon as possible. I'll ask her if we can have you over to tea when she gets back from London. I know she'll say yes."

They both stood up, feeling slightly awkward in their pyjamas, and then Robin said a hasty goodnight and was gone.

Chapter 15

Kate was walking Poppet in the garden the next morning when she spied a note by the angry-looking harpy's plinth pinned to the ground with a knitting needle. It must be from the knitting harpy she thought.

We r spirits of real peple trapped in the ston. We can only move/talk when the moon is fulle. Meet me here after mid nite the next full moon. Plse do not be frightened. Eleanor

This is was written, clearly with difficulty, in charcoal and with many misspellings. It was clear that Eleanor's spirit had trouble working her stone hands properly—which explained the messy knitting.

After lessons with Perry, Kate took Robin aside and showed him the note. "Look! This is what happened to them. Robin, they're trapped out there. Like in horrible stone cages. We have to help them."

"What we have to do," said Robin, "is take it to my mum. This is getting very complicated, and we're going to need help to sort it out. Do we know who this Eleanor is?"

"There's an Eleanor in the family Bible—she was Ivor Wyvern's sister. But she must have died long ago. So I don't know if it can be her."

"Well if it's her spirit then there's the bit about spirits or souls being immortal—so maybe it is her."

"But Ivor was the sculptor who carved those statues—if someone did this, it might have been him. So why would he do such a thing to his sister?"

"That's part of what we need to find out. Listen, I called my mum and she's come back early and has asked you to come home with me tomorrow for afternoon tea. Old English custom you know."

"Don't be silly, of course I know, we have afternoon tea here on Sunday afternoons and then only a light supper so Mrs Sykes doesn't have to work too hard on a Sunday."

§ § §

The next afternoon they took Poppet and set out after classes along the path beside the stream. In honour of the occasion, a proper invitation to tea, Kate was wearing a boho mini dress with a mandala pattern in rose pinks and goldy-yellows, navy blue ankle boots with a froth of lace around the tops and a dark blue velvet shoulder bag decorated with sequins and beads. Robin, as usual, wore jeans over boots and a tee-shirt that said Save the Tiger. His dark hair fell in waves nearly to his shoulders and was cut in jagged bangs that half-concealed his gold eyes. A half hour walk brought them to the ruin of a humpbacked bridge. "Here we are," said Robin happily.

Kate stood looking at the crumbling stonework covered in mosses and ferns and a few brambles. She shook her head. There was no house in sight. "You live here? Is there a tent somewhere, or a charcoal-burners' hut I can't see?"

"No," said Robin, "It's here, right where you see a bridge about to fall down. Now, look just to the side, look just to the left a little, so the bridge is only in the corner of your eye. No, don't stare back, just relax, and look into the trees on the left and let go of the bridge in your mind. Just see without your brain commenting."

Kate tried to do as he instructed. She focused away into the trees to the left, just the stones and stream in her peripheral vision on the right. Nothing was happening, nothing…no, wait, as she allowed her mind to let go, there it was! Not a bridge at all but a house. Still with mosses and ferns, but definitely a house, with a door to the left of the stream and built out over it on heavy stone foundations. The stream itself flowed through an oval opening with what seemed to be a portcullis coming down from the top and disappearing under the water. The roof was low and hump-backed with reddish curved tiles patterned with lichen and emerald moss and the occasional wild flower. The door was painted red and there were red geraniums in pots on either side. The house itself seemed to run back along the stream bed, appearing to cover the stream. It got a bit misty and fading as she looked.

"You see?" exclaimed Robin. "Yes, you do see it! I knew you would."

"Yes! Yes I do," said Kate. "How incredible. So how does that work? And can I look directly at it now? I'm getting a headache trying to see out of the corner of my eye."

"It's what in books they call a glamour—it just means that it's disguised like a bridge to anybody we don't want knowing about it. If everyone could see it, they'd want it for a tea shop or a gift shop or a haunted house ride or something. That's why Mum had to get the lease on the land, so Sir Hugh wouldn't be fooled into selling it. And we like our privacy. You know how the grockles descend on Devon in summer, poking into every corner and wanting everything to be Hound of the Baskervilles or Pixies or Gnomes. They'd be on this place like a flock of crows. So my father just hid it, that's all."

"I thought your father lived somewhere foreign and you never see him. And a glamour is fiction, not real — you do know that don't you? Oh, and what's a grockle?

"Grockles are what Devonians call holidaymakers." Robin grinned, looking more like some kind of super-handsome rock star crossed with an elf than ever. It made Kate shiver and she wasn't sure if it was with delight or dread. "So what are you gonna believe—the stories people tell you, or the evidence of your own eyes? That's the story," he said. "That's the story we tell. This is the reality. This is here, it's real, and my mum is waiting for us with a really good tea. Shall we go in?"

If outside was a shock to the senses, inside was a revelation. The stream didn't run under the house as Kate had thought when she saw the half circle where the water flowed under and she assumed the ground floor would be above that. Instead, once inside she saw that the stream flowed gently along between the stones of the floor. And beside it grew violets and ferns and small yellow flowers, because there was plenty of light from sky lights and big windows looking out the private side of the house. But more than that, uniquely, the house followed the stream, each room at a slightly different angle to the next. As it went over a small waterfall, so the house also fell away, and stairs beside the stream went down one or two steps into the next room. The house was only one room wide, but many rooms long as it followed the meander of the stream, and the water was entirely contained within the stone floor.

Mostly the stream was narrow enough to be easily stepped over, but every now and then it widened and there were stepping stones to get from one side to the other. In other rooms it developed into small pools and in one there was a small bridge, like the bridge on a blue and white plate, over one of these pools. In the water there were fish of many colours, spotted and striped and solid, and in some rooms jewelled dragonflies and small iridescent birds were flying around. It was easily the most enchanting place Kate had ever seen. Poppet immediately went for a drink and then splashed happily into a slightly deeper spot, pawing at where she had spotted a fish (long gone now).

"Oh, I'd never even be able to imagine someplace so wonderful." breathed Kate. "It's enchanted."

86

"Told you!" said Robin. "Yeah, it's really awesome. I thought you'd like it."

"Like it? It's just fabulous, a magical house inside and out. I think Ashley is beautiful, but this is a fairytale. I love it!"

"I'm so glad you love it. We certainly do," Maggie came into the room, putting her arm around her son and smiling at Kate.

"But it's so open, what do you do in winter or when the bugs are out?" Robin looked about to speak, but Maggie intervened, "We've got screens against insects and double-glazing in cold or rainy weather—they slide out of the walls, see." A large sliding glass came slowly across the open space that led into the garden and further into the woods. "And big shades for privacy." A long opaque material descended slowly from the ceiling.

"And there are rooms with dividers that can be closed to give privacy, lots of fire places and some heated pools for bathing," said Robin. "And some bedrooms up over the stream, not with the stream running through it, for those who don't find the sound of running water soothing (it makes me want to get up and pee all the time), or who want very dry air for sleeping, but also bedrooms with the stream running through. Come on, have the tour!"

Kate walked with Robin and his mother from room to room, each unique and each seeming to her dazzled eyes more wonderful than the last. Different rooms had different decorative schemes, some very rustic with wood and stone walls and vines growing up them, big stone inglenook fireplaces and even iron kettles hanging from wrought iron arms to make a stew or just heat water. Some with plastered and painted walls with fire surrounds from different architectural periods and a few that were carved with fantastical beasts and flowers and leaves with beams also carved or painted with wonderful patterns. The kitchen was a surprise—the same stone floor, and the stream, but here were modern granite worktops and stainless steel and cream painted cupboards with only minimal decoration.

"I think you're the most fortunate people in the world to live here," said Kate.

"You might not be quite so enchanted if you went to bed and remembered you'd left your hot drink or your book back some twenty rooms away—that's really annoying!" But Maggie was laughing when she said it.

"Aw, Mum, you know you'd just do a fetching spell. It's me that has to run back for things."

"Robin, now may not be the best time…" Maggie trailed off as she saw their expressions.

"It's okay, Mum, Kate knows about us. And, well, it's like this: Kate has been having magical experiences. She could see through the glamour with just a little help from me on how to look. It's part of why we're here. This has never happened to her before. She was so frightened when we saw the statues moving. She needs help with all of this."

"Huh? Don't do that Robin!" snapped Kate. "That whole 'I'm the guy and I was totally on top of it' thing. I wasn't the only one who was frightened. You were nearly wetting yourself! But, yes, Maggie, this is all entirely new to me. Robin says I'm 'magical' but I never had any, well, 'experiences' in New York. It only started the other night, or maybe a month ago, when the moon was full. Both full moons. And I'm finding it hard to believe now that I really saw what I saw, if you see what I mean?" Kate shut up when she realised she'd talked herself into a see/saw/seen sort of linguistic trap. She blushed.

Maggie looked at the young woman sitting by her fire and watching with wondering eyes the lively carvings on the fire surround, the beams and how they seemed to mirror the fish and creatures that were swimming in the lily pool. This child woman who, Maggie thought, had come from across the seas and thought about fate and time and gods and man. Who would have thought, though, that it would be her. Well, apparently it was indeed time.

The monstrous Ivor Wyvern would have been taught about a merciful and rational god who fixed the stars in their places and ordered the affairs of men, who had his eye upon the sparrow. He could not then have known about the unruly fiery nature of stars, or that the sun was merely a medium sized one living at the outer reaches of a spiral arm of what was, after all, only a middling galaxy. Ivor, like some others, thought of himself as above and beyond the justice of the universe. He could play at being a god on a small planet, but he would be helpless in the face of the universe. But on this small beautiful planet he had done great damage, thought Maggie. He needed to be stopped if even a part of what she'd heard was true.

All that fiery spewing and whirling, all that enormous energy and those unruly rocks hurtling through space, the unknowable unreachable depths of every blasted planet. Including ours, our precious Earth which, instead of being the gentle cup in which God's creatures could evolve gently in comfort, each in its allotted place and time, was instead as roiling and boiling a thick broth of magma and flaming interior as any star, but with a thin coat of velvety greens and blues giving the impression of a paradise. And even that thin coat turned out to be but an illusion as beneath its few, perilously few, feet of organic waste (yes, waste) it also was always on the move, being pushed inexorably to and fro so that continents broke apart and came together, annihilating what had gone before to form new Edens and new Hells.

And yet, and yet, in the human span of things all seemed ordered, and within that order there was so much, so startlingly much, that was utterly beautiful. You might know that the choir of bird song was really the war cries of feathered barbarians warning others off their patch, or that the newly hatched children of these feathered fanatics were far uglier than any of their reptile cousins, and had they been the size of a brontosaurus would have frightened the life out of any twitcher. But even then you'd be captivated by the beauty of the song.

No, the truth was that the nature of most men was to perceive beauty and order upon the face of the earth and to have his soul cry out to the heavens with heartfelt praise. Even those who knew the origins of everything, perhaps those most of all, who grasped the fiery magma, the iron core, the raging crazed groping of the stars themselves, yes those most of all were astonished by the sheer magnificence of such energy, such violence. And such is the longing of the soul for beauty and transcendence that these most of all were aware of the glory of being and, for those who thought that way, the glory of the gods.

And, having listened to Robin and also Sir Hugh about how remarkable Kate was, Maggie was almost certain Kate was one such. Kate, she'd been told, watched both the unfolding of the seasons and the night sky, read books and watched TV programmes about the origins of the universe and gloried in all of it. She was delighted that she lived in a world where rock stars were also particle and astrophysicists. She was lit from within by the excitement of finding that the immensity of a coral reef was created over hundreds, thousands and millions of years by animals you needed a magnifying glass or microscope to see. Or that many rocks had organic origins. It all thrilled her. And now she was discovering her own potential, a potential very few humans possessed—to see and possibly to do magic.

Well it seemed it was time to add yet another dimension to her delight, but also to be the cause of her sorrow. It was time to tell her the story of the dragons.

Maggie knew that it would thrill Kate to find that the first feathered dinosaurs (who would have thought that Tyrannosaurus Rex might have been, probably was, covered in tiny wispy feathers?) had not all died out or evolved into comparatively small birds. That there was in fact a sub-branch of these 'thunder lizards' who had developed in another branch of time, there to become dragons, and that such dragons were only the width of a wish away. Or, according to Robin's father Kailen, the dragons were back and tragically under the powerful influences of the being that called itself Sir Ivor Wyvern. Even the thought of him made a dark shadow pass over Maggie's spirit. There was a sudden blast of wind-driven rain against the window. A coincidence, surely?

Chapter 16

Maggie bade them sit in a small room with a view out into a walled garden. The wall across from the open French doors was a garden in itself, covered in climbing vines that were a riot of colour: morning glory, clematis, trumpet vine, honeysuckle, climbing roses, moonflowers and flowers Kate didn't recognise but suspected were tropical, all blooming together regardless of time of day or season.

Inside there was a round table set with all the wonderful paraphernalia of an English high tea—little sandwiches with the crusts cut off (Kate secretly had an email address that said wedontdocrusts@gothmail.com)—cucumber, smoked salmon, egg mayonnaise, curried chicken, and cheddar cheese with Branston pickle. Scones with pots of clotted cream and several different jams, meringues filled with fruit and more cream, and some hot sausages and small omelettes. Plus, because Kate was from America, there were buffalo chicken wings and peanut butter and banana sandwiches. Enough food for a small army was displayed on a white cloth, with pink and red flowers in a green vase, pink and green napkins and white plates with green and gold bands around the edges plus big mugs and glasses—nothing that would break if you breathed on it. There was tea and coffee and several cold drink choices too. They all set about eating and for a little while the only conversation was 'pass me those sandwiches please' and 'is there more clotted cream?'.

Where do I start? thought Maggie. Ah, it's what she's calling the 'experiences' that are top of her list, we need to get to the bottom of those and reassure her if possible. It was Robin who picked up on that, as if he knew the direction his mother's thoughts were taking.

"Hey," he said, gently nudging Kate, "No one here thinks you imagined anything—unless it's you. I saw them too, remember. And believe me, I know what I saw. Statues walking in the moonlight, and looked like they were talking too. It was really happening."

He turned to his mother: "Mum, it's a kind of magic I've never seen, or for all I know it was a kind of clockwork, but there was this slightly greeny-purplely glow around some of them, so I think it was magic. And the spell must be triggered by the moon."

"And one of the statues left me a note," said Kate, producing the grass-stained, wrinkled and smeared paper from her pocket.

Maggie read it over carefully.

We r spirits of real peple trapped in the ston. We can only move/talk when the moon is fulle. Meet me here after mid nite the next fulle moon. Plse do not be frightened. Eleanor

She looked at the hole particularly. "What's this?"

"Oh," said Kate, "That's where the harpy pinned it to the ground with one of her knitting needles. That's how I knew it was from her.

"Harpy? Knitting?" Maggie was now lost entirely in an Alice-down-the-rabbit-hole vision of knitting needles, harpies, fluttering pieces of paper, strolling stone statues, all floating by, that made no sense to her at all, but clearly were an explanation in Kate's mind. "Start at the beginning, please, because now you've lost me."

Kate drew a deep breath. "It started the full moon before last when I had what I thought was a dream, where I heard this wonderful bell, and then music and singing, and the night was bright outside, so I think I went down and out into the garden, and then it's just broken up images. I think I danced with, well, beings—maybe fairies or elves, I don't remember statues, but maybe some of them were there, or they were elsewhere. And then I came back to my bedroom and slept really late. When I woke up I thought it was a dream, but then I found the statue of one of the harpies—you know everything out there is overgrown and kind of jungle-y?—with part of Tennyson's poem about Maud on the base. And by the other harpy, the older-looking one, I found some knitting in the undergrowth behind her plinth. Those things really happened. But I really just thought the night-time stuff, the music and the dancing and everything, was all a dream."

Robin took up the story. "So we looked up the poem and then Perry said one of Kate's ancestors was called Maude and there was a scandal. We looked up the family tree in the bible and there she was—only there was a mystery about her marriage and when she died. Are there any more chicken wings?"

"She wanted to marry Ivor Wyvern," said Kate. "Her family wouldn't let her, so she ran away to live with him in this sort of Victorian-Gothic fortress he had built up the river from here. And after a few years no one ever heard from her again. Oh, and Ivor started suing the Mallory family for her inheritance, and over the boundary lines, and Uncle Hugh says that the lawsuits are still going on, which I don't understand. And I don't understand why the two harpies in our garden are called Eleanor and Maude. Ivor made them, so he must have called them that. But did he manage to catch their souls or spirits and put them in the statues? And why? It's so cruel, and they were his sister and the love of his life. How could he?"

"Maybe it was how he could keep them near him?" ventured Robin.

"But they aren't near him — they're in Ashley's garden."

"Well, maybe it's because he thought shortly he'd own Ashley and be able to evict the Mallorys. Meanwhile he was making good money by selling Sebastian the statues. Win, win. Mum, can I have another scone?"

"But it's so wicked! They're trapped, it's like being completely paralysed, but able to think and hear and

94

see—I can't think of anything more awful. Robin, Maggie, please—we need to help them!"

Maggie said thoughtfully, "Kate, I haven't come across anything like that kind of magic. I don't think it's clock-work, it sounds like what the note says—that their spirits have been trapped. We will have to research it and ask some trustworthy friends before we can begin to know what to do. The wrong counter-spell could simply annihilate them or even banish them to an outer darkness. I think it unlikely we can resurrect them as people—as living, breathing people. Even if there is a body left, that is necromancy and forbidden for good reason, not least of which is that the soul hates it. The best we could hope for would be to set them free."

"You mean allow them to die, don't you?" Kate looked deeply troubled.

"It could be what they long for, sweet girl," said Maggie. "Or they might prefer to stay as they are, we just don't know. But until I find out what was done to them in the first place there is no chance of reversing it anyway.

"But what we can begin on now is to find out who you are and what kinds of magic you might possess. Go on with the story, dear," she urged gently, passing the scones over to Robin. "What about this full moon just past? Was it the same dream?"

"No, not at all. Or, rather, yes it started the same, there was the bell that woke me up and then the music, so I went down the stairs again and across the drawing room and this time I knelt down behind the drapes at the French doors and pulled one back a little and looked out. And that's when Robin grabbed my ankle. Scared me out of my wits!"

"So she bit me," muttered Robin.

"Well, what did you expect?" flared Kate. "Something grabs me, I react. You're lucky I wasn't standing, I'd have flipped you over like a pancake."

95

"And let everything out there know where we were."

"Yeah, well, there is that. Anyway, Maggie, we were both there when the griffin, the really huge stone one from the gate, came walking past. Like really just strolling along. First there was the awful 'boom, boom, boom' of stone hitting stone as it walked across the terrace and then this humongous shadow, and then *it* with its huge eagle's head and the awful claws—we were terrified. It even stopped and looked into the window like it could smell us.

"But then other statues began to walk past, like in a Spanish town when everyone strolls around the piazza after dinner, and they were nodding and talking and stopping to exchange comments. They weren't scary at all, not even the harpies—the two of them were strolling together like old friends. But I still couldn't really take it in that it was all the statues from around the garden and they could move and talk. If Robin hadn't been there I would have probably convinced myself I was seeing things, or gone back to bed and thought it was a dream again. Which reminds me—the first one might have been real too!"

"I'm sure it was," said Maggie. "Robin told me that this one ended differently though. Why was that, do you know?"

"I don't," said Kate. "The first time it seemed I was outside with them without knowing how I got there, and we accepted each other, that's why I thought it was a dream, it was all mixed up and dream-like. This time we were hiding behind the drapes, but then one of the statues—or maybe it was a real pixie or nixie?—anyway, it spied us and it made this awful shrieking sound, really unpleasant, and shouted 'we've been seen' or something like that, and there was an awful wind and tree branches and leaves and pebbles crashed against the windows and

96

when that stopped the moon had disappeared and everything was quiet and nothing moved."

"Maybe" said Robin "it was because the statues are supposed to be secret and aren't allowed by something or someone to be seen being, well, 'alive'—there must be some sort of alarm system. Whereas when you were out dancing, Kate, it might have been garden or water sprites: they're known for enchanting humans. They would have kept you if you hadn't had your own magic you know."

"What? They would have *what*?" Kate rapped out sharply. "Oh hell's bells, I had no idea. So I was in more danger from those than the statues? You realise this is all grade A spooky sh...err, unlikely and really, really weird. I start to get my head around some of it and then you blow me right out of the water."

"Have another scone and more tea" said Maggie more in the nature of a command than an invitation. "You're perfectly right—this has got to be overload for someone who never experienced these things before. In fact, have one of these smoked salmon sandwiches—you're going to need protein, not just a sugar rush."

"Robin's right," she continued, "but since it didn't happen we have to thank our lucky stars that you're immune to that particular enchantment. So no reason to be scared about that. Now, have you had any other 'experiences' that you couldn't properly explain? Anything at all?"

"No, nothing, not that I remember..." Kate's voice trailed off, her eye catching a flash of iridescent wing as one of the small jewel-like birds flew over. "No, wait, there was a lizard, back in early spring when I'd just got here. I was watching it and being very, very still and quiet. It was just a small lizard, but then I startled it and, well, it spread wings that had been folded tight against its body—wings that were like jewels, stained glass colours that sparkled, like that bird. But it was a lizard, just a small

lizard—and then it wasn't, it was something with wings…
Anyway, I convinced myself I was imagining it because I was so tired. You see, it looked just like a tiny dragon. And that couldn't be…"

Maggie was smiling with approval like Kate had delivered a very special present that she'd been waiting for. "You saw a dragon" she said with wonder and joy in her voice.

"I did? I did! Wow… It was very small, though."

"Kate loves dragons, about as much as she loves unicorns," Robin observed happily, oblivious to Kate's glare as he ploughed on, "she's got books on them and she draws them—half the time we're supposed to be doing algebra or geography she's drawing dragons."

"Shut *up*!" snapped Kate. "You make me sound like a little girl all gooey about 'My Little Pony'—I never liked 'My Little Pony'. My dragons and unicorns are proper reptiles and proper mythical beasts. *Real* mythical unicorns have cloven hooves and beards. And dragons are very, very noble. And both of them can be extremely dangerous."

"You're quite right," said Maggie with a grin, "and now you can add to that list that they are real as well."

"Oh my stars," said Kate. "I am magical … and dragons are real. And I wasn't dreaming!"

Chapter 17

"Nicely summed up: You are, they are, and you weren't!" Robin laughed. "The thing is, Mum, what are we going to do with her?"

"Robin, your phraseology needs work," Maggie was frowning. "We aren't going to do anything *with* her, we are going to help her, and if our experience isn't enough, help her find any extra help she needs. Kate, honey, this is of course incredibly exciting and you are probably quite nervous about it too."

Kate just nodded, her expression one of wonder combined with a certain amount of shell-shock. Her eyes were sparkling with excitement, but she was pale and pinched around her mouth. Maggie passed her another sandwich and added a mug of hot tea, "Drink this, you need the warmth, and try to get round this sandwich—you hardly touched them. You've had more than one shock to the system today."

"That's witchcraft, that is," said Robin with a chuckle. "Don't mess with my mum when she's in feeding mode—she sounds sweet, but she knows what she's talking about."

With feeling like her stomach was in a knot and her throat was all but closed, Kate took a tentative sip of tea and gasped at the warmth and the multitude of flavours that assaulted her senses. "Oh, that's amazing, what is that? It isn't just tea."

"It's Masala Chai, Turkish tea with spices like cinnamon and cumin and ginger and hot milk and sugar. Great for reviving someone who's cold or ill or just overtired. And very soothing at the same time," offered Maggie.

Kate cradled the mug in her hands and sipped slowly—nothing had ever seemed to taste so good. She then devoured the sandwich and was half way through a second before she raised her head with a question. "How did you know there was magic? How did you find out? Did people teach you?"

Maggie smiled. "Many of my family are witches, or Wiccan, we've followed that path, which is very close to nature, for many generations. Some of us have some powers, some do not, a few are very powerful indeed, but almost all of us can sense magic. It runs in the family and we are raised with knowledge of who and what we are and also quite a bit about other people and creatures that are magical. There were books and lessons, and we all learnt.

"So my family knew for instance that there are faeries or the Fae or the fair folk or elves. Pixies and nixies are part of that larger family too. But none of them are considered trustworthy or even particularly kind. So when I met Kailen my family were very much against any kind of relationship. But the Fae of course are extremely attractive and Kailen was far older than I and very well versed in the ways of human romance. In a word, I fell deeply in love and there was no stopping me."

"Robin said his father was a Faerie Prince, but I wasn't sure I believed him. So he isn't human?" interrupted Kate, too startled to keep silent.

Maggie and Robin both laughed. "In a way yes, in a way no," said Maggie, shaking her head. "It's a bit like the Neanderthals and modern humans—turns out they lived together and interbred—we've all got a bit of Neanderthal DNA. Kailen is certainly human enough to produce Robin with me! But the Fae are an old, old race, they evolved at least as far back as the Bronze Age, probably the Stone Age—it's why they can't stand iron—a slight off-shoot of ordinary humanity—human and magical, not entirely human. They are considered cold and untrustworthy, but most are not much more so than your average human being. And Kailen is quite hot too."

"*Mum*!" blurted Robin, turning rather red.

"But in your case Kate, we'll have to do some digging to find out where your magic comes from. I am pretty sure the Mallorys are not at all magical. How about your mother's family?"

Kate squinched her face up in a gesture of distaste. "My mother is probably alcoholic, her family is rich but unhappy, and so is she, and I don't think she'd know magic if it hit her in the face. She might think she had the DTs. She might actually *have* the DTs."

"Oh, dear, I'm so sorry. What about your grandmother, Lucinda?"

"Well we were very close, and she never told me anything about there being magic in her family, or witchcraft. Maybe she thought I was too young or would laugh at her or begin to think she was crazy. But she had a magic touch with plants, if that's magic. She could make anything grow. And I think the four years I spent with her were the best in my life. I felt like I was healing and growing too. I miss her so much."

"Ah, sweetheart, of course you do. But that sounds promising—like she could be an earth witch. Do you know any of her family besides your father? Or family stories?"

"No, Grandmother was the last of them, at least of close family. She had two brothers, but they were killed in the war. She used to tell me she could talk to the horses, though. I thought she meant she was like that horse whisperer, but maybe she could really communicate? Oh, and I know that everyone thought she'd 'enchanted' both the Mallory boys—that's what she called them, 'the boys'. You know, Uncle Hugh and my grandfather Richard. I think she felt she may have chosen the wrong one, or there was some reason why she left Hugh and married Richard. She never told me about it, but Mother would occasionally tell me bits. She didn't like Grandmother (her mother-in-law) very much. You know, I don't think Uncle Hugh ever stopped loving her."

"What was her surname, do you know?" asked Maggie.

"Of course I do. It was Wicks, and her middle name was Maeve."

"Ah, those are both associated with Wicca. Wickes is a West Country variant of witch, yes, actually 'witch'. It's a surname around here. And Maeve is a name often associated with magic—it means 'intoxicating'. Where did she come from?"

"Somewhere in Cornwall, a small manor in the countryside."

"And did she have red hair like yours?"

"Yes, and it never turned grey or white. She had red hair and green eyes. She was beautiful."

And she was good with growing things, thought Maggie. *Coupled with the red hair and green eyes and Cornish/Celtic ancestry that pretty much spells witch. Although it could also spell Fae—the fair folk were called that by the native darker peoples, and it later morphed into faeries or fae. So she could have, like Robin, elements of both. I wonder if she knew, if her family educated her. If so, they would also have impressed upon her the importance of secrecy if what they wanted for her was a good marriage and all the things humans find important— status, security, wealth. And she certainly wasn't going to open up to a young child who might not be able to keep the secret.*

"Kate, honey, it does sound to me as if your grandmother was a witch, whether or not she practiced. There are many of us who prefer to live more ordinary lives in most ways, and if we do practice it is as loners. In fact, contrary to what you may have heard, witches are more inclined to be loners than to belong to covens. Covens I think were mostly invented by men with the hope that they would get to see young women dancing naked in the moonlight. Most real witchcraft however involves wearing serviceable clothing and doing practical things.

"But back to you. From what you and Robin tell me, you also certainly have the 'sight' and it is possible you may also have the ability to cast spells and to find your familiar. If so we need to try to uncover whatever latent talents you might have."

"Does this have to do the fact that I saw a dragon? I'm not even entirely sure I did, you know. I was so tired and I'd been grieving for weeks, I was all twisted up from Gran dying. So maybe I imagined it or there was moisture in my eyes and it made a rainbow that I thought was wings."

"Did it fly?"

Kate was quiet for a moment, then said, "Yes. Yes, it flew. It wasn't a jump and I didn't imagine it—it flew."

"Then, dear girl, you saw a dragon. And because of that you are now an important person around here. We have great need of someone with an affinity for dragons."

Robin looked puzzled, "We do? When did that happen? And why? For that matter, I'm pretty sure I would see a dragon if one presented itself. What's so special about Kate then?"

"So, have you ever seen a dragon?" asked Maggie.

"No, but I've never seen a boa constrictor either - but if one were around here I'd see it."

"Well, Robin, the thing is, there are dragons around here—and we never see them. It's because they don't want to be seen. Kate had just arrived, she was a grieving stranger in a strange land, and what did she see? A dragon, a dragon that stood still and watched her as well. It let her see it and it watched her in return. That's why I say she has an affinity for them—they want her to see them, and that means they have a reason. They have a purpose for her, I think."

Kate was looking nervous. "A purpose for me? Not as in 'virgin sacrifice' I hope? That's the only thing I've heard dragons need young women for. Other than that, the books I've read about good dragons — they save people, not the other way around. So why would they need me?"

"Ah, well, that's a story that is very sad indeed."

Chapter 18

"I learned this from Kailen because the Fae usually know what's going on in the supernatural worlds and, I am sorry to say, it appears some of them even helped with the evil that was done. Kailen should not have been sharing this outside his tribe, but we broke a lot of the 'rules' to be together and this was just another one. I, however, have never told another soul until today. It would have been nothing but gossip and very few would have believed me, plus there has been no one who could help. So to protect Kailen and our relationship I kept quiet about something we were powerless to change in any case. Now it is important that you do know what has happened to much of dragon kind."

Robin interrupted. "Mum, shouldn't we tell Kate a bit about dragons themselves first? Like what kind of dragon she saw back in the spring? In books and myths and legends anyway, there are dozens of different kinds."

"You're right, yes — we'd better go back a bit. Kate, what do you know about dragons?"

"Only, like Robin, from the books I've read, and pictures and carvings. But of course I thought they were all fiction. I know different countries or authors made up stories and had different types of dragons with different names and most of them were monsters. But I've always thought if I could meet one I'd find out that it was not a monster but just a big animal that was, well, magical. And I kept imagining friendly ones. There were books like that too. But I don't know anything about real dragons. I didn't know or imagine there were any so small as the one I saw."

"I can tell you about that one because it's the first one Kailen told me really existed, and it's called a Fae or Faerie Dragon. They aren't usually more than 5 to 9 inches long and are shaped generally like a lizard—scaly body, four legs and a tail, forked tongue and (if you got the chance to see it clearly) an arrow shaped end to the tail. Their wings are like a butterfly's and can be very colourful and jewel-like. How I would love to see one! I'm a witch, but it appears I don't have the 'sight' for that. They enjoy flowers and berries, but also eat insects and even small, very small animals. They only breathe fire when threatened. The Fae, who can see dragons, use these as messengers between themselves and other tribes. Kailen says they are capable of memorising very complicated messages and repeating them back word for word."

"They, that is dragons, *do* breathe fire?" Kate sounded breathless.

"Oh, yes, definitely, they all can, many don't choose to except as a last resort, others seem to quite enjoy it."

"How do they keep from getting burned themselves?" asked Robin.

"Darned if I know," said Maggie, smiling. "Kailen says they mix the ingredients for burning in a special stomach or some internal pouch, or possibly they produce it as a by-product of their food, like cows produce methane, and then snort it out and have some sort of sparking device in their nose or mouth that sets it alight just as it leaves their mouths or nostrils. Also their throats are coated in fire-proof mucus and their scales are quite impervious to flame, or so I'm told.

"Now, other dragon types: we'll just go with those Kailen told me about, because these are the only ones I know to be real. And there are actually only three species. If we look into the literature and beliefs of other countries it will be like what they say about Eskimos having forty words for snow—the names proliferate and the descriptions too, and where there may be only a few real dragon species in this world, suddenly there are hundreds of literary ones.

"An alternative name for dragons generally is drake or draco. It comes from the Middle English and goes back to the Greek drakon which derives from words meaning "I can see clearly". And Kailen tells me that has truth in it: most dragons see both way back into the past and can see or sense bits of the future, plus they are pitiless in seeing the truth and not dressing things up in pretty disguises. Although they are also reported to be especially pleased and happy when things are actually good. However, as to the name drake, it is most often used in English to refer to the smaller dragons. A Fire Drake for example is another name for a Wyvern.

"Wyverns are considered predatory and vicious, and this is generally true. Unlike the Great Dragons or the Faerie Dragons, they have only two legs, wings, a serpent-like neck and body and a tail armed with a vicious spike. Legend has it that those with Wyvern as a family name or with a Wyvern on their coat of arms or family crest had an ancestor that killed wyverns and possibly other dragons."

"Like the man my great-great-aunt Maude fell in love with? She ran away when her family wouldn't approve and I was told he became an enemy of the Mallorys."

"Yes, like him, and it may be the legend is true—he may have the ability to slay dragons, or have other powers over them. You're right: he was an enemy. But let's just finish with the dragons.

The third species are the Great, or Noble, Dragons. The Chinese also call them Imperial and Celestial Dragons. These can grow to enormous size—much bigger than an African bull elephant. When full grown they can be as big as a sperm whale. They are also extremely intelligent. They have four big powerful legs and claws like the talons of an eagle. Their thick protective scales come in many colours. Their tails are also thick and long with a row of spikes along the top and end in a barbed arrow-head shape that can inflict great damage. Their wings, also covered in scales, are aerodynamically designed to help cope with their weight, but they also require magic to fly. Kailen told me that to watch one of them flying is the experience of a lifetime. They breathe fire of course, but in their case they can modulate that fire from the merest breath to a great gout of flame that could destroy a large building. These are both the greatest intellects and the fiercest warriors among the dragons. And since it takes them centuries to achieve their full size, the younger ones are many different sizes, and until puberty are without many of the horns, spikes and tendrils that identify an adult. That could be why those who can see them have decided there are many different species."

"You sound like you have seen them." Kate was mesmerised at the description.

"Sadly, no, but Kailen described them so well, and he also drew me pictures. My own version of a fairy tale book, made for me by a real faerie!"

"Who are not, as you might have been taught, tiny creatures sitting on toadstools!" The voice was deep and rich like hot chocolate, and then the waterfall of flowering vines that grew against what Kate had thought was a solid wall parted and an extraordinary being walked through. He was tall and very slender, but with finely toned musculature (which was on display as he wore only a loincloth and a strap across his chest that held a quiver of arrows at his back), deeply tanned or possibly just of a chestnut complexion, with long black hair braided back to keep out of his way. His eyes were gold-green and his ears were pointed. His broad smile showed very white teeth whose eye-teeth were also quite pointed and slightly longer than those of most people. In one hand he held a bow, in the other a bouquet of field flowers, poppies and daisies, the little snap-dragons called butter-and-eggs, bee orchids and something blue Kate didn't recognise. He bowed low to Maggie as he handed her the bouquet.

"My Lord Kailen! What a surprise!" Maggie was on her feet and returning his bow with a curtsey. Then they both laughed and fell into an embrace. Kailen reached one arm out for Robin, who also bowed before he hugged his father.

For once Kate was speechless. And then his gaze shifted from his partner and son to meet hers and she realised she was staring with her mouth open. "And this is Kate, who can see dragons." It was a statement, not a question. Prompted by some atavistic insight and what she had seen Maggie and Robin do, Kate bobbed a small curtsey crossed with a bow and replied, "My Lord Kailen." It was Robin's turn to stare with his mouth open.

"Darling," said Maggie, "I think clothes would be a good idea." His laugh brought with it visions of meadows and woodland, the smell of pine needles and grass and the sound of rooks cawing. He turned and disappeared through the flower waterfall the way he had come, returning only seconds later in an ordinary shirt and jeans, but his feet remained bare.

"You're telling her about the dragons?" he queried, taking a seat at the table and accepting the plate Maggie gave him.

"As usual, you appear when you are needed," said Maggie.

"Knowing all about things we are just finding out," Robin looked rather put out by this. "You never told me about dragons!"

"You were young and angry and might have bragged to the human boys to try to make them like you," said Kailen. "But now you are older and showing more sense, and you are Kate's friend. So now it is time for you to know, and time for you to help as well."

Maggie reached to hold Kailen's hand, "I was just explaining about the kinds of real as opposed to fictional and mythical dragons. I was describing the Great Dragons like you told it to me."

Kailen took up the tale. "Maggie has told you that there are really only three kinds of dragons with which we need to concern ourselves—the Faerie Dragons, the Wyverns and the Great or Noble Dragons? That's the truth of it. There are still some Faerie Dragons and Wyverns around. But no one, not even the Fae have seen one of the Great Dragons for years now. We are hand-raising some nestlings but it will be centuries before they are fully grown. There is real fear that the Great Ones have died out, and without their knowledge and skills these little ones cannot hope to reach their potential. I understand there may be some left across the dimensions, but no one knows."

"Across the dimensions?" Kate felt like the rug of sanity had been pulled out from under her once more.

'Yes, dragons are multi-dimensional creatures. The Great Dragons came from a dimension where they were the rulers, the top of the evolutionary tree, and like so many top animals they'd developed territories and nationalities, losing their way and descended into warring factions and plundering both their planet and each other. In other words, generally behaving with all the idiocy we are seeing in humans here on our own Earth. This was untold thousands of years ago, and a number of them decided they would do better to get out. So they slipped between the pages of time into our world. Here they were endeavouring to behave as civilised beings, making a safe home place for themselves and their offspring. Having the ability to remain invisible allowed them to live here without humans knowing of their existence.

"All was going well until the last couple of centuries when humanity in its pride and thoughtlessness began to bugger up this Earth in much the same way dragon-kind had done on their Earth. Up until then, dragons had watched humanity warring away with only minor impact. But once they'd industrialised war and planet predation the Noble Dragons were afraid it was only a matter of time before humans laid waste to what is a very nice planet. They were even beginning to plan explorations to find another version of Earth that was earlier in its evolution of species but still with a climate that would sustain them. But then "It" happened." And Kailen lapsed into uneasy silence.

Chapter 19

"It? Dad, what do you mean, 'It'?"

"That's the thing, Robin, I'm not entirely sure. The Fae have been powerless to do anything about it. It involves that man you say was trying ruin the Mallorys and grab Ashley—Ivor Wyvern. We believe that over a century ago Ivor managed to make a spell that paralyses dragons, but leaves them alive and under some kind of enchantment to do his bidding. He made an enormous fortune with Wyvern Consolidated Heating & Lighting. His furnaces and heaters and lighting fixtures, all apparently designed to look like dragons, are not metal, but real dragons. The furnaces particularly cost the earth because of their size and the incredible details apparently sculpted into them, including that staple of dragon lore, the pile of gold and jewels a dragon is said to sleep on. Each one is different and unique—only the very rich can afford them, and during the first part of the 20th Century it was considered the most impressive status symbol you could possibly own.

"It is no accident that dragons feature so prominently in Art Nouveau design, that was the time Wyvern was becoming hideously rich through making dragons into household items. The very small ones, the faerie dragons, were being turned into cigarette and cigar lighters when smoking was common. Some were also turned into living jewels for very rich women to wear on little platinum chains as brooches or hair ornaments. Small to mid-size dragons (the young and adolescents of the Noble or Imperial Dragons) and a few wyverns were turned into decorative lamp posts to flank a drive or an entrance door or porch. They were being used as garden ornaments, incense burners. And a few wyverns were attack trained—not that they need training to attack, but trained to attack on command and to stop before their victim is reduced to a small, squidgy lump. So many were 'made' and sold that the Fae haven't seen a Great Dragon now for decades. Those that remain free, if there are any, are certainly hiding, or have already deserted this world and gone to another.

"Ivor decimated the smaller dragons too, he even caught a few Fae Dragons, though many still remain free. And rumour has it that he trained a sort of army of Wyverns either because they are so blood-thirsty they enjoy it, or again by coercion and magic, to protect Wyvern Hall and to keep anyone from finding the information that might allow for the un-doing of the spells and release of all the dragons, great and small."

Kate was anguished. "But this is as cruel and dreadful as what he did to the people who are now stone statues. He's imprisoned these magnificent creatures and forced them to do things that are unnatural. You, or your ancestors, knew what he was doing and you didn't stop him?"

Kailen looked both saddened and firm. "He had magic that was too strong for us. We've never known a human who had magic like that. We suspect he cannot be entirely human, but we could not get close to him and still can't get close to Wyvern Hall."

"But why not?" Kate felt her stubbornness rise. "You have magic, you know so much!"

Maggie intervened as she saw Kailen beginning to look angry as well as stricken. "Kate, the Fae cannot save the enslaved dragons because each has an iron collar or iron shackles on or are somehow 'welded' to an iron plinth, and fairies cannot stand being near iron. It makes them weak, and it burns them if they touch it. They cannot fight efficiently like this and they cannot get the iron off the dragons. In any case, it isn't the iron that enslaves the dragons, that is a spell or series of spells, and no one, not

113

the Fae or the remaining small dragons, has any idea what it is. Wyvern Hall is also warded with iron and probably with spells and the Fae cannot get in to look for a record of these spells or find an antidote or counter spell."

"The police then, or the army!" cried Kate.

"Yeah, where are the bands of super heroes when you need them," said Robin ironically. Kate gave him a look that was compounded of rage and helplessness. "Aw, look Kate, can you imagine what Sir Hugh's reaction to hearing any of this would be? Just think—there's really no-one we can call on."

Kate deflated. Yeah, she thought, the super heroes are right here—they're us, and we can't do anything. And if we did try to tell the police or the army we'd be asking for the men in the white coats to come take us away.

"I'm sorry," she said to Kalien, "I'm not an expert and should know when to keep my mouth shut. It just…it just…hurts."

He gave her a soft sad smile. "It hurts us too, well those of us that are pro-dragon. I'm sorry to say some of the Fae are of the opinion that without dragons they can get up to as much mischief and evil power-hungry games as they please. They are the Fae that give all fairies a bad name—the Elven branch. They seem to be like human narcissists—no, not the kind that sit admiring their reflection all day, a real narcissist sees all other living beings as just things to be used, played with, even tormented and broken, then thrown away. We call them Elves and ourselves the Fae to separate us in our own minds, but in fact we are all Faeries.

"Is there any way we can use that—the elves' knowledge if they helped Wyvern—to help the dragons now?" asked Robin.

"That's an excellent idea my son. And I'm not sure that it has been tried." Robin glowed.

No, like really glowed. Kate saw with some amazement that, unlike a blush, Robin actually seemed, not red-faced and embarrassed, but lit from within and faintly golden. *More things on heaven and earth…* she thought.

"But," said Kailen, "it's Kate who is the key to all this."

She started: "I am? Me?"

"A dragon has appeared to you, this hasn't happened to any human that we know of. And you are not affected by iron. It makes you, well, for want of a better word, their champion."

"But it was only one very small dragon, and the minute I moved it flew away. Surely that can't mean all you seem to want it to? I mean, I'd like to help, I really want to help—but I don't think it's a good thing to set me up as that special champion. I'm sure I'm no such thing."

"And you saw the statues moving and talking, and you can see past the glamour I put on this house. Maggie and Robin can do that too, but they can't see dragons, or rather dragons have not allowed themselves to be seen. Even by Robin, and he is half Fae. You're special I'm afraid whether you like it or not."

"It scares me witless if you want to know the truth," said Kate. "And, anyway, if Ivor Wyvern made a huge fortune selling real dragons as furnaces and furnishings—well that must mean anyone can see those. What's the difference between those he's made into 'things' and the, err, 'wild' ones you say no one can see? I don't understand that at all. Or is it because the furnaces and things are dead?"

Kalien shrugged, "We honestly don't know why they can be seen, it has to be part of the enchantments Wyvern used, because invisible dragons would hardly have made him a fortune. But we do know they are still alive somewhere in there, and we desperately want to save them."

Maggie moved over to hug her. "Kailen, she's right, she can't do all this alone, sent out to fight evil because none of the rest of us combine all her skills."

"I'm so sorry, I have misspoke. You will certainly not be alone. Every possible help and protection will be there for you. And first we need to teach you more about all of this. You may have powers we do not, but you are still a child, and no one is suggesting that you become some sort of sacrificial goat. When and if you go forth to help the dragons you will be armoured and trained and have back-up. Besides this situation has gone on for over a century — we don't have to save the world by tomorrow!"

Kate did feel as if a great weight of responsibility had been lifted somewhat. But then a new fear presented itself. "Uncle Hugh is so afraid that the Wyvern Estate is going to finally win the battle to claim everything—all the Mallory's assets, including Ashley. So maybe I have to do battle whether I'm ready or not."

Maggie gave her a comforting squeeze and laughed. "Ah, no, child. That's where I come in—I'm a witch of not inconsiderable powers and I'm a damned good forensic accountant and antiques expert as well. Kate, if I can't win the battle for Ashley Manor, I can at least slow things down for years and years. Until we find the way to win everything."

"Everything!" The word seemed to echo around the room and Robin and Kailen picked up on it too. "We'll win everything!" It seemed to swell in Kate's heart and lift her up. She found herself grinning at the other three.

"We'll be like the Three Musketeers!" She cried. "One for all and all for one!"

"Yeah, but there's four of us" said Robin. "Maybe we should be the Fabulous Four."

"Ah but the three musketeers were really four—they were the three bound in fellowship and fighting for the king, and they found their fourth who was younger and became their champion."

"Okay, so that's a lot like us, but the name is really, really misleading. But we can certainly be 'one for all and all for one!' And the high-fives went round the table.

Kate thought, I just high-fived a witch, a faerie prince and my friend Robin who is half witch and half fae — and I'm also magical and can see dragons and am not defeated by cold iron (or even hot iron)—and, and this is really, really getting weird. But I like it. I love it. I love feeling part of something important and …loving.

These wonderful feelings were interrupted by Maggie turning to Robin. "My dear son, it's time you also worked magic. I know you were extremely angry that it seemed your being a half-ling had prevented you from doing magic. I have to admit now that this was not entirely the case—it was in fact your father and I who blocked your access to magic while you were growing. Had you been raised within the Fae community this wouldn't have happened, but as you know, they wouldn't accept you. So living with me and within the human world, and full of confusion and anger as you were, it seemed necessary to keep you from injuring others or yourself with magic. Hence we set up a block. We will remove it today. I'm sorry we felt it necessary at the time, but hope you will see the sense of what we did and forgive us."

Robin was standing with his fists clenched and his head down. Kate couldn't see his face, but could see the veins standing out on his forearms as his fists tightened. He seemed poised between two poles, each electrified, and it was a heart stopping moment for her as she watched his inner struggle. Slowly his fists relaxed, his head came up and he looked his mother in the eye. "I find it hard to take in, part of me is very angry indeed. But the greater part says that is exactly why you did this to me. It still feels like an almost unforgivable thing to have done, to rob me of a birthright and leave me to struggle without it. But the degree of my own anger tells me that you had to do it because if you hadn't I would have been dangerous. I will try to curb that anger and channel it to where it can do good, just as the dojo teaches. I'm not a fool, and I'm no longer a child."

Here he paused for a long time, but as his hands relaxed he permitted himself a wide smile. "But I have to admit I'm as excited as a child to be finally getting my birthright, to be finally put in touch with magic!"

Maggie embraced her son, rather to his embarrassment, but he awkwardly returned the hug.

He turned to Kate and raised her hand high in his own "All for one, and one for all. We'll do this together, Kate, and with my parents to teach us, well, we'll get those dragons back in the skies. *Ad astra per aspera*!"

"Through hardship to the stars!" echoed Kate.

Chapter 20

A few days later it was warm, drowsy with the buzzing of bees in the long borders of the garden at Ashley, and Perry had declared an afternoon holiday because no one was concentrating anyway and he had a dental appointment. So Kate begged a picnic from Mrs Sykes and stopped off in the garden shed to pick up her tool belt.

At around the time she'd got deeply involved in the dojo, she'd also asked Sykes to help equip her for gardening and simple household repairs, so now she had a leather and canvas belt with slots and pockets to fit pliers, screwdriver, small trowel, secateurs, wire, a few screws and nails and a very small can of WD40. She'd found the belt itself plus a set of lock picks on the internet. The entire thing was, for her, the legal equivalent of a gun-belt and holsters—it helped her feel armed and confident. Confirmed Anglophile that she was, this was perhaps her only throw-back to her early childhood infatuation with cowboys.

Then she and Robin took off for the river. They waded in the shallows for awhile. Here Robin showed her how to tickle trout. 'You find one just hanging out—there's one, look. They always point upstream, probably so anything edible just gets swept down to them. Then I slip my hand in the water very, very carefully, and just hold it still until the trout gets used to it being there, then if I'm very careful I can just move my finger along its side. Look, he likes it."

So Kate tried. Her first two trout took flight as she tried to slip her hand into the water near them, but she was more careful with the third and then to her delight she managed to tickle it. It almost seemed to lean into the stroking motion.

"This is amazing, he really enjoys it."

"Then you can just grab it and, hey, presto, lunch!" said Robin happily. And there was the trout in his hand gasping in the air.

"Oh, no, I'm not doing that" said Kate, her eyes flashing.

"What's the matter? They don't bite."

"Because it's not fair to get it to trust you and then pounce."

"Nothing is fair about hunting, unless you're hunting something that is also hunting you, but I haven't noticed you being a vegetarian."

"I'm not going to figure that one out today," said Kate. "But I'm not cooking my trout either. Let that guy go, and we'll have the picnic instead."

"And then we can go see the surprise," said Robin with a twinkle in his eye.

Having finished their picnic, Robin was eager to get started. They packed up the basket and stowed it under a bush, then scrambled up a steep path worn deep between the trees, obviously in use but, thought Kate, grabbing onto tree roots to pull herself up, only by mountain goats…or children. Robin seemed to nearly skip up the slope that had her on all fours half the time.

"Isn't there an easier way to get to this thing?" she panted.

"Come on" he kept encouraging her, "this is the way I came the day I found it."

At the top they looked over a small valley toward a much higher escarpment where, almost hidden by tall trees, she could just make out crenellated walls pierced by a series of towers topped with steep pointed roofs. Unlike Ashley it was made of dark stone and the overall effect was of Gothic gone mad. It was the Disneyland castle remade by the wicked witch in Snow White and simply breathed a message of darkness and depravity and also, more simply, Keep Out!

"What is that?" asked Kate breathlessly.

"That" said Robin with suppressed excitement "is Wyvern Hall! But just wait 'til you see." And he was off again down the slope, less steep this time, and with more views opening between bushes and trees.

"Imagine," he said back over his shoulder, "I wanted above all things to find a way to get close to the castle, and I kept going and kept going for such a long time."

Kate was ready to agree about the long time, she was quite ready really just to quit now and admire (if that was quite the word) the glimpses of the walls and towers she could already see. But that wasn't what Robin had in mind at all. So keep going they did. As they finally reached the foot of the escarpment Kate stared up in dismay—it was nearly vertical and from this angle there was no sign of Wyvern Hall at all.

"Well," she said, "that's it is it? I'm not a mountaineer and you'd need ropes and crampons and … and all those things" she waved her hands vaguely to indicate equipment she didn't know about.

Robin grinned, "No this isn't it, not at all. But imagine my *extreme* disappointment when I got this far and could go no further."

"I don't have to imagine it, you idiot," grumbled Kate "I know exactly how you felt. It's how I feel right now."

"Exactly! But we don't quit now…" And he was off along the base of the cliff, again following a narrow path. At least, she thought, as she hurried to keep up, it's fairly flat here. But what the hell was he so keen to show her? The view from the other hill was impressive enough. Then they rounded a corner and there was…. "Holy crap!" breathed Kate.

"Yeah, that's sort of what I said," grinned Robin. Before them was a large polished metal statue which

121

seemed to be a modern take on some kind of mythological beast, featureless but with an air of menace mainly contributed by the huge sharp spikes haloing the 'head' and continuing down the arms to make spiked fingers.

"I call him Spike," Robin whispered, "he seems to like it."

"He...what? It's a metal sculpture, Robin, it doesn't 'like' anything."

"Wanna bet? Watch!" Robin scooped up a small rock and threw it at the statue. With absolutely no effect.

He's daft, I should know he's daft, thought Kate, *and this is all ridiculous and exhausting just to see something they do much better at the Museum of Modern Art in New York.*

But then... "Hey, Spike! Catch!" yelled Robin, and tossed another stone. And the arm stretched out and the stone slapped into it and the fingers curled around it.

"Oh, my gods," huffed Kate, as her legs gave way beneath her and she sat down hard. *That did not happen, tell me that didn't just happen.*

"Now we can go on past," said Robin. "Come on! He won't hurt you now. At least not for a minute or two." And he was off again, only turning when he realised she wasn't behind him. "Well, come on!
That diversion won't hold him forever."

She got shakily to her feet and streaked past 'Spike', still turning the rock in his claws. She then trotted to catch up with Robin, turning to look back to see the sculpted thing standing as before, arms and spikes outstretched across the path. "And how did you find out about that," she asked.

"The hard way," he grinned, pulling up the sleeve of his shirt and revealing two long partially healed shallow cuts.

"You mean...?"

122

"Yep, hadn't a clue, just waltzing on past and then, wham, those spikes caught me on the arm. Nearly passed out with fright, me. But, good, innit?"

"Oh, yeah, good, sure. Hell, what if I had a bad heart of something, Robin? What if it didn't like me?"

Don't be such a worrywart, I've experimented since. It was safe. Well, safe-ish."

"Are there more of these 'things'."

"Yeah, lots, wait'll you see, they're marvellous. Most of them don't do anything, well, most of the time they don't do anything, sometimes some of them do. But I can get round them."

"You mean some of them are active or activated some of the time, and other times others are active, and you don't know which are when? Oh, yeah, definitely bloody marvellous. Can't wait to see them, *not!*" Kate was simply furious with fear.

Robin sat down and patted the mossy bank next to him. "Come here, sit, breathe" he said. "I really wanted to share this with you. I didn't mean to scare you, well, not more than is sort of fun-scared. I wanted you to see this the way I saw it—no one, no one would believe me if I told them and no one would want to come all this way thinking I am nuts. But I figured you and I saw what happened in the garden, and you're the only human I know who's met my dad…"

That's true she thought, *I'd never have believed him, at least not before we saw the statues walking in the garden. But even then I wouldn't walk miles and miles. Hell, I'm not sure how much I believe even now. But I don't want to be dodging through them wondering which one might attack me.*

"So how do you know how to get by without being attacked? And why would you bother?"

"Because they don't want me to, that's why. Haven't you just wanted to do something because you're not supposed to? Plus the place is so spooky and so impressive, it's just crying out to be explored."

"And have you? Have you got inside?"

"Not entirely inside. Just as far as the moat. There are things swimming there, and I think there are alarms."

"But you got past these spiky things?"

"Aw, he's the only spiky one — the others are all different."

"Oh, crap," she said, "all different and with different abilities I suppose?"

"No, now that's the thing, most of them don't do anything at all, they are just there. Some are funny little things, some are big, some are even just a big granite letter or a word. But I've found two that will attack, only they won't if you go up to them and just, well, pat them."

"Are you out of your mind? How do you find out they won't attack if you *pet* them? How do you get that close?"

"By creeping up behind them, of course."

"You're nuts, you know that don't you? Why am I even here with you?"

"Because you know you want to do it—go where you're not supposed to, see things no one has ever seen, get away with stuff."

And she had to admit she did.

Chapter 21

Robin dug around in his knapsack and pulled out water bottles and some doughnuts. "Jelly or the holey one?" he asked.

"The one with the hole, jelly is too sweet."

"How can a doughnut be too sweet? Doughnuts are sweet, sweetness is the absolute essence of doughnut."

"Nope, there are *kinds* of sweet and jelly is too sweet, and doughnuts are supposed to have holes anyway. The jelly thing is a step too far, just like icing or custard."

So they finished off the doughnuts, had a drink and then Robin got up and gave Kate a hand up as well.

"Now this is where it gets really interesting" he said.

Not at all sure she liked the sound of that, Kate bent to retie her shoe and stood up prepared to argue. "How many more miles?" she queried glaring at him.

"Oh, we're nearly there, and it's almost flat, well comparatively, nearly, almost flat—look, only a gentle incline. We just sort of wind up this path—no more guardians—and we get to the gates. Then you'll see something magnificent."

Of course she wanted to see it. His grin said he could tell she did. So they set off. The sides of the path were over hung with ferns and wild roses and between them and underneath bloomed violets, primroses and poppies. Bluebells and Queen Anne's lace bloomed together as well. It was as if the seasons had got muddled and various things that normally never saw each other were all blooming at once.

"Robin, it's all the seasons at the same time along here, have you noticed? How can that be?"

"Dunno." He shrugged, unwilling to dwell on an area where he had no expertise. "But where statues come alive—and I don't think it's mechanical you know—well, who knows what else can happen? Come on, we're nearly there!"

Around another bend the path came out into a meadow through which passed a long straight drive. "Oh, you bastard!" said Kate, hitting him on the arm. 'We could have come on our bikes and not nearly killed ourselves."

"Aw, that would have spoiled it—I wanted you to see it the way I first saw it, all that tension, and then, well, Spike, and then this…!" He gently turned her away from the view of the drive and waved his arms in a sweeping gesture that took in the meadow as it swept up toward the moat and the massive gates that would have shut them off from the bridge, except they stood open.

Each gatepost was crowned with a great bronze statue of a wyvern, its wings half spread, its dragon-like head held low as if keeping watch along the drive for intruders, its long reptilian tail coiled around the pillar on which it was perched. At the far side of the drawbridge the battlements made a high wall with a portcullis almost entirely raised, but the fearsome spikes looked ready to fall. There was another wyvern in the coat of arms above the portcullis. Above the wall rose the towers and battlements of Wyvern Hall, a jumble of Gothic architecture all in dark and ruddy stone, made by someone who had probably been having opium dreams.

"Oh stars…" breathed Kate. "It's … well … unearthly, bizarre, just …oh wow. It looks so ancient."

"Yeah, incredible isn't it? But not ancient, no, it's Lord Wyvern's Gothic Revival fantasy. It's said he had these dreams—drug dreams probably—and hired architects and builders and held them prisoner to realise the dreams. But I think he probably just got hold of Pugin and William Burges and paid them a lot to get the plans

126

done and *then* he kidnapped all the stonemasons and carpenters and other craftsmen and made them make it for him!"

"Oh, right, I read that the Victorians could out-Gothic the Gothic," said Kate. "It's creepy beautiful, but it's really, really grotesque and scary too. Like those films. Look Robin, that portcullis thing past the bridge is raised. I wonder what's in there, is it a courtyard, or just the main entrance do you think?"

"I didn't go in last time I was here. Come on, let's go then, we'll try for it. Watch out for the wyverns though!"

"What, is the family home? Oh, we don't want to get a telling off." She paused in her striding across the meadow.

"Not the family, no, there's no family. Far as I know no one lives there, no one at all. No, the wyverns, those great dragon-y things on the posts."

"Oh, no, not really? They move? They're going to move? Aren't they tethered or something? Look—they have collars with chains round their necks, see?"

"So we keep right in the middle of the drive and when we get close we run like hell, ok?" He took her hand and they both stood breathing steadily. Then they walked single file, Kate first and Robin just behind her with an extendable rod he took out of his knapsack. About ten yards from the pillars they paused and he said, "Ok, when I give the word, run, keep right to the middle and run until you get near the portcullis, then stop, don't try to go through. I'll be right behind you and if they come at us I'll swipe them with this. But I think the chains are short. Now, one, two, three...*run!*"

And they ran. Kate heard the clinking of chain and the leathery whomp of wings and felt a breeze, but she put her head down and sprinted. Then she heard Robin cry out and the sound of the rod striking something, so she swung round to see him dodge just under a huge clawed foot and roll with the rod extended above him. The wyvern screamed with rage at missing him, and turned in a short trajectory to come at him again.

"Robin, run!" she screamed, unconsciously taking a few steps back toward him. He was already on his feet and digging in to sprint toward her when she felt a dreadful wallop against her back and the other wyvern's tail whipped around her like a snake, lifting her up and out over the moat. She found herself gripping the spiked arrowhead shaped end of its tail as it swung her around and back toward the stone pillar.

"Let go!" yelled Robin, "It's going to smash you against the pillar!"

"You said there were *Things* in the moat!" cried Kate, definitely caught between a rock and a hard place.

"*I lied! Let go!*"

She did, and dropped like a stone into the cold greenish-black water.

Chapter 22

The water was cold and murky so she couldn't really see anything. She pushed hard toward the surface, but just as her face cleared the water and she managed a gasp of air, something … oh, crap, some THING grabbed her leg and pulled her down. It felt like a hand, but with claws, and whatever it was it had immense strength because she was as helpless as the trout had been in Robin's hand. It was hauling her down deeper and toward the castle wall. There was a grating in the wall that was open and she was thrown up and inside, the claws leaving scratches along her calf and ankle, and it slammed the grating shut behind her. The water here was almost sludge, dank and smelling of rotting things. She came up gasping and sick, dragging herself out onto a narrow ledge. Lying there she fought for breath and then suddenly threw up a gush of stinking water. Kate lay there for some time, her eyes closed and her chest and leg throbbing with pain, trying to breathe in shallow breaths to avoid the awful stench.

"Oh, splendid, another corpse to rot and stink!" said a breathy little voice completely at odds with the cold furious words. Kate turned her head and opened her eyes. Standing in the corner of the fetid room was a being as unlike the dreadful room as could be imagined. Small and slender, obviously female, it glowed from inside the way Robin had the other day. Kate had trouble seeing its outline clearly because of the glow and because it appeared to shimmer as if it were made of water. Gagging slightly, she managed to say, "I am quite alive, and have no intention of rotting here. Who are you?"

"I am a nixie," said the little voice. "You've met one of my sisters—I fear she is in the pay of the Wyvern Master. Some of us have resisted and, as you see, the result is that I am imprisoned here in this hell hole."

"It's sickening, polluted," said Kate. "How do you stand it?"

"I would die if I could," said the nixie, "but alas we are immortal. So I sicken, but cannot die."

"Oh my stars, how long have you been here?"

"I have no idea, I cannot tell the seasons down here. It feels like a very long time, but possibly even a day in here would feel like an eternity. Watch where you bleed, young woman, you will attract worse things than my sister—things with bigger teeth."

Kate looked down and saw that the claws had indeed cut deeply enough that several little rivulets of blood were running down her leg toward the floor. She tore a strip off her shirt and bound it around her calf. "Robin said he'd lied about there being things in the moat! Wait 'til I see him, just wait…"

The nixie said, "Had you not let go the wyvern would have smashed you into the stone pillar. I think you might not have survived that, or if you had, you'd have been helpless in the moat. So he was urging the best of two bad choices. Smashed against the stone and drop helpless, or dive in and meet my sister, but still alive and not badly injured."

"That was your *sister*? That hand had a grip like iron, and awful claws."

"We are strong beings, only I am weaker now. We are water sprites, a kind of faerie, known for playing tricks on humans. Some of my sisters have married human men—it doesn't seem to work out very well. But *tricks*! Just tricks! Not these horrible things some nixies are involved in now.

"My name is Melior, my sisters are Melusine and Palatyne—you dropped in on Palatyne, she's a total bitch. Melusine wouldn't have left me here to rot. We're meant to be the spirits of sacred springs, not stinking moats, but Palatyne was always a slut. She threw you in here hoping you would die and rot, making this dreadful cell even more filthy."

"Then we'll have to get out. If you have strength, have you tried to break the lock?"

"I'm a kind of faerie, and the door and the lock are iron—I cannot touch them, let alone break anything. Just being near them, they have the effect of weakening me even more than the polluted water and not eating."

"Well, I'm human, and I have a tool belt and things that can either break or pick a lock. Let's do something about getting out of this foul place!'

"And after this foul place, how many more? How long can you fight, girl-child? Why do you even try?" Melior's voice was hopeless, sad, and somehow seductive. It seemed to bleed purpose out of Kate. After all she had only come out for a picnic in the countryside, and to see Robin's 'surprise'. Now she was—where was she? In the dungeons of the Dark Lord? In the maze without end? Being asked to be the hero when she had expected that the grown-ups would make the decisions, would educate her and, at some undefined point in the future, send her out prepared to do her part? But only a part. This silken-voiced nixie seemed to be saying she had now fallen down the rabbit hole for sure and no one was coming after her.

Then she thought of the mangled knitting that Eleanor had been trying to do as an assertion of her continuing humanity even entrapped as she was in stone with the terrible visage of a harpy. Of the sweet girl's face on the other harpy that was, it would seem, the beautiful, tempestuous Maude who'd dared all for love—and lost. She thought of Robin out there fighting the wyverns and thinking she might be dead. Of Maggie struggling with spells and paperwork to save Ashley Manor for her, Kate, and for Uncle Hugh. And of the dragons—she was the human girl who could see dragons. She'd been chosen.

Her head seemed to clear, a breath of fresh air came from somewhere, and the leaden weight on her heart lifted.

"I have no idea what comes next." she said with harsh conviction. "I will not be paralysed by what comes next! That's not right now. Right now is when we get out of here!"

And she approached the door like a valkyrie on a mission. "We won't get out that way" said Melior, "The lock and the bar are on the other side of the door. You'd need a flame thrower hot enough to melt all that iron."

"Then where?" Kate was like a grenade with the pin pulled—she'd go off in a minute.

"The grate my sister pushed you through—that locks from inside because it's to keep things from the moat out of the castle."

"Oh, hells bells and buckets of blood! It's under water, how can I pick a lock underwater? I can't hold my breath very long. Not long enough. And you can't touch the iron."

"No, it's bad, but not that bad—the lock itself is at the top of the grating out of the water to keep it from rusting away. If you edge your way along the ledge you'll see it."

"It was open though, when she pushed me through—you're a water sprite you say—why haven't you just swum out?"

"My sister is the only nixie in that moat—the other things would happily tear me into little lumps and eat me. They don't touch her because she is in the pay of the Wyvern Master."

"I'll come back for you then," said Kate.

"Sure," said Melior in a tone that meant, that will never happen.

Kate edged along the curve of the narrow ledge and came up to the grating. It was, of course, locked. The lock, which was a large and decorative piece of iron work showing swirls and lumps that looked like a face, no, that *was* a face, smirked at her. "Can't get through here," it creaked rustily. "I'll find a key" growled Kate. "No key!" chortled the lock, crossing its eyes and sticking its tongue out. Which was a mistake, as she grabbed the tongue with the pair of pliers she had in her tool belt. "Et goooo!" shrieked the lock.

"No way. I'm coming through. We can do this the easy way or the hard way, take your pick," said Kate, giving the pliers a twist.

"Ohhh, 'hit!" groaned the lock, and made a complicated series of clicking noises and turned. The grate opened.

"Thank you," said Kate sarcastically, shoving the pliers back into the belt.

There was a narrow extension of her ledge on the outside of the grating. "Nasty piece of work," she muttered stepping through into water that was about knee high. Here she was around a corner of the castle from the drawbridge and the wyverns on their pillars. So she couldn't see what might have happened to Robin, and there was no sound from that direction. But she could see the ripples in the water that was something, maybe several things, swimming toward where she stood. As quickly as she dared she turned on the narrow ledge and examined the wall of the castle. There were iron rungs set into the wall going up. A ladder! As she hoisted herself up out of the water, she heard a splashing that said something in the moat had just missed grabbing her. She began to climb.

Chapter 23

The iron rungs set into the castle wall were clearly meant for a taller person than Kate, plus they were rusty and cut into her hands. Her legs and arms ached like fire, her stomach was still complaining about the moat water she'd swallowed, and she didn't dare look down for fear of vertigo. But it was definitely a case of the only way is up. Each step meant reaching high above her head to catch hold of the next rung up and then splaying her leg against the stone wall to raise her knee as high as it could go so her foot could feel for and catch the next rung. Thanking the powers that be that at least they were equidistant apart and so far set deep into the wall, she had to rest and pant after each one.

She dared a glance upward and was rewarded to be within sight of the top—but still so long to go! *It's life or death now, it's life or death, so come on kiddo, come on, it's up because you can't go back down,* she thought. As if to underline that, there was another splash as something again leapt out of the water—trying to see where she was probably. I hope to hell they can't report back to anyone or anything she thought, with a sudden vision of being met at the top by some other guardian.

But that didn't happen. As she gained the top, her hands scrabbled for a hold in the rough stones. Again, being only about 5 foot 3 inches, she was only chest high above the wall with her feet on the last iron rung. "Crap!" She muttered, 'they couldn't have put a few more rungs in the top of the wall could they?" Digging her fingers into first one crack and then another, she moved her hands across the wide wall as far as they would go without her feet, now just one foot, leaving the iron rung as she tried to get as far onto the top as possible before she had to haul the rest of herself upward by, basically, her fingertips.

Now is not the time to give up! she admonished herself and, taking a deep breath, she pulled with her arms and swung her leg up. First one foot and leg got onto the top of the wall, and she lay panting for a bit, then crab-like scuttled her body forward and pulled up the other leg, ending up lying on her back, totally spent. *Thank you,* she breathed, *thank all the stars for getting me to that dojo, never would have made it otherwise.*

The top of the wall—the battlements she guessed, having been reading about medieval castles—was at least six feet wide. There were weeds and a few wild flowers growing out of the cracks, and even a small tree or two. So not a well-patrolled outer wall then.

And not too far away, at the corner around which were the portcullis and drawbridge, was a tower, and towers meant staircases. She got there and again there was an iron door with a big fancy snake-head lock and a lever for lifting the bar inside. She touched the lever and the lock hissed, snake-like, "Sssod offfff!"

"Sod off yourself" she said, and took out her lock picks. The lock squirmed, trying to hide the keyhole, but she jammed it open with a screw-driver and continued with the picks. A strange noise from the lock turned out to be laughter—"Sssssstop!" it hissed. "That tickles!"

"You should see what happened to the last one, tickling is nothing to complain about, and we both know I'm not stopping. You want to stop this, open up!"

The lock complied, but then, as she put her hand out to lift the lever the lock twisted one last time and aimed previously concealed fangs at her wrist. But it didn't complete its strike because Kate struck first with a hammer. A fang broke off, the lock screamed and fell silent and still. The door opened.

Inside the tower there was a wooden floor and three lancet windows, the kind that were designed for archers to shoot out at possible enemies while being protected. Kate moved quickly to overlook the drawbridge and the pedestals that held the wyverns, both of which were there, silent and still. There was no sign of Robin. A look at her watch showed her that it was about three hours since they had made a run across the drawbridge. Either he was drowned (or worse), or inside another area of the castle, or he had gone back for help. She didn't dare call out. With living locks and ferocious wyvern statues, who knew what other animate defences, alive or otherwise, might hear her?

Plus she was now inside the castle with apparently no way to get out. Both the moat and the drawbridge with the guardian wyverns were too dangerous. So now she really needed help. But how and where to find anyone or anything she could trust? Suddenly a tool belt and some potentially disabling high kicks seemed all too inadequate to cope with what she might find here. She had a strong inclination to curl up in a small ball and sob.

But... she was the human girl who could see dragons. This was the castle where the dreaded Ivor Wyvern had enslaved dragons. Perhaps there was a dragon here? A dragon that, unlike the stone wyverns, might need her help and would want to help her. Possibly she could communicate with it. But first she had to find one. Which was not going to happen by staying up here. So a tool belt and some Taekwondo would have to do. She was also beginning to feel hungry and thirsty. Thirsty—there was a water bottle in her tool belt, and it hadn't leaked. *Take sips*, she told herself, *only a few*. This wasn't the kind of dwelling where she might expect to find a well-stocked kitchen or even clean water if, as everyone said, no one lived here.

So Kate made her way to the spiral stone staircase that wound down and down, pressing herself against the wall because there was no railing. *I don't mind heights,* she told herself, except of course she did. So, careful not to

136

look any further down than the next step, she inched her way. Arrow-slit windows set at intervals let in some light. Where they stopped and the dark began, she paused to find her torch and put it on pencil beam (so as not to alert anything that might be down below) to shed a spot of light on the next step down. The trouble with the torch was it made the rest of the dark seem that much darker, and she had to keep herself from putting it on full beam and sweeping it around. Although between the noise of her movements (so much louder in the deep silence) and the little beam of light anything meant to guard within the tower was probably entirely too aware of her already. Just then the little beam of light showed, not a stone step below but a blank space. And her foot was already hovering over it! She stopped dead and carefully shone the light down and - oh, thank gods - the next step was there. Without a handrail however it was a very scary manoeuvre to get down across the missing step. But she made it, except with something of a thud and a huh! exhale as she landed. At that point she decided that there was no longer any point in keeping the beam narrow and low because anything in there with her would know for sure it had company. So she put it on wide beam and shone it all around. It was a great relief to see there was absolutely nothing in there but herself, and also that she was nearly at the bottom.

Soon she was on the floor and facing yet another door—wooden this time, but with great iron hinges and the now expected big lock. This one seemed to have the face of a fox. It snarled at her and showed some enormous teeth, but Kate was ready—pliers grabbed an eye tooth and started to twist. The snarl turned to a whimper, like a whipped puppy. It took her by surprise, and she nearly dropped her hold, but she figured that the keyhole for the fox lock would be behind the teeth, and that unless she made it give up it would never just hold its mouth open while she picked the lock. "Okay, I know that hurts, and I

137

don't want to have to remove your teeth one at a time like in that film *Marathon Man*. But, believe me, I will if you don't just open the door. Because once your teeth are gone, I can pick your lock, and you'll have endured torment for nothing, see? So let's just skip all the torture and unlock okay?" Inside, because of the whimpering, she was curdling her own blood to be doing something so painful to another being, whether or not it was actually alive. But she was a rather different person than the Kate who had been worried they might get told off for trespassing by the inhabitants of this place just hours before. The fox lock subsided, shut its mouth and made the requisite clicking noises as the tumblers turned. The iron bar moved smoothly back in its slots and she could lift the latch. Sunlight blazed in, momentarily blinding her, and she moved quickly back into the shadow. From here she peered out into the main courtyard of the castle.

It was big, and was mostly laid to grass with gravel paths through it. Unlike a real medieval castle, it was not a space for gathering villagers when under attack or for mustering troops in time of war. It was a recreational space with a central fountain that she recognised as being a copy of Bernini's Fountain of the Four Rivers (but without the obelisk) in Rome. Only this one was not made of travertine marble, but black stone, possibly even onyx, and when you looked closer the gods of the rivers were more like devils, with curling horns and cloven hooves. Some of the animals looked more like demons. But no dragons. Perhaps he only wished to work with live dragons, and the dragon was not born that could spout water all day without choking to death. Still, as demonic as it appeared, it was also quite beautiful and showed the hand of a master sculptor. There were actually flower beds and these were full of black and gold flowers, real ones. The black petals shone with the dark rainbow colours of a magpie's wing and the gold was shot through

138

with apricot, red and orange. The surrounding castle was a gingerbread confection of towers, turrets, crenellations and pointed Gothic windows all in mainly dark stone with red stone outlining the windows and doors and battlements. Gilded statues and gargoyles were poised as if about to take off (and remembering the wyverns, Kate feared that maybe some of them could).

So she made a wide careful circle around the fountain and kept a wary eye on all the gilded statues of heraldic beasts as well. On the other side of the courtyard was an open door (well, that makes a change, thought Kate) leading into another courtyard garden, this one very different from the saturnine black, red and gold of the great courtyard. Here was a sunken garden laid out with a central pool where gold and silver fish swam under water lily leaves, and low box hedges, carefully clipped, each enclosing beds of flowers in shades of peach, apricot, pink, lavender, white and blue. In the centre of each enclosure was a tree covered in white, pink or peach blossoms. The scents were beguiling. Even the walls here were of beige limestone and the Gothic ornamentation around the windows was picked out in spring green and silver. It was an enchanted bit of loveliness amidst the fearful mass of the rest of the Gothic pile.

There were birds as well, singing and flying about, including several white peacocks. But one bird in particular caught her eye—iridescent wings, a body tapering to a tail with an arrow head at the end. Not a bird—it was the lizard, no, a *dragon* such as she had first seen in the wood at Ashley Manor. It flew toward her and when it knew she had seen it, it flew across the garden toward a flowering tree where it landed on a branch about the same height as her face. She approached it carefully. Instead of flying away, it startled her by speaking in a tiny, whispery voice. "You are Kate. You shouldn't be here so soon, but as you are the Dragon King says he wants to see you now."

"The Dragon King? Do you mean a dragon, or the man who controls the dragons?"

"The Dragon King is a dragon, the King of the Great or Noble Dragons. He is imprisoned here, but he is still the King. He wants to talk to you."

"I need to talk to someone who can help," said Kate. "Take me to him then."

"He's in the cellars. He can't leave," whispered the Faerie Dragon.

"Where, where?" demanded Kate. "The cellars are huge—I could be looking for weeks."

"No miss, you'll find him all right, just follow me and if you lose sight of me, listen for the huffing and puffing."

"Oh crap," said Kate. "Does he breathe fire?"

"Of course, he is a dragon. But he won't hurt you. Now let's go. He wants to meet you."

Following the tiny dragon, Kate ran through the sunken garden and down a covered passage where she found the door that led directly into the cellars. It was, of course, locked. This lock, which was another large and decorative piece of iron work, displayed a demon's face, complete with curling horns. "Can't come in," it wheezed.

"Oh, I think I can" growled Kate. The lock opened its mouth and a puff of sulphurous smelling gas came her way. Luckily a small breeze also sprang up and most of the cloud by-passed her, the little that got to her made her eyes water and burn.

"You little monster, poison me would you?" And she hit it back with a spray of WD40 from the small can in her tool belt. The demon lock coughed and choked horribly and vomited some greenish fluid that smoked and seared a hole in the stone by Kate's foot. But the door was now open.

"Nasty little creep," she muttered, finding her torch and setting off. It was a longish journey through corridors and rooms, sometimes seeing the little Fae Dragon ahead of her, sometimes making wrong turns. A journey punctuated by dead ends and some peculiar areas where unpleasant noises and smells emanated from iron gratings in the floor and other rooms where fluorescent fungi cast dim light on the walls. She finally lost sight of the Faerie Dragon entirely. She was listening for the huffing and puffing. Finally she heard it, and headed in that direction. It got slowly louder and it seemed the chill of the cellars was gradually replaced by greater warmth. Finally she rounded a corner and the great furnace room under the main hall was revealed.

Chapter 24

Up against one wall, there was the big black furnace with its rainbow sheen barely visible in the light of her torch. It must have been polished recently she thought, but as she got closer she saw that what she'd taken for polished metal were really deep azure and navy blue scales full of colour and radiance. The furnace was in fact an enormous dragon, coiled into a large mound resembling a huge beehive on four feet, each foot ending in golden claws. It was making the puffing sound. She stopped at what she hoped was a safe distance and said clearly, "Dragon King of Wyvern Hall, it's me, Kate. You wanted to see me."

From the middle of the blue black scaly beehive there was movement and slowly the huge head rose up on a long snake-like neck. "Yes. I did." His head was about twice as long as she was tall, lizard-like but 'decorated' with spikes and frills and two backward-facing horns that came to sharp points. Where the rest of him was in darkest shades of blues, purples and blacks, his dark head had touches of turquoise and gold and azure, something like the sea at sunset.

As the Dragon King unfurled himself, Kate couldn't see any wings. "Oh, no!" she cried in pain and shock. "Your wings are gone —have they amputated your wings? Oh, I'm so sorry, oh, gods."

The dragon king opened his beautiful golden eyes wide, and then he opened his enormous mouth and …laughed. It was a terrifying sound, and accompanied with a small gout of fire. But he meant no harm. "No, child, no, my wings fold down tight and fit along the curves of my body so well that unless you look closely I appear not to have them. But they are there I assure you. Don't trouble yourself, I am trapped here, but I have not been mutilated … he wouldn't dare. It is as much as he can do to keep me enslaved, to injure me would have been beyond even his power."

His great golden eyes were looking at her with interest and intelligence, but also with warmth and, it seemed, approval. Kate felt oddly as if she were in the presence of a very big dog who also happened to be a university professor, or perhaps a particle physicist (the most inscrutable intelligence Kate could think of). Intelligence, power and benevolence seemed to radiate from him.

She was observing him in return with great awe and curiosity. He was, in a word, huge. Great Dragon was no misnomer in any way. As he had uncurled himself from his 'beehive' configuration—it occurred to her later that he'd been curled in on himself with his tail over his face much like a dog would curl up into a ball to sleep—his true length and height were overwhelming. From his feet to the top of his shoulder must have been about twelve feet, and then his flexible neck reared another eight feet or so. His head was perhaps ten feet from nostril to the top of his horns. His body was covered in scales in every possible shade of blue, and each one shimmered like silk. His legs were relatively short for his massive frame, and ended in feet that were quite different front and rear. In front, although he was standing on them, they more resembled hands with four 'fingers' and an opposable 'thumb' each tipped with a golden claw. His hind feet were three-toed, with longer golden claws. His tail was at least the length of his body and was ridged with pointed 'thorns'. Almost nothing would survive a swipe from that tail. Next to him Kate felt truly insignificant and absolutely tiny. The length of his head alone was nearly twice her height.

"So," he said, "You have arrived all by yourself with no help and with, it appears, great risk to yourself and some damage as well. You are early in this narrative, and unprepared for the tasks ahead of you. I do not know quite what to do with you under these circumstances."

"Well, Noble Lord, if you don't know, I certainly don't. I was foolish to think getting into the castle was a game. And now I don't know how to get out. Or how to help you. I've been told I am the human being who can see dragons, I've been told this makes me important somehow to saving dragons. But I have no idea how."

"You remind me a bit of Joan of Arc, a simple peasant girl who had a vision that she was to save the King of France. No one could have believed she would succeed, yet she did."

"And got burned at the stake for a thank you," said Kate. "Thanks, but no thanks. And I haven't had a vision. I saw a dragon, the same kind of dragon that found me here and showed me where to find you. It is Maggie and Kailen who have the vision. Only it was going to be a process, I was going to be trained, we were going to make a plan, a plot, put together an army—oh, not an army, but gather minds and people who could help. A posse—we were going to have a posse. We were going to undermine Wyvern Industries and somehow find out how Ivor Wyvern enslaved dragons and undo that. And then Robin and I thought it would be fun to get across the drawbridge and look inside. *Fun*! Oh, friggin' son of a sea cook! I almost died, Robin may be dead, and it's all my fault!" A sneaky tear crept out of her eye, and she wiped it away with the back of her hand.

"You and Robin…good, there is someone else who knows you're here. No (he raised one clawed digit toward her in a gesture for silence), I believe I would know if this Robin had perished here. I have my spies. And having adventures is what childhood is all about— or," peering more closely at her, "teenagers as I believe you must be. Some fault, perhaps, but not grievous fault. And we can perhaps make use of this. Because to have

144

something to work with your 'posse' needs information, and I can give you some you wouldn't get elsewhere."

Kate could actually feel her backbone stiffening as something like relief and a bit of courage seemed to wash over her. "Noble Lord, yes, we know so little. Well, Kailen knows the most, but nothing that really helps us. We didn't know you were here. We have no idea how to free you or the others. We need so much help…"

With a slight puff of smoke and smell of sulphur that Kate interpreted as suppressed laughter, the Dragon King said, "That makes two of us. I too need so much help. But please young woman, much as I appreciate the *politesse*, if we are to work together you must stop called me Noble Lord, or I will have to respond by calling you My Dear Young Lady, and we'll never get very far that way. My name is Chen Shi. It's Chinese, as it was in what is now China many centuries ago that dragons first crossed the dimensions and settled. The Chinese made us gods and Chen can be translated as Morning or Dragon and Shi has a number of auspicious meanings including Time or Season, Real, Honest and Stone (as in strong, impenetrable). So it could mean Morning of the World or The Season of Change. Honesty and Strength are implied. Good, isn't it?" the last was said with a twinkle in his great golden eye.

"However," he continued, "Many of the English-speaking beings whom I have known over the centuries call me Chauncey. I understand it is meant to be endearing, is easier to pronounce and I suspect it is intended to keep them from being terrified! I rather like it. So please call me Chauncey."

"Thank you, Great, err, Chauncey," said Kate. "I want very much to learn things that can help you and other dragons—and the stone statues that Ivor Wyvern put in Ashley Manor gardens. But I want to get out of here alive too. I cannot go over the bridge with the wyverns on guard there, and the moat is full of horrible things set to kill me."

An ugly look of anger passed over Chauncey's face, his lip curled back and smoke again came from his nostrils. "That man is evil incarnate. But never despair, there are beings in here that are mine—the little faerie dragons that even Ivor has not managed to hunt down, and possibly some nixies that still owe their allegiance to me and mine. Some birds also will come."

"Oh, yes, there is a nixie trapped in fearful poisonous sludge in the dungeon just off the moat. Her own sister lives in the moat and is helping to hold her prisoner. It was the sister who grabbed me in the moat and threw me into the dungeon with Melior. She is wasting away but cannot die. I must get her out. I promised."

"It is never wise to promise what you may not be able to deliver, young Kate. But I will think upon it and find a solution if there is one. How, in fact, did you get out?"

"I … I tricked the lock on the grating that led back to the moat. All the locks are animate faces. This one stuck its tongue out to taunt me and I grabbed it with pliers and, err, twisted as hard as I could. It screamed and opened. I'm afraid I did similar things to the rest. I was taught to ask nicely, or rather mostly not to ask at all, just accept what I was given. But when you're given a stinking poisonous dungeon and a taunting lock, you don't accept."

"Wise thinking," murmured Chauncey.

"But Mel wouldn't come out that way, she knew if she was in the moat there were things that would tear her apart."

"So if you go back you could probably deal with the lock on the door?"

"Oh, yes, I think I could. So far none of them, even the poisonous one, have been able to stop me."

"Excellent," breathed Chauncey. "You may be lacking in information, young Kate, but you certainly aren't lacking in skills. Little Melior has been one of the few nixies who sided with the dragons. And I have hated to think of her in that poisonous environment."

"Kailen said that this Lord Wyvern discovered how to entrap and paralyse dragons to make them into..." Kate paused to think how to phrase this without distressing Chauncey or wounding his pride. "Into household and art objects. But you don't seem to be paralysed. Why can't you just get up and go? And how did anything, let alone a mere man, capture you?"

"If I tried such a thing I would be subjected to a truly painful and incapacitating sort of electric shock. Believe me I tried, and after recovering each time from the great illness that succeeded the shock, I finally made the decision to bide my time, do this job, and wait for a combination of circumstances that would allow for my release and the chance to exact retribution. The Great Dragons live for many centuries. The past century has been only the blink of an eye to me. And as I have a photographic memory, I have entertained myself by re-reading favourite books."

"But how did he catch you?"

"He sent a message—through channels he should not have known existed—that he had in captivity three of my very young children. That each day that passed without my appearance before him, he would slowly torture one of them to the point of death, then revive it, and torture another the next day, and so on..."

Kate thought she would be sick, in fact she sat down rather suddenly staring up at Chauncey with an expression of horror. "So you came here and he freed your kids?"

"So I came here and subjected myself to his will … and he turned my children into paralysed statues that he

147

sold at the Great Exhibition." said Chauncey in a soft voice that barely hinted at the sorrow and anger he felt. But Kate picked up on it. She reached out and stroked his front foot, tears now streaming down her face.

"But I understand that those dragons that are entirely paralysed, although alive and able to hear and see and think, do not feel pain. I have been told this. I pray it is true."

"So do I," whispered Kate.

"As for me," said Chauncey giving himself a mental shake, "I and other 'furnaces' and those dragons made into cigarette or cigar lighters and other household appliances have to be able to move and to take in fuel (that is, to eat) in order to do our jobs. But move out of our prescribed orbits as it were and we are subject to intense pain that knocks us unconscious, so we have learned to wait, hoping that time will provide a way out."

"Perhaps that time has finally come," said Kate in a quiet voice. "Already we have Kailen, Maggie and Robin. I'm sure Kailen can muster some trustworthy Fae, and there will be others I'm sure. Plus they have said they will train me in magic, whatever that entails. And with Ivor Wyvern dead, we can apply our brains to finding out how he enslaved you, or find mages that can reverse his awful enchantments or alchemies or whatever it is he has done to you."

"Dead? Ivor Wyvern dead? Oh, no, my dear child, you are missing what is perhaps the biggest piece of this hideous puzzle. Ivor Wyvern is not dead. Ivor Wyvern is as immortal as I am, and, hidden away, continues his crimes to this day. No he isn't dead…and his powers are far beyond any you might expect."

148

Chapter 25

"But…but that's not possible." Kate was stunned.

"I'm telling you Ivor Wyvern is still alive, and I should know," Chauncey said grimly.

"That would make him about 200 years old! And surely that's impossible."

"He is an alchemist, an inventor, a magician, a genius, he has enslaved dragon kind! What is to say he hasn't also found the equivalent of the fountain of youth? Besides, I am not entirely sure he is actually human. But I know he hasn't aged."

"So you've seen him?"

"Oh, yes. Off and on he appears and gloats. I am, after all, the Dragon King. Whatever his accomplishments in the dark arts, having me to heat his horrible castle is quite a trophy. It amuses him that I am here, resting on a bed of old iron and rusting garden furniture while his other 'Wyvern Dragon Furnaces' are nested on beds of gold and jewels and precious ornaments, as in the legends. He hasn't aged a day since I first knew him either. I suspect he is also doing magic here, very dark magic. I am grateful that he comes only rarely, as seeing him does nothing for my peace of mind."

"Maybe he sold his soul to the Devil?" ventured Kate.

"I wouldn't know, I am not of this world, and the world I come from didn't follow that exact superstition. Does this world actually have devils? In all my years here I've never seen one."

"Yes, I think you have… you've seen Ivor Wyvern."

"Touché." breathed Chauncey.

"That's French. What does it mean?"

"It means I acknowledge you have made a very good point. In French it is part of the language of fencing—when your opponent touches you with the point of his sword."

"Thanks. But it does totally change things. We—Robin, Maggie and even Kailen I think—all believed that he was long dead, the castle was empty and only his lawyers were a threat to Ashley Manor. So we thought, once a safe way in and out was possible, we could come here and either free you or find the antidote to the poisons or enchantments that keep you and the others enslaved. At least we hoped we'd find something. Or that, because Maggie is a witch and so am I—and I'm the one your little dragon chose—we could free you in some other way. And free the statues."

Chauncey said, "You spoke of statues before. I know he has turned some dragons into statues, and light fixtures and lamps, but these are not what you're talking about, are they?"

"No, not paralysed dragons. Ivor was—err, is—an artist and a brilliant sculptor too. But he did terrible things after he sculpted someone. I'm not certain how, but he transferred their soul or their spirit into the stone statue. And those that decorate Ashley's gardens become animate—they can move around and talk—every full moon. Among those seem to be his sister Eleanor and the woman he loved, my great-great-aunt, Maude Mallory. He made them into Harpies, but they have their own souls, and they seem to be very lovely people. Would he have killed and dissected them to take their souls? Or taken them while they lived? Would it have hurt a lot?"

"My dear child, I have no idea. This is different magic to that which he used to vanquish dragons. I don't know how it's done. I don't, sadly, know what he does to enslave me. Except that both are equally evil and self-aggrandising."

"So what can we do now? If we start messing around with his enchantments it's bound to draw him to—well, probably annihilate all of us. I don't want to end up with my spirit trapped in a statue. I don't want to end up dead either. And I'm not sure I could stay sane under any sort of torture. He sounds like the scariest thing I've ever heard of. But no wonder he's still fighting the Mallorys to get Ashley—it's because it's still him, not just 'an estate' or lawyers. I need to tell Maggie. I need to tell them all. It changes just about everything. Not that we've made a real plan yet. I guess it's just as well we haven't. Oh, twenty bleeding hells, I wish I knew what to do."

"I think you're doing very well indeed. And you're quite right. You need to tell them everything you now know. I think you need to do that as soon as possible. I'll still be here, I'm not going anywhere." This last was said with the dragon equivalent of a wry smile.

"But I don't know how to get out! The only way is the bridge over the moat and that's guarded by the wyverns on the pillars. That's how I ended up inside—one of them was about to smash me to bits against the pillar, so I jumped into the moat and got grabbed by, well, Melior said it was her sister, P-something. And I nearly drowned, but she threw me into that stinking pit where Mel is trapped. Anyway, swimming across the moat is definitely not an option, not for me or Mel."

"What about other guards or automatons? Did you see anything else that was set to attack you?"

"No, nothing. Other than the animated locks, and I fixed them all right. I was afraid they might have an alarm system, but nothing happened. There were some butterflies and birds and even a white peacock, but they were real I think, and harmless. And the little dragon that told me to come to you of course."

"Then let me think. Forget the moat. If you can open the lock on the door to Melior's cell, then bring her back through the castle to the big entrance with the portcullis and the drawbridge. I'll send the fae dragon with you to show you the way. Only if anything or anybody else appears, she will hide, because she would be turned into a paperweight or something equally depraved, if he got to know there is a free dragon within these very walls. And it's extremely important she remain free—there are very few of us now, and I depend on her for news and information. It's how I knew you were here in England, and I expected that someday you would come here to me—just not so soon."

"But the wyverns will attack us surely? And they are deadly." Kate was far from believing escape was possible.

"So they are, so they are. Let me think… Possibly they are set to attack only things coming in, not going out. But we don't know, so 'possibly' isn't good enough."

Kate was beginning to feel quite desolate. Here was the giant Dragon King helpless himself and seeming to be at a loss to think of a reasonable plan to get her out either.

"If only we could just fly over the walls and the moat—in films most super villains have helicopters stashed away on a landing pad. Does he have one? Oh, never mind, I haven't a clue how to fly one anyway."

Chauncey looked at her with renewed hope. "Flying, yes, that could…well, it could work."

"No, it couldn't. I don't know about nixies, but I can't fly. That's not an option." She heard the flat denial in her voice and wished she could be more positive.

"No, not you, nor Melior," said Chauncey thoughtfully. "I am thinking that a large flock of birds, big birds, yes, crows, could attack the wyverns and distract them so completely that you and Mel can make a run across the drawbridge with very little danger. Or at least less danger… There's a large colony of crows not far from here and they are friends of mine. I'll get Cora, the Fae Dragon, to go tell them what's needed. Crows are big and very intelligent and very brave—an entire flock circling the wyverns' heads, going for their eyes—they'll be so occupied you can get away."

"Yes, yes! I can see that it could work. I hope Melior can move fast enough, she seems very weak. I hope I can move fast enough... And that the wyverns can't. I do wish it were more than a good chance—I can't help wishing it were a certainty."

"Then let's think of it as a certainty. We are magical creatures —we will do a simple spell: Melior will certainly run fast enough. So will you. And the crows will be very successful indeed in distracting the wyverns." Chauncey's eyes seemed to glow more golden and she felt a kind of heat and a kind of certainty. Testing herself out (what did she have to lose?) she stared back into those eyes and said with equal certainty, "The crows will protect us, and we will run very quickly. We will pass over the bridge in perfect safety." Was that a sort of spark she felt? Her fingers tingled and looking down she saw they were giving off tiny flashes. "Oh, stars! It's magic."

"Feels good, doesn't it?" rumbled Chauncey, with what had to be a smile on his huge face. "Yes, young Kate, it's magic. Now let me call my little dragon. Cora, come here please, I have need of you now."

Chapter 26

The little faerie dragon came and, much to Kate's amazement and delight, settled on her hand where Chauncey could see and speak to her.

"Cora, I need you to fly to the rookery and tell the crows that I need them to do a very specific job. Tell them it could be dangerous. But tell them also that this could be the beginning of freedom for the dragons and the overthrow of the evil Lord Wyvern, so it is of great importance. Tell them I will not forget it.

"Then you must come straight back here and guide Kate through the castle, first back to free Melior from that dungeon and then guide both of them to the main entrance. When you get Kate and Melior there, the crows must then descend upon the two guardian wyverns at the drawbridge. They must chivvy the wyverns, flying around their heads, trying to put out their eyes, blinding them in a cloud of feathers and distracting them from the nixie and the human who will be running for their lives across the drawbridge. It is imperative that these two make their escape, my gentle Cora, or all hope for us is lost. When you have seen what happens, and I trust it will be successful, then come back here to me and tell me all. You are a fine Dragon, Cora, a brave friend. Do your best."

"We are all going to do our best!" said Kate, vague memories of Shakespeare's Henry V speech before Agincourt seemed to percolate through her, adding certainty and courage to her voice. "And it will be good enough, because we have made a spell."

"Yes, we have made a spell, a spell for success, a spell that ensures that all of these steps will be carried out and the result will be that Kate and Melior are free and can return to Kate's friends to plan the downfall of evil and the resurgence of dragon kind. So Cora, do not be afraid, and fly now as quickly as you can."

As they watched the tiny dragon flying away down a corridor, Kate said "Is it okay to ask you some questions while we wait?"

Chauncey snorted some smoke and made a noise that could have been a chuckle. "Of course you may ask. It is not always possible that I will answer."

"So you are the furnace that heats this entire place? Do you do it by breathing fire?"

"I am *not* the furnace—I am forced by circumstances to do the work that would otherwise be done by such an appliance, yes. And, yes, when I am working it is my job to take in fuel and turn it into fire that I then breathe out into the network of pipes that heat the castle in cold weather. Or upon the occasions that it is occupied, to heat water also."

"So they have to give you food?"

"Ah, food. Yes they have to give me food. Food is what I consume to live, just as you do. But in my case it also contains ingredients I can use to create fire. You might be surprised that dragons can cultivate very sophisticated palates and enjoy all the wondrous culinary delights this world has created over the millennia. It is much better now than when we first 'came through' from our previous world and had to fight with the remaining dinosaurs and the first birds over carcasses. Those are not days I would chose to relive. But it's been a long time since I tasted the delights that refined cuisine can provide. Wyvern supplies me with a sort of dog kibble, a so-called 'balanced diet' that keeps me healthy and strong enough to do the work. And drinking water as well of course."

"Oh that must be so … well, boring."

"It is boring, but I am not bored, I have a perfect memory, so I read to myself in my head. And remember better days. Although it is true that before the better days there were other rather awful days when we saw our entire world disintegrating."

"Kailen said you come from another world, or universe."

"Indeed, dragons evolved in a parallel universe where the cataclysmic event that wiped out the big dinosaurs here—you know about that, yes?" Kate nodded yes. "In our world it never happened. Hence the dinosaurs continued to evolve, and one line developed much as humans did from apes, and these became the dragons. Mammals never really got a look in, so no humans. But as with humanity, dragon kind developed large brains, and yet kept the raging hormones, so that what had begun as battles between individual males over females became ensconced in time and tradition as war. Ultimately the more peacefully inclined, the emotionally intelligent and those that were considered odd and were bullied and slaughtered, these Dragons gathered together and over a period of many years understood quantum and the nature of time itself and were able to escape their warring race and slip down another leg of the trousers of time into this world. At the time we arrived, all was relatively peaceful, if lacking in culture."

"Another leg of the trousers of time?" queried Kate. "That sounds like a fantasy author I love, Terry..."

"Pratchett!" finished Chauncey, grinning. "Exactly, Sir Terry Pratchett. Didn't really comprehend quantum, and didn't get his big dragon exactly spot-on, but he knew more than he knew he knew, if you understand me, and I greatly enjoy his books. They're all up here" and he tapped the side of his head with a golden claw. "I have a totally photographic memory."

"But if you've been trapped here for over a century, how did you get his books?"

"The crows and a pair of ravens! They bring me all kinds of things. They are rather unsophisticated in their choices, but over time I have read many, many thousands, possibly millions, of books. And tasted some rather astonishing things too. And been gifted with some truly execrable plastic err…things. They are extremely intelligent for the size of their brains, but it can be hard to get them to concentrate, so I take what I can get. In any case it has resulted in a close relationship — you know that birds descended from reptiles?" Again Kate nodded yes. "It has helped us to establish a bond. And that means they will help us soon now."

"I think I'm more astonished by knowing that you read Discworld than I was to find out that dragons actually existed in the first place. But I think it's wonderful. It means you're not just a monarch, you've got a good sense of humour."

"You think monarchs are lacking in humour? You know, perhaps you are right. In my experience, many rulers, whether hereditary or elected, seem to be sadly deficient in that particular virtue."

"That's what I thought. But in his book with dragons he talks about the sort of things the little swamp dragon eats—sounds totally yuck."

"It would sound that way to a human, wouldn't it? It would kill you or make you dreadfully sick, and you can't produce fire in any case. I can eat a Steak Diane and Potatoes Anna with a crisp green salad and Peach Melba for dessert—or sushi with miso soup and green tea ice cream—with great pleasure, but they do not fuel my fire. That requires an assortment of, well, fuels, not so different from what that young swamp dragon—Errol isn't it?—consumes.

"However, the ghastly Ivor Wyvern has a very good business head along with his penchant for torture and conquest. So to feed his patented line of Wyvern Dragon Furnaces sold by Wyvern Consolidated Heating and Lighting, he has developed a fuel — also patented as

Wyvern Best Dragon Brand Furnace Fuel — and convinced the purchasers of these ruinously expensive "furnaces" that they must be run only on this fuel or they could go wrong and be impossible to repair. Hence the need to purchase only his fuel. And where does he get that, you ask? Why, through the efforts of Wyvern Rubbish Collectors Plc which gathers refuse for slightly cheaper rates than most rubbish collectors and sends it off to Wyvern Recycling to be turned into this rather expensive fuel. But it comes in very attractive large bags, so no one suspects its origins.

"Although dragons may develop refined tastes that can cover the output of gourmet restaurants and even sometimes hire human chefs, they, like starving animals and people everywhere, can live—if poorly—on almost anything organic. And dragons have the added ability to digest organic materials such as oil shale and coal. So people who own one of his dragons could actually feed it their garbage. But Wyvern makes sure his products are sold with the understanding that only his fuels can be used. He makes money coming and going."

"Dreadful—everything I hear about him makes him more dreadful." Kate suppressed a shudder. Then she surprised him.

"Chauncey ... do you understand quantum?"

"Do I ... what?"

"Understand quantum—I'd like to know how it works."

"No, no actually I don't, not as in actually *understand* in order to explain. But ... I know a dragon who does. Someday..." And Chauncey was very relieved to see Cora returning.

Cora settled on one of Chauncey's horns and Kate heard her little voice chattering away in a language she didn't understand. She was sure it was language and not just animal noises because Chauncey was nodding almost imperceptibly and asking questions, also in this language. When Cora had finished, Chauncey turned to Kate.

"Cora says the crows agree and are taking up positions hidden in trees as close to the wyverns at the end of the bridge as possible. She says the drawbridge is down—well, it always is actually—and the portcullis is up. Hummm, that isn't always the case—I wonder if the despicable Lord Wyvern is expected? Ye gods and little fishes, that would be a disaster. You must leave quickly, as quickly as possible! Ah, yes, as soon as they see you by the portcullis the crows will attack the wyverns en masse. The wyverns are always facing outward, so they won't see you crossing the courtyard and hopefully will be so occupied by the attacking ravens that they will miss seeing you entirely. But you'd better go quickly, free Melior and impress on her how important it is to move really fast."

"I hate leaving you like this, but, okay. Cora— let's go get Melior!"

"We will meet again, my brave Kate, and then the world will be a better place. Run!"

And Kate ran. She ran through the huge chamber and down underground corridors twisting and turning, following the rainbow flutter of Cora's wings. Just as she was getting breathless she smelled the stink of the dungeons. Skidding to a stop by the big iron door that sealed Melior in, she reached for her lock picks. But where there had been animate locks on the other doors, here there was just a simple deadbolt with a knob. When she touched it however it gave her a shock that made her entire arm feel numb.

Quickly she tore a strip of cloth off her shirt and wrapped it around her hand, then took the pliers to the knob—a sizzling and sparks showed it was still dangerous, but the pliers had rubber handles and the electricity didn't get through to her. She had to use all her strength on the knob which obviously hadn't been used in a long time.

Finally it opened and, still gripping with the pliers, she pulled the reluctant door open.

Melior was crouched on the ledge above the pooled sludge looking terrified. She was shaking and whimpering. Kate felt they didn't have time for her to coax Melior out, so she simply walked in and took the nixie by the arm with one hand and her arm under her shoulders. "I'm sorry you're scared, but we have to go *now*."

And half-lifting, half dragging, she propelled Melior out the door where Cora was perched. Seeing the tiny dragon, Mel suddenly seemed to get a grip and started to move of her own accord.

"Good, Mel, great! Follow Cora—we're getting out of here!"

And hand in hand the two young women ran. Even with her breath and her heart pounding in her own ears, Kate could just hear the faintly squelchy sound of Mel's feet hitting the stones. Again Cora flew in front, making turns Kate didn't remember from her trip down to meet Chauncey. Two flights of stairs, stopping briefly to catch their breath on the landing, and they were in the short hall leading toward the door that blocked their passage into the beautiful courtyard garden full of gentle colours so at odds with the rest of the castle. On the other side of that was the central courtyard with its access to the tunnel through the great outer wall to the portcullis and the drawbridge. But here was the poisonous snake head lock, only on this side it was in the shape of a beautiful art nouveau maiden's head and arm with the keyhole in the middle of a flower held in her hand. Melior stepped forward and, in her breathy little voice said, "Sister, let us pass." And the lock turned and the door opened.

"Wow!" said Kate. "That's amazing."

Melior looked pleased. "It's only because whoever made this must have used a nixie as a model. When the art is good, a tiny portion of the model is, well, incorporated, no, not, ah … imprinted perhaps? Anyway, we recognise each other and that bond meant she would do as I asked."

"Well it makes my job easier," said Kate. "Now we need to run for that tunnel, but I think stay out of direct sight of the wyverns on the pillars, just in case they look this way. Let's go for it."

She felt tiny claws digging slightly into her shoulder and looking down sideways saw Cora perched on her shoulder and intended to come with them.

"You must be tired of flying so much," guessed Kate. "Hang on then, here we go."

Spell or no spell, faith or magic, it all worked. They ran at an angle that kept them concealed from the wyverns until they got to the mouth of the tunnel through the great portcullis wall. Kate stepped forward so that she could be seen and heard one deep sharp *kraa!* followed by a wall of sound as over a hundred crows exploded from the trees and torpedoed toward the Wyverns, who virtually disappeared under an avalanche of birds. Kate and Melior sprinted across the bridge and between the pillars, heads down and running as if their lives depended on it—which of course they did. Even well out of reach of the wyverns on their chains they ran on and on, until a curve in the road hid the castle and the wyverns under their cloud of crows from sight. Then with one accord, they turned off the road into the trees and collapsed on the ground panting. At least Kate was panting. Melior just seemed to be breathing a bit more heavily, and her lovely naked body with its look of a shimmery haze around it made her look very like an art nouveau painting—all those lovely shimmery young ladies caught between adolescence and adulthood with a come-hither radiance that yet wasn't sexual, just sensual. Definitely look, don't touch. The horrible stench she'd had to live in didn't seem to have touched her either—she neither smelled bad nor looked like she needed a bath. Unlike Kate who was now hot and sweaty and still carried

161

both the smell and the stains of their dungeon. *Supernatural definitely had its advantages* she thought.

Just as she was thinking of getting to her feet and making a start on the journey back to Maggie's house, they heard a car.

"Down, get down!" commanded Kate and they flattened themselves down behind the gorse bushes into the bracken. She managed to keep one eye still on the road, and saw the great black car with a wyvern for a hood ornament and a black and red crest of wyverns like that carved above the portcullis of the castle. She also caught a glimpse of a hawk-profiled man with jet black hair sitting in the back. *Oh shivering sea-cooks,* she thought, *it's him, it's Ivor Wyvern. Thank you, Chauncey, for warning me and getting us out of there in time.*

Chapter 27

After waiting for some time to make sure there weren't more cars or anyone coming back, Kate, Melior and Cora regained the road. As they walked along Kate realised that she didn't actually know the way back to Maggie's cottage in the woods outside the Village of Ashley. She had come with Robin that morning—it seemed like years ago now—through the woods and scrambling up cliffs, and she really had no idea where this road went. Although she rather thought it would come to a crossroad that would be signposted to Ashley, she became aware that walking through the village with a dragon on her shoulder and a naked young woman who shimmered wasn't a real option. Or, given that it was possible that both would be invisible or perhaps look like something else (a bird and a—a what?—a young woman with clothes on?), there was still the fact that she herself was extremely dirty and stinking like a sewer, covered in scratches and with a bloody cloth bound round her leg. She could not allow the village to see her like that because that would mean Uncle Hugh would know and be very upset, and she didn't have a believable lie to tell him. Plus she would get Robin into *so* much trouble!

And what about Robin? Was he okay? Chauncey had said he hadn't died or been imprisoned or been within the castle or the moat at all because Chauncey would have known. But what had happened? He could have been injured or even killed outside. But somehow she thought not: he was clever and strong, and possibly had magic she didn't know about. He must have gone back home she thought, home where he could find help. Oh, please, don't let them try to break into the castle! Because that would surely mean she'd lose three of the people she loved, and the only people she knew who were also magical.

As they walked she explained all this to Melior and Cora. Melior knew the cottage because in the past she had happily inhabited a sacred pool not far upstream from it. But she had no more idea than Kate how to get there from the road they were on (a road that remained deserted—apparently no one, no one at all, wished to go to the castle even though everyone believed it to be deserted).

Cora, however, as a creature with wings who knew her way around the entire area doing reconnaissance for Chauncey, did know the way to Maggie's cottage, a way that would avoid the village. So with Cora flitting from branch to branch they set off through the woods and fields.

Mel stopped when she found a small stream to immerse herself in the water. "A nixie who dries out is a shrivelled nixie," she said when Kate complained they were losing time. "That's how that slut Palatyne caught me. She sent word that Lord Wyvern had captured her and kept her in a birdcage just out of reach of water—an exquisite torture you must admit, within sight and smell of that which would save her but unable to reach it—and that if she couldn't escape, she would dry out and shrivel up slowly and horribly. But it turned out she was one of the traitor nixies and had offered to help him capture me, because Palatyne said I knew about anything the Fae might be planning against him and what spells they might be weaving to free the dragons. She, Melusine and I are triplets, so naturally I rushed off to rescue Palatyne from such a slow and painful death. But instead I was trapped by her and incarcerated. I'll wager anything you like that Wyvern was going there to torture me for information I don't even possess if Kate hadn't rescued me."

"So you don't know anything about how to rescue Chauncey and the others?"

"Nothing at all I'm afraid."

"And the Fae—do they have plans or spells?"

"You need to ask them."

"I did, I asked Kailen, and he said the Fae were under the impression that the dragons were gone. So I guess they think that those that have been enchanted into objects and appliances by Wyvern are lost or dead, that they can't be saved."

"Ah,"said Melior. "But Chauncey knows otherwise, doesn't he? He's quite alive. You said he knows in his own case and guesses for the others that with the right reverse enchantments they can be saved."

"Yes, this is something the Fae don't know, it's what we must tell them and convince them if necessary that they must work to find these reverse enchantments. Or help me find them. We must pray that there are records of these, that they do in fact exist."

"Wherever there is an enchantment or spell there must be a reverse spell. It is a universal law. I believe a human said 'for every action there is a reaction.' It is the same for magic, there is always the reverse because there must be balance."

"That's Isaac Newton's Third Law, 'For every action, there is an equal and opposite reaction'," quoted Kate. "Apparently he was also a magician. And possibly the most original mind ever born, plus obsessive, compulsive and, well, weird. I learned that from Perry, who has studied Newton a lot."

"Perry? Who is Perry?" Melior twirled on the spot sending out a liquid shimmer. Her natural tendency to brighten at the thought of a human male was showing.

"He's my tutor, he's brilliant and, come to think of it, he does have a great interest in legends and myths and magic. Peregrine Sinclair. He's a scholar and loves research. I'll bet he could help, if he can believe that magic really exists. I know he *wants* it to exist, but I don't think he actually believes it, let alone knows it."

"We will convince him," purred Melior, causing Kate to look at her with new eyes. In her mind she was beginning to see a sort of coalition forming, and it was indeed made up of odd elements. Melior, far from being the small helpless victim Kate had thought her until then, was turning out to have considerable depths. Perry might have some interesting 'scholarship' ahead.

Just then Cora flew back toward them. "Hide, hide!" she cried in her tiny voice. "Something is coming up ahead. Hide, and I will go find out who or what."

Kate and Mel scrambled for the shelter of hazel bushes and bracken while Cora flew on ahead, concealing herself by flitting from shadow to shadow. Quite shortly she came back, her entire body and wings seeming to glitter with the strength of her feelings. "It's Robin and Kailen! They are coming to save you. But I told them you have saved yourselves!"

Now Kate could hear the sound of voices coming closer, and Robin followed by his father came into view around some trees.

Kate was running so hard, and then she literally crashed into Robin running the other way, and they fell to the ground together, laughing and crying and talking over each other.

"Kate! Oh, Kate! I thought you were dead. I thought... I thought it was all my fault. Oh, Kate!"

"Robin, I couldn't find you. I didn't dare cry out. I was inside the castle, Robin. I was so scared, and I was so angry. Robin, I found him! I found the Dragon King!"

166

Chapter 28

There was a long breathless silence as Kailen and Robin took in what Kate had said.

"Is…is he dead?" asked Kailen, but with desperate hope in his voice.

"No, no, he's alive! Just somehow enchanted to stay where he is, doing the job of a central heating furnace. He can move within limits and he is fully awake and thinking—boy, is he thinking, he's a genius!"

"Oh…he's alive…oh, we hoped. We kept hoping…" Kailen's eyes seemed moist with unshed tears. "Does that mean others may be alive?"

"Chauncey says he believes they are alive, all of them. Enchanted, enslaved, but alive."

"Chauncey? What is that?" Kailen sounded baffled and even outraged.

"Err… okay, look — it's what he told me to call him, all right? He says it's his name amongst his English friends. It's sort of close to his Chinese name — but I don't remember that exactly."

"Young woman, you met with the Great Dragon King, the oldest and best of the Noble Dragons and you tell me he wanted you to call him Chauncey? I think someone has drugged you, I think you have been brainwashed. Maybe there are no dragons, they just made you think he was there! And you spent the afternoon—while we thought you were injured or dead—conversing with a furnace!" Kailen was looming over her shaking with suppressed feeling, tugging at his long hair and looking like he'd like to murder something. The happy shock of being told the Great Dragon King was alive was replaced with doubt and dismay. The Fae had believed for so long that the dragons were gone that hope was, in some ways, more than he could bear.

Robin grabbed his father's elbow, pulling his hand down and taking hold of it. "Dad! Dad, no! Kate's not drugged, she's not hallucinating. I know her—this is Kate. She tells the truth! She always tells the truth, even when you don't want to hear it. Why are you so upset? Nothing wrong with being called Chauncey, is there?"

Kailen looked at his son with puzzlement as the anger and anguish slowly drained out of him. "No, son, I suppose not. It's just... just that this wondrous creature, the Great Dragon King, he has almost been worshipped amongst those of the Fae who admire dragons. It is just—well, it's not fitting that he should have a sort of nickname and that he should ask a human child to use it. I am finding it virtually impossible to take in."

"Virtually, but not entirely, hey Dad?" grinned Robin. "I know you use language exactly, like all the true Fae, and every word has meaning. And every bloody gesture and all those formalities...ah, never mind. So *virtually,* but not *entirely* impossible—Kate, that means he's getting his head around it. Don't get all bent out of shape because he thought you were imagining things."

Kate was so tired and so glad to see them both that she actually had only been confused by the sudden transformation of Robin's father from ally to interrogator. She was so tired now that she couldn't really grasp why Chauncey's name should be the source of so much confusion and outrage. In fact, she felt as if she were possibly falling, she needed to sit down... So she did quite suddenly. As her eyes closed she heard her own voice whispering "His name is Chen Shi." And she passed out.

When she came to, she was being carried like a child in Kailen's strong arms and they weren't far from the cottage. Suddenly Maggie was with them, tears pouring down her cheeks, her arms outstretched in an effort to embrace them all, all at once.

168

"Oh, Kailen! Robin! You saved her! I was so frightened, so frightened for you all." She was shaking with relief.

"No, Mum, Kate saved herself! We found her with the nixie walking back through the woods." Robin was slightly crestfallen, but believed in giving Kate the credit.

"It's true, Maggie my love, Kate and the nixie were being guided by Cora back here. But Kate is injured and she's exhausted." said Kailen.

"Cora? A nixie? Where are they? And what is Cora?"

"Cora is a Fae Dragon and the nixie is Melior who used to live in the enchanted pool near here. I think perhaps she has gone there for the healing and refreshing properties of the pool. Cora is up in the tree right there." Robin and Maggie both shaded their eyes and stared. Maggie suddenly stopped and passed her hand several times in front of her eyes murmuring something. It was a spell for calmness and clear sight. She then looked again, slightly off to the side of the tree.

"Oh, I see her, I see her!" She breathed in wonder. "Hello Cora, thank you, my beautiful friend, for helping the people I love."

Maggie turned to Robin, "You are half witch and half Fae my son. Do as I did and say—she whispered in his ear—and then look to the side just as you showed Kate when you taught her how to see past a glamour." Robin did as she said and his concentration was replaced by a look of wonder. "OMG, it's a Dragon, I'm looking at a Dragon. That is so cool. Err—and beautiful. Thanks Cora, you rock."

Cora responded by leaping into the air and doing a back flip before flying over and landing on Kate's hand as if to bring their attention back to the exhausted heroine who, although conscious, was visibly drooping. "Chen Shi loves Kate, he thinks she may save him." she said in her lovely high voice—it could have been bird song except you could hear the words.

"I'm an idiot," muttered Maggie. "Kailen bring her inside and lay her on the sofa. I've been making healing potions and food while you were gone. I didn't know what you'd find. Oh, Gaia, earth goddess, I'm so grateful you're all back. Kate, darling, we'll have you feeling better soon, I promise."

Kate was gently lowered onto a couch spread with squishy duvets and pillows, and lay back with a feeling of extreme relief. She'd done it and she was still alive! Her leg, though, where the malevolent nixie had clawed it, was throbbing and she felt somewhat nauseous. She said this to Maggie, who unwrapped the bandage and saw with concern that the wounds were looking rather as if they were infected.

"Where did this happen?" she asked.

"In the moat, it was filthy and this horrible thing grabbed me and it had claws—they did the damage. Later Melior told me it was her turncoat sister who'd gone over to the evil Lord Wyvern. I swallowed some of the moat water too. Maybe that's why I feel sick now."

Maggie was taking her pulse and then passed her hands over Kate's face and down her body. In their wake Kate felt a feeling of peace and relaxation coming over her.

"Robin, go get the glass with the green liquid please, and there's an ointment next to it. Bring those and some clean cloths. Oh, and a bowl with warm water too."

She gave Kate the glass and told her to sip it slowly. Meanwhile, she dipped the cloths in the water and gently bathed the cuts on Kate's leg. Kate had tensed expecting pain, but whatever soothing Maggie had done also kept her from feeling any hurt. Maggie inspected the cuts carefully, washing them again using something that

170

smelled strange but not unpleasant, then coated several bandages with the ointment and carefully wrapped the leg. Kate was still sipping the drink, which seemed slightly minty and slightly like camomile tea, but felt her grip slipping. Robin noticed, and caught the glass before it could drop.

"Mum, she's passing out again!" But Maggie was okay with that. "She's just going to sleep now, so she can heal."

But Kate remembered something she must tell them, so hauling herself back from the edge of blissful unconsciousness, she said, "You have to know—Ivor Wyvern isn't dead! Chauncey told me. He's still alive and he's very very dangerous!" And with her message safely delivered she let go and slipped like the trout she'd held only a few hours ago, back into the gentle waters, and down and down, far from fear and danger and pain.

Chapter 29

Kate was asleep, but she'd left consternation in her wake. The message she'd delivered was making Maggie, Kailen and Robin struggle for belief and understanding. However they looked at it, it was the worst possible news. A powerful magician was alive and apparently as full of power as ever.

It was Robin who suddenly said, "Wait…wait a minute. If he's alive this could be good news. We capture him and force him to tell us how to undo the enchantments. If he was dead we might never find those spells!"

He didn't get the reaction he expected. His mother looked green with fear and his father looked full of doubt.

Maggie said, "Robin, you must *never* under any circumstances go near Wyvern Hall again. That monster has much more power than anything we can devise. You would be killed. Or… tortured. Or turned into a statue. And we couldn't stop him! We don't know anything that could render him helpless. Kailen, tell him!"

Kailen put his arm around her and faced his son. "Robin, your mother is right. You must not go there again, nor Kate, nor any of us.

Then he turned so he could face Maggie as well, holding her by both arms, he spoke calmly, trying to infuse her with some calm and, possibly, hope. "At least not until we learn more. We must know the extent of his power and we must devise a plan. I cannot trust most of the Fae, many are unconcerned, some are traitorous, and only a very few stand firm with me. That is not enough to make up any kind of fighting force, even if we knew what we would be fighting. It is knowledge we need now before we can even think of formulating a strategy. And I honestly don't know where to turn for that knowledge."

But Robin, although somewhat sobered, was full of ideas. "I do, I know ways to find things out. The statues in Ashley Manor garden regain consciousness or come alive every full moon. The one Kate thinks is Eleanor—that's Wyvern's sister—has even left a note asking Kate to meet with her. And another is Wyvern's wife Maude, she's Kate's great-great-something aunt. They must know loads about him and his powers. There are the other statues too—he imprisoned their souls in his sculptures and they might some of them know things that could help. At least they have reason to hate him, which puts them on our side. He's made a stone army, and if it can I bet anything you like that it will turn on him!

"Then there's Perry, our tutor—he loves research. He may not be magical, but I'll bet he'd love to know it's real, and he'd be mad keen to do something more exciting than teach a couple of teenagers. Oh, and that nixie—Kate rescued her from the dungeons—she hates Wyvern. And the little Fae Dragon, Cora. She goes in and out of Wyvern Hall a lot doing what she can for Chaun—err—Chen Shi. She must know loads of stuff. And you heard her say the Dragon King thinks Kate is destined to save him. If that's so, then Kate is the lynchpin here—all of this has been waiting for her to arrive. Think of it, none of us knew anything about any of this until Kate got here. And since then it has all just been exploding!"

Both his parents were taking all of this in. Maggie was still extremely worried, but also there was something growing in her as she saw her child taking up a stance full of intent and hope. Kailen also seemed to be infused with something of his son's passion.

"That's what I'm afraid of, darling, it's all just piling up as if behind a dam, and that could break and wash you all away with it." Maggie went to her son and pulled him close. "I hate what I'm hearing, I hate what this animal, this demon has done. And I know as a witch that things of power are stirring in so many places around here. But as a woman I just want to keep you and Kailen and Kate safe. There are premonitions and intuitions lately that seem to speak of a battle to be fought, but nothing I can pick up tells me who or what will win."

Kailen came to hug them both. "Robin is right though—there are untapped resources we have not considered. After all we have just become acquainted with this awful knowledge. So long as Wyvern doesn't know that we know, we will have the chance to gather information and make decisions based upon it. And now we will have reinforcements we never considered. The Fae have been concerned and fearful about the fate of the dragons for many years. Now that we know at least some are alive, and especially the Dragon King, we cannot simply turn our backs. In fact I think we won't be allowed that option…Wyvern will learn that Kate and Robin were there and if he follows up they will be in jeopardy. So it may become a question of who strikes first, not a choice to opt out.

"Look, it is well past sundown. I suggest we all get to sleep and tomorrow when Kate is awake we can find out everything she knows and also seek out the nixie. And we must approach this Perry as well. We have to use our time wisely to pool knowledge and resources. When is the next full moon?"

"June 20th, Kailen. that's next week."

"So that's when Kate will meet the statue that is Eleanor. We must see if we can join that party."

"And it's virtually the Summer Solstice, so all of our powers as magical beings should be increased." Maggie was sounding more positive. She knew that a gathering of magical beings at such a time could result in more than the exchange of some information, much as that would be welcome. But to put their heads together with these living statues at such a time could be extremely fortuitous.

"Mum, I'm hungry," Robin, his eyes drooping with the need to sleep after his adventures and his fears, also needed refuelling. It became a raid on the refrigerator and then each of them did a quick heating spell on the soup, but used a toaster for the bread ("it gets hot but soggy when I do the heat spell"). Soup, sandwiches and gingerbread with clotted cream plus hot drinks were consumed quickly and the dishes left for the next day. When Robin hit his bed he was asleep almost before he could pull up the quilt.

But Maggie went off to the bedroom where Kate was sleeping and gently woke her with a hot drink. When Kate shook off the wooziness of sleep she asked what time it was.

"Time for going to bed, lovely girl, but I thought you'd really appreciate a hot shower first to get all the castle moat grunge off, and some soup and bread to fill your stomach before you head back to a nice clean bed for a proper sleep. Shower's just through there, lots of towels and a robe. I'll be out here just in case you feel dizzy or anything."

Kate found sluicing herself clean under lovely hot water, with great smelling soap and shampoo was just what her body and mind wanted. Twenty minutes later, wrapped in a white towelling robe she was towelling dry her hair and found that Maggie had laid a small table with soup and fresh bread and butter. She simply wolfed it all down, and again a feeling of well-being came over her. "You put spells on this?" she asked Maggie.

"Only simple ones when I cook it, just another small ingredient to the mix and helps with digestion and feeling well."

"It works," said Kate simply.

She paused: "Maggie, there's something I want to try to say. I was so scared today, but I also—how can I put it—once I got out of the cell by the moat and then when I overcame the other things, and actually met Chauncey—err, Chen Shi—and then got away! Well, I think I feel like someone who is so very different to the kid who arrived here a few months ago. Someone powerful, someone to be reckoned with. I know that sounds like bragging, but really I'm mostly grateful, because it's what I always wanted—to have substance. I mean, it's horrible what has happened, and I hate to think of all the damage and pain this man, this thing, has caused, but I still feel good about me. Maybe I shouldn't if that's the price?"

"You didn't cause any of this, you just discovered it, and it needed to be discovered if there's to be any chance of changing it. We have that chance now, and it's because you are here. And most people don't feel they have much, um, substance, until they are tested and aren't found wanting. And you haven't been found wanting. You deserve to feel good about yourself, you've earned it."

"Well, that's a relief, because it was pretty awful in so many ways, but there has been the warm bit inside me that has been saying just that—you've been in trouble and you got out, you did this yourself!"

"And tomorrow we will sit down and start making plans, but first you need to go next door to a nice clean bedroom that doesn't smell at all of dank moat water and get a good night's sleep. I just happen to have another of those green drinks here in a thermos, and it should help you nod off as well as fighting off any possible infection you might have picked up."

Chapter 30

The smell of frying bacon intruded on Kate's dream in which she and Robin, dressed in unlikely costumes as a medieval man and his maid, were about to take an embrace to the next level. For a moment the two images were confused in her dream—Robin in doublet and hose presenting a tray of bacon and eggs to her as she sat on a green bank embroidered with flowers—or was that her dress? Dreams fled as her stomach growled. She opened her eyes to a sunny room with cream walls and fabrics in shades of green. Bacon, there really was bacon! She noticed a tee shirt and leggings laid out on a chair and pulled them on, stopping in the adjoining bathroom to wash her face. Then she followed her nose through a number of rooms with the stream flowing through them to the kitchen where Robin was piling plates with scrambled eggs and bacon, Maggie was buttering toast and Kailen was attending to a hissing coffee machine. There were also croissants, pots of jam and honey and some steaming mugs of tea, including herbal tea and Chai Latte ready on the counter.

Maggie was in what Kate thought a fashion magazine might have called "What the stylish witch wears at home"—a long loose gown in shades of terracotta, gold, flame reds and some shots of deep green. Looking more closely you could see that it was actually a flowing pattern of symbols and spirit animals. Her blond hair was pulled back into a loose chignon. Robin was wearing a black tee shirt that said "I Will Make Better Mistakes Tomorrow" and torn jeans and flip flops. Kailen had on what appeared to be his uniform—black top and trousers that were as iridescent as a beetle's wing, his long hair in all its braids tied back.

"Hey Werewolf! You're up!" Robin flashed her a big grin. "Werewolf? Oh…' Kate stared down at her tee, which featured a large werewolf and the slogan "Always be Yourself. Unless you can be a Werewolf, then always be a Werewolf." She grinned back. "I'm hungry, really, really, hungry," she growled low, but ended up coughing.

Maggie laughed, "Well, at least I don't have to ask if you feel ok."

Kailen said, "Coffee or tea?"

"Oh, coffee please, can you do a cappuccino with that machine?"

"Definitely, it's what Maggie likes," Kailen pulled a new mug out of the cupboard.

A few minutes later they were all mostly through their first coffees (Kailen had tea) and making inroads into bacon and eggs, toast or croissants with sweet butter and honey.

"From our bees" Robin told her proudly. "I've learned how to calm them when we want honey—but we always leave them plenty. And Mum's been teaching me about why we tell them about what's been happening. But I expect that when we tell them what happened to you, and that you-know-who is back, or rather never went away, they are going to go mental!"

Kate snorted with derision. "You-know-who? Oh, do we have to do the whole Voldemort thing? He-who-shall-not-be-named and all that codswallop? Actually, would he know somehow if we did say his name? 'Cause I'd like to curse his name and him, but if there's some magic that will backfire if I do that y'all need to tell me right now, okay?"

Kailen laughed, the first laugh he'd managed since they'd realised that the situation that had been a background worry had become the foreground threat. "Not any magic that I know of, sweet Kate, I think the dreadful Lord Wyvern is going to have to discover us like anyone

178

else, by asking questions and following up leads. But it is also quite possible that he feels so invulnerable after all these years of being still alive without anyone—at least anyone we are aware of—knowing, that he will simply brush away your trespass like an irritating fly and go on as before. In which case it may well be that pride goeth before a fall. A catastrophic fall if we can manage it!"

Kate brightened at that, "Oh, good! I was afraid, you know. I was very afraid that if he is still alive we are all, well—doomed. We need to find out about him—Eleanor and Maude will know, they will know his character and his weak points, err, if he has weak points. Crap, he simply *must* have weak points."

Robin let out a 'whoop' then, and shouted "I told you, I told you she was the lynchpin, and she would be ready for whatever came. Kate, we talked some after you fell asleep. Err, how are you by the way, how's the leg?" But he went on before she could answer. "I said we had to talk to them, the harpies, and maybe the other statues too—they probably really hate him. And Perry, we need to recruit Perry, he's the utter super spy when it comes to ferreting out intelligence if it exists in a book or on the 'net. Leg's all right, yeah?"

Kate couldn't help smiling. "Yeah, the leg's okay. Your mum, whatever she put on it, it's nearly as good as new. And that green stuff I drank? I've never slept so well, and no bad dreams. I was sure I'd have nightmares. But maybe living a 'daymare' keeps the night ones away. Oh, where are Melior and Cora?"

Maggie reached over to put her hand over Kate's, "Cora's gone back to Chen Shi to tell him you're safe and that we will be planning how to free him, and the others. She's not really a great brain, she's so small, Cora, but she can memorise messages very well indeed. And we think Melior is back in her pool which is just upstream a bit from here. Robin and Kailen are going there after breakfast to see if she'll come down here, or we'll go there and find out as much as she knows. I think you got her out just in time—Wyvern may have visited the Hall specifically to question her. But the most important thing is to talk to Eleanor and Maude at full moon, that's only a few days from now. Robin has the idea that maybe we can turn those statues into a stone army and point them at Lord Wyvern if they hate him more than they're scared of him. We would also like to undo the enchantment on them, although hopefully they might fight first if that proves to be useful. But it's information gathering for now."

"My bet is that Perry will be leaping for joy to go all super-spy," said Kate. "If there's anything in old documents or new ones, or on the 'net—he'd love that. He's such a romantic, I've seen him sitting by Maude—the harpy statue—and talking to her. He confessed he was so enamoured of the Romantic Poets and some of the later Victorian ones like Tennyson, that the thought that our Maude could have been Tennyson's Maud really got to him. Of course, he doesn't know that she is really in there—he thinks it's just a statue and a romantic story. Wait until he finds out! And I wonder, can Maude hear him, between full moons, that is?"

"Do you really think he can believe?" asked Kailen. "My experience of humans is that they read about magic and fantasy, as they call it, but if you confront them with a reality they somehow explain it away. Very useful of course as it means so many of us can walk amongst them without having to work hard at spells and glamours to disguise what we are. If a human can explain it away, almost all of them will—they can stare straight at a unicorn and believe it's only a white horse with possibly an injury to its head. Your lovely uncle, Sir Hugh, for instance—a troop of us —the Fae—were just having a bit of a party in that pretty wood with the good view of the Manor and Sir Hugh came along and thought we were just maybe a coach party in fancy dress pretending to be fairies or, actually, he thought we were pretending to be 18th Century lords and ladies. Have to say he was very gentlemanly about it. Didn't try to drive us off his land or anything, in fact he just asked that we not start any fires or cut down any trees and off he went."

"I'm almost certain Perry would believe, if we could show him any proof at all, if he could see it. But, oh my stars! Uncle Hugh! He must be going mental because I'm not back and I didn't call. Quick, Robin, I need your phone! Oh, crap, what'll I tell him? What can I say?"

Maggie, putting her hand over Robin's phone so it didn't get to Kate, said, "It's not a problem, Kate, I called him yesterday evening and said you and Robin had been hiking and you fell and cut your leg a bit and felt a little feverish. I said I did a bit of first aid and you were exhausted, so you were asleep and we felt it wise to let you stay that way. He knows you're here, he knows you're safe and he expects you back later today or even this evening."

"Oh, that's a relief. It's like Kailen says, Uncle Hugh wouldn't be able to, well, encompass the idea that magic is real or that statues have living beings in them. Or dragons! He'd never believe in dragons! I'm so glad he's not worried. But, Maggie, *where* does he think I am exactly? You have a glamour on this house so it looks like an ancient bridge, nothing more. So where are we supposed to be?"

"You are a bright one, darling girl," said Maggie with a grin. "We are in the cottage I rented near Exeter while I work on plans to build a cottage right by that very old bridge. Sir Hugh doesn't actually know where I supposedly live at the moment, and as he can always reach me when he needs to, I don't suppose it bothers him."

"Well, before I go back we'd better put our heads together with a reasonable description in case I need one. Robin, can you pass the croissants?"

Chapter 31

After breakfast—Kate had thought there might be a nice dishwashing spell, but it turned out there wasn't, or at least Maggie wasn't letting on, so Kate and Robin washed up—Kate and Maggie sat down with Maggie's computer to make a list while Robin and Kailen went upstream to talk to Melior.

"Men aren't nearly so good at making lists," commented Maggie. "They either think they can remember it all or they just hare off and act first and think later. Not so true of Kailen, and I have to say I'm very pleased to finally see Robin taking after him more. Robin was such a delinquent, and I think that was because he's a halfling, neither witch nor Fae. The Fae won't really accept him and I'm a loner witch, I don't like what I've experienced of covens—they start off all right, but seem to dissolve into bickering and one-upmanship, like so many groups. Probably because they don't have anything important enough to present a united front against. But it's left Robin out in the cold and he was acting out a lot before he met up with you and Perry.

But it turned out it was Robin last night who brought me and Kailen to our senses when we were feeling like the roof had caved in. I was sick with fear at the thought of Ivor Wyvern (doesn't that name seem a little -err -squirmy?) He scares the crap out of me even now, but yesterday I just sort of froze. Kailen was a bit more sensible. We both said you and Robin were never, ever, going back there again, but then Kailen said, well, not until we had enough information so that we could free Chen Shi and maybe the others—and even take down Wyvern.

After that we were at a loss because we hadn't any information and no ideas on how or where to get any. But that set Robin off—*he* had a lot of ideas, good ones. Just like yours. So what we need to do now, you and I, is create an action list and then work out what needs to be done first and second and so on."

"And what can be done simultaneously and who should do what," finished Kate. "It sounds like we're planning a campaign."

"That's exactly what we are doing—planning a campaign and then we'll set about recruiting people and beings to do their parts. With luck, and some of the concealing spells we have, we should get everything well underway without that depraved monster having any inkling that his 'creations' are about to turn on him. I am beginning to get a better feeling about this. Oh, and when Robin and Kailen get back we must take you out and introduce you to the bees and you can tell them your adventure. They can get quite stroppy if they aren't kept in the loop, and they can be all kinds of helpful if you trust them with everything. It's hard to explain, but the 'hive mind' can really help."

"You're very different from the adults I'm used to," said Kate. "I can't think of any of them who wouldn't be saying 'We'll call the police' and certainly forbidding me to have anything more to do with anything even potentially dangerous. Well, except Grandmother, she wouldn't want me in danger, but she never treated me like a half-wit either. And if she were here now she'd be sitting and plotting with us I'm sure. Robin said I'm the—what was it?—the lynchpin here and everything is because of me, and Chauncey said that to Cora. And you guys haven't said, oh, no, you're not, you're going back to America where you'll be safe. That's what most people would say."

"You're the girl who can see dragons, you got inside Wyvern Hall and proved the Dragon King is alive and brought back so much information—and a nixie. And we aren't just adults, we aren't entirely human—and neither are you in the ordinary sense—we know a potential rallying point when we see one. And this threat won't go away. If Wyvern has really enslaved virtually all the dragons on this Earth, he may get bored and want to enslave and torment more species, certainly more humans. He's definitely holding an awful grudge against the people of Ashley Manor. He might be satisfied with just ruining the estate and possibly grabbing the land, but we have to doubt that—he's going to want more personal vengeance. So as a Mallory you wouldn't be safe in any case."

"It's not that I don't want to be safe. I'm terrified of the idea of magic that can torment and enslave, but I don't want to be safe like ordinary folk say to kids—stay in your room, don't go out, leave this to the grownups. Ugh. So in a peculiar way I'm glad I've been given this role. Besides I love Chauncey, he's mega in every possible way! I want so much to help him, and his children and the other dragons."

"Chen Shi has children here?" It was a new thought to Maggie.

"Yes, it's how Wyvern caught him—he managed to ensnare several of Chauncey's children, young, smaller dragons, and somehow was able to get a message to Chauncey saying that if he didn't present himself at Wyvern Hall, Ivor was going to—how did he put it, it was appalling—oh, going to torture one at a time to the point of death, then bring them back and do it again until Chauncey turned himself in. But that he'd free them if Chauncey cooperated. So he did. He's been there ever since, enslaved, with only limited movement, being a central heating furnace."

"And the young dragons?" asked Maggie, fearing she already knew the answer.

"Ivor turned them into what look like iron or bronze statues and sold them at the Great Exhibition. Chauncey says that's why there was such a craze for dragons of all kinds in Art Nouveau, that's the decade—

1900 to 1910—when Wyvern started selling them for furnaces, statues, fireplaces, lighting fixtures and even cigarette and cigar lighters. Lots of other designers began to incorporate them in jewellery and door knockers and all kinds of art—but those were manufactured things, not real dragons."

"The Fae have been totally stymied as to what really happened to the dragons—they'd decided that they were dead. Now we know. Knowledge is power. And knowing they aren't extinct—except for the Faerie Dragons, the Fae knew there were a few of those, but they never met Cora obviously. Or if they did, she wasn't talking. Perhaps because they are powerless to undo the curses alone," mused Maggie.

"Curses?" asked Kate.

"Curses, enchantments, spells, all part and parcel of the same thing—magic. Powerful magic in this case. It must involve some rather complex spells, and in that case there's every chance they are written down. Which means that, if we can find them, we will either find the counter-spell as well or be able to create one. It's all about balance, where there is a spell, there has to be a counter-spell."

"That's exactly what Melior said, about balance. But it does sound very Hogwarts," said Kate a bit doubtfully.

"Which is why we witches—those who can actually do magic anyway—and the Fae keep a low profile. In this day and age we might not be burned or drowned or otherwise tormented, but we'd be a laughing stock, as are so many so-called mystics and fortune-tellers. And I can tell you that the Fae do not take kindly to being laughed at."

"Neither do I," said Kate, remembering her early childhood when it seemed everyone, starting with her mother, made fun of her and how she had felt what amounted to impotent rage at the unfairness of it. I

186

wonder, she thought, if I had access to magic then, what I might have done to them? I'm pretty sure it would have been a big overreaction. "Maggie, do most children of the Fae and witches—or even young dragons—know how to do magic? I mean, if I had known how, I probably would have hurt the people who hurt me."

"It's really like with any children—there's a certain tendency not to understand entirely the results of one's actions, and even quite nice children, before they properly understand consequences, can do things that hurt other beings. Children with magical tendencies, even magical powers, do these things and hurt things—maybe it's just to smash a vase or make things jump off shelves, but it can be that they hurt people or animals when they themselves feel hurt or angry. It's the feelings that need to be addressed as well as the powers. So it's a matter of raising and training. It's interesting that you didn't have any magical tendencies or experiences until you moved to Devon. It may be that your magic is strongly rooted in the West Country. There is a history of that. I wonder how your grandmother — Lucinda—I wonder if she lost her magic when she moved to America, or if she simply never felt it when she lived here either?"

"I don't think she ever thought of herself as a witch, maybe her family didn't tell her, or thought she had no power. But I'm sure she did—she could make anything grow and she was so insightful about people. But she would probably have described that as having good instincts," said Kate thoughtfully. "But will you and Kailen train me, like Robin and I train at the Dojo? So that I can work magic but not get out of control?"

"Very like the Dojo, actually—practice, practice, practice." smiled Maggie. "Yes, we will. And Robin too. We'll have to get Perry's cooperation with that because it's going to eat into school time. And we need Perry to help with the research. If he proves impervious to belief in magic, or if it freaks him out too much to be useful, we will apply a few forgetfulness spells. But I don't think it will. I used to employ him, and I recommended him to Sir Hugh to be your tutor. I've sensed the possibility that he might have some magic in him, or at least be able to accept that it exists.

"I think … no, actually I'm certain Perry will be intrigued and even delighted to know there is real magic, and then he'll really want to be involved—in fact, you won't be able to stop him. Perry is, well, he's like a super-nerd and super intelligent and would be over the moon to belong to our secret group. Plus if you want to get a computer hacked or have someone who can play any of those games at the top level, he's your guy. I've heard he goes to Discworld Conventions and ComicCon, and I'm gonna make him take me along to the next one if we can— once we've saved the dragons." Kate was grinning with the pleasure of getting to include one of her favourite people. She had no doubts, none at all. Maggie was relieved to see it.

So, sitting side by side, the two witches made their list and then read it over.

1. <u>Kate Mallory</u> — The Dragon's Champion—the girl who can see dragons and is resourceful and courageous. Has good self-defence skills and the beginnings of magic powers. At 16 she is of an age to learn quickly. Will be taught magic and more self-defence.

2. <u>Maggie Spencer</u> — 'hedge/loner' witch. Skilled at spell casting and aware of auras and can do really good forgetfulness spells. Is learning to see dragons. Is a really good forensic accountant, which may make it possible to thwart Ivor Wyvern and all his lawyers legally as to ruining the Mallorys and acquiring Ashley Manor. If not, then older ways will be used.

"What older ways?" asked Kate.

"I'd rather you didn't have to know," sighed Maggie, "but if needs must you will learn them."

3. Kailen — Fae prince and powerful mage. Skilled fighter. Can see dragons. Is unusually (for a fairy) skilled at arbitration, which will be useful to bind certain of the Fae that he feels he can trust into a unit that can fight if necessary. Capable of twisting the truth very believably — as are all the Fae, but we can trust Kailen, and we cannot trust the rest, not entirely.

4. Robin Spencer — Halfling (half witch/half Fae), good at martial arts, excellent liar. At 16 is just itching for a quest or a fight or something to go out and win. The problem will be to channel this without antagonising him. Will be taught magic along with Kate. Will be Kate's protector and champion.

"Oh, hey," objected Kate "He'll be impossible if you tell him that!"

"We are dealing with a teenage male ego here, and it needs a little boosting since you are the Dragon's Champion and that automatically relegates him to a secondary roll. This should please him," explained Maggie. "And I know you won't let him order you around."

5. Peregrine Sinclair — a human being with intelligence and researching skills and a romantic heart. Possibly can be taught some simple but effective magic. If not, certainly some self-defense, and a few classes on who to trust and who not to trust.

6. Cora, a Faerie Dragon — very loyal to Chen Shi, reasonably intelligent, a great messenger and scout, and seems also to bond with Kate.

189

7. <u>Chen Shi (Chauncey) the Dragon King</u> — a Great or Noble Dragon, who, if we can free him will certainly round up a fighting force of other freed dragons. In the mean time, the single most valuable information resource.

8. <u>Melior, a nixie</u> — so never perhaps to be entirely trusted. But her own sister betrayed her and she suffered gravely. Kate saved her. So if nixies are capable of loyalty, perhaps she will be loyal to Kate. She will be ready to go to war with Palatyne, but we need to turn that to our advantage. She must hate Wyvern as well. If she can't be trusted to take an active part, then we must hope she is grateful enough not to betray us.

9. <u>The two harpies</u> — Eleanor and Maude, almost certain to be on our side, but we must be sure —since one is the sister and the other the wife of Ivor Wyvern — that they do not harbour fond feelings for him in spite of what he's done to them.

"Kate, they want to meet with you," said Maggie. "It will be up to you—and Robin, if they will accept his presence and possibly me as well—to feel them out and gain their trust and loyalty to our cause. So, they go high up the list of Things to Do.

10. The rest of the <u>Ashley garden statues</u> — These are a very mixed group, but all apparently (except perhaps the griffin and the other mythical animals) have a real reason to hate Wyvern. They could be a real fighting force, since they are stone.

"As for the rest of Ashley," said Maggie, "Sir Hugh and Bates and Sykes the gardener and Mrs Sykes — we need to keep them entirely unaware of this. Thank goodness for screening and forgetfulness spells. Kailen and I will perhaps just weave a sort of screen around them,

190

something that protects them from knowledge of what's really going on — humans are pretty good at that anyway, so that might be the most natural. And we won't have to intervene in every incident where they might see what they shouldn't, just keep a general eye on it. That might be something I can teach you as well, Kate. It is relatively simple magic, and since you live there you are best placed to keep an eye on things. Although a lot of the time you may be here, so if we can't come up with a reasonable explanation for that we might have to get a sort of facsimile of yourself up and running at Ashley. Again this will operate using spells."

Now, a list of what to do:

1. Between now and the next full moon, Kailen and Maggie start teaching Kate and Robin how to use magic. You can help us to weave the protective spell around Ashley's other inhabitants.

2. Approach Perry — Kate, that's you and me to begin with, then if/when he wants in, we introduce Kailen and tell him about the statues and dragons.

3. Start using some school time to help Perry research old documents and volumes in the library and on-line.

3. Next full moon Kate meets with Eleanor and Maude and exchanges information and hopefully enlists them in our plans. They may have an enormous amount of information and we need as much as we can get. We need to find out also if they can hear if they are spoken to between full moons.

4. Unless Wyvern becomes alerted to what is happening (and the drawback there is Palatyne who could possibly tell him that you escaped with Melior — she might see it as to her advantage). I don't think his wyverns are capable of

coherent thinking and speech. Well, if all goes smoothly without alerting him, and if we can acquire information on how to release Chen Shi and the other dragons, then I think that our move should be made at Samhain — that's Halloween. That gives us almost five months to prepare ourselves. If we can't acquire the spells however, we will just go on looking until we do, and then make our move.

"That's as much as I can think of right now," Maggie said, pushing the pad of paper away. "We will undoubtedly think of more, and things will change as we go along. The real necessity is to be flexible and try to see, not obstacles, but opportunities. You and Robin should be quite good at that. I think teenagers were made to overcome obstacles. We older ones are not as flexible perhaps."

"You make it sound like Parkour or Freerunning," laughed Kate. "Actually, that isn't a bad idea, to learn some of that."

Later, when they were telling Kailen and Robin all of this, Kate had looked up Parkour and filled them in on it. "Parkour is all about moving through your environment efficiently and naturally. People jump, climb, and vault over obstacles in their path. Their goal is to get from point A to point B as efficiently as possible. The word "parkour" originates from the French phrase *parcours du combattant* —it's the obstacle course-based method of training used by the French military. Today people do it for fun, but it was actually developed as a tactical skill and way to build the fitness. We might think about using it."

"I know who already does it," said Robin. "Perry! Along with mountain climbing. Honestly, he really does. You don't get the muscles he's got just surfing the internet. I'd love to learn."

192

"Me too," said Kate. "We'll get him to teach us by telling him it's a really hands-on way to graph equations. He'll love it!"

Chapter 32

Robin and his father made their way up the stream from the house to find the sacred pool where Melior lived before she was lured to Wyvern Hall and imprisoned. They hoped they'd find the nixie there since she had disappeared shortly before they reached home, and their guess was that she was missing her pool.

Coming around a curve in the water they heard a lilting soprano singing a wordless tune both beautiful and forlorn. Ahead they could see the widening of the stream that was the beginning of a pool.

"She's there," breathed Robin. His voice had taken on a deeper tone and his eyes were glowing gold. Seeing this, Kailen came to a stop and put his hand on his son's arm. Robin tried to shake him off and move on with a strength that was not usually his. Kailen had to take him by both arms and turn him forcibly away from the pool.

"Robin, look at me." Robin was twisting his head toward the pool and the seductive song. "Robin, listen to me *now!*" Kailen's voice had also taken on a deeper and resonant timbre. Robin slowly turned his head toward his father and some of the tension went out of his body, but Kailen kept his tight hold as Melior's compelling song continued to pull at the teenager.

"Melior is a nixie, and they are known seductresses of men and boys. She is possibly just letting out some of her feelings of loss, fear and unhappiness about her imprisonment and the treachery of her sister. But that song has the effect of drawing you, who are half human, and you could be enchanted. You must understand, Robin! Listen to me! Shut out her song—use your head, boy. If she, even inadvertently on her part, draws you in, you and she will become useless to our quest to free the dragons. Robin, a man enchanted by a nixie, is just that—

enchanted—and forgets all of his earthly duties and even his passions. So let that song go now, you have the power to do that. I will have words with her as well. She's an elemental, and as such is not used to governing her own feelings at all. But either she must or we must avoid her altogether."

The glow in Robin's eyes and his fierce resistance relaxed as Kailen's words sank in. He shook his head like a dog shaking off water and was once more in charge of himself. Even so, Kailen demanded that he stay where they were, while Kailen went forward alone to talk to the nixie.

As Kailen rounded the curve of the stream that opened into the pool Melior's tune came to an abrupt stop. She had been sitting on a moss-covered stone with her feet in the water and braiding her long white-blond hair. Now she glared at Kailen, who smiled rather grimly. "You were perhaps expecting Robin? I tell you right now you need to re-think that idea. He is not for you, and should you attempt such enticements again you will answer to me."

"He is such a pretty thing, and so eager to learn of love, and I have been so mistreated and tormented, it seemed but a small thing to comfort myself, Lord Kailen. But, as you say, he is yours, and I will not therefore reach out for him. I cannot of course speak for him..."

"No, but I can, and he will not be wandering this way on his own, believe me. Meanwhile, we have come to ask you if there is anything you know that could help us in our efforts to undo the inestimable harm Wyvern has done over the years. You are the only being beside Kate and the Fae Dragon Cora that we know who has been inside Wyvern Hall. Anything you know could be important."

"I know that my sister Palatyne has, like some other fairies and elves, gone over to Wyvern, that she now lives, apparently by choice, in his foul moat. Although how she can bear it I do not know, unless he has worked magic on her. Possibly he has enslaved her and she is not malicious out of choice, although of the three of us she was the one with the most uncertain temper. You know that we are triplets, Melusine, Palatyne and I? Melusine seems to have disappeared, I have not had word of her for many years.

"I know that the moat is also inhabited by a selection of monsters such as I have never encountered elsewhere, all with great claws and sharp teeth, all eager to rend and tear. I have no idea whether he made them or captured them or enticed them. I know too that along with the bronze wyverns set as guards on the gate posts he has an army of the living creatures, the only dragons that have willingly been enlisted to do his bidding. But they are not very bright, have no speech and exist only to fight, so they are not particular about who they work for. They are not fond of the other kinds of dragons, rather like the faeries of the Un-Seelie Court are enemies to the rest of us.

"What I do not know is why Palatyne laid the trap for me—I can only guess that it was at Wyvern's order. But what he thinks I know or could do—I have no idea what that would be."

Kailen thought this over. "Could he think that you, living here on Ashley land over the centuries, might have knowledge of the family or the history that he could use as leverage in his quest to destroy the Mallorys? Or, contrary-wise that you know something about *him* during the time he spent courting Maude and sculpting statues back in the 1860s—something that could be used against him? Were you ever tempted to seduce him—did you seduce him? And if so, how did he manage to get away without, as is so often the case, perishing as human men do if they leave a nixie? Come, Melior, this is a most grave business, and anything you might remember about him could be something no one else knows, something that could help us."

Melior looked at him from under her lashes, trying to judge what might be to her advantage in this exchange. She did owe Kate a debt and she knew these folk were Kate's friends, but she also was craving for some recompense for her suffering. So she remained silent.

Kailen felt he could almost see the wheels turning in that beautiful head. He too thought hard and came up with what could be a potent threat. "Melior, you know that if Wyvern succeeds in acquiring Ashley it is almost certain that in his fierce hatred of this place and this family, he will destroy not just the Manor, but the surrounding lands. And he will be very angry that you escaped him, whatever his reason for wanting you, so he would take personal pleasure in destroying this stream and your pool—your sacred pool. If you tell me what I can see you are holding back I can promise that we will do everything in our power to protect you and, more than that, my partner Maggie will be protecting the land—she has the power to do this. You owe Kate for her bravery in releasing you rather than just running for her own life. Share this secret with me, and you will have repaid that debt and we will do everything in our power to keep you safe here. Is there anything else we can do?"

"Try to find my sister Melusine. I have no idea why she has been missing for so many years. We have lived our separate lives for centuries, but we are triplets and have usually always known where the others are. I have been concerned.

"As to what I know from the past—yes, there is one thing. I did not think it was important when I thought that Ivor Wyvern must be dead these many years as any mortal man must be. But then Kate discovered that he lives still.

"This is what happened back then in those days when Victoria was Queen: I was interested in this saturnine young man who spent so much time at Ashley.

He was mysterious and I was attracted to his darkness. I did indeed attempt to seduce him, and I doubt not that he would have succumbed to me, but at the point that he was ready to fall, there was a change in him. We were sitting here, and I was leaning into him and whispering all the wonders that he would experience with me, and he was clearly taken with it all. But then...it is hard to explain...then something happened and he changed, his entire manner became still and he stiffened. He drew back and looked at me as if I were something abhorrent, something that would ruin him (which I suppose could have happened had he been really human). You see, that which looked out of his eyes at that moment was not human. It was old and hostile, and...knowing...as if it could see through me easily and knew all about nixies and the dangers of our charms. So what I know now is this— Ivor Wyvern is a two-part being—there is the human with artistic talents and hunger for power and love (though I think his idea of love is not humane) and there is this other being that lives also within the man and which is very dangerous. Or, together they are very dangerous. And I think it must also be the reason he is still alive now, looking not a day older. And if this is all so, then the reason he wanted me was to silence me, because I may be the only being who knows that this is not a man at all but a two-part monster.

"I can tell you I was greatly relieved when this thing I had mistaken for a callow human youth simply got up and went away, for I wanted nothing more to do with whatever he was. And now we know he or it is still alive. I do hope you can protect me. Because it now occurs to me that Wyvern may have taken Palatyne mistaking her for me, and then she sold me out to save herself. And this may have been Melusine's fate also. We are identical triplets. If this doubleness of his is the seat of his power and must be kept secret, then he might think that even a small chance

198

that I spotted it was sufficient to take me and keep me from ever revealing it."

Kailen was shocked. Fairies were so long-lived as to be nearly immortal—they could be attacked and killed, but they did not age and die as ordinary humans did. Dragons were immortal also. But for a human being to be or have become a two-part being that was now possibly immortal, or at least didn't age, was a new kind of being, and clearly an extremely dangerous one. Particularly as they didn't know what this second part of Ivor Wyvern was or could do. That it had frightened Melior was clear, that she was now very worried indeed was also clear. Not for a moment did he doubt her—she was a faerie and an elemental and she would never be fooled by a simple change of mood in a human. "Was this being, this second part of Ivor Wyvern—that is, have you any idea what it is or was before it joined with him?"

"No, Lord Kalien, none at all. All I could see was that he changed in a most profound way without, mark you, actually changing his appearance. What showed most clearly was the difference in the eyes, and they had become cold and ruthless and—as I said—very old, ancient. Also entirely impervious to my seduction so, by definition, not human. I have no idea as to the identity of something that could become part of a human being and remain so. I know of no supernatural being that can do that."

"Nor do I," said Kailen. "But what you have told me is very important to any threat we can mount against him, or it, or them. I am sure that combining our strengths we will be able to identify what or with whom Ivor Wyvern has joined and then we can seek out its weaknesses." He wasn't actually sure at all, but felt it would help to give Melior, who was looking rather terrified, courage. And anyway, they simply had to find out. That's what they were doing after all—gathering information before they could formulate a plan of attack, or (he hated to think) of defence.

Chapter 33

Kailen walked back to Robin with more on his mind that he could have wished. What Melior had told him added an entire new dimension to what they were facing. Although in a way it made complete sense because the idea that a human being, no matter how extraordinary, should be able to enslave dragons, rip the spirits from bodies and imprison them in sculptures, and otherwise practice a level of dark magic that was out of his entire experience. Well, that had seemed to be the case, but on thinking it over it made much more sense that this human man had made a deal with some devil that allowed them as a combination to do what neither could do alone. That there was sufficient anger and power there to fuel the darkest magic was certainly the case. He could understand the anger at the Mallorys for refusing Wyvern's suit for Maude, although really not the extent of it. But why they were inimical to dragons he had no idea. What kind of creature would hate dragons so? Maybe that knowledge lay with Chen Shi. It might also lead to the identity of the creature in residence within Ivor Wyvern and once they knew that, it could lead to the sort of spells used to enslave the Dragon King.

He found Robin sitting by the stream, dangling his hand in the water and looking extremely bored and refusing to meet his father's gaze. As they walked back to the house, Kailen tried to explain more carefully the dangers involved in dalliance with a nixie.

"So you see, my son, that had you followed the instincts she aroused, you might have been lost to us all. As a halfling, had you decided in future to leave her, you might survive that, although fully human men do not. But in the meantime, you could have spent years literally 'away with the fairies' while we here are fighting a war to save both the dragons and the Mallorys—to save Kate—and if possible the statues. And you would have no part in it. And I wouldn't have got from Melior the incredibly scary but useful news she has just told me."

"Couldn't you have trusted me!? I am, as you say, a halfling, so, yes, I wanted her, but I think I could have controlled the situation because I'm not just some dumb human kid. She so clearly wanted me, she's very beautiful, she's very experienced, so I wouldn't be tempted to take advantage of some human girl. And why would it keep me from fighting in this war against the evil Ivor? It could have worked!" Robin had clearly been working out his arguments and really believed them.

"Robin, I saw and felt the change in you. You were not making your own decision, she had made it for you. The human part of you was totally overcome and the Fae part wasn't having any influence at all. And had the two of you joined, she'd have had you away from here, away from me and your mother and my Fae kin and from Kate and Ashley Manor. There are more realms that you know, and she'd have taken you to one and we'd never have found you.

"You simply wouldn't have been here to help, and you'd have taken the heart out of Maggie, leaving her grieving and stricken. We all have important parts to play in this coming conflict, and some of yours are to help Kate and not cause your mum to grieve and lose her power. Melior is an elemental, she was hurt and frightened, and she saw seducing you as a bandage on those feelings. She wasn't thinking of the repercussions at all. I have made her face them, and she will not be trying to acquire you again. I'm sorry, but you'll just have to put up without a sex life for a bit longer. Or find some local girl, be sensible so she won't get pregnant and—what is it the Rolling Stones say?—'get your rocks off'.

"*Dad*!" Robin was playing at shock, but he'd capitulated and recognised the wisdom of what Kailen said. "But, wait, you said that Melior gave you really scary news? What?"

"We're almost home. Let me tell you, Kate and Maggie all together, because I think it's going to have a really big influence on what we do from now on."

"And you got this from *Melior*? She seemed a bit, well, vague and ditsy to me."

"She actually didn't know what she knew, so you're right in a way. And like all of us she thought he was dead. Knowing he's alive and not aging, she has realised something she, possibly only she, knew about him was important, and also dangerous for her. I've promised we'll do everything in our power to protect her. With the provision that she doesn't mess around with you!"

"Yeah, yeah, you've made your point. I won't mess with her either, she's totally out of bounds."

They had reached the house now, and found Kate and Maggie printing out copies of their lists—one of people and one of things to do. One look at Kailen and Maggie came to him with concern in her eyes. "You have discovered something, My Lord, something of import I think," she said, falling back naturally into the older way of speaking that they used for greeting and for serious matters.

"My Heart, I have, something so startling that I have been struggling to incorporate it." And Kailen gathered them around a table and told them the story Melior had told him of the duel nature of Ivor Wyvern and how the hidden being was both ancient and very powerful.

Kate, Robin and Maggie were all aghast at this news. As much as it went toward providing a possible explanation of how Ivor Wyvern had lived on for nearly two centuries without visibly aging, it also added an extra and—almost certainly—exceedingly dangerous dimension to his powers. They needed to find out what this being was, and thereby its powers, even perhaps its motivation. Kailen, with centuries of knowledge and experience of supernatural beings and Maggie, with her witch's sight and voracious intelligence—neither of them had ever heard of such a pairing, or what kind of being could accomplish it. Kate and Robin of course hadn't a clue. Kate was sure that Chauncey would have told her if he had known. That left them with research. Which led straight to recruiting Perry. The big question—whether he could believe them—had been pondered upon by Kate and Maggie, and they had developed a plan.

§ § §

Monday again, and Kate and Robin were with Perry in the library. Maggie was due to come over at lunch time ostensibly to talk to Perry about Robin's progress. Meanwhile it was geometry, and the theorem about the hypotenuse.

"Why," asked Robin, "do we have to do geometry on a Monday morning? Mondays are bad enough, and then you add geometry."

"Well, I figured it this way—Mondays are the pits, and none of us are all that keen on maths, so I thought we'd get two of the worst bits of the week over with together, and the rest of the week will be a breeze comparatively," offered Perry. "Anyone have a better idea?"

"No maths?" queried Kate.

Perry looked doleful, "That would mean I cannot tell you the story of how your lurcher Poppet got her name. And I was looking forward to that."

"Oh, come on, Perry! How can that have anything to do with maths!"

"If we get to grips with the hypotenuse then I can tell you why your dog is called a lurcher. Because they go together." He held up his hand, "Honestly, I'm not having you on. You'll see."

So they tackled the hypotenuse. Perry was busy drawing with chalk and talking "The hypotenuse is the longest side of a right-angled triangle, the side opposite to the right angle. A right angle is a 90-degree angle, remember? The length of the hypotenuse can be found using the Pythagorean theorem. Don't flinch so hard Robin—theorems don't bite. This theorem says that the square of the length of the hypotenuse equals the sum of the squares of the lengths of the other two sides.

"Okay, that's it, you two! Come out from under the desks and stop laughing! It really is easy if you pay attention. After all, I'm total crap at maths, and I understand it. Just stare at the blackboard, okay—it sounds hard, but if you look at it, it's totally easy. So here we go—as an example, if we make this side of the right triangle have a length of three (which when squared is nine) and this one has a length of four (when squared, sixteen), then their squares add up to twenty-five. And, here we go, the length of the hypotenuse is the square root of twenty-five, that is, five."

"Okay," said Kate. "I can actually see that. But what about my dog—should I have called her Pythagoras? I don't think so."

"Nope, it's why she's called a lurcher. That's any other kind of dog crossed with a sight or gaze hound—these are dogs that hunt by sight, not smell, and they include Greyhounds, Whippets, Wolfhounds, Borzois and Salukis." Perry had already loaded a series of dog pictures into his laptop and was now flashing them up on the screen. "They're built for speed and mostly have a strong hunting instinct." Kate was, as with anything to do with dogs, all attention.

"I think," said Perry, "that Poppet is a cross between a Greyhound and a Border Collie." Pictures of each dog showed side by side. "She's got the shape and size of the first and the colouring of the second. And they are said to be the very best kind of lurcher, combining the intelligence of the collie with the speed and skill of the greyhound."

"Now, lurcher doesn't mean what you see in old horror films, the mummy staggering and lurching. But lurcher means this." He turned back to the blackboard and drew a small four-legged figure with arrows showing it was running along the two sides of the right triangle. Then he drew a bigger stick figure running along the long—the hypotenuse—side. "See the rabbit or hare is trying to get away by zig-zagging this way and that, and because they're so fast they often do get away, even from a gaze hound, which will also follow it on this zig-zag path [he drew several more right angles going off up the board]. But they don't often get away from lurchers—which in old English dialect is supposed to mean *lurker*, or *thief* or maybe *prowler*. Okay any guesses on what they do?"

Robin looked at the animals supposedly running first this way and then that, and said "I think a very bright dog might see that if he ran straight along the long line— the hypotenuse—he would intercept the rabbit right there when the two lines come together, because he'd be taking the shorter way. So is that 'lurching'?"

"Exactly, that's 'lurching'. And a dog that is clever enough to figure that out and fast enough to do it is a lurcher. A good lurcher takes the hypotenuse of the triangle to intercept its prey. They are incredibly clever and fast."

"And Poppet is a lurcher? She doesn't seem interested in chasing anything but me or her ball. Oh, and butterflies." Kate was sceptical. "And I really wouldn't want her chasing things down and killing them either. But

I can see she looks like a lurcher, yes. I just won't tell her about the hunting and thieving!" *Or*, she thought, *maybe I will—maybe she could be a man-hunter, if we have one on the run.*

Which reminded her that Maggie would be arriving in a couple of hours and they were going to recruit Perry into their 'magic circle' or 'enchanters' army'—or just add him to their presently very small numbers and hope that he understood and would go along with it. Really she hoped he'd be wild with enthusiasm, except they were asking him to join in with something that was almost certain to get very dangerous. Maggie was prepared to show him some spells and she was bringing Cora in the hope that with the right coaching he could see her. That should be all the convincing anyone would need. As to the possibility of interruptions—they planned to take a walk down to the stream that led to Maggie's house, hoping that if Perry was willing to be enlisted, they could end up there, far away from the ordinary folk of Ashley Manor. Both Kate and Robin were on tenterhooks about this first attempt to recruit a non-magic person with the intention to teach him and use his proven research skills even if magic was beyond him.

Chapter 34

The next lesson was astronomy and map reading—sky maps and earth maps, it all tied into maths a bit as well, but was more palatable than most maths because they could grasp the usefulness of it. Although Kate was all for just using a sat nav for earth-bound travel, she was fascinated by the star and sky maps. Still their minds kept straying to when they might have Perry as a compatriot.

At last it was lunch time and Mrs Sykes delivered the usual soup and sandwiches to the terrace outside the library and the sweet was brownies (Kate had brought her Grandmother Lucinda's recipe with her from America). And then Maggie and Poppet arrived more or less together (Poppet always came in time for lunch). But rather than concentrating on the food, Poppet was circling around Maggie looking up to where Cora was perched on Maggie's shoulder. This caught even Perry's attention. It seemed as good an opening as any.

"Hello, Maggie, I've never seen Poppet so interesting in something that isn't food. You must have something very attractive about your person." Perry said.

"Hello Perry. Yes, I do have something attractive to Poppet. Dogs can sometimes see or sense what people can't."

"Well, I admit that whatever it is I can't see or otherwise sense it, Maggie. Mind telling me what it is?"

Both Robin and Kate were controlling themselves with difficulty—it seemed important not to be laughing now when they wanted Perry to take something unseen seriously enough to see it.

"I'll hopefully do better than that, I think I can help you to see what Poppet is seeing. Hold still for a moment, please, and let me put my hands over your eyes." Maggie did as she said, and under her breath she murmured a spell for clear sight and a wish to the goddess that Perry might be blessed with the sight to see a dragon. Perry must have had super-sharp hearing because he caught his breath and, though he didn't move, he whispered "Did you just ask that I be able to see a—okay I'll go with it—a *dragon*?"

"Yes, exactly," said Maggie firmly. "Open your eyes and look now. Nothing to fear, she's quite small and gentle."

"I'm game," murmured Perry with a grin that said he expected a joke. But then his eyes opened and there, on Maggie's hand—was a dragon. Cora was only about nine inches long, and she had her tail curled around her legs, but her wings were half unfurled and tiny puffs of smoke were coming out of her nostrils. And she was making sure her iridescent colours were completely on display, shimmering in the sunlight. Perry literally staggered, and had to sit down rather suddenly. Cora took this as an invitation to fly over to him, and he automatically put his arm and hand out as you would to a tame falcon. She landed. And Perry was enchanted. "Oh my gods, I never would have believed... It's so beautiful. Is this perhaps a relative of the collared lizard?"

Maggie, Robin and Kate all grinned in congratulation at each other. Perry was clearly hooked, even if he was scrambling in his head to connect the impossible to the possible—just as Kate had once done.

"She could be, possibly, but very remotely. She is what she looks like—she is a dragon. She is a Faerie Dragon, called that because they are so small. This one's name is Cora. It is a great honour actually that she is allowing you to see her—even if I helped a little. I think you must have a soul that has longed to see the unseen, believe the unbelievable."

Perry was nodding assent, but without taking his eyes off Cora. Finally he raised his eyes and looked at

Kate and Robin. "You can see her too, can't you?" They nodded. He turned toward Maggie, "So this isn't about Robin's progress, is it?"

"No, it's not. It's about—well, beings of other worlds, dragons and witches and fairies and—magic. It's about magic and magical beings."

Perry lowered his arm slowly, so as not to startle Cora, who moved very like a bird would do, up his arm toward his shoulder. "You are telling me these things are real? That you did a spell to make me see a dragon?"

"I helped you to see her, yes, and with a spell, a prayer, what you will. And yes, these things are real."

"But…you're an antiques expert and, and…an *accountant*!"

Now Maggie laughed, "Yes, yes I am—*and* a witch *and* a healer! Very dull, accountancy, is what you're thinking. Not really, it's detective work a lot of the time. And there's nothing in the laws of the universe that says I can't be all these things. And the mother of a child whose father is one of the Fae."

"Robin—Robin's father is a faerie? And I'm guessing we are not talking about the ones that sit on toadstools or march for gay pride. We're talking the old inhabitants of this world, the ones that were here before iron?"

"Bravo!" came from Robin, who just couldn't be quiet any longer. "Exactly those faeries."

And from Kate, "I said he'd know all sorts of things, and would want to know these are real, didn't I?"

Still looking rather shell-shocked, Perry gave them a warm if slightly shaky smile.

Kate had an issue however. "But, Maggie, why is that a few days ago only I could see Cora, but now you and Robin can and now Perry? I thought dragons stayed invisible to humans."

Cora flew over to Kate's shoulder and said in her tiny musical voice, "For safety and to move freely in this world dragons arranged to be seen only by the Fae, but because of 'the horror' Chen Shi told me to make myself visible to the people who can help. I didn't know you were the one when I first saw you, I was looking you over, but then I saw that you saw *me*! I was so startled I flew away. But that's how I knew you were chosen, so when you ended up in the castle I sent you to the Dragon King. Since then he has told me I must be visible to those you choose."

Kate, Robin and Maggie were all nodding, but Perry was sitting with his mouth hanging open, dumbstruck. Finally Cora noticed and she gave a trill that might have been a laugh and flew back to him. "Yes, I can talk too," she announced and sat once more in his hand.

"We should take a walk," said Robin. "We don't want Sir Hugh or any of the Ashley people finding us like this—if they overhear, they'll think we're bonkers."

"So they aren't chosen to 'help'?" asked Perry.

"No, because, unlike you, they don't have any belief or longing to know the unknown." said Maggie. "So what we are doing, what we hope you'll help with, has to be kept from them."

They were walking now, down through the garden, and along under the trees to the stream where they turned and followed along it.

"So what exactly are you doing? And how am I supposed to help?" Perry was finding his feet fast in more ways than one, and having got to grips with dragons and magic, was ready to face—what was it Cora had said?—the horror.

It was Kate who answered. "It's all involved with Maude and the statues in the garden and the Victorian Gothic monstrosity that was built by a monster—Sir Ivor Wyvern."

"The one whose estate is still fighting to ruin Sir Hugh and take Ashley?" asked Perry. "Where Maggie is fighting back."

"The very one, he married Maude—maybe, there's no record—and he sculpted the statues, and he made an enormous fortune selling dragon furnaces and lighting fixtures. Only those furnaces and fixtures aren't made to look like dragons—they *are* dragons, dragons that are enchanted and enslaved."

Perry was very quick—he asked, 'But if human beings can't see dragons, why can they see these? I mean, obviously they must be corporeal things to be sold."

"Chen Shi says that some part of the curse that enslaves them has also stripped them of the glamour that kept them invisible." said Kate.

"Chen Shi?"

"That's the Dragon King," answered Robin. "Wyvern had the colossal nerve to make him—the King of the Great or Noble Dragons—into the furnace for Wyvern Hall. Kate met him there when she got inside a few days ago."

"Oh my lord," breathed Perry. "I've read a lot about the Noble Dragons—they were thought, or the myths were thought, to originate in China. Incredible beasts and incredible powers ascribed to them. And you've met one, the King?"

"Yes, and he told me that Ivor Wyvern isn't dead—that, like dragons, he has become immortal. Chen Shi doesn't know how, but Ivor Wyvern, who was born somewhere around 1826, is alive and still looks like a man in his prime—but he's nearly 200 years old! So it isn't his estate, some fusty old lawyers, trying to destroy Ashley and the Mallorys, but Ivor himself with all his rage and power. And we—those of us who know the truth and have some magic or some abilities that can be useful—need to destroy him to save the dragons and our home. Oh, and the statues—after sculpting them Wyvern enclosed their spirits in the stone. We think he must have murdered their bodies. What he has done is beyond awful—it is as Cora says 'the horror'. And we aren't safe if he finds out we know, which we think is only a matter of time."

Perry was now shaking his head slowly is if trying to take it in. He looked stricken. "Maude" he said, "she is in there, inside the harpy? I've sat and talked there to her, because I love the poem—she might have heard me? I can't bear that she is trapped. Well, of course we must do whatever is possible. And all of you—you can do magic, but what can I do?"

"Research," Maggie was quick to say. "We have no idea what enchantments were used to do this to people and dragons, but they must be quite complicated spells. And if so they will almost certainly have been written down. As a witch I know that for every spell there must be a counter spell, just as to do complex magic requires sacrifice, because there must be balance. You are our librarian, our font of knowledge about all sorts of esoteric subjects. And what we don't know you will know how to find out. If we are going to have a chance of freeing these beings we must undo the curses, and for that we need the counter spells. We are hoping that they may just reside in a library in London, or even Ashley, because back when Maude was in love with Ivor there was much coming and going between the houses. By Hecate, it could even be lurking on the Internet somewhere. If all else fails, then we must find a way to get you into Wyvern Hall to the library there, or Ivor's private chambers. We must find these documents because enchantments like these are far beyond my knowledge and also far beyond that of the Fae according to Robin's father. And Chen Shi and all of his kind, except a few Fae Dragons like Cora, have all been enslaved now for over a century. That's why we need you quite badly. We'll all help, but you will be able to guide us."

"We'll get you a tee-shirt that says 'I'm a Librarian, so Beware' if you want," said Robin with a grin.

Perry grinned back, "We could even find a use for the hypotenuse!"

"Tee-shirt with 'Watch out, I've got an Hypotenuse, and I know how to use it!' " cried Kate.

The break in the tension was as welcome as a cool breeze on a hot day and they continued up stream without feeling like the weight of the world was on their shoulders. Kailen met them coming down from the house by the old bridge. Introductions over, Kailen brought them back down to earth with a thud. "Then there's what I just found out yesterday—Wyvern is not only still alive and looking no older than he did in the 1860s—but my source tells me he is actually inhabited by another being—something ancient, powerful and evil.

"Oh, so on top of everything else Wyvern is a Chimera. That's just the icing on the cake, is it?" Perry wasn't sceptical, just feeling overwhelmed.

"You know what this being is? A Chimera? I know about the chimeras that were supposed to be a combination of a lion, a goat and a snake, but how do you know this is what is part of Wyvern?" Maggie asked.

"Huh? Oh, no, I don't actually know what other supernatural being can be part of Wyvern. I was thinking of the scientific use of the name 'chimera'—they have found some human beings who have two different DNAs—and some innocent people have been accused of a crime and some criminals have got off because their DNA didn't match that found at the crime scene. It happens when someone has an organ transplant or total blood or bone marrow replacement—or occasionally when the person was a non-identical twin and somewhere during the early pregnancy—in other words, while sharing the uterus

214

of their mother—this living person's cells encompassed or devoured the twin—which is a lot more common than you might think. Anyway, it's a person, perfectly normal in all other ways, who contains two different DNA profiles.

"The connection to chimerism just sort of shot into my mind and, well, shot out of my mouth. But actually I don't know if it has anything to do with this case of two different beings—two different personalities or intelligences?—sharing the same body. Which should be impossible...ah, no longer a word I will be using, I guess! Unless it's a really exaggerated case of split personality? How can your source be so sure it is two different beings?"

"Because the source is a nixie—a water spirit, a kind of fairy—and can tell when one bit of this, err, person is, well, a human being and the other is a supernatural. She was in no doubt, no doubt at all." Kailen was sombre.

"I'm not sure my research skills are going to find the answers you seem to need," said Perry, also sounding deeply serious.

Maggie was quick to reassure them, "It's a case of sifting as quickly and thoroughly as possible through everything we all can think of—including talking to Chen Shi and any other supernaturals we can find. It could include fairytales or folktales, some of those have truths buried in them. It might include scientific journals—follow up on chimerism and also look into the theories on parallel worlds or universes. Chen Shi told Kate dragons developed on another Earth and became scientifically advanced enough (or maybe magically advanced) to bridge the gap and come into this Earth many eons ago. Maybe something else also 'came over'. It's not so much having to find out exactly what this other being is, maybe it isn't all that important to get a name and history, but if we can somehow grasp the extent of Wyvern's powers and what he used to defeat the dragons, then find or develop a counter-spell, then we can free the dragons. And it's likely that at that point the dragons can take it from there."

Kate broke in, "Perry, you've seen Cora—she's tiny. But the Noble Dragons—I met Chen Shi and, although he was all coiled around himself, even the length of his head was about twice my height—his entire body would be about the size of a brontosaurus I reckon. And they breathe fire and they are armed with spikes and almost armour-plated with scales. A few of these that aren't paralysed—Wyvern and his body-buddy might not have an answer for them. So we need to find out how to free them and maybe our job is done."

"Body-buddy—yeah," said Robin. "Kate, that's awesome. That's what we call it until we find out what it really is. Perry, we all dig in and work like demons to find everything we can. My dad will go off asking questions of the supernaturals. We'll hit computers and libraries and all the attics at Ashley…"

"And not go near Wyvern Hall!" Maggie interrupted. "You can get answers from Chen Shi via Cora."

"Mum, we won't go there, not now, but it may come to that. So part of our research has to be how to get in and out safely and where to look for the spell books or whatever Wyvern and Body-Buddy use. Because much as you want it to be otherwise, it's almost certain those were never at Ashley Manor, and let's face it he/they won't have donated them to the British Library."

"The internet…" Kate began.

"There wasn't one back in the 1890s or 1910 or whenever Wyvern and BB enslaved the dragons." Robin shot back.

"I know that! But what if, for security, in case of, oh, a fire or robbery, Wyvern and BB decided in the last few years to set up some secret, encrypted account with all this stuff stored in it? That's what countries and secret

216

agencies do now—they don't just keep paper copies. Everything Maggie knows about the lawsuits is available on the internet if you know how to look. So Wyvern is using 21st Century methods now along with magic and ancient stuff. Maggie, sorry, I know I'm supposed not to know that you can hack things…"

"Never mind, Kate, it's all just part of our pool of resources now. I'd have said if you didn't,"

Perry coughed and actually raised his hand. "Umm, I'm also a very good hacker, I may not be world-class, but I'm good. It was tempting to use it fraudulently, but luckily I got this job teaching you guys, and well, I'm ready to have a go at it. I'm also really good at covering my tracks."

Kailen spoke up, "We seem to be concentrating on these spells being written down—but what if they haven't been? What if this Wyvern plus supernatural being combination can simply do this magic and for them it is not so complex? If the—what do you call it?—this Body Buddy—is from another dimension and comes complete with magic or, for all I know, potions we do not understand?"

"Then," said Kate "We take them captive and torture them." There was a dead silence and they looked at her with shock.

"What? I'm supposed to be the good witch? I'm the one that got held captive. That castle is foul. The wyverns nearly killed me and Robin. I've stood by Chen Shi and heard what they did to his children. And to the statues in the garden. These are not people, these are evil incarnate. If we can actually hold them, if their magic isn't too strong for that, then I say we do whatever is necessary to get them to set the dragons free, and then we destroy them."

Maggie came forward and put her arms around Kate. "We will pray it doesn't come to that, especially as there is doubt that we would prevail in a straight fight, but if necessary, yes, we could try to do that,"

Kailen, Perry and Robin exchanged looks. "The female of the species…" whispered Robin. "But I agree." Kailen and Perry nodded their agreement too.

"Still," said Maggie, "there's a lot to be done before it comes to that. Now that we have Perry our next mission is to talk to Eleanor and Maude and any of the others who might help."

Chapter 35

On the night of the full moon that also fell on the night of the summer solstice the mixed band of co-conspirators crept into Ashley's garden at about 8:30 pm. The full moon was due to rise at approximately nine pm, at which time, because it was the longest day of the year, the sun was still above the western horizon, sunset being due to occur at about 10:30 pm. This conjunction of the full moon with the longest day of the year was a rare and momentous occurrence, and any magic would be increased, hopefully to their benefit.

They came quietly and gathered by a garden pond enclosed in a high yew hedge so as not to alert Sir Hugh or Bates or the rest of the inhabitants of the Manor. Maggie and Kailen had cast a general glamour over the entire estate, but it would not conceal the humans. Here they waited nervously for the rising of the moon because that should trigger the animation of the statues scattered throughout the garden. So much seemed to be riding on this meeting that they all were anxious not to scare the supernaturals away or otherwise cause some kind of riot.

Kate had been nominated to go first into the garden around the big fountain where the statues seemed to gather because she had been 'called' before. She was periodically checking her pocket for the note from Eleanor that she intended to present as a kind of ticket should any other statue or being challenge her arrival at their garden party.

Kailen was beside her as moral support, being a supernatural himself and therefore probably acceptable. Maggie, Robin and Perry were sitting on a stone bench

219

placed so people could enjoy watching the koi carp and water lilies. Melior was swimming among the koi and flashing glimpses of her shimmering body at the young men on the bench. She had, however, promised Kailen that she would not try to enchant Perry, not on this of all nights or on any other occasion because he was so necessary to their plans. Melior was incapable of refraining from flirtatious behaviour, but she quite understood that they had an overwhelming need to work together, so enchanting either Robin or Perry was totally out of bounds. As usual she was as the gods made her, shunning clothes. The others were dressed in a kind of cross between combat and party mode. "Combat" because they really didn't know what they might face amongst the many animated statues and "party" because it was in essence a real "garden party". So Kate and Maggie both wore handsome light-weight trousers with good pockets covered by pretty floral tops (Kate in green, Maggie in blue) that were cinched at their waists with 'jewelled' belts that helped disguise that they were hung about with useful tools. Their hair was bound back with gold clips that could double as rather lethal hat pins and they wore light ankle-high boots that were indeed made for running. Kailen wore his usual slightly iridescent black and could depend on his strength and his magic. Kate realised for the first time that Kailen looked a bit like the young Keith Richards. Robin wore a red open necked shirt outside his jeans, covering a belt with a holstered knife and black boots, also with a concealed knife. Perry, his blond hair combed back, but flopping forward as usual, was in a dazzling white dress shirt and navy blue trousers, with a knife in a boot holster.

Robin and Perry desperately wanted to pace about, but were constrained by the need for quiet and secrecy. Maggie appeared to be meditating. It was, after all, a holiday of importance to witches. They were all hoping that once Kate was in conversation with Eleanor (and

220

hopefully Maude) she would be able to introduce the rest of them without panicking any of the other statues.

Looking at how bright the sky still was, although streaked with beautiful sunset colours, Kate asked Kailen, "What if they don't come out until it's well dark—what if they wait until midnight?"

"Then we will wait also," said Kailen, "but I doubt that will be the case—the conjunction of the full moon and summer solstice is rare and it is likely that the statues will be animated the moment the moon clears the horizon here—and I imagine they will be very happy to finally see the sun even if just for a little while."

"But," queried Perry, "won't the other people here see them?"

"Enchantments on a night like this are very powerful, we can be sure that the other inhabitants here will not see a thing." Maggie had come out of her trance or prayer and replied with certainty.

"Then maybe I won't see anything either." Perry looked crestfallen. "I'm the only one here that is just human without any magic."

Maggie laid a comforting hand on his shoulder. "You can see Cora. If Kate gets to explain about us to the statues I think you will be able to see them as well. See and hear them as animated beings, that is. It may be that Kate is the conduit, the chosen one, what she says goes within this community of imprisoned spirits."

"Well, we should find out soon, I suppose," said Perry.

"After all," Maggie encouraged, "we don't actually know that you don't have magic, we haven't had the time to educate you in simple spells or heightened senses. You are very receptive to recognising what most people would blank out. That's a promising start."

"The moon is rising," announced Kailen. "Kate, we will go out now into the fountain garden where it will be easy for Eleanor to find you."

"I'm suddenly so nervous," quavered Kate, and Maggie gave her a quick hug.

"Go on, girl, you can do this, don't forget Eleanor wants very much to talk to you." came from Robin.

"And we mustn't let her down," from Perry who had had the last two days to get immersed in all that had happened, including the knitting and the note.

"I hope they'll let you all join us," said Kate, "I hope they see it as helpful and not threatening."

"Only one way to find out—look, the moon—we go now." And Kailen took her arm and off they went through the hole in the yew hedge and into the brightness of the fountain garden, where both sun and moon shone at once.

As they came near the fountain in the centre the harpies appeared from the other side where they usually stood facing each other on their plinths, as did many of the other statues along the long beech avenue. Both Harpies were sculpted according to the classic idea of these ravenous mythical female creatures: each had a woman's head and upper body, but with the addition of great wings. Their lower body, legs and feet were like those of an eagle, ending in massive talons. But Eleanor's face, middle-aged, was twisted into that of a woman enraged and all humanity had gone from it. Under the scrap of stone drapery that Victorian sensibility dictated must cover them, her breasts were pendulous and shrivelled. Her wings were bat's wings and her arms ended in hands that were twisted and also had long dangerous claws. Still these hands held her knitting, a symbol of her determination to hang onto her humanity, and her twisted face attempted to smile. Maude, on the other hand, had the face of a beautiful young woman, a face that could smile easily, her wings were

222

feathered like an angel's and her lower body was also feathered as it blended into legs that ended in the great taloned feet of a bird of prey. Her drapery covered a young woman's upper figure with her arms ending in very human hands, although tipped with claws. She was carrying a book.

"Look, Maude, it's Kate" said the one with the terrible face who clutched the ravelled knitting in one taloned hand. "Kate, Kate, we're so glad you're here. We were worried you might not understand or be afraid of us." Her voice, Eleanor's voice, was warm and kind in such contrast to the sculpture she inhabited.

Kate pulled free of Kailen's arm and ran across the lawn toward the Harpies. "Eleanor? It is you, isn't it! And you are Maude! Oh, hello, hello!" And she would have flung herself into an embrace with Eleanor, but the Harpy put out a hand to stop her.

"I fear you will bruise yourself on this stone, nor do I dare embrace you, dear Kate. Believe me we are as we once were inside, but this stone is a terrible inconvenience and I could hurt you without even knowing it. We may touch only carefully. Ah... don't be sad young friend. It is hard for us to feel sad on this special night of the year when the moon and the sun both shine for us."

Maude broke in, "Is this beautiful fairy your friend or betrothed? I have heard that fairies can be espoused to humans."

Kate turned red, something she hated but did so easily as a redhead. "He is my best friend's father and a sort of mentor. His name is Kailen and his partner is Maggie, who is a witch. She and Robin and Perry are waiting behind the yew hedge by the koi pond to find out if it is okay for them to join us."

"Perry? The Perry who sits at my feet and talks to me about Tennyson and Shakespeare and how he hopes that by teaching you he will learn himself and maybe go on to achieve great things?" Maude was all but jumping up and down and her wings were fluttering, her hands clasped in front of her as if praying it would be true. "Yes, of course they must come out, we want to meet your friends." Maude, whose face was young and beautiful.

The three behind the yew hedge heard the invitation and ventured out. Perry and Maude hurried toward each other. Maude was quick to speak, "Please, please do not be embarrassed that I could hear what you were saying, I was so flattered that you would confide in me, even though you couldn't know I could hear you. It was frustrating not being able to respond. But tonight I can! I am so pleased to meet properly."

Perry stood before this apparition in stone, beautifully rendered down to the last tiny feather, the folds of drapery and the talons on her feet (Ivor Wyvern was indeed an artist of rare ability) looking stunned. "I have sat talking to you for hours, and now I find myself bereft of speech," he finally managed. "I have only just been, how shall I say, 'initiated' into this circle, and am finding it all a bit overwhelming. But I am glad beyond measure to meet you, Miss Mallory."

"Maude, please call me Maude, you have done so often enough." Maude's reference to his soliloquies as he had sat beside her mute stone presence made Perry blush. She put out a stone hand as gently as she could and tentatively touched his sleeve. "We are friends already, let it be so."

Meanwhile other statues from the long beech walk were appearing in the fountain garden and the sound of chatter could be heard over the plashing of the water. Most were clearly extremely curious about the small group of humans standing with the harpies, but were giving them space to converse in privacy.

"Did Wyvern make all these statues?" asked Robin.

224

Eleanor answered, "Yes, all of them. And co-opted our spirits or souls and invested the stone with a sort of life. Trapped life, a dreadful thing to have done. But my brother was never really right in the head, or kind, and he grew into a genuine monster of depravity."

"Did every one of these people offend him or do him harm, then?" asked Kate.

"No, dear, not all of them, not at all. They were simply his models and then he did this to them. We are lucky, all things considered, to have this reprieve every full moon, so we have had years to talk amongst ourselves and tell our stories. Although Maude and I have kept certain parts to ourselves."

"Because we were his family and he did this to us out of enormous anger and hatred," Maude filled in. "The others, poor things, are just innocent bystanders in the path of a madman. But we both defied him and for that we paid the ultimate price. I shudder to think there was a time I loved him so madly that I threw away my reputation and any chance of a normal life to follow him."

"Love can be a kind of madness," Maggie laid a consoling hand on Maude's arm. "Particularly when you are young and it is first love. Then it can be madness indeed. And I believe he also loved you, if you will, 'madly'."

"But why, why did he transplant all of their spirits into his sculptures?" cried Kate.

"I think," said Eleanor, "he wanted 'friends'—he was so peculiar that essentially he had none. He both kept himself apart and also those few who ventured near soon found themselves uncomfortable and made off again. This way, he had a literally captive audience with whom he could talk and exchange ideas. It's why he gave us the power to move and speak at full moon—he wanted to stroll in a beautiful garden with beautiful and intelligent people under the moon, exchanging ideas and behaving in a manner he had read about in places like Renaissance Italy. He was doomed to disappointment there, however."

"Why?" asked Robin.

"Look around you," Eleanor made a sweeping gesture. "There is Socrates, over there is Shakespeare, Pliny is just coming down the beech walk now, and over there is Newton. He made a sculpture garden of the greatest minds and the most beautiful gods and goddesses, see, there—Venus, Apollo, and even Neptune."

"Only we ain't," came a voice from behind them. Turning they saw Shakespeare, except his voice was that of a Devon farm labourer. "He thought he could make a fine likeness of the Bard and then plonk me in it and I'd somehow *be* Shakespeare. Only I'm just Tom Jenks from up Morchard Bishop way. I took care of pigs, me. I can't even read!" And the man laughed bitterly. "Served him right," he added.

"It's the same with them all," said Maude. "Ivor thought by willing it so, or working dark magic, he could make anyone do or be anything. He simply thought other people were things he could manipulate and if he said, you, you look like Socrates, I will make you into Socrates, then it would be so. Well, he could transfer their spirit or essence or soul into their statue, but he couldn't change that essence—we remain ourselves. In a way that has been the salvation of many of these poor souls, to know they thwarted him in the end. Otherwise I fear more would have gone mad."

"But have some gone mad?" asked Kailen.

"Yes, a few. Poor Plato just wanders, he hasn't spoken for decades. But not many of us, although for all I know it would have been a release."

"I think not," said Eleanor, "I don't think madness is a good escape, there is so much that is dark about it. I feel those poor souls suffer more than the rest of us."

"Are they dangerous?" asked Perry.

"Not generally, occasionally one has tried to run out of the magical perimeter apparently intent on finding Wyvern to do him harm, but they cannot get out, and with sunrise we are all immobile once more."

"Vile, it's vile," said Perry. "But why, if he wanted company, did his magic not make it possible for you to stroll and converse every night?"

"I think probably he didn't want *that* much company," said Eleanor with what could be called a smile on her twisted features. "Or possibly there are limitations on the type of magic he used. Certainly once he discovered that his beautiful sculptures of the world's finest minds didn't contain anything but quite ordinary minds, and those were not inclined to friendship with their tormentor, he stopped visiting the garden at all. It's many decades since we saw him here."

"What I want to know is—why are you here?" queried Robin. "Why aren't you in the gardens at Wyvern Hall?' At the same moment that Kate came in with, "And what I want to know is what spirit did he put into the griffin from the gatepost? It nearly scared me to death last full moon."

Tom Jenks aka Shakespeare, who was still within earshot of their group, interjected angrily. "That poor beast. It's an eagle in there, and it don't understand why it can't fly. That's cruelty if you like, trap a poor dumb bird in that body. If I could shed the spells he put on me that kept me from tearing his heart out, I'd have kilt him once for myself and once for that pathetic bird."

"Maybe sometime soon you might get that chance," said Kailen, "and now Mr Jenks, if you will excuse us, we need to converse more privately. We'll return to this beautiful garden afterward and I hope maybe to talk with you again." And Kailen ushered the five of them and the two harpies back to the archway in the yew hedge that led into the small garden with the koi carp pool and the wisteria trees. "We'll have privacy here if you don't want all the other statues to know your full history," he said.

"What about her?" asked Maude on seeing Melior swimming lazily among the fish. "Is that a mermaid? No, I see she has no tail. She's very beautiful. Can we trust her?"

Laughing, Melior came over to the edge of the pool. "I am Melior. You can trust me to hate Ivor Wyvern. We are all here tonight because we are looking for ways to defeat him. That is why I am here. And is that what you want too, Wyvern's Maude?"

Maude made a small bow, and replied, "Forgive me for not addressing you directly, I'm sorry. And yes, Melior, that is what I want too."

"And the statues are all here at Ashley because...?" Robin interjected again.

Eleanor answered, "Because when he was creating his sculptures they were meant for Ashley Manor gardens as Sebastian was then designing them. Sebastian paid Ivor, who had a rising reputation as an artist, and that's how Ivor got to know Maude. Plus, when he became enamoured of Maude, Ivor also had his eye on the estate, he thought it would be a lovely place to be a part of. He genuinely tried for some time to ingratiate himself with Maude's relatives."

Maude chimed in, "Wyvern Hall was under construction at that time, and as you might have seen, it is located on a crag coming out over the river, so there isn't a place for a formal garden spreading out around it. I admit that as a young woman with a taste for the macabre I thought Ashley rather anodyne and boring, altogether too sweet actually. When I was reading Byron and Dracula and Mary Shelley's Frankenstein and that American writer, Edgar Allen Poe, part of Ivor's attraction was that he seemed to embody so much of that edgy, dark quality.

If only I'd known what that all really meant. But I didn't of course. Back then I was excited by that Gothic monstrosity just as I was excited by him—he had such talent. Genius is exciting.

"A few years later, after I had run away and joined him in living in the Hall, I began to find the unrelieved Gothic darkness, all that dark stone and red brick and heavy oak, quite oppressive, so Ivor made me a beautiful courtyard garden, even resurfacing the walls with white marble and golden limestone, all pastels and lightness of touch in the planting and the pool. Again his genius could encompass that kind of an expression. But I fear it was just a sort of stage set where I was to act the part of the beautiful chatelaine. Cracks were appearing in the relationship by then, and the garden brought only a brief reconciliation."

"And then what happened, my dear?" prompted Maggie.

"Then Eleanor went missing. She was my only friend by then. Suddenly one day she wasn't there. I asked Ivor where she had gone, and why she left without saying anything to me. He told me she had suddenly developed a fancy to see Italy once more (we used to travel there fairly regularly). It was Eleanor who used to counsel patience between us, but later she began to tell me that she was becoming afraid of her brother and that perhaps we should both consider whether we might be in some sort of danger living there. It was shortly after that that she was just…gone. I didn't believe Ivor, even though I still wanted to. And without Eleanor, and with Ivor treating me more and more like a thing he owned, or even a bit like a cat with a mouse it is just playing with—well at that point our liaison broke down."

"You never got married then?" asked Kate.

"No, my sweet, we never married, it would have been hard to find a clergyman to officiate and it turned out that Ivor couldn't abide them anyway—maybe, being a devil, he would have combusted or something. And I, I in my impetuous rebellious youth, thought not being married was very romantic. Just like Mary Godwin, author of Frankenstein, living in sin with Shelley, you know. I was an idiot of course. But so many are."

"And Eleanor, why did you suddenly go away?" asked Robin.

Eleanor said, "Ah, but I didn't go away at all."

Chapter 36

I'm Ivor's older sister. When he was ten and I was seventeen our parents were killed in a carriage accident. Ivor was already a difficult child, sullen, withdrawn and prone to temper tantrums.   When our parents died it was discovered that our comfortable life was based on a lie—our father had somehow squandered his fortune and was in debt. We—Ivor and I and a distant relative who was brought in to oversee us—moved from a family estate with elegant properties in both London and the country to a very basic townhouse in a lower middle class area of London. We were not totally poverty-stricken, but every penny had to be watched.

It quickly became apparent that the cousin who was supposed to look after us had a taste for gin. No, this is no time for niceties—she was a drunken sot who spent the food money on gin and most of her time passed out in her room. I very quickly took over the running of the household, and removed the keys from her and hid the monthly allowance. Within weeks she declared we were not worth her time, and left.

I tried with Ivor—I tried to give him love and stability and as close to our old life as I could on a severely curtailed income. But Ivor became even more strange and reclusive, he hated the 'common' school that was all we could afford (although he had previously hated the expensive public school as well). He got good grades in subjects he enjoyed—art, history, English and Latin—but was constantly in trouble for fighting and, later, for stealing. He rejected any attempts on my part either to love or to chastise him. As he got older I had to give up any pretence that I was *in loco parentis* because, honestly, I'd become more than slightly afraid of him.

Then, seemingly overnight, our fortunes—or, rather, Ivor's fortunes—took a sky high leap. One day I was cooking cottage pie in a damp kitchen, the next it seemed we were back in our parents' mansion, only now it was Ivor's. By this time he was nineteen and I was twenty-six, an old maid who kept house for my brother. But now my brother was handsome, rich and displaying a prodigious talent as a painter and sculptor. And it seemed I had no memory of how any of this had been accomplished. I tried to question Ivor about this, and he told me I had developed a high fever and been delirious and comatose for some weeks. During which time, he told me, he had discovered that the fortune we thought lost had been simply hidden away by our father and once this was cleared up we could live as we had before. When I told him I found it very hard to believe as surely I would have some memory of my illness (and I had none], he threatened that if I persisted in that line of questioning he would have me committed to an institution for mental defectives. So I said nothing more, and after awhile I convinced myself that probably I had been so ill that I really couldn't remember. Plus who would want to return the near squalor we had lived in for those ten years?

We rented a comfortable country house a few miles from here, and Ivor set about making plans for a huge mansion in the fashionable Gothic style. Ivor's outstanding ability as a sculptor brought him to the attention of Sebastian Mallory, who was renovating the gardens here at Ashley and was interested in getting Ivor to create a series of gods and goddesses to line the beech walk leading to the fountain garden. Ivor convinced Sebastian that a sprinkling of great men of science and philosophy would be a good balance for the Dianas and Neptunes, so he did them as well.

For a few years I was delighted that Ivor seemed to have found himself, that he seemed to make friends and that people flocked to buy any painting or sculpture he produced. They were indeed first quality, he was very talented, and I was happy that he was happy—it made for a much better life. Then he and Maude fell in love. It seemed it would be the most natural thing in the world for them to marry. But Sebastian refused. I learned later that Elizabeth saw through my brother and sensed he was dangerous. But Maude was very high spirited and wanted excitement, so after what seemed ages while she, and to a lesser extent Ivor, tried to win over her brother who was her guardian, one day she just packed her jewels and a few clothes and turned up on our doorstep. Ivor was delighted. Spitting in the eye of the establishment suited him just fine. And by that time any vestige of good feeling between him and the Mallorys was long gone due to the acrimonious fighting over Maude. It became apparent to Ivor that the Mallorys thought he wasn't good enough and this, as it always had, enraged him.

The doorstep where Maude arrived by this time was at Wyvern Hall. Ivor had gone ahead with his plans, and this, his very own Castle of Otranto, had taken shape very rapidly on the crag he bought to reproduce the idea of a medieval fortress castle on an unassailable rock. I didn't meet Maude at first. Once living in Wyvern Hall I again was detecting the kind of strangeness and instability that used to frighten me in Ivor, and I took for my rooms a suite as far as possible from his.

It was actually nearly a month later when I met her as she was exploring various bits of the Hall. I was—back then—horrified to find they'd been living in sin for weeks, sharing Ivor's bed and taking their meals in private in his sitting room. As I also ate alone in my sitting room this could have gone on even longer if Maude's sense of adventure hadn't led her to go exploring.

But she is such a delightful person I soon stopped judging her and only wished for them to be happy. I made it my business to befriend her and make her feel welcome and for perhaps the first time in my life I had a close woman friend. We were—are—very different, but we got on very well. I tried to encourage her when Ivor was moody or angry, trying to be a listening, non-judgmental ear for this young woman who, in spite of being still very much in love, was finding living with Ivor to be difficult—as did everyone sooner or later.

Things went on like this for several years. Ivor was now about thirty-eight or -nine, Maude was only twenty-six. But we were noticing some unsettling things. Ivor appeared not to age at all. By the time Maude was twenty-six she had changed slightly, and there were a few worry lines in her face. I of course was now in my forties and looked it. When Ivor reached forty-two there was still no physical change. It was perplexing. Also he spent more time away from the Hall and was sometimes in a vile temper when he returned.

Maude and I were as close as sisters, and we would sometimes, in my rooms where we hoped we wouldn't be overheard, talk about the ways Ivor had changed and the ways he hadn't (that is he wasn't getting older). Maude still loved him I think, she always said so, but I was beginning to say that perhaps we should be thinking about some kind of escape plan if we should need one. I thought her brother would mount a rescue if she sent him word, although she said she never would. I suggested that perhaps we should plan a trip to Italy, just the two of us, and once we were safely away from the Hall we could think about our options more clearly. She was willing to consider Italy because we both loved it, and Ivor seemed too occupied with his business or his art to be free to take us. But she was not ready to see that Ivor might be really dangerous and we might be better off not to come back again.

I haven't mentioned our staff—a place that big requires a number of maids and footmen, a cook, gardeners, boot boy—well, we had the minimum. By living out of wedlock, Ivor and Maude had put themselves outside polite society, so we didn't have visitors. Ivor was not very sociable even at the best of times, and now things we—Maude and I—knew nothing about were making him more irritable than usual. So he didn't want the place full of servants, he wanted his privacy.

We had a coachman and several boys to see to the horses who lived over the stables, and Ivor got one of them to pose for a marble sculpture of the young David with his slingshot—totally different from Michelangelo's colossal David, but really wonderful. I took to standing quietly at the back of Ivor's studio to watch the work—if I was silent he would let me watch occasionally. Then the work was finished and Ivor set the life-size statue up in his own study, a place we were never allowed to enter. That same week, the young groom who'd posed for the David disappeared. Our coachman was very put out. Ivor let it be known that the boy had simply left, apparently in the night, without a word to anyone. But then I overheard something terrible.

As I said, Ivor's study was off limits to everyone. But I was in the library which was adjacent to Ivor's study and the door was just slightly ajar. I was looking for a needlework book I had ordered when I heard the young groom, the one who was supposed to have left. He was weeping and shouting at Ivor. Something to the effect of "What have you done to me? Why am I here? This isn't my body!" And then he just sobbed and cursed. I dared to peek through the crack in the door and saw it was the statue that was speaking. I was so shocked I nearly fainted (those awful whalebone corsets, no room to breathe). Ivor was standing in front of it and grinning terribly at the young man's misery. I suddenly felt sick with rage and galvanised to come to this poor groom's defence, although what I really could have done I don't know. I was just so sick of the atmosphere of mystery and strangeness, and now there was clearly someone, or something, in deep trouble.

Something quite terrible had been done, although I wasn't sure what. So I burst into Ivor's study waving my book and shouting "What have you done?" Just that, nothing more. Ivor turned on me like a wild animal surprised just as it was killing its prey. "None of your damned business, you stupid woman." And he went on about how he'd tried to keep me safe by forbidding me access to certain areas (like the cellars as well, but I had no desire ever to go down there), but now that I'd seen it was too late and what had happened to the groom would happen to me. He hit me then, hit me over the head with a bronze panther he kept on his desk. I just dropped.

I think he kept me imprisoned and drugged for some weeks while he sculpted *this* (waving her hand to indicate the harpy body she inhabited). Then he killed me, or…or did some magic that lifted my spirit out of my body, and my body died. It may have really looked like that old saying 'giving up the ghost'. Thank goodness I didn't feel any pain. I vaguely heard him saying things, chanting things, and another voice joined as well, but I could see nothing except what seemed like the flicker of flame through closed eyelids and then—then I was looking out of the eyes of this statue. And I have been here ever since.

And that is when I knew that my brother Ivor was evil incarnate.

236

Chapter 37

The small group were visibly distressed that Ivor would so easily dispose of his sister, in spite of already knowing he must have done so. It was hard to grasp that he was so entirely without normal human feelings. Eleanor's phrase about 'treating other people as things' stayed in Kate's mind. Kailen was more inclined to take this all in without much visible emotion, perhaps because many of the Fae themselves were prone to treat people as things, and he had more experience of it.

But again it was Robin who asked, "But by this time Wyvern was enemies with the Mallory family—so why are you and Maude here in the Ashley gardens?"

It was Maude who took up the story.

§ § §

He brought us—the harpies—here in dead of night and set us up in the gardens on plinths he must have created earlier. It was many years after my brother Sebastian died. Elizabeth was a reclusive widow by then, and the children had all flown the nest, even Andrew the eldest who had inherited—he was overseas exploring and mountain climbing. By the time he returned he must have thought we'd been purchased at some point in the past and he never questioned it. Before that we'd been kept for many years in an empty room on the ground floor of Wyvern Hall. We never saw anyone for all those years. Do you know that some spirits, well our spirits anyway, will continue to think they feel hungry, and regret the meals they cannot eat, for some years after they have no bodies? I was constantly thinking about toast with honey. It stopped finally, thank goodness.

But before Ivor also dispatched me, after Eleanor disappeared, it was a strange period of time. I wasn't aware of what Eleanor had seen, the statue of the young David. I believed that the groom had simply left one night, as I was told. But although I still felt love and some passion for Ivor, he turned away from me, and I was installed in a suite of rooms that overlooked the beautiful courtyard garden he had made as a gift to me. The rooms were opulent and beautiful also. I think he remembered my peacock dress on the night he met me and our infatuation was kindled just by looking into each other's eyes, because he had the rooms decorated in peacock colours, with shot silk in changing colours of blues and purples, greens and gold. And rich plum velvet on the couches. The paintings all featured peacocks, either as central subjects or as small reminders in landscapes and gardens. One room was an exquisite library, fitted with intricately carved shelves and thousands of books. I couldn't understand why he would take such care to surround me with beauty and reminders of our early days while becoming virtually estranged from me.

Several times I tried to talk to him, but he simply said this was how it had to be at this time, and I would oblige him by not pestering him and not seeking out his company. As I knew him to be prone to rages and violent outbursts over what seemed to be small things, and without Eleanor to comfort and advise me, I did as he said.

I have thought since that possibly he was seeking to avoid having to dispose of me as he had Eleanor by keeping me away from him. I wondered for a long time why he didn't just send me away, but I think now that since I 'belonged' to him and he still had feelings for me he could not do that. Also he would have risked me making friends in some foreign place and saying too much, or even returning to my family, which would have been a complete betrayal in his eyes.

But I was hurt and felt betrayed myself and took to brooding. I also became quite insomniac and started walking about at all hours of the night. At first I only kept to my rooms and my garden, then I expanded my wanderings to the big public areas and finally the dusty corridors and even the cellars. Whatever fears I might have had of these places previously seemed to have left me, and I found solace in just walking and walking without thinking. It might have been a form of self-hypnosis to get away from the pain of my life alone in what had become a prison.

And then one night, as I roamed the cellars— which are vast and on several levels with what seemed miles of corridors and so many, many rooms which I suppose were store rooms—most were locked—this one night I heard screams, high keening cries of such pain! And Ivor was there, where the screams were coming from, and I could hear him laughing. I went cold all over and thought I would be sick, but then I gathered myself and moved forward. You understand that these cellars were so large that had I not been in just that corridor at that time, I never would have heard anything. Now, just as Eleanor had done, I was moved to somehow intervene. Having no idea what was making those terrible cries, still I wanted to help them. And now also I wanted to make Ivor stop. It was as if my eyes were finally open and this not only revealed his nature, it killed my love.

All of this was happening within me as I came to the entrance to a high-ceilinged cavern where there was a dragon chained down on what looked like a huge rack, the kind used for torturing people by dislocating all their joints. The dragon's long neck was stretched out painfully and Ivor was slicing it with a knife and lapping the blood and biting at it—and it was screaming.

Ivor himself was bloody about the face, chest and arms. And he seemed to be in a sort of blind ecstasy. It was appalling and stomach-turning. I couldn't help but note that this dragon was coloured like a peacock, which made my revulsion even more acute. It appeared to be about twenty feet long, head to tail, enormous to my eyes, but I've heard since that it was young, just a child. A child being tortured.

And Ivor—who had been my love, my mate—was consuming its blood and revelling in its pain. Before I could think what I was doing, I ran forward and grabbed his arm, the one wielding the knife, and screamed at him to stop. Stop! Stop! I cried. And he turned without a word and plunged the knife deep into my breast.

Chapter 38

"The rest is similar to what happened to Eleanor. I was not dead after all, but wounded, and eventually recovered a kind of consciousness to find myself tied to a bed. I say a 'kind of' consciousness because either from a fever or drugs I seemed to be hallucinating most of the time. I thought at times I heard Ivor arguing with someone else, but never saw anyone. Once I thought he was weeping over me. He seemed to be consumed with anger some of the time and with sorrow at others. Although I wasn't in physical pain, I was so sick with the pain of his betrayal I only wanted to die.

Apparently he spent most of his time sculpting my harpy, this one I inhabit now. And, like Eleanor, one day I was in this semi-conscious state and the next I was looking out the eyes of this mythical beast. So there has been no death for us, we just go on and on. I thought I had long ago come to terms with it, but telling you has brought it all back."

And Maude, having held herself together throughout this tragic story, now put her hands up over her eyes and turned away. Her stone body could not shed tears but she was clearly crying. Perry was at her side in an instant, holding her unyielding stone as Maude rocked back and forth. Eleanor also came over and held her friend's head against her own breast.

But it was Kailen who approached her and took her hands in his. "Maude, this is important—did you, when Ivor turned on you, or at any time before that, sense another presence within him? Did you think, this cannot be the Ivor I know—did you see a change?"

Maude raised her face to him and said, "I did upon occasion think he was possessed by something demonic.

241

And when he turned from tormenting the dragons and stabbed me so coldly without a word, his eyes were entirely 'other' if you understand me. But I put that down to trying to excuse the man I once loved from his acts of inexcusable cruelty by trying to believe he was possessed. I know that he was entirely capable of those things. But still I cannot quite reconcile them with his love for me (because once he did love me) and even when he forced estrangement upon us he kept me in luxury and with so many reminders of our love. Maybe that was a refinement of cruelty, but my heart—if I had a heart—obviously the heart is part of spirit and not a beating thing at all—so I still say 'my heart' does not quite accept him as entirely a monster. He wasn't a monster with me, but perhaps only with me."

Kailen said, "You have confirmed what we heard from a supernatural who knew him. It was not your imagination that thought him to be possessed. Ivor is host to another being, something that joined with him to give them both unimaginable powers that I am guessing would be impossible to either alone. And this other being is described as impossibly cold, calculating and ancient."

"That *is* what I saw, but I thought it was only what I wanted to believe, because it was so hard to think, as Eleanor does, that he was purely evil. I believed that finally. I heard him crying, but again put that down to having hallucinations. But, oh, it would be a relief to me to think there was some shred of remorse in him, some bit of sadness. That the tears were real after all.

But… it is also horrifying to have to believe that he harbours some other being, something you say that is ancient and evil. Do you suppose it took him over?"

"We don't know that one way or the other, just that they co-habit the same body and work together. We have no idea what this other being is or was before it decided to join with Wyvern, or when or why it did so. We don't know if it was a forcible takeover or a joining together freely on both sides. Perry called it a chimera, but then retracted that, saying it reminded him of a medical condition whereby an animal can actually be partly one animal and partly another and there are ways to test for that. That is science however, not magic, and the two animals must be of the same species. This, on the other hand, we believe is powerful magic, and although it appears to have something to do with chimerism we don't think this other being was ever human."

"I don't know whether to be relieved that Ivor might not be entirely to blame for his despicable cruelties or further distressed that I was intimate with someone who was actually two someones. It makes me feel despoiled and unclean. "

Perry, close by her side where he had been gently stroking her wings, said, "But you had no idea then of what he was, so you are innocent in all of this. You have no reason to feel soiled, you could not be that. Look, even Ivor has made a beautiful creature for you to inhabit. It may be a harpy, but it is as beautiful as you were and appears to be mostly angelic."

"With claws though," said Robin. "Still, in this world it might be that an angel with claws is a good thing to be." Which finally brought a tremulous smile to Maude's face.

And Eleanor laughed, if rather sadly, "Yes, it's clear he was still fond of her, insofar as he was capable of fondness. With me he was simply furious, as he had been so often during our lives together. I was so often saying no or criticising or telling him how to behave. Had I been his parent he might not have hated me so, but to have that from a sibling—well, he never could abide being thwarted. So he took every scolding and every criticism and wove them into the very fabric of my harpy. On the other hand, it seems he couldn't bring himself to kill me outright, and gave me a kind of afterlife. At least Maude and I have had each other over these long years, and that has been great comfort to us both. And I have always been fascinated by bats and thought them the most unusual and interesting mammals, so my wings don't distress me as I believe Ivor meant them to. And my harpy might be a travesty of womanhood, but I can identify with the anger she expresses. Knowing even a small part of what Ivor has done makes me want to find a way to end it."

Maude now raised her head and spoke with new resolution, "Yes, I do too. We all feel this way. My love is dead—hell, we are all dead—but we suspect that there are living things that continue to be tormented. A lust for that kind of thing is an addiction."

Maggie stepped forward. "You know then that Ivor Wyvern still lives? We only found this out a few days ago. We were unaware until then, and thought that the trouble his lawyers continued to cause the Ashley estate was only posthumous instructions. And we didn't know that he had somehow captured and enslaved the dragons."

"All the dragons?" asked Maude. "I only saw that poor young one."

"I found the Dragon King in the cellars of Wyvern Hall. He is totally helpless except for enough movement to allow him to function as the central heating," said Kate. "He told me Wyvern had the power to capture and enslave dragons, and indeed had actually driven them to a kind of extinction—not dead, but helpless and being used as furnaces and lighting fixtures or just statues or garden ornaments. He made tons of money that way, selling them."

"Only a few Fae Dragons, like Cora, have been left free, probably because they are so small and good at hiding," added Robin.

Kate continued, "And he told me that Wyvern is still alive. Nearly 200 years old and still alive! Said he

244

came to the castle occasionally to gloat over his capture of Chen Shi most of all. Then I saw him—Ivor that is—in a big black car being driven to Wyvern Hall. He really looked just like a man in his thirties, no older at all."

Kailen said, "You say 'we all feel this way'. Do you mean the other statues here? If so, would they fight?"

"Oh, yes, I think they would. But you heard what Tom Jenks said—we are all under some sort of spell that keeps us confined within the garden. It sounds like several spells to restrict movement are being used, or maybe variations on one spell." Eleanor was thinking hard.

"We would love to help, but when I was transferred into this statue I could not hear anything of what was being said, or see anything at all. So however it was done, I have not the slightest knowledge of it. And Maude has said the same. We don't know how it was done. We didn't want to know. But now…now we wish we did!"

"So," said Perry, "our first order of business is to somehow find the spells used to bind you and the dragons. There must have been something like a summoning spell used as well to get all the dragons to come to Wyvern. Hunting them down would have taken much too long."

"I hadn't thought of that," said Maggie. "I know some very fine old summoning spells. Maybe the one Wyvern used is one of those, or something related, to bring the dragons to him. But possibly one of the other people trapped in their statues might have heard something when their spirits were being transferred—if we can only get part of something to work on, maybe we can tell which branch of magic he used, which language or part of the world. It would make sense that when he was mastering magic he would follow a particular school. In which case all the spells would be from that one."

"I would bet it comes from wherever the 'cold pitiless' thing that co-habits with him comes from. I bet that BB brought the magic, but needed Wyvern, a human, or at least a body, to work it. There has to be some reason why they joined up." Robin was bouncing with pent up excitement at the theory he'd come up with.

Perry was excited by that as well, "That would explain why they need each other, but that may not be the only reason. Did Ivor have a particular interest in dragons earlier in his life?"

"Not that I ever saw," replied Eleanor. "He was more interested in art, he wanted to be an artist. Well, being Ivor, he wanted to be a *great* artist. I don't remember any interest in dragons or mythology. Certainly not in dragons as captives."

"He never mentioned them," said Maude, "but obviously he became deeply involved with them in hideous ways. What is this BB you speak of Robin?"

"Oh, that's what Kate and I have called his co-inhabitant. BB for Body Buddy."

"It just sort of slipped out," said Kate, 'and it stuck. Better than calling it the "cold, ancient, evil being" because I'm scared enough already without constantly reminding myself of just how horrible this being is."

Perry spoke again, "And we found out that the dragons are not of this world. Err, I mean that literally, they come from a different world, a parallel Earth according to what Chen Shi told Kate, and learned how to make the transition from that one to this one. So I've been wondering if this BB didn't come from the same world. If he is another supposedly mythical being from that world and maybe these two species have a hatred of each other. Suppose he came here to find a willing partner to help him conquer the dragons?"

"But what would he give in return?" asked Eleanor.

"The usual devil's pact—money, power, live forever, great talent, recognition—Ivor was suddenly the most celebrated artist in England, right?"

"Yes, yes, he was, for all I know he still is, and it did happen quite suddenly. Too suddenly."

Kailen broke in, "Time passes, all too soon our ability to converse and exchange information will be gone until the next full moon. Eleanor, Maude, do you think we might safely question the rest of your companions in duress to find out if any remember any of the spells used to transfer your spirits to this marble? And also if they would, if they could, like Tom Jenks, fight the evil with us. I ask because of the possibility that one of them could perhaps be a spy."

Maude and Eleanor looked at each other, then nodded as one. "We have had hundreds of nights like this one to walk and talk and get to know these people. All of them are united in hatred of what has happened to them. Even if it has endowed us with a kind of immortality, it is not worth the price we paid, deprived of an ordinary life and love with family and friends. And Ivor abandoned us here over one hundred years ago now, once he found out we loathed him. He has not returned, nor has anyone of us been absent. So, no, there is no spy. And yes, I believe if we introduce you they will be uplifted by the chance, any chance, to repay him for this evil. They will tell you what they know. We never, I think—is that right, Maude?— talked about the actual kidnapping of our spirits. It is a painful subject. So we don't know if one or more might know something helpful. If they do they will tell you I feel sure."

Chapter 39

The group re-entered the big fountain garden with its long herbaceous borders via the archway in the yew hedge and found that many of the statues were standing around near that arch, chatting amongst themselves, but waiting, it appeared, for them. There were about two dozen of them, and another dozen or so still strolling. Probably it felt good just to be able to move.

Jenks, having been the only one to speak to them previously, had made himself a kind of spokesman. "We was wonderin' when you might be coming back. Time, as they say, marches on. Won't be too long now before we have to get ourselves back to our resting places well before the sun comes up. Have you come to help or just to jabber?"

"We hope we can help, and that you can help us," said Maggie. "Eleanor and Maude have told us you all hate what Ivor Wyvern has done to you and wish to see him pay for his crimes. But to help us do that we must find out how he managed to transfer your spirits, your very being, from your human bodies to the statues you now inhabit. So we have a question for all of you—what do you remember about that process? Can you remember anything about what happened to you and how he did it?"

A number of the statues simply shook their heads, a few turned their backs. The Goddess Diana, with her bow and quiver of arrows, spoke. "We mostly have tried to forget, it was for all of us the most awful thing that ever happened. Although he sculpted us over a period of years, every time it was the same. Once the statue was finished we each got a note saying if we came to his studio he wanted to give us a bonus because his work had gone well and we, each of us, had been good models. So we went. And that was the end of our human lives."

"He showed me the finished statue I'd been the model for. He reached out to shake my hand," said Socrates, "saying we'd done good work together. But he hung on, and then I found I couldn't pull free. He hit me with something, and I blacked out. Next thing I knew I was tied to a table or something and he was saying things in a language I didn't understand—it was guttural and ugly. There was a rope or a braided cord going from my body to the statue and as I watched a sort of flame came from my body and started up along this cord—it was a flame or a light, it was red and green and black — how black could be a flame I don't know. And then everything went black, and when I was conscious again I was no longer in my body. In fact I could see my body lying there, and it looked collapsed, sort of dried out and—well, it was horrible to look at. I knew it must be dead. That was *me* lying there and I was dead. For a few moments I thought I might be going to the afterlife, to heaven or even to hell. But then I realised I was seeing from the perspective of the statue. The cord had also shrivelled and hung like a dried out worm. It was hideous and disgusting, but Wyvern was beside himself with the evidence of his success."

A beautiful statue that Kate recognised as Helen of Troy from the name inscribed on her plinth took up the tale. "I was a school teacher in Exeter. My name is Martha. He sent me a note that he had some fine details to finish and asked me to return so he could make sure of my features. I went, why wouldn't I? I was flattered that he had me as the model for 'the face that launched a thousand ships'. There was tea and biscuits, but the tea was drugged and when I woke up I was also bound to this table and had the cord stretching between my body and the statue of Helen. Wyvern was chanting some gibberish that sounded to me like it might be related to ancient Babylonian (I studied to be an archaeologist, but there was no work for me then, because I was a woman).

"I have to admit that when he first appeared here at Ashley to walk with his statues under the full moon I did talk to him a few times. He was literate and interesting and I had not had that kind of companionship in years. But he became enraged when I dared to disagree with some pet theory of his, and I quickly realised what the others had been telling me—he was wicked, and none of us should in any way satisfy his desires. So from then on I refused to speak to him. And as you know after awhile he stopped visiting us. Luckily for me the man that inhabits the statue of Hercules turned out to have also studied archaeology and ancient languages, so we do have some great talks in our field. And the other folk here—well, we have all banded together in a 'misery loves company' sort of way and a common bond of hatred for Wyvern."

Perry asked her, "Would you say this language could have been Babylonian?"

"I'd never heard it spoken, but I would say that is what it reminded me of."

"Was he reading it out or did he have it memorised? Could you see if he had a book or scroll?"

Martha pondered a few minutes. "I am trying to bring back a clear picture of what I could see at that point. I was foggy with that drug, but I do remember I could feel something scratchy along my arm and when I looked down it was sheets of parchment or possibly even papyrus. So yes I would say he was reading from it, or at least referring to it. I couldn't see the writing, although I think I saw some line drawings, some pictures."

"So not bound in a book?" said Perry. "Although I suppose that doesn't mean it isn't now. Could you see any of the pictures clearly enough to have any idea what they were?"

"I thought they showed something similar to what was happening to me—a bound person attached by some kind of cord to an upright person."

250

"You have given us excellent news, my dear," said Maggie. "That these spells are written down somewhere is so important. It means we have some chance of actually discovering them and even the counter-spells, or possibly using what's in the spell to produce a counter-spell."

Kailen looked around at the other statues. "Does anyone else here have anything to add to this? Anything, however seemingly insignificant, however small, any memory could be so important. If you can't think of anything now, please, if you are conscious within your statues during your enforced period of quiet, search your memories for any bit that could help. Not just the period of your transfer, but what Wyvern might have talked about during the time he was sculpting and you were modelling."

"Also if he ever said anything about dragons or other mythological beasts," said Kate. "Or if you ever heard him talking to himself or seem to argue with himself, or a voice that didn't seem to be his."

A heavy-set (well, fat actually) statue in medieval costume came forward. "I be Walter Taylor, he made me into Falstaff he said. He used to talk about dragons some, said he wouldn't have believed them real, but he had proof now and he were delighted with how they could be used. Me, I didn't really understand a word of it. And that's why I think he talked about it, because he figured me too stupid to understand. He were right o' course, I didn't really. But I be taken by him saying that they kept him young. It were such a strange thing to say. My friends here have said, well, having an interest is supposed to keep you young, but I don't think that were what he meant."

"Oh my god, that's why he was drinking their blood. Maude, what you saw, him cutting the young dragon and drinking its blood. That's how he's stayed the same age. Dragons are immortal, Chauncey told me, they virtually can't be killed. So Wyvern must be using their blood to keep himself from ageing." Kate was moved to

251

hug Maude who patted her very carefully on the back. "You guys are awesome, truly awesome, you've helped so much. We're going to beat this thing!

"Maggie—think, if we can free the dragons, Wyvern won't have any fresh dragon blood, he'll shrivel up like a mummy and die!"

"Or, Kate, he could shrivel up like the mummy and not die. Go stalking around like in the film." Robin was walking stiffly with his arms stretched out.

Kate laughed, "You know that isn't real lurching, Robin."

"Maybe I'm hypotenusing." And with an exaggerated moan he intoned, "I'm the hypotenuse, and I'm coming to get you!"

Kate obligingly squeaked and mimed terror.

"Enough, you two," said Kailen, coming over all parental. But a lot of the statues were laughing. "Aw, let 'em be. Us haven't had a laugh in so long," said Tom Jenks. "Does the soul good you know—and we be nowt but souls nowadays." Kailen smiled.

"Take a turn with us around the fountain," offered the beautiful Helen aka Martha from Exeter, "Enjoy the last of this perfect night. We will then take ourselves back to our plinths and await the dawn."

"We're so glad to have met with you," said Socrates. "You give us hope."

"Can you hear us if we come and talk to you? We know you can't answer, but can you hear?" asked Kate.

"Oh, yes, oh my, the things we have heard over the years!" laughed Diana.

"That's wonderful. That means we can come and tell you about anything we find out."

Perry already knew Maude could hear him. They walked together and he said he'd come every day and talk to her about what they found out, and just to chat, so she wouldn't feel so alone.

"I don't feel anything really," replied Maude. "When no one is talking I seem to just doze or even sleep. I don't feel physical pain, and my mental pain, though it has been stirred by all this, is mainly an old and gentle ache, often not there at all." Seeing him look downcast she made haste to reassure him, "But I have cherished the times you have sat with me, and I look forward to seeing you. I am grateful that I do not feel imprisoned in my harpy, but that doesn't mean I don't enjoy having someone talk to me, especially you. You have done me the honour of confiding in me and that is a lovely thing."

Chapter 40

"What we have to do is see Chauncey again—soon!" said Kate. "We have to tell him how Wyvern stays young."

"No, that's a terrible idea. He can't do anything to stop it and that will hurt him so much. He'll go mental!" Robin was pacing around the library waving his arms with the intensity of his argument.

"We need the spells, Chauncey may know them, or know where they are. We have to see him," Kate maintained.

"Well, we can't see him — you *know* that. You're the one who nearly didn't get out alive. That kind of luck doesn't happen twice." Robin was looking grim.

Kate was mutinous, "We can find a way. We'll get the architect's drawings—there have to be ways in that don't involve the wyverns or the moat."

"Now that sounds like a good idea." Perry had just come in and was dumping an armful of books and copies of newspaper cuttings on his desk. "But first we need to find out more about these people who were—I suppose the ordinary world would say kidnapped and killed."

Perry had made a list of the names and former addresses and occupations of all the statues, and as near as possible the date they were 'turned'. He'd made a blown-up copy and taped it up on the blackboard. One thing they had told him was that they wanted to know if possible what had happened to their families, wives, husbands, children, parents. And what had been said about their disappearances. "We owe them this at least, to find out what was said and done at the time." he said.

"Even if it might upset them?" asked Kate, catching on a little late that not all information should be shared.

254

"We can filter it slightly if we think that's necessary," said Perry. "But I think it possible that their human emotions have been somewhat dulled over the years. They are certainly capable of emotional feelings— although not physical ones, which is good — think how painful standing completely still would become after only a few hours. But unless they are stirred up, as often happens during their moon lit nights, it seems that when they are on their plinths they can easily fall into a doze or a trance or sleep and feel nothing. But these disappearances must have been reported in the papers at the time, and even for sometime after. And there's a chance that we can learn helpful things from those reports as well."

"If they all posed for sculptures by Wyvern, who was famous then, wouldn't there have been an investigation that connected him to all those disappearances?" asked Robin.

And they set to reading the clippings and checking in the local records and some history books that covered that time in Devon hoping for revelations they could tell the spirits in the statues.

"I have to admit I'm surprised. Our reading so far hasn't turned up anything like a big outcry let alone a murder investigation," said Perry. "Or any mention of Wyvern at all. But since it also seems that he used mostly working-class people, or vagabonds or tramps in some cases, mostly they would have been considered to have 'moved on' and no records kept. In the case of Martha/Helen, the school teacher, it turns out she had already accepted a post in Lincoln and it was during the school holidays that she posed for Wyvern. She apparently never mentioned that to her family in Exeter because it would have been considered a wanton act to pose semi-nude and with no chaperon. She would have lost her job and her reputation would have been ruined. Her family thought she was hiking with friends in the Lake District, and only became alarmed when the school in Lincoln wrote asking where she was. By then it was too late to trace her. So far not one of these people has been reported as a crime, just as disappeared. Some of them aren't mentioned in any records at all."

"Not much has changed then," said Kate sourly. "If you're poor or homeless you don't count. New York was full of people who just 'disappeared'. And even now if you're female and act like Helen did a lot of people think you deserve what you get. Sometimes I just hate the world."

"Well at least we can tell them something, and we can tell Cora what we've learnt and she can tell Chauncey," Perry said. "That's what he told you to do, Kate. He knows that for the present we can't do anything about his captivity. Sounds like he has a similar attitude to the statues—he's stuck so he makes the best of it. But I wonder if he knows that Wyvern is a dual being? Or if he does, maybe he knows what kind of being the other one is. These are questions I'd really like some answers to."

Perry was pointing out the different names of the statues as he talked about them when Poppet put up her head and started wagging her tail and Robin hissed, "Danger, Sir Hugh approaching."

Perry instantly pulled a string that let down a large European map that entirely covered the list of people and references. "And here," he said, using the pointer to outline an area in middle Italy, 'is where that ignorant Giorgio Vasari declared that the Renaissance began after what has been called the Dark Ages ever since. But if we're discussing art—and we are—the Renaissance really began in northern Europe, in the Low Countries. They were even using oil paints while the Italians were still using tempera—that's egg yolk mixed with pigment,,, Oh, good morning, Sir Hugh!"

"Art history, hey? Always liked a good painting of goddesses by—oh, what's the fella's name?—did Venus on the half shell dontcha know."

"That's Botticelli, Uncle Hugh," said Kate, getting up to give him a hug.

"But what's this about the Renaissance not beginning in Italy, Perry? Ah, hold on... I know where you got that. That art fella on BBC 4—funny guy, walks a lot, said that what they called the Flemish Primitives were anything but. You've only got to look at that Ghent thingy—triptych—I mean, even I can see that might be the best painting in the world. Just my opinion of course." But Sir Hugh was beaming with the knowledge that he had one-upped Perry.

Sir Hugh, although ostensibly of the hunting and shooting variety of English country gentleman, hadn't, as some thought, entirely ignored his education, and took a decent First in Art History at Oxford. In his old age he also enjoyed watching a lot of BBC 4 documentaries, occasionally objecting strenuously with the presenter. Hence his occasional habit of dropping a piece of obscure but entertaining information into conversation. He did so now.

"Did you ever see the extraordinary St George and the Dragon by Bernt Notke in the church in Lubeck?" he now queried. Perry shook his head.

"Is that some rock 'n roll band? From Lubbock, Texas, like Buddy Holly?" asked Kate, sliding her notes on the statues under her text books. "I always wondered why St George wanted to kill dragons. Dragons are *good*!"

"No, Lubeck in Germany, and Bernt Notke was a 15th Century artist. Huge, great, really beautiful, but scary dragon. One of the best sculptures I ever saw. I was there in 1966 after I left Oxford. Why kill a dragon? Because dragons stood for black arts and the devil I guess. In the medieval mind anyway."

257

"Terrible slander, saying that about dragons," said Kate.

"What?" demanded Sir Hugh. 'Whatever do you know about dragons?"

"Oh...I don't, not really, I've just always liked them." Kate was flustered at how close she seemed to have come to revealing something, anything, about the reality of dragons. Not that Uncle Hugh would have believed it.

"Well, you're in good company—a lot of kings, emperors and noble families include dragons in their coats of arms. Symbols of bravery and strength and, in the orient, supernatural power, wisdom, strength, and hidden knowledge, also protection, since dragons are indomitable." Sir Hugh was beaming pridefully with being able to impart knowledge to his sometimes know-it-all niece. "And Maggie tells me that a dragon, well, a symbolic dragon, is a great help when you need the truth to be exposed, such as during legal disputes when someone is making false claims. She is surrounded by dragon symbols in her office here and when I asked her why, she explained about that. I didn't know your mum was so superstitious, Robin. But, well, I figure, we need all the help we can get, and if dragon symbology helps Maggie with this fight, then I'm all for them.

"What's next on the study agenda?" he asked, turning to Perry. "More fine arts?"

Perry shook his head. "No we're about to embark on some study of the local architecture from the cob and thatch cottages to the High Victorian Gothic. And of course Ashley as well—it's from the reign of Charles II isn't it?"

"That's it," beamed Sir Hugh. "We've got all the architects' drawings for Ashley here in the library. Victorian Gothic—that's another thing, that hideous pile up river, Wyvern Hall. My great-grandfather Sebastian had a copy of those plans too, you know. I think he was planning on using them to try to get in and rescue his sister, Maude, after she ran away or was kidnapped or whatever. When Sebastian died his wife was supposed to have destroyed them."

There was a suppressed groan from Kate and Robin, which surprised Sir Hugh. "Why should that upset you kids? It's an evil looking thing and I wish we could destroy *it*, not just the plans."

Perry intervened, "Because it's a perfect example of Victoria Gothic for us to study, Sir Hugh, and naturally the kids are more interested in a building that is nearby than something they may never actually see."

"Well, I hope you never have occasion to see this one either!" stormed Sir Hugh, "That evil bast …err, beast's works should be levelled and strewn with salt!" Then he grinned like a boy. "Ah, but the plans weren't destroyed. I found 'em years ago in the attics. Used to spend a lot of time up there when the weather was too foul to be outside."

All three listeners looked at him with real excitement. Used as he had got to being sidelined by the younger generation, Sir Hugh was regaining something of his own lost youth basking in their interest. "Come on then, last one up the stairs is a, a… Ah, never mind, that would be me anyway."

Chapter 41

So the four of them set off, Sir Hugh in the lead because getting to the attics wasn't entirely straight forward.

Entry in fact was up the back stairs and through an un-used servant's bedroom up under the eaves. With only Bates and Mr and Mrs Sykes in residence, bedrooms had been given to them on the first floor so they got decent light, heating and space, all of which were at a premium in the old servants quarters in the attics.

Sir Hugh moved a small dresser out of the way and gestured to a dusty and cobwebbed door behind it. "Through here is the entrance to treasures unknown and unexplored. Or at least they were until I explored 'em. Found things I brought to your mother, Robin, to sell. Some pretty good stuff tucked away up here. Helped to keep Ashley going. And a great way to spend rainy days."

They all stooped slightly to get through the door, and entered a vast space, virtually the length of the central wing of the house, in perpetual twilight. Vast it may have been, but also crowded with furniture, boxes, toys and books, garment bags hanging on rails and vast piles of unknown objects looming out of the dark corners. The immensity of the job ahead of them was apparent. Thank goodness, thought Kate, it isn't hot this week—we'd have baked up here. As it was everything was coated in dust and draped in cobwebs. She shrank back from these, disliking the feel. But there was no getting round it—everyone was needed to sift through the piles and check the drawers and boxes. Sir Hugh admitted rather shame-faced that he no longer had any idea where he had first found the plans or what he had done with them after looking them over. All he could be certain of was that he hadn't taken them back downstairs.

"I think," said Perry, 'that our first job is to bring up some bottled water and other drinks. A few snacks. Good torches. And cotton gloves if we can find any, so we won't be damaging anything valuable with fingerprints and spreading dirt. Is there any electricity up here?"

"Don't think so," said Sir Hugh. "Might be an outlet in the bedroom. If so, we could get an extension cord and a lamp."

"I know where to get the gloves," volunteered Robin. "My mum keeps a pile of them in case she's called on to examine anything potentially valuable. She's here today, isn't she, Sir Hugh?" At Hugh's nod of agreement, Robin said "I'll go ask her, shall I? And get those drinks and snacks. Mrs Sykes likes me, no problem."

"I'll get Bates to look out a torch or two and an extension cord and a lamp. I hope plugging something in up here doesn't blow a fuse, can't think of the last time we switched anything on here. Still, live and learn." Hugh turned to follow Robin, returning shortly with the lights.

Robin came back a few minutes later with gloves—a great relief to Kate who hadn't been looking forward to handling the dusty cobwebby piles—and drinks and snacks. Plus his mother. Maggie raised an eyebrow at their surprise. "You didn't think I would miss out a chance to paw through this treasure trove, did you? What are we looking for exactly?"

"Perry here is teaching our young 'uns about architecture of this area and I remembered that I once found the architect's plans for Wyvern Hall up here. Perfect example of Victorian Gothic, Perry says. Perfect example of the devil's own residence says I, but who am I to stand in the way of education?" Sir Hugh, however irate he sounded, was looking as excited as Perry, Robin and Kate.

Maggie exchanged a look with the three others that said plainly, Ah ha! Now we could be getting somewhere. But all she said was, "And who knows what else we might find. Let's get going!"

And indeed, dust and cobwebs notwithstanding, it was a treasure trove. Boxes that contained hats, each wrapped in tissue, hats whose styles covered two centuries—Kate and Maggie were both enchanted and Maggie set them aside to be taken downstairs. "These," she explained "could potentially fetch thousands in the right auction. And I'm your girl when it comes to the right auctions."

The same held true for much of the contents of the garment bags—dresses of many different periods and for many different purposes, mostly in good condition. Some went with the hats. "Eureka" shouted Maggie, "Sir Hugh this will pay a lot of back taxes and get you a car you can afford to run."

Then there were shoes, and then gloves. And some jewellery. All went into the pile to go into an empty room downstairs and be carefully assessed. Then Kate found the stuffed animals—Steiff animals of all kinds, some according to Maggie dating back to the start of the company around 1850. "These will also make a small fortune, they've been packed carefully and haven't got moth," she announced jubilantly. Kate was cuddling a giraffe, and Maggie decided not to part her from it.

But this wasn't getting to the papers. There were enormous piles of papers, and some filing cabinets as well. Perry was methodically going through the piles, in spite of sneezing and watery eyes. "Allergies" he muttered, "Well faint heart ne'er won fair lady."

"Who would that be?" asked Robin. "You won't find any fair ladies in those piles."

"Maude of course!" stage-whispered Kate. "He's doing this for her ... well partly for her."

Hours later they had made some startling discoveries. A complete skeleton, all correctly wired up.

262

"The last person to try to find things in this great pile of stuff," said Robin. A beautiful if shabby rocking horse. "Another one for the auction house" said Maggie. A mummified cat. "So that's where he ended up" said Sir Hugh, stroking the fur lightly with one finger, "we thought he'd just run away." But the papers continued to hide their secrets. This didn't really disturb the hunters, who could see that essentially the Mallorys never threw anything away, and this meant the architect's plans had to be in there somewhere.

As indeed they were. Robin had been looking into various corners and boxes in a desultory way, when he opened what he thought was a very elegant leather-bound book inset with what might be jewels to find it was a fake and had a storage space inside. Here folded into quarters were the plans. "Oh, of course, now I remember," said Sir Hugh. "I thought they might someday get thrown out with all those old papers in piles, so I thought I'd better put them somewhere safe. I meant to write it down, but I forgot. Well, I was only about 12 for heaven's sake."

"You're a hero, Uncle Hugh!" said Kate, hugging him. "You made sure they would stay safe and you put them into something obviously valuable so they wouldn't get thrown out by mistake."

"Well, Kate, enjoy studying Victorian Gothic, but really I'd just as soon never lay eyes on them again—too many awful memories." And Hugh stripped off his cotton gloves and left taking Maggie with him so they could discuss the possible value and sale of the many other things they'd found. And they hadn't looked through but about a tenth of what was stored up there—there would be treasures to come. But meanwhile, there were dragons to free, and the only way to do that would be to gain access back into Wyvern Hall.

Well, that was part of it. The other part they hadn't figured out yet—how to undo the spells that Ivor and his

Body Buddy had used to enslave them. There was every chance that it would turn out to be a number of different spells to suit the types of 'jobs' the dragons were sold for. And counter-spells would either be given, or between them they would have to invent them. "Say them backward?" suggested Kate.

"We'll certainly try that when we find the spells that enslaved them," said Perry.

"Do you suppose they are up there in Ashley's attics?" asked Robin.

"Doubtful," said Perry. "If they are written down, they are almost certainly in Wyvern Hall."

So it was back to the architect's plans. Perry photographed them and entered them into his and everybody's computer and mobile phone so they could learn them well. A minor hiccup occurred when Kate pointed out from her own knowledge that there were certain differences between the plans and the building itself. The garden for Maude was shown as a much smaller space with what looked like storage sheds built against the walls, and there was no sign of the cream limestone and marble that faced its walls.

"Easily explained," said Perry. "She wasn't there yet to request a garden of her own. That was made some years later. Does it mean you can't access the big courtyard from this space?"

They poured over the images and saw that there was the passage Kate remembered connecting the two. So that was okay. They paid particular attention to the layout of the cellars—Kate had only vague recollections of these as the passages she followed seemed to wind and twist, with many locked doors along the way. The large area where Chauncey now played central heating furnace was there, located under the central hallway of the castle. A huge space to house this huge dragon and central so that all the pipes could spread out through the walls. With many branching passages leading off it. There was the moat and the castle entrance with the portcullis and drawbridge with indications of the posts for the wyverns to stand guard upon.

Perry was pointing out an area at the back of the Hall to show them how, with the proper tools, they could gain access from the rear without alerting the wyverns or the creatures in the moat. It did mean climbing up the nearly vertical cliff face that was at the back of Wyvern Hall, but Perry had surprised them by saying he had spent several holidays in the Alps scaling vertical rock faces—for fun! He knew all about the proper clothing, and ropes and other climbing equipment.

He said "I suggest you two fit in some time to learn wall climbing at the Quay Climbing Centre — it's the south west's largest indoor climbing wall in the huge space of Exeter's old electricity building. I'll come along if you like. Then we'll do a little outdoor cliff scaling on Dartmoor. After that we can collect the tools we would need to break into Wyvern Hall from that side and practice climbing with those on our backs."

Kate and Robin looked at each other—this was getting very real.

Chapter 42

The next day Kate came into the library, waving a sheet of paper. "Cora has brought me a message from Chauncey! Look, I've written it down just as she told it to me. Thank the stars that Cora has a perfect memory for conversation when she is actually listening. And of course she listens intently to Chauncey.

"Anyway she told him I am worried about him and wanted to come to see him. But as you said, he warns me not to try. Not now, he says. And then he quotes from Hamlet, only not exactly, because I looked it up. He (not Hamlet, Chauncey) says:

I could live in a nutshell and count myself a king of infinite space. But, Kate, my dear child, I do not, like Hamlet, have bad dreams. I have good dreams, and even better visions for the future. So I do, as I always have, count myself king of infinite space — in all truth in the past, just for now, within my mind only, as in a nutshell I must dwell. Soon in reality once again I am sure. Dragons live virtually forever, this is but a moment.

And Cora tells me that Ivor Wyvern is a dual being — that Melior and Maude are sure his human body is inhabited by another entity, something you and Robin refer to as the Body Buddy. Very droll.

But I have thought upon this and it occurs to me that there is another being from the world we dragons came from that might have the intelligence and power to also pass between worlds. It is something that this world would call a Chimaera—not the DNA reality kind—but a supposedly mythical beast made up of several different kinds of animal. In the case of the race I am thinking of, this is a beast that can change shape at will, but that must use other intelligent beings to actually carry out its dark magic. Dragons and Chimaeras were at war for eons in our other Earth, and the Chimaeras lost badly. Although they were shapeshifters, they couldn't become something that could fly. Myths from this Earth say they could breathe fire, but the ones we were at war with could not. You could say they were badly outgunned by the Dragons. And the dark magic they could do wouldn't work except when they inhabited another intelligent and facile body, such as a human one. There weren't any of those, since mammals never got a look in because the reptiles (us) weren't wiped out by the asteroid that struck this Earth and left the way clear for mammals to develop. The other big intelligent beings with useful 'hands' were us, the Dragons, and they couldn't inhabit us.

So they were stuck with small animals with hands like some lizards or big animals that had brute force but not too much in the way of brains, easily vanquished by dragons. Hence I believe the last few Chimaeras simply ran and hid as best they could. If any or even just one had the knowledge we used to come here, to this Earth, and found a human being it could co-inhabit with—that would explain the hatred of dragon kind and also where Wyvern got his frankly astonishing ability as a dark mage.

That could be the explanation for this entire strange series of events. Wyvern, with his love of art and determination to become a great artist plus his hatred for so many people, meets with a Chimaera who loathes dragons. Hence the capture of the dragons here which he couldn't have done on our old Earth without a partner to do the necessary parts. It could also explain Wyvern's apparent immortality — Chimaeras, like Dragons, are immortal.

Keep me informed, dear child, I have every confidence that you and your trusted group will find answers that can overturn this dreadful — and I use dreadful advisedly — double being and give dragons back their freedom. Might I be so bold as to ask that when (I say when, not if) you find the counter-spells that bind us, that you free me first. I can then fly you however far and fast to free the others, and I know they will take heart at seeing me alive and powerful once more.

"And that's the end of the message. He seems full of confidence, and I wish I were as confident. I hope he's right about the flying far and fast, because we'll need as many dragons as possible to face Ivor and his awful Wyvern army. I hope that imprisonment hasn't weakened his muscles — what if he can't even walk, let alone fly?" Kate was voicing her fears to Robin, Perry, Kailen and Maggie, who'd all gathered to hear the message.

Maggie spoke up, "We can't know for sure, but I suspect that, being magical creatures, dragons can probably recover their strength in ways humans and earthly animals cannot. But if he should be weakened, Kailen and I can both work spells for strength and agility. In fact, as they don't entirely depend upon being with the subject, we can begin to do those now. We can in fact do a spread of spells to all enslaved dragons wherever they may be."

Perry stepped forward and said, "If it wouldn't knock the power out of these spells, might I be allowed to try as well? Is there another way to test for magic than to try to do it? If I am not gifted in that way, I know I have plenty of other possibilities to help. But I must admit that to be able to work magic seems like a wondrous thing and, like Robin — although I never suffered from not being able to — I have a child-like wonder and excitement at the possibility that I might learn to do this."

Maggie laughed, "The more the merrier, Perry. Why shouldn't you try? As a human being who decided that witchcraft was my chosen way of living, I wasn't sure that I could do magic, but it became obvious after a bit that, as they say, you don't choose magic, magic chooses you. And it starts sometimes early, sometimes late, can be extremely powerful or only a small talent. But like any talent, say for music, the more you practice the better you are likely to be. I know there are those who would keep magic a deep secret with only the very few practitioners allowed, but I think that it could be inclusive and help many people develop more of their potential in other areas. The thing is, I was doing magic when I thought it was just coincidence. Now I know it is not such a rare talent as all that. However, you must not be disappointed if you do not have this gift. As you say, there are so many other ways in which you are helping."

Chapter 43

Maggie suggested they meet that evening in the wild garden on the hill above Ashley. Here they gathered in the clearing where Kate, only a few short months ago, had lain crying for her dead grandmother and had first seen the Fae Dragon, Cora.

Surrounded by ferns and woodland flowers and trees now in full leaf, the three humans and the Fae prince and his son, the halfling sat cross-legged in a circle. Maggie presented each of them with a stone on which was carved a glyph or sigil. Each was different. For Kate there was a recognisable dragon carved in amethyst, for Perry a sigil that meant "I am calm, open and energised" in jade, Robin got a glyph for safety and strength in obsidian. Kate and Robin also got an obscure extra tweak on their glyphs that granted them peacefulness — Maggie knew that her son and Kate were too keyed up and could easily start throwing darts of extra strength and anger around without recognising it. And Kailen got one for focus on turquoise. He grimaced at this and threw a quizzical look at his mate, because he alone except for Maggie understood the meaning of each stone. She simply grinned at him, knowing that however powerful he was in war, in peaceful pursuits he was liable, like all the Fae, to have meandering thoughts.

For Maggie herself there was a sigil on quartz, grounding her as the conduit through which the energies of the others could pass to the dragons, all the dragons anywhere. She had also drawn in the earth before her a rune to protect her from being overwhelmed by the emotions the others might feel, because she was the channel, and it was vital that a channel be clear and unaffected by what might pass through.

"None of these glyphs or runes is directly related to healing for the dragons, they are meant to protect you and increase your own powers, such as they may be," said Maggie. "The healing must come from your own thoughts and feelings. Kate, Robin, Perry—try to quiet your mind and let feelings and thoughts of healing take over. Perhaps imagine throwing a net or a soft blanket out to the universe, asking that it be taken to those who need it most, envisioning the dragons, all dragons anywhere. If this is too vague, imagine arrows of love, or images of light and stars, or snowflakes of healing energy going out into the world, seeking dragons. Imagine, for instance, a snowflake or a flower or a golden dart of healing power that you send out with the intent of reaching a dragon. You may if you want also envision a particular dragon.

"Kate, it might increase your power to think of Chen Shi as the recipient or possibly his imprisoned children. None of you have to try to conjure up an exact image of a particular dragon, particularly as you have never seen any but Cora, but it could happen that any of you might find that certain dragon images appear before you, in which case, accept these and send out healing in whatever way you find suits you.

"If your mind begins to wander, pull back and let your mind go where it will for a bit, this may be a respite from the intensity of your reaching toward the dragons. You will do much better just to be quiet inside and ask, as St Francis put is so well 'Lord, make me a channel of your peace'. This will free you of self to some extent and allow the energies around you to find the way through you to the dragons. I say 'energies around you' because this is a place of peace and power both. And it is these more than any other elements that will have the most efficacy for quieting a trapped dragon and then restoring power.

"Anyone have any questions at this point?"

271

Robin looked up from where he'd been studying the ground. "What if my mind is full of anger and the urge to send arrows of flame at the wyverns and at Ivor Wyvern himself? Because that's what it's full of."

Maggie wasn't surprised, she'd felt an almost visible heat emanating from her only child. "Tie those up in a net of spider silk, the strongest 'string' on earth, imagine tying it tightly with your anger and the flames inside. Now put them in a strong box and lock it. Then give it to me or your father. Err, also the key, my son! We'll keep it safe until it is time to use it. Then you'll get it back, stronger and more powerful. Trust us. You will get to use this. Only not now. Okay?"

Robin almost visibly deflated a bit and was calmer and more focused. "Okay. Got it. I can do this."

"The mind picture I have is of Cora," said Perry, holding the white jade in his hand. "I don't know if it's a vision or just common sense, but I think she, being so small and having to fly so far and memorise long messages... Well, plus the risks of getting caught. Anyway, I feel like I should be sending healing and strength to her. Is that useful, or am I blocking any ability to cast my net or blanket further?"

Maggie turned her senses from Robin and tuned into Perry. She saw an opalescent glow around his hand where he held his stone. "I can see clearly that you are in fact attuned to both your glyph and stone and to your purpose. This is real power, not an intellectual endeavour, my friend. Go with it. Cora does indeed need your help."

She turned her attention to Kate, who appeared lost in contemplation of her stone, and saw that there was a rainbow hued channel going straight from her to Chen Shi. *Holy Hecate!* she thought. *The girl doesn't even need me as a channel, she's going straight for it. That's power! That's just incredible power! I wonder if he can feel it, and if he knows what it is? Surely, surely he does. Oh, I hope so.*

Kailen was doing it his own way. An accomplished bowman, he was sending out golden darts of strength and calm. Totally focused, she noted with amusement. Warlike power turned to quiet purpose.

Looking back at Robin she saw to her intense relief and pleasure that he was now deeply involved in sending nets of—crikey—flowers? Yep, flowers—out into the world in a general way that pleased her for his sense that the universe would see that they got to where they could help.

That was her job: she gathered Robin's flower nets, Kailen's darts of strength, Perry's loving intent and sent them out where they could do the most good. With her symbolic feet firmly in the earth for balance and her witch's senses flung wide as a channel she took the power, love and healing that these good folk were broadcasting and sent them carefully and purposefully to their intended recipients. It wasn't easy to be focused upon recipients that could be anywhere, but she brought up inside herself as much of the essence of dragon as she could and poured the power upon it. And felt a rebound of relief and thanks coming back like a wave. *Yes, they can feel this, and now they also know there are friends out here. There's nothing quite like knowing you aren't alone.* So she channelled a message of her own that simply said: WE KNOW. YOU AREN'T ALONE. FEEL SAFE. HELP IS COMING. And again the wave answered with relief and thanks and two words: WE WAIT.

Chapter 44

Kate was totally involved with her rainbow channel. She could feel, see, even taste the textures of it as it ran from her core toward Chauncey. She felt herself being pulled toward it as well and instinctively drew back. *It's a channel for healing and strength, not something I'm supposed to run along* she thought. *It's for sending, not for travelling.* But she watched with fascination as it seemed to simply grow from her out and out. Feeling it connect at the other end, she carefully poured out what was to her the essence of healing—love. Thoughts and feelings of love. Images of softness and comfort, arms around a child, gentle warmth and whispered words of calm and steadiness. She thought a bit and sent forth images of her grandmother Lucinda potting up seedlings, Lucinda reading her bedtime stories and Lucinda calming a bird with a broken wing. Then she sent images of herself with the starving puppy that would be Poppet, and the hugs she got from Mrs Sykes and her Uncle Hugh. And, remembering that she had read it was medically proven that laughter could help the healing process, she sent images of some her favourite passages from Discworld books, knowing Chauncey loved them too. She sent blankets strewn with flowers and others with stars, and the best comfort food she could think of, hot buttered toast with honey, masala chai, split pea soup, and brownies with clotted cream. She didn't exactly know what Chauncey would find most comforting and healing. So she sent what was most dear to her, that which gave her the greatest comfort and had helped to heal the dark and dreadful lonely places. It was the most honest she could be.

Light came back, waves of light, and warmth like a breath. And she could feel without words Chauncey's welcome and happiness. They were actually in communication! Her mind reeled slightly, but she righted it and, as if she'd been doing it all her life, opened a receptive channel beside her sending one. What she was getting was very similar to what she was sending— amazement at the two-way communication, welcome and kindness. Suddenly there was his voice in her head— "Child, you outdo the masters of old, you have made a channel for a dragon, you have done what no one dared to do for fear of being overwhelmed. I promise I cannot overwhelm you. This is not a matter of size but of power and esteem, and we are evenly matched in this. I confess to being amazed. But thank you, thank you for the gifts you send. They comfort my soul, they heal something important within me. I know this is your intent, I can tell you it works."

It would be wrong to say that Kate received this with the reverence and manner in which it was sent. No, she was Kate, she was American, she was 16. So she leapt to her feet, punching the air and shouting, 'YES! Way to go!' at the top of her lungs. The other four were startled out of their communing with the infinite and turned toward her with shock on their faces. Kate blushed. It was an awful blush that seemed to start at her toes and wash upwards.

"I ... I made contact with Chauncey..." she mumbled, subsiding once more to the ground and burying her face in her hands until she felt the heat fade. *I've totally screwed that one up*, she thought. *They'll think I'm an idiot. Chauncey will think I'm an idiot.*

"I assure you I do not think you're an idiot, although I know a few dragons who are so full of themselves that they might. I think you are a wonder of a human being. The one we've needed. If I could leap up and punch the air, I think I would also do that, because this is a special day indeed."

"You're talking to him!" said Maggie. It was a statement, not a question, but Kate answered anyway.

"Yes, and he's talking to me. He just told me he doesn't think I'm an idiot. Thank the stars, because I feel such a fool."

"For celebrating such a marvellous achievement? Of course you're not a fool. If this were a football match and you'd just scored an important goal, that would be an appropriate response. What you have done, it seems to me, is the magical version of that goal—and none of us were looking or we'd have been on our feet as well." Maggie was smiling and applauding with silent handclaps. "I suspect this is a unique moment in the annals of magic. You've done quite naturally what no one has done before, or if they did, we don't know about it. Well done."

Robin leapt to her side, giving her the embrace of a football player after a goal. Kailen and Perry were with Maggie, holding their arms in the air. Even in her combination of elation and embarrassment, she somehow sent this all to Chauncey. "Well done indeed." he responded. "And this will give Cora a rest if we can keep doing it. Can you keep doing this?"

"I have absolutely no idea!" said Kate. "Maggie, how do I keep doing this?"

Maggie came and joined in the hug. "You made a channel, sweet girl, and you sent love and healing to Chauncey and when you felt him respond you somehow made a second channel that he could respond through. I've served as channel for other people's sendings on many occasions, but I've never seen anyone just go ahead and make channels and use them. Instinctively you seemed to know everything you needed. I can only suggest you keep following those instincts."

Kate found the ground coming up to meet her and would indeed have fallen if Perry hadn't caught her. He and Robin eased her to the ground. "Are you okay?"

"I'm just suddenly a bit dizzy. I think if I just sit here it will be better." Maggie came over with an energy drink.

"I think I may have overdone it slightly. But...BUT...I do remember what I did. I remember, so I can do it again. It was—it was all quite simple really. Just exhausting."

Chapter 45

The next day Kate, Perry and Robin spent pouring over the architect's plans for Wyvern Hall, making notes of what Kate could remember and matching that with the drawings.

It was typical of Ivor of course to interfere and add many things his architect hadn't included—but Ivor had been the client after all. They found a number of alterations in the plans labelled IW and in some of the correspondence that passed between them, Ivor was quick to criticise what he didn't like or when his architect didn't incorporate a change exactly as Ivor expected it. When it was explained that Ivor's addition couldn't be done exactly as he wanted, he simply demanded a way be found. Usually it was. Occasionally, but only occasionally, Ivor would accept a necessary compromise.

It was a strange castle that the drawings revealed. Unlike most Victorian Gothic piles, which tended to have plenty of bedrooms and very few bathrooms, Wyvern Hall had only four large suites of rooms, each with a bedroom and en-suite bath, sitting room, and dressing room. Two of them also had libraries. These sumptuous suites of rooms, all interconnecting but not connected to each other, took up the space on the first floor that would have been occupied by up to 20 bedrooms in a castle whose owner planned on entertaining a lot (which was after all a usual function of a country house). In addition to these there were special rooms on the third floor usually occupied by servants and in the towers. These appeared to be laboratories or studios and some were serviced by elevators leading to the cellars. A huge attic room with windows that captured the north light was clearly meant to be Ivor's main painting and sculpting studio. An elevator and a sort of dumb-waiter led down to the ground floor by

278

a side door where materials could be delivered. There were also a series of vents and pipes installed that after deliberating over them for some time Perry guessed were meant to be a ventilation system that would perform as a sort of air conditioning in summer and connect to the central heating in winter.

What there weren't were any servants' quarters as such, not in the attics or the cellars. There was a large kitchen with several rooms off of it. Several were pantries and one a cold room, but there were two rooms, a sitting room and a bedroom with bathroom that were clearly meant for a cook.

"Where are the bedrooms for the servants?" asked Perry. "It appears the only servant in the house would have been the cook. Not a parlour maid or a footman or someone to clean or help the cook. There are a few bedrooms for the people who took care of the horses over the stables, but with nothing in the house at all then household servants must have been housed over the stables as well. I can see that he didn't intend to have guests, but even if just for himself and his sister and Maude there must have been maids!"

"I don't think they needed people for those jobs," said Robin. "Ivor had the ability to make automatons and if he could power them with magic, then they could have done the servants jobs."

"Oh, stars," said Kate, "They are like that Spike we found? They could still be there, what if I'd run into one of those?"

"I think Chauncey would have warned you, like he did about the wyverns. Probably they are 'stood down'— that is, they are turned off, when he is away," Robin said. "They are probably stacked up in a storeroom and just come out when the master is in residence. Very sci-fi."

"Robots" said Perry, "real honest-to-god robots. Wow! This guy is really ahead of his time. Perfect evil overlord stuff. They must have been either very good simulacrums of people to fool Eleanor and Maude, or he might have done a spell so they saw them as real people. Because they might have said if they were served by robots. It's all very complicated."

"Or dead people," said Robin with relish. "If he could transport souls into sculptures, maybe he could re-animate the dead and then just pile them up in cold storage between times."

"Stop, just stop!" cried Kate. "This isn't one of your video games or a film. This particular evil overlord is not someone we should admire, he's our deadly enemy. Anyway, there was one other human there—the cook. It must be that magic isn't good enough to conjure up a good dinner."

"Yes, the cook. I wonder what happened to the cook—or cooks?" Perry was pondering. "And if one got to retirement age, what happened to him? Surely Wyvern didn't allow anyone who lived there to leave in the ordinary way."

"Maybe he could hypnotise them to forget?" said Kate hopefully.

"My fear is that the cook, or cooks, are amongst the garden statues we didn't already speak to," said Perry. "Possibly one of those that wouldn't speak at all. Anyway, what we need to know is how to get around inside and how not to trigger any alarms or arouse any of these servants, whatever they may be. We have the plans, but that's just the beginning, we need to get inside safely and then search out the spells Wyvern uses. We've only just started."

"Yeah, but part of that 'safely' thing is to know who or what is inside that could keep us from finding them, or hurt us or kill us." Robin's excitement was now turned to dead seriousness.

"Wait, I know," cried Kate. "I can talk to Chauncey…he might know. If he gets messages from Cora and from the rats and crows, he could know what the servants are and what we do to avoid them, or any alarms. Maybe he can see the plans through my eyes? Anyway we already know that I didn't set off any alarms or meet up with any soldiers or servants or—yeah, okay Robin—zombies in the cellars. That may mean none of these things are animated until Wyvern is there."

"And if Chauncey doesn't know?" asked Perry.

"Then we're no worse off than now and we can take this up tomorrow. I'll open the channels to Chauncey tonight, before I go to sleep, since doing it tires me out. And report back tomorrow."

Robin had been thinking. "Listen, you should really come over to our house for the night. You've only ever channelled Chauncey the other night, and it did affect you quite a bit. Wouldn't it be better if you had my mum there with you to sort of monitor things and step in for back-up if you feel overwhelmed?"

Kate nearly snapped that she would be fine, thanks very much, when she realised that that exact response proved that she wasn't entirely fine at all. So she nodded her agreement and said to Perry, "You need to give us a project that I can tell Uncle Hugh requires that I spend the evening and then the night at Robin's. He's not going to go for me doing a sleepover with a guy at our age."

Perry grinned. "Project, huh, that requires staying late, so you might as well stay over? Okay, astronomy—Robin you and Kailen have a telescope, right? Then I want you to plot a star map. No, no, you don't have to actually do it. I can do one up to show Sir Hugh if he wants to see it. But it's a perfect reason to have to stay overnight at Maggie's."

So that's what they did, and later on, curled up in bed with cocoa and her tablet with pictures of the architect's drawings, Kate settled herself and made the channel to Chauncey. Maggie was there in a chair, ostensibly reading a book, but ready to help if needed. Again she saw her channel as a rainbow and soon felt the warmth and welcome from the ancient dragon. So she created the second channel, and could feel him reaching out from his end to make the connection. With an almost audible click they connected and Chauncey's voice appeared in her head.

"Hello youngling, we meet again—is this like wifi?" Kate laughed and Maggie looked up with a question in her eyes. "I don't know, I don't know how wifi works, or how this works—but I suppose it's similar, yes. Chauncey, can you see me, or tune in to the pictures I want to show you?"

"I don't know, these channels seem to be sound only, or, wait, let's see...there, I have removed the obstacle. Now I can see you." And as suddenly, in her head she could see him as well, not the entirety of him, but his head, nodding benevolently.

"What was the obstacle?" she asked.

"Just a small adjustment in my own head. It was similar to rolling up a window shade I suppose. No more than you, do I understand the exact workings of this magic. But, what the heavens and hells is that room you are in? I've lived all this time and never seen anything to match it!"

"Oh, this is the queen's room. It's in Maggie's house and I asked her if all the bedrooms—there are maybe fifteen, maybe twenty, she says she can't remember—anyway, if they all belonged to people and she said no, not really, they just called them various names to remember them by. So I asked if I could sleep over in this one. Isn't it just incredible?"

Chapter 46

The room Kate and Maggie were in was called the Queen's Room, as in Queen of the Fae. It was what Kailen had described as one of the Faerie Queen's favourite rooms, and Maggie and Robin and he had decided to replicate it as closely as possible at the cottage just for the fun of it. And although incredibly beautiful and startling, it really was fun. Imagine this: a room like a forest glade, where the trees and shrubs were every green nature ever created, where the moss covering the ground was starred with tiny flowers and colourful mushrooms and the stream that ran through the entire house ran here also. Now add flowers, butterflies, dragonflies and birds and fish—all moving and changing colours so that one moment they would all be in soft tones of peach and gold and cinnamon, then change so subtly that at first you didn't realise they were now showing silvers and blues and snowy whites, and yet again to reds and fawn and oranges, even to deepest navy with black and greys. This shifting pattern could have been nervous, but was mostly slow and sensuous and soothing.

The furniture seemed to be part of the forest itself, with the moss segued into deep velvets, the trees wove themselves into chairs and tables and there was a beautifully realised bedstead bedecked with animals and faeries, but not carved as such, simply appearing out of the wood. The sheets were silken and changed colours as you watched as well. It became apparent over time that the colours and the activity of the various animals was tied somewhat to the moods of the inhabitants, but also that if things got too excitable it seemed the room itself would exert a calming influence. Altogether it was the most definitely enchanted and completely enchanting room Kate had ever seen.

283

"It took me and Kailen all of our combined talents at magic to make this," Maggie confided to Chauncey and Kate. "Once we worked out the basics though it really runs itself. The Queen has never been here, and I hope she never comes because she isn't trustworthy, and she'd make trouble just for the fun of it, but her taste is excellent and I like to think she would find our re-creation of her summer bedroom a fitting tribute. Her magic is much more complex than mine, and even Kailen's (which is why she is queen of course). I'm glad you asked to stay in it, we don't spend enough time here, and it is a lot of fun just to be here and watch."

"Are they real, the fish and the birds and all the rest?" asked Kate.

"Oh, not entirely—they are more a sort of dream. A real bird or butterfly or fish (except some squid perhaps) couldn't tolerate the changes, even magical ones, which would allow for such a succession of colours and patterns. We simply created them a bit like a Disney film—I think if you watched very closely for several days you would see patterns repeating."

"But they have substance—that butterfly landed on me a moment ago, and so did that little bird, and I could feel them."

"Ah, well, Disney doesn't use magic. We do, so proper three-dimensionality isn't so difficult."

"I see you have wonderful powers, both of imagination and witchcraft, and I am glad to know it," said Chauncey, his voice now apparent to Maggie as well as Kate. "I am delighted to see something not just of my own imaginings, and even more that it tells me there is so much real power available to our endeavours."

"Ah," said Maggie, "you see behind the scenes as well as the pretty play. You are right, Kailen and I are a force to be reckoned with. But then we find Kate, who has more raw power than any of us alone or in combination."

284

"I do?" Kate was furious to hear her own voice coming out as a squeak. "I mean, I didn't know that. Surely it's not true. I don't know how that happened, I didn't before, I only dreamed."

Maggie put out a comforting hand, "We'll guide you, don't worry, you won't be alone with this. Look, try this—think of a colour combination that is different to what is going on here now and then just project it outward into the room. It's quite sensitive. The room, that is."

Kate grinned and made a stab at colours she hadn't yet seen in combination here. Everything became gold, bronze and beige … and rippled. Then as if the sun were setting the western wall blazed with vivid pinks, oranges and golds as the 'sky' overhead became that beautiful deep blue green that occurs just before it goes navy and black. Two white swans flew over and in their wake came the darkness and then—the stars. Chauncey, watching from his prison, blew out a puff of appreciative smoke and Maggie clapped softly.

"But," said the ever-doubtful Kate, "if you've programmed the room to react to someone's thoughts or feelings, wouldn't it do that for anyone who was here?"

"I can assure you absolutely not." Maggie replied. "There is nothing in our 'programming' as you call it that could have created these effects in response to someone's thoughts or even demands. If these are the effects you imagined, then you are definitely magically responsible for them."

"They are what I wanted to happen," breathed Kate a little shaken. "But I can't say I truly expected them to. Err … that ripple was my surprise that it worked!"

Chauncey asked, "Is it the case however that only in this room are such effects possible, or could Kate go into your kitchen or out into the garden and create such a scene?"

"We've not tried her out in that way," answered Maggie. "Neither we nor she has any real idea of her powers. I suspect that it would require the magic already in this room to augment her or anyone's powers to create these effects. But, honestly, we don't yet know."

"Imagine," said Chauncey, "how helpful it might be to create a realistic but false environment, perhaps to screen other things happening. There could be many ways that could aide us."

"Like walk past the Wyvern guards without them seeing us." chimed in Kate. "Total cloak of invisibility. Oh, this is so Hogwarts!"

"Remember that ripple though," chimed in Maggie. "There you are walking across the drawbridge past the wyverns and suddenly your concentration is interrupted, even if just for a moment, and wham!—there goes your invisibility. Not to mention we don't know if you or anyone could distort reality on the move. Or if it worked on how the wyverns perceive things. They could smell you or just about anything."

"They could certainly smell you and also I would imagine detect some 'disturbance in the force'," contributed Chauncey. Seeing Kate's confusion as she recognised his reference, he chuckled, "Yes my American friend, I've seen Star Wars. On an old video tape in a machine that had been thrown away and on which I am now sitting. There is gold in old rubbish too."

"So you're saying we can't create a false reality that would work to protect us from the creatures that guard the Hall? That means it's back to scaling the cliffs, and I don't think I can do that with magic." Kate was downcast.

"And I've never found any spells that allow for flying, at least not safely. Witches do not ride broomsticks or otherwise fly that I know of," commented Maggie.

"Why are you having to get into Wyvern Hall? Aside from rescuing my good self, and it's a bit early in

286

the planning to be thinking of that. We don't have the counter-spells."

"That's why we need access to the Hall, to find the spells and counter-spells. Look, can you see these pictures of the architect's plans for Wyvern Hall?"

"I can, but I have never seen most of the actual building itself you understand, so I'm not sure what you want me to identify."

"We're looking for ways into the castle, and think we have found a way by climbing up the escarpment at the back where there is no moat and no wyvern guards. Then we need to know about possible servants or guards inside the castle and how to avoid them."

"I have never seen any human beings other than Wyvern himself. As to other beings, Cora and a few other fairy dragons visit me, as do the crows and ravens. And the rodents, I have had some interesting conversations with the rats. Ah... *the rats.*

"Kate, listen to me, it is dangerous both to climb vertical cliffs and to break into the Hall. And after that you would have to spend weeks searching out every possible hiding place with no guarantee of finding anything useful and danger dogging your every step. It is both hazardous and wasteful. Besides, I have just had a much better idea!"

"But Chauncey, we need human eyes, ears and hands to find something like these spells, they could be in a book, or a drawer, or locked in a trunk or hidden in a false wall or an ordinary safe. Cora and the fairy dragons can't deal with any of those." said Kate.

"Rats, my lovely Kate, rats!" Chauncey was nearly crowing with delight at her amazed face. "How do you think I got that old video recorder working—not with these hands!" Holding up his enormous front legs to show her his equally enormous hands. "Rats did it for me— they've got very good hands, very clever, and clever minds too. Much more clever than most people believe. The only better animal I can think of for the job would be an octopus, and it would never survive long enough out of water. Not to mention I don't happen to have one.

"So rats it is! I have legions of rats available to me, and they will do whatever they can. No really good opposable thumbs of course, but using both front feet and working together they can open most locks and many drawers, and even manipulate large volumes. As to locked doors, that's rarely a problem for a rat—they just go through the walls and make a hole in a baseboard behind a large piece of furniture. And they can climb almost anything. Things they can't—well, the ravens or crows can fly up. And the ravens bring me things. They can manage things almost as heavy as they are for short distances.

"Then, if we are extremely fortunate in finding them, I can send the ravens to you carrying the papers or scrolls with the spells. Or if necessary you intrepid climbers can come and check out the likely places where they might be hidden. Rats are much better at finding secret hiding places than any human could be. If they are here we will find them." Chauncey beamed benevolently.

"That's brilliant, Chauncey! That would certainly save us from having to come and go a number of times into the Hall. But if they don't find anything, or can't get in certain places?" asked Kate.

"Then you'd better learn how to climb, young Kate," rumbled Chauncey. "But at least we can narrow things down and eliminate so much. And meanwhile, if you have half the powers Maggie is guessing you do, then learning to use and control them would be top of your to-do list I think."

"Definitely," said Maggie. "Kate, tomorrow school is going to change. You, Perry and Robin are all going to be getting a cram course in everything magical that Kailen and I can teach you. And learning as much as possible about how much and what kinds of abilities you have.

"Chauncey, now that you can be in contact with us, shall we meet every evening to update ourselves and share what we've been doing?"

"Most definitely my dear Maggie. The only caveat would be if and when Wyvern is here. It is of course imperative that he doesn't get wind of what we are doing. Knowing I'm in contact with the outside world would ring all sorts of alarm bells in his already paranoid brain. I believe we must work carefully to keep the monsters in the dark."

Chapter 47

As usual, Perry, Kate and Robin were in the library at Ashley Manor the following morning. Unusually, Maggie and Kailen were also there. Or, Maggie was there and Kailen was there 'in essence' because, as one of the Fae, the iron in the spiral stairs and the walkways for access to the upper shelves would have made him feel ill and blunted his magic had he actually been in the room.

In addition, though any number of explanations for Maggie's presence would suffice, the presence of a tall, dark man with his hair drawn back into dozens of braids and wearing only a loin cloth and a bow and quiver of bronze-tipped arrows would not have been so easily explained. So Kailen was there by using FaceTime (magic wasn't always the most efficient way to connect, in this case wifi and iPads worked as well or better), while he himself sat in comfort in one of the gardens of their house over the stream.

The library itself was one of Kate's favourite rooms in Ashley Manor, as wonderful in its way as any of the magical rooms in Maggie's house. An oblong room rising up three stories through the house, it combined elements of the Medieval and Rococo with some Victorian Gothic—and what should have been a hodgepodge of styles somehow resolved into a room of pleasing proportions. It wasn't cosy, it was grand. The cast iron that would have troubled Kailen so much was present in abundance in the beautiful spiral stair rising up past shelf after shelf, with openings off it to cast iron walkways giving access to what seemed numberless shelves of books. The cast iron of both stairs and walkways was embellished with a wonderful forest of plants and animals, including any number of mythical beasts. All home to many, many thousands of books, all shelved by subject, which were indicated in some cases by the kind of plants or animals or other decorative detail in the ironwork. All of this richness was topped by a domed ceiling rising up yet again with windows all around giving light and airiness to that upper area.

And the dome itself—that was a wonderful meringue of Rococo plasterwork centred with a fresco painting of the muses of all the arts in a delicious palette of nature's own colours, the cerulean of sky, the pastel palette of sunset, the spring greens of a garden fit for goddesses, who were there: Calliope, Muse of Poetry; Clio, Muse of History; Euterpe, Muse of Music and Lyric Poetry; Erato, Muse of Love Poetry; Melpomene, Tragedy; Polyhymnia, Hymns; Terpsichore, Dance; Thalia, Comedy, and Urania, Muse of Astronomy, all dressed as Greek maidens and each with her identifying emblem.

Kate knew them all from her many hours lying on her back both on the splendid Savonnerie rug before the fireplace (also with a cast iron fire surround imitating a forest) and on various levels of the shelves—she had studied them and looked them up and applauded the artists who seemed to get their plaster and paint to embody these creatures of myth.

The usual curriculum was shelved for the foreseeable future while the new courses were laid out before the three students.

"No more algebra, geometry or trigonometry!" crowed Robin. 'Now we get to make things—err—move? Or transform? Oh, okay, Mum, I see the way you're looking at me, I'll shut up now." He grinned at her and folded his hands in pretend meekness. She couldn't help laughing.

"We need to find out what areas you are gifted in, for which we need to do some testing." As she spoke Maggie was handing each of them several small stones, some were gem stones, some granite or slate or limestone. This time there were no inscribed symbols on them.

"Oh, no, Mum—more tests?" Robin was mock-annoyed.

"Oh, yes, my child, more tests. But you will enjoy these. The secret is to not allow yourself to get frustrated, or try too hard or force things. I believe the phrase used to be to 'hang loose'. The harder you try, the less you will be open. Magic uses its practitioners as a channel. So that requires you to relax and allow that channel to open. Tension serves to narrow or dam a channel.

"That also means magic can be quite dangerous to those who practice it. Attune yourself to dark magics and you can become as something blasted by lightning. So in addition to making yourself a channel, you need to clear your mind of dark emotions: the obvious ones like anger and revenge and envy but also those that are more subtle — ambition, desire for power or fame. To be a proper channel for power is to become aligned and open to the forces of good in the universe. It is not to claim power for yourself, but to be a vehicle, in some senses a servant of that power, and so it is obvious that to become a servant of the dark is as destructive to you as it might be to that which you wish to destroy or claim power over. In other words, my dears, don't go over to the dark side!

"In our case it means that our anger and pain and feelings of sorrow and lust for revenge against those that have hurt us or those we care about—those feelings must be shelved. Later, when you have become adept at making a channel and being able to focus the power that comes through—when you have mastered this and mastered your own emotions, then and only then can a sudden blast of anger turned outward be used to light the force you have channelled and use it as a weapon when necessary. But that is down the road a way. So, no fireballs, not for awhile yet. This especially means you, Robin!"

292

"Aw, Mum, I didn't even know I had any magic until you told me I did and you'd bound it. We might have a serious talk about that by the way—no one asked me, you know! So don't go on about fireballs at me, okay?"

"You used to set fire to your bed at least once a week!" said Maggie with a grin. "We couldn't leave you to incinerate the place, let alone burn yourself. We had to do something!"

"What? When was that?" Robin was gob-smacked.

"When you were a few months old. I'm afraid having a little talk with you wasn't on the cards then. And I was in London studying and leading what was supposed to be a normal life in a rental apartment. 'Oh my, whatever would the neighbours think?' " Maggie's smile said she knew that phrase was standard issue for young teens the world over to describe how circumscribed their lives were by parents who didn't understand.

"Anyway, my love, you get to go first. You already made a channel that allowed nets of healing flowers to flow as the universe directed them. Now I want you to relax into that space you found the other night and, taking those pebbles one at a time, see what picture comes into your mind and try to project that out to us. Don't worry, your magic, whatever it encompasses, is freed of any shackles now. So whatever is in you to do you should be able to do. Only stay away from fire! And that same warning applies to you all."

Kailen laughed, "Apprentice wizards set fire to listed library—what a headline! I can only echo Maggie's warning. Nothing fiery, even if one of these stones seems to indicate fire. At that point just put it down and tell us what appeared in your mind."

Robin looked distinctly uncomfortable to have to go first. It crossed his mind that, after all, maybe his powers weren't up to much. Part of him so wanted to impress, but he understood the bit about pride and he tried to calm himself by looking at the small scatter of stones in front of him. Did any of them call to him? Nada, zilch, nothing. He turned his head away and reached out blindly for a pebble. This one felt slightly rough and with a shallow depression on one side. He didn't look at it, he closed his eyes and felt it all over, his fingertips noting the subtle differences. His inner vision was filled with a picture of a jug, one that was of a reddish-brown clay decorated with a pattern of triangles and painted with rather sickly green stripes. He imagined himself reaching out and picking up the jug with his free hand and gently placing it on the table in front of him. He could feel it now — just as he felt the pebble or shard in his right hand he felt the shape of the jug with his left. There were gasps from Perry and Kate. Robin opened his eyes and saw that the jug was indeed there, on the table, with his left hand resting on it. "Holy crap," he breathed.

"You did it—you made something appear!" Perry was pounding him on the back.

"Did it come down a channel like something out of a tube?" queried Kate. "Why a jug?"

Robin shook his head. "No tubes, no, I just felt the shard here and it gave me a picture of this jug and I reached out with my other hand and picked it up and put it here. It was all so simple. But there was no jug and now there's a jug. Why the jug, Mum?"

"Because this shard must have been a part of a clay jug just like this one. It was telling you what it was and you made a channel for a similar jug to arrive here.

Perry said, "I think it's from a prehistoric period and possibly not British—it could be something that was traded for tin a few centuries BCE, or it could be an antiquity sold at auction to someone around here and it got broken. But now we have a whole one." He reached out to touch the jug and his hand went right through it. Again the

294

rest gasped, this time Maggie as well. "Well," she said, recovering herself, "it would appear that this jug is only Robin's to hold. Robin, can you try to give it to Perry?"

Robin picked up the jug and offered it to Perry. This time it was substantial. "Well, I'll be damned." he breathed turning it gingerly in his hands. "But isn't there some law of nature that says if this is here now, it's not somewhere else? Like in someone's curio cabinet or a museum?"

"I honestly don't know," replied Maggie, "I'm an accountant, not a physicist. Okay, I'm a witch too. I suspect this has not been on this plane of existence before or your hand wouldn't have gone through it at first, Perry. And if it's only magical it will go back to wherever such things go, but as I think it may be tied to the shard that conjured it, it may stay here. Kailen, what do you think?"

"Beats me," her partner answered, grinning. "But I'm for burying it at a crossroad with a stake through it."

"Oh, Dad, you can't—it's magical, not evil," said Robin, feeling protective of his first magical object.

"Well," chimed in Kate, 'if you two don't know, then is Robin magical in ways you don't understand?"

"That is quite possible," replied Kailen, "As the son of a witch and a faerie he is likely to possess each of our magics and to have or to develop new ones of his own. It's one of the reasons we bound his magic until he was old and settled enough to handle what will definitely be some surprises."

"Ha!" exclaimed Robin to Kate. "You're not the only one with powers you never knew you possessed. Now there are at least two of us. We can be The Dastardly Duo and fight evil wherever we find it!"

"Maybe you'll be the Terrible Trio," said Kailen. "Perry, I'm counting on you to put the boys in the ascendency on the male side of being magical. Let's see what you can do."

Perry had been feeling that he might just as well give up before he started as he'd spent some time staring at his pebbles without really seeing them, and realised that he was very, very nervous. That was never going to allow him to become a channel. He thought of how he had held the jade in his hand and it had soothed him and he had made a connection to Cora. Now he brought his attention firmly forward to the different specimens before him. It had been easier when he was given one—now he must choose. He extended his hand, not closing his eyes as Robin had. He felt he needed every sense he had. Each of his stones appeared to be a gem stone of some kind. He ran his hand gently just above the little collection and...felt one reach out. No, that was not quite it—but it was somehow letting him know it was there. He lowered his hand to it and grasped it gently. Turning it over he saw he'd picked up a round emerald green stone with six rays of lighter green coming from its centre. They were so symmetrical he wondered if he'd been drawn to a synthetic stone or man-made trinket.

He closed his eyes and felt the emerald in his hand. Thoughts were scattered here and there through his mind—a man-made object would lead to another object, a synthetic might lead him to plastic, which he instinctively shied away from, it felt so cool and at home in his hand. He felt it change just slightly and a small hummingbird appeared in his mind's eye, its throat coloured like the emerald, all glinting feathers shining and glowing. He extended his other hand and the bird gently stepped onto his finger. He reached out and let the bird perch on the edge of the jug Robin had conjured earlier. This time there were gasps of wonder and gentle clapping from the watchers as the exquisite bird appeared to them. It shook its feathers and flew to Kate, as if saying, okay, two of us have exhibited ourselves, now it's your turn.

296

Maggie was looking quite impressed and pleased. "Perry, it seems you have a gift for living things. This lovely bird is from Ecuador, as is the stone. But I have to say I am quite impressed with both of you—you not only have shown us what it is you experienced, you have given it reality, or allowed it to take on reality. I expected pictures either projected outward for us all to see or appearing in our heads, as Chauncey did with Kate and me. You have given us the reality. Kate, are you ready for your try? You know how to create channels. Shall we see what one of these pebbles says to you?

Kate also felt absurdly nervous, staring down at the seemingly random collection of small stones Maggie had set before her. She wondered how Maggie had chosen them, if they were specially designed to bring out the talents of her fledgling witches or if they were just a random collection. Maggie wasn't telling. Kate stared at the handful, noting that they were all seemingly beach stones, worn smooth, of various colours and shapes. She ran her hand over them, touching them lightly, then, different to the boys, picked each one up and held it for a moment. After that she looked once more, and now her witch's inner eye, her channel, opened and what she saw was indeed water, water like staring into the ocean. The stones seemed to be scattered across the bottom and fish of various kinds, but each seeming to be of a similar colour and pattern to a stone, swam around. She pulled back and saw that it was huge, it was the ocean—she couldn't bring that forth to the table. But she reached her other hand out and passed it over the vision in her mind, and the area shrank down, glass sides appeared and it was all only about one foot by two by two. Still, a lot of water, a lot of mass, she couldn't lift it. Or could she? She brought her hand back, keeping her other hand over the real stones on the table, and then used both hands to shape the aquarium on the table, where it grew under her hands like a living

297

thing, complete with pebbles, water and fish. Again there were gasps and clapping.

"I couldn't lift it out of my vision, not with all the water and fish, it was too heavy, and I would have flooded the place. So I had to create it already in place for you to see," said Kate. "It isn't taking the vision from my mind and transferring it, I had to make it new. I hope that is okay,"

"Oh, my stars," said Maggie. "It's more than okay, it's almost miraculous. I've never seen it done that way. You used all the stones and you made them part of the thing you called forth."

They all sat contemplating the table now hosting an aquarium, a pre-historic jug and a small iridescent bird. The three students were both pleased and in awe of what they'd managed to do. But it was Robin who put into words what they were also thinking. He stood up and began to circle around in front of the fireplace, gathering his thoughts.

"Mum, Dad, it's incredible that we have each brought something from, well, nothing, or from some contact our minds made with these stones, it seems like very strong magic. But... well, okay, what's the point? We can feel something and it puts us in touch with another part of it, or something related to it and we can actually manifest that new thing. But I don't see how that relates to finding what we really need. What can we touch that would lead us to the spells that Wyvern used to enslave the dragons? For that matter, this seems sort of random—I got a jug, but Perry got a bird, the bird isn't part of or closely related to the emerald. And Kate saw all her stones in the sea and made an aquarium to hold her vision here. It's all confused. It's not carefully connected and it seems almost random. I mean, I could have got the person who made the jug and Perry could have got a ring with an emerald, or Kate just one fish. I'm not trying to say this isn't amazing, it's super amazing, but it doesn't seem very useful. And we didn't do any spells—hell, we don't *know* any spells!" Robin, who had been pacing and waving his hands around as he marshalled his thoughts, now sat down. "Oh, crumbs, I'm sorry, I don't want to spoil the moment, but this is confusing."

It was Maggie who put a comforting hand on his shoulder, but Kailen who answered via the iPad. "You're absolutely right, of course, as practical magic goes this is hit or miss to say the least. But it's how Maggie and I thought we might find out more about each of your talents without imposing a strict regime of spells or potions or anything at all that would keep you from just flying free to produce something magical. We didn't even chose the stones you got—we made it as random as possible while still giving you something to focus upon. And we got what seem to be very random results. Certainly not practical for the battles we must wage.

"However, we got so much amazing talent and information—with this we can help you shape your magic, adding spells and even potions. But we now have a sort of base on which to build."

Maggie spoke up too. "Perry has a wide-ranging talent using, if only subconsciously, so much of his knowledge—how else explain how a rare emerald would transform itself into an iridescent bird where the only commonality is the colours and the country of origin? Robin, you have an affinity for things of the earth—in other words, mineral as opposed to animal or vegetable things] and possibly for made things as well—so shaping a jug could equally become shaping a weapon. Kate, you saw an entire world—the ocean—and then you transformed it into something that could be safely placed on a table top without damaging any of the components. That is quite stunning and original. By which I mean I don't know of any witch who has ever done anything remotely like it. It must have so many possible applications." Maggie made each of them feel that what they'd achieved more than met her hopes and that building upon their raw talent would be like giving an artist the right tools for the job.

But it was Perry who came in now. "I'm more delighted than I can say to find that I have these abilities. But how did you know that I might? I certainly didn't. You knew your son was, and you sensed that Kate was, but I wasn't exhibiting any talent for it at all."

Maggie laughed. "Perry I've been watching you first as my assistant in the auction house, then when you came to help me at the antique shop. No, you had no idea that you had magical abilities. But I watched as you intuitively matched things together, as you followed some trail known only to yourself tracking down a reference or a record, as you made exact valuations and identifications of objects. All of what most might have called just an instinctive talent for research I could see was more than that. Statistically—and never forget I'm a whizz of an accountant—your success rate was way above the best others could do. I thought then that you were using magic, but I couldn't 'see' it clearly as such. Indeed I thought at the time you would have an aptitude for material, man-made things like art and antiques. But I was sure you had magic, the kind that made far-reaching connections. The surprise was to find that you have such an affinity for living things as well as man-made things. Rest assured that when I suggested you as a tutor for Kate and Robin I was as sure as I could be that you would also be magical."

Chapter 48

"Can I try again? I have an idea," said Kate. "I won't use the stones, please."

"Go ahead, Wonder Woman," said Robin. "What about a Great White Shark?"

"Oh, don't be silly," Kate spoke without thinking because she was already lost in her inner vision. She was envisioning the nine muses on the ceiling, but trying not to envision the painted figures but real goddesses, one in particular —Clio, Muse of History. She was working her way through the tangles that separated fact from fiction. And it was fiction in a way that she was after. She didn't want what had happened to Ivor—the spirit in the statue of Shakespeare that was really just the Devon farm labourer who posed for the statue. She didn't want to call forth the spirit of the woman who posed for the Clio on the ceiling. Good grief, that was *necromancy*! And she wouldn't want to do that, ever! No, she wanted the 'real' Muse of History, i.e. the mythical one. Which is why she wasn't focussed in on the painted ceiling, but internally, sending her channels outward as a million probing tendrils feeling for something that would indeed be the Muse of History.

If I'm going to do magic, Kate reasoned, I *have to let go of mythical versus real and be open to the possibility that something that has existed as an idea, a legend, a myth for all these centuries will have a reality somewhere, just like dragons, and it needs to be one I can talk to. What Terry Pratchett would call an 'anthropomorphic personification'.*

Her mind collided with another! Oh! she squeaked, startling her table-mates. "Ow!" came the reply, "Who in Hades are you?" And the Muse of History appeared. She was old, but erect and sharp-eyed. Kate saw a Maggie Smith lookalike in a white flowing robe and a diadem of laurel leaves, carrying a book. Kate stood up and made a curtsey, "I'm Kate Mallory and I need your help." And with those words the rest of her group could see Clio, Muse of History, in the room.

"Oh, what a very fine library!" commented Clio, staring around her. "And the Muses on the ceiling—well, I can't say we ever looked like that. I can't say I ever looked like this, either." Her hand passed over her face and down her robe. "Human form is not my usual dwelling of choice, and if it is occasionally a necessary habitation, I wouldn't choose to be so, err, ancient."

"Dwelling?" queried Robin.

The Muse of History stared down her fine aquiline nose at him. "Boy, stand when you address me!" Robin did as he was told. *Definitely Maggie Smith*, thought Kate.

Clio turned back to Kate. "With what do you need my help, and—out of curiosity—how did I get here at all?"

"I, err, I suppose you could say I summoned you, or conjured you up. I did it because we need help with an historical event. Can you see back through *all* of human history?" asked Kate.

"I can, at least that part of it that has happened since man first created me. One day nothing, the next, fusst! there I was, Muse of History, observing…well, everything. But if you need help, why not just read history in any of these thousands of books? It's a lot of trouble to summon me they tell me." She visibly preened. Kate thought it better not to tell her that actually it hadn't been all that hard.

"Because what we need to know is not in a book, it wasn't a great event done by famous people. But the results have been catastrophic for a few people and could be for many more. We want to know how it started. If you witnessed it, we will know how it started and we can make plans to end it."

"Oh, no! You cannot go back and change history. I can promise you that is catastrophe if you like, ask anyone who's tried it—never works, always ends badly. I have to step in actually, and eradicate the intervention, which also means eradicating those who intervene."

"Oh, we don't want to change what has already happened, we just need to know what happened to start it and that knowledge we hope can help us to cope with it and find a way to end it. As of now we don't even know what really we are up against. That's the starting point. We need to know that."

The Muse of History sat down at the table, where Perry had courteously pulled out a chair. She gave him the barest nod of recognition. "I'm not some djinn you conjured out of a jar, here to do your bidding you know."

"We apologise if we've disturbed you or made things in any way difficult," interceded Maggie. "We are in great need, there have been such cruelties done to people who are innocent of any wrong doing and it's been going on for over a century. We would be so grateful if you could help."

"When and where did this event occur?" The Muse was inclined to be gracious when met with gratitude.

"In the mid-19th century, we think, and in London. We know it was in London."

"A time of great events and many smaller cruel ones, how do you expect me to find one amongst so many?" Clio was dismissive. "Now if you had a name…"

"But we do! It's Ivor Wyvern and he, we think, went from genteel poverty to great wealth and power virtually overnight. And we think it was due to something supernatural."

"Ah, Wyvern…Wyvern…" Clio was apparently scrolling something through herself, she had that inward look as she sifted. "Here, and, umm, here… Wait…whoa, that was a distinct dip in reality there. Yes, your Wyvern was clearly, umm, maybe not so clearly…"

With the look of someone recalled from far, far away, she settled herself and brought both hands palm down on the table with something of a bang. "If I had seen that clearly at the time I would have intervened I can tell you. But it appears that even I, Clio, Muse of History, had the wool pulled over my eyes, erm, so to speak.

"But what I do have is this." And before them appeared Wyvern walking down the street, a young man, late teens or early twenties, in 19th century dress, stopping outside a grand house. And what they heard was this:

"In there," said a voice whose owner they couldn't see. A very young Ivor Wyvern went up the stone stairs past the stone wyverns and under the coat of arms carved into the stone lintel.

He was saying, "It belonged to my grandfather, before my imbecile parent got his hands on his inheritance."

"Well, it's yours now." said the other voice.

"Won't people notice?"

"People see what they want to see."

"No" said Ivor. "They have sharp eyes and sharper tongues when it comes to sudden wealth and elevation of station. They won't accept this. There will be too many questions."

"Well, let's just say there will be a slight adjustment to the timeline. You've always been here sort of fing. You'll get used to it *very* quickly once we've done the contract and all that stuff."

"And *then*," said Clio with distaste and even anger, "there is a disturbance in the time line and it became just as that voice said—he'd always been there. I missed it! The only way that could happen would be if something of great power was messing with it and could shield it from me. And that is intolerable. I will *not* be having with it!"

Perry couldn't quite leave that alone. "But isn't it true that it is the victors who write the histories? Doesn't that change the truth?"

"Oh, truth, pah! What's truth? As you say, the victor gets to propagate his version of the truth. That's just part of history. History is…everything …the lies, the betrayals, the truth, the versions of the truth. I can show you things that actually happened. What you make of them, that will be your 'truth'. But the real truth? I'm not in that business, I just record things, and leave it up to you and these," a wave of her arm took in the library and all its books "to sort it out and disseminate the latest 'truth'."

"If you can show us what actually happened, can you follow him, or them, now? We think what happens next may be crucial." said Kate.

"I *can* do that. But why should I?" sniffed Clio.

"Because it would help?" offered Kate a trifle helplessly.

Maybe it was what Clio saw in her eyes, maybe it was simply a whim (gods and goddesses are very prone to whims), but she inclined her head and, in a gesture that reminded more than one of the people present of the Ghost of Christmas Yet to Come, she pointed a bony finger and Wyvern's study appeared with Ivor and the Chimaera talking. And they saw and heard the entire exchange, including the contracts and the 'merger'. Plus they now knew for certain that Ivor was a double-being and the identity of his alter-ego, his Body-Buddy was a Chimaera Mutabilis calling itself Proteus. This fitted with what Chen Shi had speculated, and now they knew it to be true, and how it had been done. And why there was this vendetta against dragons.

"Ah, I see, yes, a most formidable power," murmured Clio. "I knew it couldn't be just another jealous god who messed with the time-line like that and concealed it from me. I would like to wipe him and his nasty power out of history, so I would!" And with a furious swipe of her arm she erased the scene and startled the rest of them.

"So is that what you just did?" asked Robin. 'Eradicate the Chimaera? Restore the time-line?"

"Ummph! I'm afraid I can't do that. Not anymore. This little blink of the eye that changed things for Ivor Wyvern is like a pebble dropped into a quiet pool. Catch the pebble just as it hits the water and you change history back into its designated path at that moment. Change it now and all those ripples—over one hundred years of history—will be wiped out and changed to whatever it might have been. Everything, everything would change. And not necessarily for the better. You all might not even exist.

"If I ever intervene when some nincompoop messes with the time-line it has to be *at the very moment.* Then I can wipe it away and history continues as it should. But now—however much I wish to destroy that puffed-up foreign interloper swanning in from another reality like he owns the place—I cannot. It would literally destroy this world. No, this one you have to handle, just as you've been planning. I hope you have some good plans. This is not going to be easy, not easy at all. If I can be of some more help, I will try to find information for you, but I can't dirty these hands you understand." And with that she simply faded away.

"Get her back!" demanded Robin. "She can show us how they enchanted the dragons and what the spells are."

Kate was looking exhausted. "I don't know if I can, or if she would…"

A faraway voice called back "The bastard screened that from me too, there's a blank, just a blank. You'll have to cope. There's something in a store room, look in the cellars, or maybe the attics… A room with no windows I think…" the voice faded away.

Kate looked up, dazed. "I think she's embarrassed to be seen by humans unable to find her references. She's a goddess, she doesn't like being fallible, she really, really doesn't like letting us see that. I'm not sure she'll be available again."

"How do you know that?" asked Perry.

"I can, err, sense her feelings, there's a lot of embarrassment, and that's covered over with a really thick blanket of anger."

"But *we* didn't catch her out, that Proteus did. She shouldn't be angry with us." Robin was pretty angry himself.

Maggie gave Kate a hug. "You did wonderfully well, getting her here, amazing. Robin, she's not angry with us, she's furious at being deceived, but she's mightily embarrassed to have to discover that in front of a bunch of humans. We've seen her make a mess of her job, if you will, or being made a fool of, and however politely we treat her, she won't want to see us again, ever."

"That's the trouble with bloody anthropomorphic personifications—they are as touchy, more touchy in the case of gods, even than people. Take on a human form, get a double dose of human sensitivity. Thin-skinned as hell, your average god." Kailen was extremely put out that they wouldn't be getting any more help from the Muse of History when it had started out so promisingly.

But just as they were convinced they would never see her again, Clio suddenly appeared in their midst, looking as if she'd been through a wind tunnel, hair wild and garments torn. She was looking furious. "I couldn't help myself, I thought—that evil bastard Proteus should be eliminated. I did what I knew was not allowed, was in fact impossible. I just said to myself, bugger the timeline, this is Earth's enemy, not just yours, and I went after him. But time won't be toyed with like that, not in such a big way. Just as I told you, it would have ripped up this reality and skidded the whole of history in another direction. So various doors were slammed in my face. However, I did manage to get this scrap of nastiness." She drew from her robes what looked like a fragment of skin, dripping with blood. "Make of it what you will. It won't solve your problems, but it could strengthen your resolve." She dropped it on the table like a soiled towel. "And that's me done. I need a rest—being bounced around in a black hole is not something I intend to do ever again." And she was gone.

They stared at the grisly object on the table for a bit, then Maggie put her hands over it and the vision appeared.

Ivor, an older Ivor, was standing over a dragon chained down on what looked like a huge rack, the kind used for torturing people by dislocating all their joints. The dragon's long neck was stretched out painfully and Ivor was slicing it with a knife along its neck and lapping the blood and biting it, and it was screaming. He himself was bloody about the face, chest and arms, dragon's blood, not his. And he seemed to be in a sort of blind ecstasy. Then Maude appeared from behind Ivor screaming Stop! Stop! And he turned and without so much as word plunged the knife into her breast and Maude fell to the floor.

And then Ivor was screaming: "You…you… fiend, monster, abomination! You've killed her! She was MINE!! She was everything to me. You… you used my body, my arm, my magic—you destroyed everything for me!"

The entity that was Ivor and Proteus stood over the slumped body of Maude, the poisoned knife protruding from between her ribs. The young dragon chained to the rack, its neck dripping blood, was quiet and shocked.

"She had no business being down here, you know that, you know that she would have loathed you for what we were doing. There was no way we could allow her to see this and live. You know that's why you estranged yourself from her in a vain attempt to keep her safe." Proteus was cold and pitiless. His opinion and care for humanity was low to the point of non-existence.

"We could have worked a forgetfulness spell, I would have soothed her mind and she would forget." wailed Ivor.

"No we could not, she would not—she was a woman of high emotion, she would not forget."

Suddenly, Maude's body gave a gasp and a shuddering cry. Her hand fluttered upward toward the knife in her chest.

"She's not dead!" cried Ivor, dropping to his knees and clasping her hand to keep her from further injuring herself. "We must help her, we must get help."

"That isn't going to happen. Anyway, you know the knife is designed with a poison to allow it to pierce dragon scales, and that will prove fatal to her in time. There is nothing a human doctor could do."

"Then we must do something, reverse the poison, give an antidote, *save her*! She's mine! She's mine, I *will* have her!"

"She will hate you henceforth—she will never be yours again. You should make her a statue in which her spirit can dwell where you can visit her. Send her to be with Eleanor. Sister and bride, how fitting. And you and I will be free to pursue our ends without fear of discovery."

"You cold, miserable, pitiless bastard! I should never have trusted you with dominion over my body even to give you the pleasure of the dragon's pain. You have deprived me of the one person who truly loved me. I will never again allow you to hold sway here."

"As if you could stop me! Must I remind you of who here is the real immortal? If I leave you, you would fall to bits like a dead moth. We are joined only because I will it. You would do well not to forget that." Proteus' voice was cold and certain, but Proteus himself was not so certain as he sounded. The watchers in the library could tell because in this vision they had access not just to what was happening but to what these beings were thinking and feeling as well.

Ivor's skills in the black arts had progressed. Ivor's abilities and Ivor's talent for evil had grown, certainly with the help and encouragement of Proteus. But they were now no longer entirely strengths that the Chimaera bestowed, but some at least were strengths Ivor alone possessed. It was only Ivor's human insecurities that made him still depend so much upon his Body Buddy. Insecurities that Proteus made sure to nurture at the same time as he encouraged Ivor's talents. In truth the Chimaera was no longer certain that Ivor would crumble both mentally and physically if his dark twin left him. Still, no time just now for wandering thoughts, they must keep this human woman alive while Ivor prepared what would be both her memorial and her tomb.

Proteus turned his attention to stopping the coursing of the poison through Maude's blood and steadying her heart. At the same time he did roughly the same thing for Ivor, soothing the poison of doubt and anger, steadying his purpose and lending strength to their body so that Ivor could carry his love, his possession, to a comfortable resting place in his studio where he could nurse her and work on the sculpture that would be her final resting place. Sculpting and painting were the two things closest to his heart, and those on which he refused to use magic. Because his talent was real, and his alone, and it would be, he felt dimly, an abomination to sully it with magical shortcuts. This did not stop him from the savage

310

pleasure he took in the black art of transferring a living soul into one of his creations. That, he'd convinced himself, was something else entirely.

The vision faded, and the soiled cloth or skin upon the table also simply curled up like a dried leaf, then scattered to dust that blew away. The five around the table sat stricken at having witnessed first-hand the reality of Maude's story as they had heard it in the garden all those weeks ago. Each and every one of them felt like no amount of hot showers would serve to wash away those gruesome images.

Clio was right, it didn't solve the problem, but it made them yearn to visit all the torments of hell on Ivor Wyvern and Proteus.

Chapter 49

Robin and Kate were wading in the river, balancing precariously sometimes on the stones and pebbles on the bottom as the rush of the water tried to bowl them over. Kate was still thinking of her encounter with the Muse of History and discovered yet again one of the laws of nature—when your balance is precarious you need to be paying careful attention to where you put your feet and not let your mind wander. Her foot slipped into a gap between stones, and she went crashing face down into the water. Robin was there in an instant, lifting her, but her ankle was trapped between stones and she yelled as he turned her. "My foot, Robin, my foot, it's caught!"

"Oh crap," he breathed, as he managed to lower her so her head was safely out of the water while he felt down her leg to where her ankle and foot disappeared between two stones. He tried to move one but it was deep into the stream bed and held in place by others. Frustrated, he sent an angry gesture at it, wishing it away, and was astonished when it lifted out of the stream bed and simply rolled away. Kate pulled her foot free, and was scrabbling in the water trying to regain her footing. Robin wrapped his arms around her and lifted her up.

Suddenly they were face to face, bodies pressed together, with the water flowing around them at thigh height. Kate felt pleasure suffusing her body, the warmth of Robin's hands supporting her back was spreading wonderful feelings. She was looking into his eyes and found there the same feeling of surprise and wonder that she was experiencing. Before either of them could say something stupid and ruin the moment, Robin moved one hand up to cup the back of her head and kissed her. It was a long kiss. Planets were born and died during that kiss. The shock of it, the sweetness of it, the feelings that were awakened in parts of them they thought they knew, but were now exhibiting previously unknown intensity of sensation.

"Is this magic too?" asked Robin when they finally broke apart. He helped her to the bank, where they sat on the moss under an oak tree and watched the water, carefully not looking at each other.

"What, like you moving the stone to free my foot? No, I think it's a different kind of magic, our magic maybe." Kate was staring at his hands, the hands that had moved a stone with magic and held her so protectively. "I mean our magic together, just for us, between us."

"Just for us," Robin repeated, taking her hand in his. With his hair wet his pointed ears showed and his golden-brown eyes with their slight up tilt made him look less human, more like his father. He pulled her into his lap and kissed her again, holding her protectively and easily. She had had no idea he had such strength and gentleness together. The wise-cracking Robin who was her best mate and fellow trouble-maker seemed far away. This was a new person, someone strong and calm and even more trustworthy. She abandoned herself to his embrace.

Later they walked back along the path toward the junction of the stream with the river. "I wish I'd brought Poppet," said Kate. "She loves to swim."

"I'm kinda glad you didn't," said Robin with a grin. "Can you imagine her bouncing all over us while we were, uh, getting to know each other better?"

Kate laughed. "Oh stars, yeah, she would have been doing that. Talk about spoiling a moment! Still, I will bring her here soon so she can play in the water."

"Meanwhile, we need to collect Perry and go to the climbing wall. How's your ankle?"

"I only twisted it slightly. You did just the right thing, not trying to twist me around. And getting rid of that rock—that was so cool." Kate gave his hand a squeeze.

"Did you see that? I thought I'd had to leave you pretty much face down in the water."

"No as in 'see it' exactly, no. I felt it and I could feel you'd used magic. Just think, if you hadn't been able to do that, we might have had to choose between me learning to breathe under water or spraining my ankle!"

"I want to say, 'aw, it was nothing'…but I was totally astonished. I just felt this strong need for it to move—I mean, I was so scared you could drown or get badly injured. Anyway that need seemed to go from my centre down my arm and out at the rock—and it just went. That felt so good. That you were okay, that was so good."

"And it could be so useful—just think, you need to move something and it moves. That could be the turning point in a battle." Kate was again thinking of the probability that they wouldn't be able to get rid of the evil that stalked them all without some kind of a face-off. It would be wonderful if they could do it all by stealth, and they were all determined to make that happen, but she knew they all doubted it too.

§ § §

The climbing wall was not one of her favourite things, she'd always had a thing about heights. When Uncle Hugh had taken her to Cornwall to see where Lucinda's ancestors came from and just to enjoy how lovely it was around the south coast near Falmouth, they'd gone to the north coast also, to see if they could see any seals. Kate remembered a book where a young woman had sung to the seals from the window of her castle on the north coast, and she'd always imagined singing to seals and having them come to her. They didn't find that castle, because she'd mixed up the north coast of Cornwall with the west coast of Wales, but went to Tintagel instead, which was magical in its own right, being said to be where

King Arthur was born. Then stopped along the coastal cliffs where Kate embarrassed herself by having to crawl on her stomach to approach the edge where it dropped over a hundred feet to the sea below, as she simply couldn't bring herself to walk to the edge and look down.

So she didn't look forward to the climbing wall, even though they were safely roped. She knew better than to look down, but it still seemed her whole being knew it was an awful drop.

"Why can't I use magic to levitate myself?" she had asked Maggie, having confessed her fear of heights.

"Because levitating or flying, even if you can do that—and I imagine you probably can—well…there you'd be high up the side of your cliff using magic, and if you hesitated even for a second due to fear of heights, you'd lose the magic and really would fall. Much better to prepare yourself with practice and ropes and crampons, or whatever things you'll need. You can use your magic to calm yourself and to minimise your fear."

"Better surely to take fear away entirely?" Kate was imagining how free she'd feel without any fear at all.

"You'd be in desperate trouble in no time. There are people born who can't feel any pain. You would think that was a great blessing. But they don't usually live all that long—they can get appendicitis or cut themselves severely and not feel a thing. Pain is a friend if it makes us take care of an illness or injury, or even better, try to avoid them entirely. The same with reasonable fear. Totally fearless people—and there are those too—don't usually make old bones either. They put themselves in situations that are almost designed to kill them. No, take your fear, examine it, question whether it is a rational fear or an irrational one. If the latter, I'll bet you'll find the magic that will dissipate it. If the former, then do whatever is needed to protect yourself. That's how to use fear. Just like magic, don't let it use you."

"You always make such good sense, and you always have the answers I need," Kate had said leaning in to embrace Maggie.

So far however, her fear of heights was only diminished, certainly not gone. She couldn't even imagine the day when she'd enjoy conquering that blasted wall, let alone scaling the escarpment that might be the only 'safe' way into Wyvern Hall.

Chapter 50

Every evening after she'd tucked herself up in bed, Kate opened her channel (what Maggie called a witch's third eye) to Chauncey and reported the events of the day. At first she'd tried to limit these to what she thought he would find important, but he kept asking for more details of her day, what she did, how things looked, how she felt. She realised he was hungry to participate in daily life, and with his photographic memory not just for books but for all life events he could easily pick over things that were relevant to their search and ultimate goal and things that simply gave him something interesting or entertaining to think about. Plus it increased their bond to share so much. Bonding with an enormous dragon who, if he were to be believed, was millions of years old, was not something Kate had ever imagined. (So far her hopes for this kind of bond had centred on dolphins and seals and possibly wolves.) But it was proving very educational and entertaining for her as well. Plus it gave her access to all sorts of knowledge and power, including what Chauncey could muster, in spite of his enslavement, of his own great power, to provide her with extra strength for working her magic or even climbing a cliff. It was the least he could do for his adopted daughter, he told her.

"Does this make me a dragon too?" she asked him when he'd announced that he'd adopted her and would do so formally as soon as he was free. "Will I have your powers? Will I fly?"

"In every way that counts," he had replied. "But it's only what you already possess. Except the flying, you won't fly like a dragon, you won't look like a dragon, and you won't suddenly grow wings. But what you do have in common with a dragon is courage, magic, empathy (although sadly I cannot say every dragon has that important quality in abundance). That is why I have decided to adopt you, because you are very like the best kind of dragon—strong but not cruel, a fighter but only when necessary, intelligent (although not so intelligent as a dragon, but I can let you borrow from me if necessary), and courageous."

"But I'm often frightened, so I'm not really very brave." Kate admitted with furrowed brow.

"What idiot taught you that bravery was lack of fear? Every being who hopes to stay alive had fear built in—it's the flight part of fight or flight. It helps us survive when running away is the best strategy. Only what the Vikings called Beserkers had no fear, and that's because they were severely mentally ill. So they were set up as sacrifices in the front lines or as a rear guard while the rest escaped, to slaughter as many of the enemy as possible before they were inevitably slaughtered themselves. No, daughter, bravery is when, even though you are afraid, you face what comes and deal with it as best you can. I'm happy to say you had your Grandmother to nurture that in you, and now you have me."

Despite difference in size and shape, Kate was coming to think of Chauncey as someone who would have been a fine match for her grandmother. Indeed she often felt much as she had with Lucinda—loved and protected and encouraged.

Tonight she told him about walking in the river and how her wandering mind had allowed her to lose her balance and get her foot trapped between rocks and how Robin had used magic successfully to free her. At which point she came to a halt, and felt a blush rising.

"And then the young Prince finally kissed the Princess!" said Chauncey with a verbal flourish and a large grin.

"You're not supposed to be in my head like that!" snapped Kate turning even redder. "We agreed —private is private."

"Ah, sweet girl, I didn't need to invade your mind, it is written all over your face. But I am delighted for you. The two of you together are formidable and with a romantic link even more so."

"I'm not entirely sure about the romance thing…" mumbled Kate. Suddenly talking to Chauncey seemed altogether too much like standing before a parent or a headmaster. "But, there's one thing…I'm feeling so happy, happy in a way I've never felt before. And about Robin of all people! I mean, well, everybody daydreams about who the special person might be, and I was still waiting for someone new to appear—only it was Robin! And now it seems like it could only *be* Robin. But what I'm worried about, guilty about, is being so happy when you and all the dragons are enslaved, and the statues as well and we all may be going into a very dangerous fight. And yet I'm so…happy. Can that be right?"

"Love makes the world go 'round," said Chauncey with a wink. Seeing a head over ten feet from nostril to horn tip winking at her was, well, an experience. As much as she felt she was getting to know Chauncey, he constantly surprised her.

"In all honesty, my dear child, family is what we all need, and a sense of family is what gives us the courage to go into battle and fight like avenging angels (or devils — same thing really) for their survival and safety. You have been the catalyst that has coalesced all of us disparate individuals and species into a family. And a sexual interest is a very strong bond. As your adoptive father, I say go for it! Sex is one of the most powerful forces in any universe. It will help you when the manure hits the hurricane."

"I wasn't thinking of using sex as a battle strategy," mumbled Kate. "But okay, yes, I'm really infatuated, and it's a surprise, I wasn't expecting it."

"Nice surprises are to be treasured. We certainly get enough of the other kind."

"You're right of course. But if you think I'm giving you all the details just because you get a bit bored living in that cellar—well, I'm not. But I'm glad you're happy for me. I'm happy for me too. I hope Maggie and Kailen are okay with it."

"I am never bored! I can entertain myself for centuries if need be." growled Chauncey. "As to Robin's parents, anything that stabilises their son will please them. Like you, he has tremendous powers, and they've been anxious as hell. You are a steadying influence, or rather, caring for you as he does is a steadying influence. You don't have to do anything but love him. And he you of course. Then together you will be more than the sum of your parts."

"Forging a super weapon with sex appeal" Kate couldn't help but smile at the vision it presented. Just like in a graphic novel, or anime, she could see the super-hero vision of her and Robin back to back, facing a circle of Wyverns and demons. Plus Chauncey overhead, hovering with his great wings in a protective posture while one clawed foot grabbed a demon in a death-grip. With a kind of internal flip of a switch she projected this out to Chauncey, who laughed long and hard.

"I will love to see this coming true. And I do believe it will."

"How are the rats doing with the search for documents?" asked Kate as she did every evening.

"Nothing relevant to the spells, but, hells, bells and buckets of blood, what an enormous empire that dreadful animal has gathered in a mere hundred and fifty years!"

"I love it how you think one hundred and fifty is a short time span. That's about two lifetimes for a human. Anything relevant to Ashley in those about his empire?"

"Yes, most definitely, and I've sent them to Maggie. She can, I trust, do wonders with those. The thing I find personally maddening is the vast amounts he charged for one of us—one of the dragons, that is—the big ones. And even a tiny fairy dragon cigar lighter cost the equivalent of a Faberge Easter Egg. Although it is worse to think of them imprisoned, it's pretty damned enraging to think that his personal fortune was built on our slavery."

"A lot of the vast fortunes of humans also started with slavery of other humans, and from what I can gather, a lot of the richest people in the world are still getting richer by making other people poorer. It really makes my blood boil. I love my dad, but I think he's one of those plutocrats too, although he lost most of his fortune through bad investment. And as for my mother, well, she doesn't care about anything but her own personal comfort and pleasure—and to keep her that way takes a lot of money. It makes me grateful that I've got the family I have now, one made up of witches, faeries and dragons and even rats and crows and ravens. I can trust you guys."

"And I you, my daughter, and I you." Chauncey's rumble was contented.

With that they said goodnight and Kate shut down her channel. She thought she might try opening a channel to Robin, but on second thought she didn't. Even though she knew that if she managed to connect, he would accept the 'call', she felt shy of the face to face, or even being the first to send an email. That was definitely the downside of having him for a boyfriend—suddenly she hesitated to be first to make contact, which had never happened before. *We've got to find a way to stay best friends and one of the gang while being*—she hesitated even in her own mind— *in love.*

Chapter 51

It turned out after a number of rather fraught classes where Maggie and Kailen attempted to teach Perry, Robin and Kate the basic essentials of doing magic safely, that their talents differed quite a bit.

All three had perfectly understood the principle of action-reaction and also grasped the idea that turning someone into, say, a toad or a bird would be possible, but leave a lot of extra mass lying about that the practitioner had to deal with in a humane way. That is: one hundred and sixty pounds of human into a two-pound toad won't go. Or, will go, but you're left with 158 pounds of 'stuff' and this must be kept safe from harm until the spell wore off or was reversed. And rejoining this human-recently-toad with his 158 pounds of 'stuff' wasn't nearly as easy as performing the toad spell in the first place. It was in fact very complicated indeed. Hence, no toads, boys and girls, no toads. Unless you want a 160 pound one, in which case that is a whole different world of trouble.

Anyway, a basic rule of magic safety was don't mess with silly tricks, because pull one of those on a friend and you might not find reversing it to be possible.

Doing evil magic damaged the practitioner, even when that was a necessary evil—such as possibly eliminating Ivor Wyvern. However, there were safeguards. One being that you never went up against evil alone. Never being a word that had some elasticity in it, as in when you're out alone and faced with a depraved enemy, then disabling or even destroying them is sometimes necessary.

"In other words," said Kate, "the whole thing is mutable, changing to fit circumstances, and we will be doing this by the seat of our pants most of the time no matter how many classes in magical philosophy we get. Just like real life actually."

Maggie laughed ruefully, Kailen shrugged his shoulders. But Perry applauded and Robin bowed to her.

"I fear that just about sums it up, Kate. So, let's get back to how Maggie and I see your strengths as practitioners," said Kailen.

"Perry, you have real strengths in the area of spell-casting, using spells already devised and possibly making up new ones, or altering others to better suit circumstances. Your power is in language and also in your real affinity with other beings, so you will be able to call upon the birds and beasts of the field and forest to come to you and do your biding to some extent. Hence, if it comes to some sort of war between us and the Wyvern forces, you might for instance call upon flocks of birds to harass or carry messages or even drop small bombs. Or herds of cattle or deer to charge. Don't laugh Robin, large animals en masse running at you, some with sharp horns, are formidable. Perry, you also have the intuitive power to soothe and help both humans and animals with your mind only and, we believe, from a distance. That can be very helpful when trying to encourage someone in danger.

"Robin, you have the ability to call objects to you and to wield them in many ways. You can also create objects out of materials lying around you—turning sand into glass for instance, or calling forth an entire object from a fragment. In this respect you combine your mother's earth-witch talents with some of my own abilities to activate inanimate matter. As you have grown in compassion and understanding, these potentially lethal powers will, I trust, be used only as needed. All of this you do from instinct. Unlike Perry, with his facility for language and making spells that way, you will use intuition, need and intention.

"Kate—ah, Kate. It would seem your spell-casting is powerful, but not so much a function of your quite extensive vocabulary—more like Robin's, a function of intuition and need. In your innermost self you are aware of the many tendrils of being that link all things in this world, animate and supposedly inanimate. In many cases you have only to feel or wish to make it so, but again these are tied to need.

"Becoming a channel and then shaping vast things, this is powerful stuff. Also potentially dangerous, as you can yourself become 'part of the one'—that sounds a bit Zen, I know, but I would alert you to beware of the seduction of that channel you can open, beware of the possibility of its becoming the equivalent of a black hole, sucking you down. Sometimes witches of your persuasion have indeed 'disappeared' in this way and they don't come back.

"So I would suggest that you do some protective spells—easy to master, using words and objects like a circle of protection—before you seek to open any powerful channel and call forth power. However, if there isn't time to create a circle of protection, then the simple words '*Conserva me*' or a plea to Diana, goddess of nature and the moon '*garde-moi en sécurité*' can be said, shouted or just thought as you face danger and reply with magic. You could also ask that of Gaia, primordial mother of all life. Chose one or all, use them in extremis. When you are able to plan ahead, however, a circle of protection and one or more magical friends should be your choice.

"Over to you Maggie."

"You really need five practitioners to make the strongest circle," she said. "One at each of the cardinal points for Earth, Air, Fire and Water and you in the middle, casting the circle. However a single witch can cast a circle without much to-do or even any materials."

Maggie then took them through the process of creating a circle of protection. "This is a basic circle casting which can be performed quickly and easily without the use of tools. Okay, relax and breathe deeply. Imagine making a channel to receive divine, white light. You can widen this channel at your will. Now, open your arms, palms facing out. With each in-breath, visualise yourself pulling down pure, divine light through your channel, and as you breathe out you channel this light out through your palms to create a protective shield around you. You may feel a tingle or buzz, or get goose bumps, or you could feel light and uplifted. All of these are signs you have connected with the, for want of a better word, divine. Now hold your dominant hand outstretched and pointing to the edge of the circle. Spin around clockwise three times, mentally marking out your circle with the divine light. Then raise your arms above your head and say: 'I ask the God and Goddess (or The Powers That Be) to bless this circle so that I may be free and protected within this space. So mote it be.' You are now ready to cast your spell or perform your ritual. To close your circle, hold out your arm and spin around anti-clockwise three times and feel the protective light dispersing. Thank the Spirits for their presence and declare the circle closed."

Each created a circle of protection using this formula. And they then took turns at aiming various magical weapons at a large rock.

Perry stepped up and used a well-thought-out spell to create a blast that shattered chips off the rock but left it essentially unmoved.

Robin presented the obstinate rock with a shower of stone spearheads, designed to shatter it, but the stone remained intact, if battered.

Kate thought briefly and sent streams of water across the intervening space with such force that, against the laws of nature, tunnelled under the rock and presently tumbled it over. "One to me, I think," she commented.

"My next move was going to be to call an elephant," said Perry with a grin. "Although where it would have to have come from is anyone's guess. Pretty sure I shouldn't be summoning animals when I don't know where they are to begin with, might be cruel."

"Yeah, like picked up from the African plains and dropped here." Robin laughed. "Not sure at that point that your average elephant would be willing to shift a rock."

"Or," said Perry, "I could do that bird trick from mythology, taking one crumb of stone away every year, until the stone disappeared. Or was that the bird dripped water on the stone? Either would involve turning a few seconds into a few million years, of course."

"Of course," Kate agreed. "Like that would work in time to foil a villain. I don't think so."

"Hey, we're talking immortal villains here, we could foil him immortally, or eternally. Whatever." Robin was laughing again. The truth was he was delighted with finally having power, and being treated like an adult by his parents. And even more delighted to just watch Kate and feel that, should the need arise, he would lay down his life to keep her safe. Although in truth, it would appear she could probably keep herself safe without his help. Still the memory of her slim body fitting neatly against his, like a custom-made jigsaw puzzle—the missing pieces were now in their proper place and he experienced a feeling of wholeness he'd never known. So, yes, the perpetually discontented, disaffected youth that had been Robin was now glowing with a feeling of belonging.

It was at that moment that Kate looked over to him and smiled a smile that was just for him. And he could hear her inside his head. *"Thanks, Robin, I felt that too— how we fit together, how it makes us happy and that makes us stronger. I always thought of strength through anger, but strength through happiness and belonging, that is grace…how fortunate we are!"*

Chapter 52

Kate was lying under a tree in the wild garden deep in thought. She'd been mulling over the way she did magic, as Kailen had described it, by intuition and need. And spells, she thought, I'm good at spells. But spells were something you carefully prepared beforehand when you had some idea what you'd be up against. That was fine for getting into Wyvern Hall, she would have a veritable arsenal of spells prepared against the wyverns and the 'things' that made the moat into a killing ground, plus any conceivable surprises that might lie in wait as she followed the trail to where Ivor and Proteus had concealed the spells they used to enslave the dragons.

But, once there, other than opening and retrieval spells, plus protective spells and a few that Robin called her 'cherry bombs', she would have to rely on her intuition and need. These had indeed worked well for her in practice, but in a situation of great danger, where fiendish protective spells were a given and an actual attack could not be ruled out, well, the bottom line was she was afraid. *Be afraid,* she was thinking, *Be very afraid. That's from some book or film.* She couldn't remember what.

She texted it to Robin, who answered almost immediately "It's from The Fly, Geena Davis says it. But you're saying it. Are you? You are, aren't you? I'm coming right over."

That's what she loved about Robin. No messing about with 'don't worry' or 'I'll have your back' or even (the worst) 'there's nothing to be afraid of, silly', just 'I'm coming right over'.

And within a few minutes there he was. And she was in his arms, and he was stroking her hair and kissing her neck. And holding her, holding her not just with his arms but with his entire body shielding and protecting her, and he had thrown up a protective shell around them that glimmered faintly and made the world outside seem slightly out of focus. She relaxed against him, and the tears came and she was shaking, which astonished and embarrassed her, but didn't seem to faze him. Her wise-cracking pal and companion in mischief was murmuring, "Let it go then, let it all out, that's my girl, that's what you need. Go on, sweetheart, I've got you."

And some minutes later as they sat together under the tree and he supplied tissues and she was laughing in a slightly shaky way, he said, "You've been wound tighter than an overwound clock, sparks literally flying off you. I knew you'd have to let go, I'm so glad I was here."

Kate pulled herself together after a bit and said, "I am afraid, I'm scared out of my mind really, but I thought I could just stuff it down and get on with what needed to be done. Only I couldn't. I was beginning to think I might crack. Thanks, love, you're right of course, I needed to let it go. I was fighting the fear so hard there was very little left to fight the other things. I'm going to be afraid, but maybe now I can use it."

"Fear can be very protective, fight or flight, and when the time comes you'll probably have to do both. If anyone can, you can. Oh, and I will have your back! And...I'll be afraid too, scared sick probably, but we can do this. Didn't you once say to your uncle that you didn't believe you'd been sent all the way to England just to have to give up? And now that it has turned out you're the lynch-pin in all this, well, it would be really crap if you'd been made the 'chosen one' and not supplied with what you need to do the job. And once Chauncey is free then we have an ally who will scare Ivor puke-green and Proteus back through the dimensions I'll bet."

"I just hope I'm not the bloody chosen one as in the human sacrifice," groaned Kate.

"Do you really think that's what you're destined for?" queried Robin.

"No, not really, or, not much. But I wanted to say it because it's the last bit of the fear I've been hiding—that I might be the pivotal person, but only to be a sacrifice. Truth is I hate pain so much, I'm so scared of it. It's one thing to get hit in the dojo, or even fall and cut yourself, the adrenalin is going, so it doesn't hurt much at the time, and usually only aches later. But...but to be made helpless and tortured—the helpless part, I'm so afraid of that."

Kate shuddered and ducked her head, almost whispering, "Afraid I'd do anything, say anything, to make it stop. I read books where ordinary people are brave beyond anything anyone could expect of them, as if it just kicks in when needed. I don't believe that in real life. I don't think I would get through that. I'd break."

"But you're not an ordinary person! You're not entirely human at all—you're a witch, a magical creature." Robin's hands on her shoulders seemed to give forth strength.

"But I think, since like you once told me, fear paralyses, that we'd better get to work on some good protective spells, including protection against pain under dire circumstances. I don't believe that you are intended to be a sacrifice, if I did I'd take you and run—and to hell with Ashley and your uncle and the dragons.

"Look, I understand your fear, and the best thing for that is preparation. We'll get my mum and dad to help put together some anti-pain spells in case of capture or being wounded, and some disguising spells so we don't get seen in the first place, along with all the ones I've been thinking up for sending the evil army to perdition and freezing Wyvern or something similar.

"Because we both know on some level that we've all come together, our strange group, to do a job, and that it isn't an accident. So stop believing failure is something that could happen."

Kate managed a smile. "You're right of course. I can't believe that any more than I could believe that I came here just to have to go away again. So we aren't running away. After all, I do believe in faeries." Her face, turned up to meet his gaze, was warm and full of trust and sly humour. "And here you are!"

Chapter 53

Every evening Kate would contact Chauncey and find out what, if anything, the cohorts of rats and ravens had unearthed. If there was anything even moderately interesting she would send a sort of mental screen shot to Maggie. Then it was up to accountants to try to run down the sources of funds or what was purchased under expenses. Spells or proto-spells were sent to spellchecker sprites. These folk did not check spelling and punctuation, they were expert at spell casting and historic spells, and are able to 'test drive' spells to see if they were authentic, accurate and efficacious. So far there had been some excitement when a spell for paralysing animals was found, but it proved to be a dud, and tweaking it resulted in a nasty explosion where one faerie's wings were burnt quite badly and the rest of the team had to quit research to apply healing spells for several days.

Then came the night when Kate 'tuned in' to Channel Chauncey and he was grinning (honestly a rather awful sight, all those teeth in a head the size of a small boat).

"Good news!" he boomed it out. "The rats found a casket, but it's enchanted and touching it knocked one of them right across the room."

"Is it all right?"

"The rat—yes, he's bruised and shaken but he'll live—rats are tough. But it means that whatever is in there is really important. I'm willing to guess that it is the spells."

"Couldn't it be some important land deeds or maybe very expensive jewels?" asked Kate.

"We've found plenty of that sort of thing, under lock and key of course, but nothing with a potent spell protecting it before. If Wyvern hasn't be-spelled those other things, then this has to be even more precious. And I'm betting that means it's the important spells."

"So that means we need to get in there and get them! We've been perfecting protection spells and even an anti-pain spell just in case things get nasty. We're as ready as we'll ever be." Kate's heart began to beat somewhat faster and she felt a sheen of sweat. Ready or not, her body was reacting.

But Chauncey held up a cautioning claw. "I think we need to move very carefully here. If that container is enchanted to repel boarders so to speak, then it could also be enchanted to let Wyvern know it's been disturbed. In which case he'll be down here with an army of wyverns and some very nasty spells. Or maybe just the police to arrest trespassers. Or it could be rigged to totally destroy the next being that touches it. Is one of your number able to decode or otherwise figure out what spells are in operation from a safe distance? Or, like bomb squads, disable the spells that guard the casket? Without disabling the spells inside? We need more information before we go in mob-handed."

"You've been watching too much television again." said Kate. "But, dammit, you're right, we can't just rush the place and grab it. Besides, if it is the spells, it probably doesn't also have counter spells and that's what we really need. Which means we have to make them. Time, time, always time. And if you're right about Wyvern then we don't have much time. He could just come and take the casket away with him and hide it somewhere else."

"Unless he needs it here. There's something that I haven't mentioned … about every two years he comes and does the spell again. Prior to that I will have been getting slightly more movement and strength back, but he renews the spell and I am enthralled once more. So maybe he has to have that spell here."

"But then you've heard the spell? You have a photographic memory, you'd remember it, right?"

"I fear not, dear child, no. He first does a simple sleep spell or something anaesthetic, or possibly just knocks me unconscious. I fear I just wake up once more totally enslaved."

"Well, that's a bloody shame. What about all those other dragons he's enslaved and sold? What if they regain strength and movement?   That would ruin his entire business—and they'd be rampaging all over. Does he have a specially trained army of repair people who go around doing 'maintenance' every few years? Because it hasn't happened—that would have been a huge news story."

"I do not know. But, thinking about it, I doubt very much that he has a staff of human beings going around making sure his 'products' remain enthralled. Wyvern as I know him—and I know him better than most because he comes to talk to me—is reclusive and doesn't trust people or want much to do with them. He works under the radar. It's one reason he talks to me—I am a creature to match wits with, and it pleases him to remind himself of how intelligent and powerful I am, yet he, only he and his verminous partner, can keep me helpless.

"Although, wait, just wait a minute. Kate, there is something, if only I can remember it…   You see, for so long now I have had no hope of being discovered at all, let alone rescued, so I have let a lot of what Wyvern says just sort of pass over me. I didn't want to get too excited about some small gem of information he might let drop—and he does drop them, it seems to be part of his pleasure in having me captive. He means to torment me with them, and it works. I find that becoming excited and hopeful about each little drop of information he releases only left me troubled and more helplessly angry. So I have let them just slide away. I have not however lost them entirely—they are here in my brain."

Chauncey then spent some minutes sifting through his mental filing cabinets. Kate could hear him muttering to himself as if he were going through the attics at Ashley "down here maybe....no, not there, somewhere I never go any more...yes, down there where I've put up the 'no-go' signs... it would be there, where I hate to think..."

He resurfaced from his mental wanderings. "I've got it. It's from a long time ago when he was making all the dragons into 'things'. I asked him how he was going to manage keeping them all enthralled and what he'd do if any got loose. I was hoping, you see, that they might. But he told me—oh, this is absolutely crucial—he told me that by enthralling me the spell was designed to enslave every other dragon in this world. That they would come to him here at Wyvern Hall under an enchantment and then remain here like so much raw material to be turned into whatever he wished and sold. And that so long as he renewed the spell upon me periodically so would all the enslaved dragons, no matter how far away, also have the spell renewed and reinforced.

"So quite aside from wanting the glory (even if private) of keeping me, the Dragon King, as his personal slave, it also made it possible for him to control every other dragon through the mystic bond between me and all the others. The only ones exempt from this are the fairy dragons and the wyverns—I have no ethereal bond with those. The faerie dragons he captured he had to enchant separately, and the wyverns, well, apparently the Wyvern family has some bond of their own with those. At the time he told me this, I was mourning not only my own sad state but that I'd been duped into captivity and thereby was responsible for all the others as well. So I did bury that memory as being too painful and maddening.

"But, now, Kate, now, it will be our salvation. Because if you free me, you automatically free all the others! I can think of nothing more wonderful.

335

Chapter 54

It was late September and the season of theatre and other indoor entertainments was kicking off. Sir Hugh saw that there was to be a production of *The Merry Widow* at the theatre in Plymouth and got tickets for himself and Kate, thinking it was time her musical education received a wider input.

"It's the most famous operetta by Franz Lehar, and full of beautiful music. Yes, when I was your age it was the Beach Boys and Elvis and then the Beatles and Rolling Stones, but I was raised with opera and operetta in the house, and I love that too. I thought you might enjoy this one particularly as it is full of glorious costumes and really lovely music. And it will give us a chance to dress up a bit ourselves and have an evening out," he told Kate.

It was true that she mostly ran around in tee-shirts and trousers and could hardly remember the last time she'd had dinner in a restaurant, let alone gone to a play or musical. In New York, yes, but certainly not since she arrived in Devon. But Kate loved her uncle, so she was definitely up for it. Plus, as she told Hugh, "Grandmother used to listen to operetta and opera too, so I have heard some, I think I've heard *The Merry Widow*. And I'd love to get dressed up and go out for dinner."

The dress she chose was a long-sleeved scoop neck cotton with a fitted waist and a bell-shaped skirt ending just above the knee. Mainly apricot, it was decorated with multi-coloured flowers and leaves spreading from the waist up to just below the bust and in a border around the skirt. It was one of a handful of stylish frocks she'd brought from New York at the beginning of the year but had no reason to wear until now. Heels and a bracelet and earrings from Lucinda completed the outfit.

Hugh was plainly delighted with her appearance and she thought he didn't do so badly himself in a dark navy suit with a striped shirt and regimental tie. They were having an early dinner at a restaurant near the theatre when Hugh was startled by the vibration of his mobile phone in his pocket. He'd only got it as a present from Kate a few weeks before because, as she told him, it was important to have it with him when he went out hiking the estate or was away so if anything went wrong, either with him or any of them, he could get or give help.

He was not at ease with the blasted thing, even after she and Perry sat him down and played with the settings and tried to get him comfortable with texting and making and sending calls. Calls weren't so bad, but texts—they tended to infuriate him as his big fingers didn't get the hang of the tiny keyboard that appeared on the ridiculously small screen. Kate would send him several texts every day hoping to get him used to answering, but mostly he just ignored them.

"If there's trouble and you need me, text me where you are and I'll just come and get you. By the time I managed to text you back with a sensible message I could have got there three times over!" And that was the end of his attempts to text. Kate had made sure he had all their numbers on speed dial however, just in case he was in trouble himself. Now he fished the vibrating phone out of his pocket and stared at it as if daring it to defy him. It was however just a text from Perry saying that he wouldn't be at Ashley on Monday, so school would 'out' for the day.

Hugh read it out to Kate and then suggested they might use the time to go to Exeter and see his attorney about getting Kate her permanent residence status.

"Uncle Hugh, I got the message from Perry hours ago, and so Robin and I want to take Poppet to the river and see if she'd enjoy swimming. It's going to be sunny on

Monday, and the rest of the week could be rainy. Can we do the lawyer another day?"

Hugh was not used to having his ideas contradicted so out of hand, even by Kate. Maybe especially by Kate in this instance.

"I have noticed you and Robin seem to be spending a lot of time together outside of school, Kate, and I'm not sure it is a good idea. He might come to think there is more going on than is wise." Hugh wasn't used to the parental role either, but he was pretty sure of his ground here. Although he had nothing but praise for Maggie, her son was a different matter. Robin's reputation as a wild child and possibly even involved in criminal activities had reached him (on the basis that a lie or half-truth is up and running before truth can even get its boots on). He had been happy to help Maggie out when Robin needed a place to learn but didn't want his great-niece involved with a juvenile delinquent. But, just as with Poppet, who had appeared before Hugh could arrange for the "proper" sort of dog, Hugh had decided a bit too late to try to intervene.

Kate's green eyes flashed rather dangerously as she met his eye and stated categorically, "I don't think Robin just *thinks* there is more going on, because there is more going on. We *are* involved, and I'm over the moon about it. I don't see what you have against him, but whatever it is, it's not true. He's the best friend I've had, and now we're becoming more than friends and it's lovely. Isn't that how it's supposed to work—friendship growing into something more? Not just some crush on someone you just met? And Perry can vouch for him one-hundred percent in case you need references. Plus Chauncey can too...oh..."

"Who's Chauncey for heaven's sake?" growled Hugh.

"Err, sorry, forgot, a friend of Maggie's who thinks very highly of Robin. But he's not someone you know. But, please let's not argue about Robin. I swear he is very honourable and all that, and those things he did at school—well that was just because he was unhappy there. Anyway, he makes me happy."

"Okay, Pumpkin, I won't say anything more. But please be careful. He may not be the shining knight you think he is just now. After all he's only down here because he was expelled. That's not a good sign usually."

"Uncle Hugh, I was asked to leave three different schools! Besides, Grandmother told me you were expelled from the same school as Robin. And Grandmother would trust Robin, I know she would. Honestly, Uncle Hugh, there's nothing to worry about. But if you like we can go to the lawyer on Monday. I'll postpone us taking Poppet to the river. I'd love to be a legally permanent resident because I really want to stay here. And maybe we can see the Cathedral again?"

Mollified by her willingness to compromise, Hugh was content that he'd sounded his warning and that all would probably work out as it should. A really good wine and his favourite lamb chops confirmed his good mood. Plus *The Merry Widow* was possibly his favourite operetta.

As Hugh had hoped, Kate was entranced with the performance as well, costumes and music delighted the eye and the ear. Particularly the Vilja aria. But she was puzzled by what its inclusion might mean. After the performance, as they drove home in Hugh's old but beautifully maintained Jaguar, she asked him what exactly a Vilja was.

"It's a wood nymph, or sprite or sometimes called a dryad, m'dear. Why do you ask?"

"Well, it's the most beautiful song in the operetta, but it also seems out of place, it's not at all part of the plot as far as I could see."

"Ha! You're absolutely right, Kate, on both counts. All I can figure is that Lehar had this extraordinary piece of music and they fitted it in with Hanna, the Widow, singing it as an entertainment for the Grand Duke's birthday. That sort of thing would have happened. In the days before records or radio or telly it was quite common for people to play instruments and sing to entertain each other, so that part fits. But the subject of the song? No idea why she would sing about a Vilja."

"Me neither," said Kate, "unless she was trying to tell Danilo that their love is like that. Are water sprites and tree sprites related do you think?"

"Now whatever put that in your mind? I have no idea, but I know when I was a youngster I wanted desperately to believe all those, and fairies, and centaurs, were real. As I got older I still harboured a longing to see something. Met some gypsies in our wood one time and, for a moment there, I kind of convinced myself they were maybe fairies—the fair folk y'know—they were dressed in such wonderful colours and seemed almost ethereal. But then they were just Romany after all. So I bid them good day and asked them to be careful about fires and went home. Always stuck in my mind though."

Kate thought, *you were right about the faeries—I remember Kailen telling me this story—but I guess you were too given over to the 'real' world to let yourself see what was sort of 'unreally' there.*

She said, "The song says humans and faeries or sprites can fall in love. Do you think that's true?"

Hugh smiled a long ago and faraway smile. "I think it must be true in mythology (if that isn't a non sequitur) as it is written about so often. But it is probably a metaphor for falling in love with someone human who is very beautiful and unobtainable, or if obtainable you don't keep him or her long."

340

"I heard Maggie told the village that Robin's father was a faerie."

"I'm sure she just meant to replace an unpalatable truth—that she'd had some love affair and Robin was the result—with one that would take the village's attention away from her being an unwed mother into the realm of fantasy. Here in the West Country it's surprising how many people still believe in the supernatural. It seems to have worked—no-one makes any remarks about them. But of course nowadays no one necessarily gets married before having kids anyway. However, I don't recommend that to you!"

"I can assure you that's not something you need to worry about, Uncle Hugh. I'd love to know there are wood sprites though—at least I think I would."

"Seems to me that most supernatural stuff, if any of it is true, revolves around very unpleasant, dangerous beings. Like that Wyvern, he was a monster, and I'm still trying to deal with the fall-out from all those years ago. It's like he's still around—now that's supernatural evil if you like. Though I must say Maggie with her accountancy skills seems to be making some headway. You can't say accountant and supernatural in the same sentence, so if she's got his measure, then he can't be a supernatural monster, just an ordinary human monster I guess."

If only you knew, thought Kate. *On second thought, best you don't know.*

And the rest of the drive home passed with them alternately humming and singing some of *The Merry Widow.*

341

Chapter 55

Sir Hugh and Kate returned to a scene of chaos at Ashley. Lights were blazing and there were three fire engines in the stable yard where smoke and flames were coming from the stable building. Half of it was collapsed and the rest was soaking wet with the water that had put out the flames in that area.

Bates, Sykes and Mrs Sykes and Perry were standing in the courtyard, kept back by some police.

Hugh came to screeching halt, jamming on the handbrake and exiting the car at unheard of speed. 'What the hell is going on here?" he roared in the voice that used to be able to carry over a force 9 gale. His faithful retainers rushed to him even before the policeman got there. But the uniformed officer did intervene. Sir Hugh turned on him furiously. "My hunter, my old Beaumont — where's my *horse*?"

The policeman seemed to be blown a step back by the force of Hugh's cry. "He's, he's okay, Sir Hugh, he's in the field."

Bates, dressed in a waxed jacket and wellington boots over his pyjamas, rushed toward his old friend and employer. His face, mostly blackened with soot, showed the white streaks of tears, and one hand was clearly burned. "I got him out, him and that sheep he's so fond of. Them's okay, Sir Hugh, don't you go worriting now. But I couldn't get to them hens, Sir, I'm afraid the chicken coop went up like a firework. I couldn't save none."

Hugh, seeing the state of his old friend, embraced him gently in spite of the soot and, turning to Mrs Sykes, ordered, "Take him inside and get this hand bandaged. If you think best, call the doctor."

"I tried before, Sir Hugh, but I couldn't get him to move," she said as she led the now quiet Bates away.

"Poppet! Where's Poppet?" screamed Kate racing toward the fire fighters. It was Perry who reached her first, enveloping her in a hug that effectively stopped her.

"It's all right, Kate, she's inside the Hall, I shut her in the kitchen so she couldn't get hurt. And the firemen have the fire under control now, it won't reach the Manor." he said firmly. But then he bent his head and whispered, "I saw what happened. There was a dragon in the sky and it swooped down and blew fire like a huge blowtorch. Bates is right, the hen house just ignited, whoosh, and then it spread quickly to the stables—all that straw. But a dragon? I thought we were saving the dragons? This thing wasn't paralysed and it was trying to kill us all!"

"Two legs or four?" whispered Kate.

"Err, what? I, oh, there were two legs. Yes, two. Why?"

"It's a wyvern, not a dragon, or anyway a very stupid kind of dragon, and Ivor Wyvern has an army of them. He must have found out something, or guessed something, and he's attacking Ashley. Why didn't it go straight for the Manor I wonder?"

"It's all stone and slate on the exterior, nothing very flammable like the stables and the hen house. It just made the one pass like a low flying fighter plane and blew out a jet of flame and soared off again. Maybe it's like a warning shot." answered Perry. "He wants us to know he knows we're on to him."

"That means we have to move faster. Somehow we have to find the spells."

A high-pitched howl came from inside, followed by a sharp bark.

"Oh, that's Poppet! I've got to go to her, Perry. She must be so frightened."

Perry put in a call to Maggie, where it went straight to voice-mail. "Maggie, Perry here. A wyvern has

343

attacked Ashley Manor—set the stables on fire, then flew off just like a jet fighter. The fire fighters have almost got it out. No one hurt, but badly shaken. I'm the only one who saw what happened, but if they decide that it was arson, what am I going to tell them? Plus it means…"

Maggie picked up and said "It means Ivor Wyvern is aware of at least some of what we're doing, and he's sent a warning or maybe meant to destroy the Manor entirely. Which means he knows Kate is involved in this. Yes, I'll be over with Kailen and Robin as soon as we can. Don't tell the police anything. Don't let Kate say anything either. Bye."

Kate was sitting on the floor in the kitchen with Poppet half in her lap, half sprawled across the floor. The dog was feeling much better now that she knew her beloved person was okay and with her. Kate was absently fondling the pup's ears while she tried to clear her mind to make the channel to Chauncey. She had considered for a bit before trying it, but decided that even if Wyvern was there with the Dragon King he would be unaware of her presence in his mind. But it took awhile for her to be calm enough to open the channel and she breathed a sigh of relief when Chauncey's enormous face appeared in her mind's eye.

Chauncey however was agitated, it showed in his eyes, which were more red than golden and his scales were behaving like a squid's skin—patterns flowing over them in variations of blues and blacks, with touches of red.

"Kate, I see you are all right. Wyvern is here, and he is very upset. He hasn't come near me, but every living thing in the castle is reporting he is angry and frustrated."

"Chauncey, he sent a wyvern to destroy the Manor, or maybe just to warn us off. It set the chicken coop on fire, which set the stables on fire. But not the Manor, the fire department got here and put it all out, and it didn't touch the Manor. And nobody was hurt, except the chickens were burnt. And Bates, Bates got a burned hand when he rescued the animals in the stables—Uncle Hugh's horse and a sheep that keeps him company, the horse that is, not Uncle Hugh. You know, horses are herd animals and a horse alone can get very neurotic, so some horses get other kinds of animals for pets to keep them company. I heard of a race horse that had a pig that had to go to every race with him or he wouldn't be any good for racing. And sometimes they have a donkey, or a pony, or... Kate was talking fast and in a jittery way, and Chauncey could see that she was shivering. Once she'd done her 'job' of making contact with him, something in her let go and she was all over the place with delayed reaction.

"Kate, enough, slow down my dear child, slow down now—you are all right. Hug your dog, sweet girl and listen to me. I would hug you if I could—imagine I'm hugging you. There, see, it's all better now. No one died, well, except the chickens. But everyone else, even Sir Hugh's horse, is alive and well. And the Manor still stands. It was, I'm sure, a warning. Which means that somehow he's become aware that you are aware of him." A chittering could be heard, and Chauncey's great head turned and bowed toward the floor. Kate could hear him responding with soft noises and the occasional snort and the odd word of English like, 'Yes, go on.' And then he raised his head and looked at her with great sorrow.

"I have just heard from the rats that Ivor saw some evidence that they were searching—because without really dexterous hands rats and ravens aren't always capable of putting things back just as they found them. And it made him go to the moat and call for Palatyne to find out if there had been any intruders. She told him about you, Kate. She didn't know your name, but she described you. She told him you had escaped from the dungeon with her sister and, even though she didn't know if you were still in the castle or escaped entirely, it has made him aware that you were here and had been on the loose inside. So of course he thinks it was you who has been searching. That explains the attack on Ashley Manor. The rats don't think he knows the casket has been discovered. They followed him, keeping inside the walls as much as possible, and he did go to check on it.

"Apparently thinking it is safe, he has begun to calm down. However, I am sorry to say that he killed Palatyne for letting you get away. Even though she threw in her lot with him, it might have been because of some threat he held over her. And that she didn't kill you but only threw you into the dungeon with her sister, and that you both escaped—that makes two beings on the loose who might know too much, and was reason enough for him to murder her. You must take every care now, Kate, because he will come after you. I think it is time to take this warning of his and use it to mobilise and attack before he can hurt you or those you love. He'll be around to see me soon, but he can't hurt me and he can't tell when I'm lying, so I'm safe enough. I will however try to find out as much as I can about what he thinks he knows."

Chapter 56

The next evening they gathered in Maggie's house intent upon making a final plan. They would make their move as soon as possible, with the intention of getting to the enchanted casket. Chauncey's rats had described their route exactly and he had told Kate who wrote it down, every turn, every door, every place that might hide a guard or a wyvern. They knew exactly where it was and had to get it quickly, before Wyvern either moved it, or he rained down death and destruction upon them.

They had been going over a number of possible ways to nullify the spell that protected it for some time, searching through Maggie's family grimoires and everything Maggie and Kailen could remember about undoing spells. But after several hours of heated discussion it didn't really seem to be leading to anything but a fistful of possibles and maybes. This, they agreed, was not going to be good enough. Particularly if the spell included an alarm if a magical being tried to destroy it. Most really heavy-duty spells did have such an alarm. Or if destroying the protective spell also destroyed the contents—if indeed they were spells, as they fervently hoped—that could so easily happen.

They were all sitting there looking shattered when Robin spoke. "What about we forget the spell on the casket for the time being and see if we have or can make a really strong, unbeatable, protection spell for whoever goes in to get the thing? Something created to protect them when they pick it up and run with it. That way, we have it in our hands and away from the Hall and can work out how to open it without being in so much danger of being discovered. There must be such a spell, yeah?"

His father looked at him with an expression comprised of astonishment and pride. "That is a really good idea. Maggie, that's possible!"

"It might even be possible to include a levitation spell that would mean the person didn't have to actually touch the casket but could sort of move it along without having to set off its protection spell," offered Maggie.

And then came the argument about who should go into Wyvern Hall to get it. Kailen argued he should be the one to go because of being a warrior and very nearly immortal, with centuries of magical training. Robin said he should go because he was both a witch and a faerie and knew all sorts of unarmed combat moves and could undoubtedly run faster than any of them. Both Maggie and Kate looked appalled at these ideas—sending the men they loved into what could be unimagined dangers. Maggie said she should go because she was a very powerful witch with great spell-casting skills and could adjust a spell to suit the circumstances really quickly. And she could weave a disguising spell to look like a little old lady who had somehow just got lost inside the Hall (not all that helpful since the place had never been open to the public, but might give pause to an attacker who would have gone straight for the throat of a strong male invader). Kate said she should go because she'd already been through so many of the passageways and rooms in the castle, and she knew how to get through the locked doors. Plus they'd been telling her for some time that she was the lynch-pin who had discovered most of what they knew already, and now they were saying that she was their most powerful practitioner of magic. It made sense that she go if she was strongest in these areas.

But then Perry spoke up. "I may not be the strongest witch, I am not immortal or a warrior, I'm the least talented in many ways. But I have these advantages—I am young and strong, I can run as fast as

348

Robin, I have some talents in defending myself. I'm a damn good rock climber. Also it may be that Wyvern or the spell he cast is set up to expect one of you—strong, magical beings. Possibly someone like me, with more limited powers, will go unnoticed and be able to con the spell into thinking me a harmless being. My disguising spell will be that I am just myself, a tutor, someone of no account. And finally—if I am lost in this endeavour, I am the least important. I am single, so if I die there is no one's life that will be torn asunder by grief. You four will still be here to work on opening this magic box and, once you have the spells, creating a counter-spell and going in armed to the teeth to free Chauncey and all his kin. That is the bigger job, that is what it all depends upon. To get the casket is just the first step, and all of you will be needed to do the rest.

That spread a pall of silence for a few moments, but then Kate spoke quietly. "I think you'd find that we would all be torn up with grief if you died, Perry. You're one of us, we're one with you. We don't send what you seem to think you are—our expendable member—to risk themselves like that."

"No," said Robin. "We don't. We send me—because, like Mum says, it would be much safer and really cool if whoever goes to get it can then move it along without having to touch it and set off that spell. I can do that, I have found out that's one of the ways my magic works best. If I need something to move I can get it to do that by pointing at it and making it my intention. I've walked around the house with the toaster or a big book moving a few feet in front of me for practice. I thought it was such a super thing to be able to do, but I didn't have a real purpose for it, unless it was to make the army wyverns just move away at my command. Now I know it's perfect for this job. And I won't get hurt. Mum would kill me if I did!"

"So would I!" said Kate, coming and putting her arms around him. "This is not what I want you to have to do!"

"You don't get to be queen of the world quite yet," said Robin, holding her gently and speaking softly into her hair. "Someone has to do this, and it should be the person with the best skill set for the job. And that's me."

Kate waited for Robin's parents to object. But they didn't. She looked around at the rest of them feeling a bit dizzy and sick, but they were nodding agreement with Robin. The magic he had done that moved the rock away from her trapped foot in the river—the magic that marked the start of their love—now made him the chosen one for this dangerous, awful job. Somehow that must be wrong. But deep down she knew it wasn't wrong. And that if anyone could do this, he could. And that from now on they would all be risking themselves in ways they would never have believed. Time had run out.

§ § §

Later on, tucked up in bed, Kate opened the channels that allowed her to converse with Chauncey. This time she found him looking alert and almost cheerful. She told him their plan for liberating the casket, and he approved. He cautioned her that they must wait until Wyvern and his driver had once more vacated Wyvern Hall, but that, he said, would happen tomorrow.

"How can you be certain?" asked Kate. "Maybe now that he knows I exist he will stay and plan an attack."

"Because," said Chauncey, "ever since Maude died he has never lived here—he only lived here permanently while he was supervising the building and decorating and then again when they lived together. Whatever happened between them, she is possibly the only human being he ever loved. I think that after she died, he

350

has used this place only to keep me and therefore all the dragons enslaved and possibly to do various dark magics."

Very dark magic indeed, thought Kate, but carefully didn't say. Ever since they'd learned that Wyvern returned periodically to drink the young dragons' blood in a sadistic ritual that made her feel ill just thinking about it, she and the others had been careful that Chauncey shouldn't know about it, because such painful knowledge when he was powerless to do anything would just be cruel. They needed him positive and strong for the moment when he could rise up, and all his folk with him, and make Ivor Wyvern wish he'd never been born.

Chauncey was still talking. "We've had our visit—the couple of hours he seems to look forward to when he comes to gloat over how he keeps his prize monster enslaved. And I of course was encouraging him to brag, which he loves to do. So I have found out that he believes himself and this fortress of his are completely impregnable and he is leaving tomorrow strong in the knowledge that whatever you might or might not have seen, you are essentially harmless. I'm not sure he sent the wyvern as a warning or just because he was furious. Ivor Wyvern has been known to act first and think later. That fire might have been just a bully hitting something in a rage. And he seems to believe that no one at Ashley will associate it with him. Sometimes I think all he has to do is look at me lying here on old furniture and scrap iron and he feels more powerful. He feels, as he has felt for these many years, invulnerable. I encourage him in these feelings. It makes him stupid.

"Plus, of course, he is supposed to be long dead, and really shouldn't be seen around the area much. Anyway, he is going away again, and you all will have your best chance of getting in and getting the casket. He won't be expecting that. I doubt he will add anything to the wyverns and guarding spells he already has. His isn't

351

the kind of mind that expects others to be as bright or expert or capable as he is. It's his own hubris that will be his downfall. He thinks you are only a child, Kate, and he seems unaware of the forces massing against him. So you must come soon and retrieve the spells. If we are fortunate perhaps the counter spells will be there too, or if not, you will be able to create them. I hope so, I must believe so. Because if I am free, then all my kin are free as well, and *he* is finished."

Chapter 57

Two days later, in the morning hours before the sun would shine on that side of Wyvern Hall, Robin and Perry were half way up the almost vertical escarpment overlooking the bend in the river that protected the castle from the rear. Several ravens were circling in a general way, occasionally pointing out a good next toehold or warning them away from a crumbling bit. This was very helpful, particularly as for Robin it was his first attempt at a real rock climb. Perry was leading since he had quite a bit of previous experience climbing rock faces. They were each outfitted in dark climbing gear, helmets and harnesses and were roped together. Robin was fit, but felt that various muscles were going to be extremely sore, because they were already complaining like mad. Perry above him seemed to be out for a walk in the park. Robin gritted his teeth and moved up again using the handhold the raven had pointed out to him. He very carefully did not look down. The one time he did had proved not to be a good idea, and they were a lot higher now. Surely nearly there.

Perry achieved a ledge, narrow, but allowing him to rest with both feet on it and body pressed against the rock face. "Up here Robin, come up and you can rest those muscles for a few minutes. We're nearly there."

Robin carefully following Perry's directions and found himself standing in relative comfort with handholds to steady himself, but without having to bear weight. They just stood there and breathed. Perry looked out and up, but Robin didn't. He laid his cheek against the rock face and enjoyed the coolness against his hot sweating face.

Perry said, "I think we need to make our way a bit to the left—there's a cleft there and it leads up to the top without any overhang. Where we are now, if we go straight there's a bit of an overhang. I don't think you want to deal with that on your first climb. Plus little lips that stick out like that could just give way when we put our weight on them. So we'll go for the cleft over there and that should get us to the top without any trouble."

Their plan, such as it was, was to find a small door that the ravens would lead them to, get in (using Kate's tried and proven lock breaking methods) and Perry would wait with the climbing equipment out of sight, but keeping watch, while Robin followed the map and the escort of rats that Chauncey had promised. As far as they knew the only dangers were the wyverns and the creatures in the moat. And the enchanted locks, but those Kate had shown Robin how to manage. There were the strange modern sculptures on the path Robin and Kate had taken so many weeks ago, some of which were booby-trapped, but it appeared these were an aberration, something Ivor had experimented with perhaps, probably in the 1950s, but decided he didn't want or need in the grounds or the castle itself. And there were no servants—Ivor came seldom and stayed only a short time, so he and his chauffeur brought everything they would need with them it would seem. Robin wondered how much the chauffeur knew about his employer, and if anything about the dragons. It would make sense if he didn't, Ivor couldn't afford another human being with knowledge like that.

Meanwhile, there was the rest of this bloody cliff to scale. It turned out to be easier than the first part once they were in the cleft. They could lean against one wall and run their feet up the other, then shift and move their torsos. It put the load elsewhere and gave some of Robin's muscles a bit of a rest. Finally Perry was at the top and rolled onto the flat. From where Robin heard him whispering, "Oh, holy flaming hell!"

"What? What's wrong?" Robin hissed.

"Nothing, we're okay. It's just I've never seen Wyvern Hall before. It's a nightmare! Just what I'd

354

imagine the devil would create if Victorian Gothic were his thing, which, actually, I imagine it could be," responded Perry, leaning over the precipice to help Robin up the last few feet and over the edge.

Robin just lay on his stomach panting for awhile. "Awesome" he finally said. "Just awesome. And if possible I never want to do it again."

"We have to go back down you know," said Perry.

"Don't remind me just now," responded Robin. "I want to lie here and think how scared I was and how I'm on solid flat ground now. Dammit, why don't we have flying spells?"

"Maybe there are such things, but it would appear we aren't skilled enough, or as Maggie keeps saying, they have their own difficulties. I would hate to be several hundred feet up and go into a downward spiral I couldn't come out of. I know what I'm doing when I'm climbing." Perry was taking himself out of his harness and unhooking the rope. "Since you can use intention and projection to make things float and move, maybe you can revise that to make yourself rise into the air."

"I will be trying that as soon as we get back with the casket. I was surprised to find out what the rats found was just a dull metal box about the size of an ordinary document box. I somehow expected it would be inlaid with gold and precious stones."

"I think they wouldn't want to draw attention to it—and it's the contents that are precious," said Perry. "Up you get, we shouldn't just hang around. It seems there isn't anything spying on us, but I wouldn't want to count on it. The sooner we are out of this open area the happier I will be. Although honestly I don't fancy going inside this monstrosity either—all that dark stone—who would make such a thing? Don't answer that, I already know."

They tucked their climbing equipment into some bushes, blessing the arrogance or ignorance that had led

Ivor to dispense with rotations of guards patrolling the parameter, and made their way quickly across the parched ground to the back of the castle. It wasn't far, maybe ten yards or so, and then they made their way along the wall through weeds and nettles looking for traces of the small door said to be set down a flight of stone steps.

"Oof! I've found the bloody steps," said Robin, sinking nearly out of sight amongst the weeds and brambles which had overgrown the area. They had gloves and knives and hacked a way clear down to the door. Here, as expected, was another of those be-spelled locks. Robin touched it with pliers whose handles were encased in rubber against electric shocks. He was staying well to the side, which was wise, as the keyhole spat out a gob of something that when it touched the ground immediately fizzed and ate a hole in the stone.

"Ha! Any more where that came from?" Robin poked the lock again. Nothing. Nevertheless he carefully used the pliers to try to turn the handle. It didn't move.

"Okay, be like that," he muttered and gathering intention and propulsion he aimed at the handle, which resisted only minimally before turning. Another well-aimed thrust of magic opened the iron door, which scraped alarmingly along the stone floor.

"Good thing you didn't inherit Kailen's weakness in the presence of iron." said Perry. "I hope to hell that Ivor didn't see fit to use an old-fashioned alarm system."

"Kate didn't run into anything like that," said Robin, "and our feeling is that Ivor is so confident of his magic, or should I say his and Proteus' magic, that he wouldn't even think of something as mundane as an electronic alarm."

Perry had been thinking. "No guards patrolling, no extra magical beasts to sniff us out. There's no need me keeping guard out here, I will be more useful coming with you, I'll have your back." Robin didn't argue, he felt very relieved. All he said was, "Two heads are better than one."

In the gloom of the underground passage they checked the map with a pencil torch and started off. Shortly small squeaks let them know that the rats had found them and were prepared to lead them through the maze of passages. This made the going much quicker and they didn't worry about making a wrong turn. Finally they reached a flight of stairs and, on getting to the top, were on the ground floor of the castle. Here they paused to become accustomed to the light once more and then set off again along a hall off which were some rather splendid rooms. But the rats pressed on, and so did Perry and Robin. Up a back flight of stairs and a servants' back hallway led them along toward what turned out to be another door. It wasn't apparent at first, having been disguised as an ordinary part of the wall, which was papered in an Escheresque pattern of Wyverns all interlocked—making a perfect disguise for the door itself.

The lock was part of a wyvern's mouth, open to spit flame, but this one the rats and ravens had dismantled—various toothmarks showing that the lock had indeed put up a fight. There was also a blood stain on the floor, so some animal or animals had been injured or possibly killed in the effort. Perry breathed 'Brave fellows" and his wish became a cloud of feathers that settled on the floor, turning to tiny white flowers as they covered the stain. The two largest rats came and sat on their hindquarters with their paws lifted in front of him. He extended his hand and they ran up his arm to sit on his shoulder, leaning against his neck and patting his cheek — the nearest a rat could come to embracing him.

Robin was already inside the room. It was quite narrow with no windows, probably fitting into the wall itself, so that no trace would appear either on the plans or from any usual ways of measuring. It was lined with shelves on which lay some folders and many boxes for documents and possibly for jewels or gold. They were all plain, serviceable metal, varying only in size. Robin and Perry stared around them using their torches, unwilling to chance touching anything but unable to tell which might be the important box. The rats, however, knew, and Perry quickly got the idea that if he pointed at a box the rat that now sat on his forearm would either display no movement or move its head slightly to indicate direction. Thus it directed him to move to the right and up two shelves and then along to the corner of that shelf where one box rested. When Perry pointed at it, the rat made nodding motions of its head and drummed on his arm with its front feet.

"That's got to be it, then" said Perry, automatically reaching toward it. At which point the rat gently bit him on the wrist. "Ow! Oh hells bells, I got so excited to find it that I forgot we can't touch it. Thanks, my friend." he said, stroking the rat gently. It ran back up to sit on his shoulder.

"Okay, then, Robin, let's find out what happens if you can lift it from what we hope is a safe distance. Ready to try?"

Robin grinned. "As I'll ever be." Inside he wasn't feeling all that ready—who knew what kind of magic the spell on the box would release when it was disturbed? If it was programmed to respond to touch, they were safe enough, but if to any kind of movement, they could be in for a nasty surprise, or even a fatal one.

"It didn't kill the rat that touched it—only threw it down and stunned it, which could have been the drop to the floor. If that's the force of the magic, hopefully we'll be okay at a bit of a distance. Only one way to find out. Perry, go outside and stand with the wall between you and it. Just in case this all goes wrong we need you in one piece to send for help or get me out of here."

He watched as Perry stepped back through the door and to the side, but then saw he was carefully peering round the edge of the wall to see what was happening. "No bloody peeking—what if it sends explosive bolts? Could take your eye out. Get back and stay back. One of us has to be able to call for reinforcements or do magic healing or whatever it is you can do. Good. Stay there!"

Quieting himself, as they'd been taught in the dojo as well as what he'd learned about doing spells, Robin sent a questing wave of intention, gentle as a feather, toward the box. This magic 'feather' stroked the side of the box and there was no resulting quiver let alone an explosion or darts of fire. Then he moved it along the front toward the lock, just visible as an ordinary looking keyhole in the front of the box. As it got within a few millimetres of the hole, the box vibrated just slightly. The feather backed gently away, still touching the box. The box became still once more. Robin gently moved his magic over the rest of the surface, around the sides and back to the front, where he carefully rearranged his spell to flatten and strengthen his 'feather' into something like a flat shovel or a spatula, all the time keeping it in contact with the base of the box. The box remained inert.

Sitting there on the shelf, a plain dull metal box only a few inches high—it seemed to Robin suddenly that all this care he was exercising was rather silly. He could just take a couple of steps and pick it up! He had already raised his foot when he felt a scrabbling on his trousers and looked down to see a rat pulling with teeth and paws. It shook its head at him wildly. He felt dazed for a second and then realised he'd almost come under the influence of a spell of such cunning that he might have destroyed himself. His own spell had disappeared. The box hadn't moved, yet somehow it had sensed danger and seemed to have mesmerised him into forgetting everything and just going to grab it. Which meant that doing so would be very dangerous indeed. And that the protections around this box were much more impressive than he'd thought. Still, it hadn't seemed to react directly to his 'feather' or his 'spatula'. Maybe it was programmed to react to the presence of a large warm body in the room.

To test this, he retreated to the doorway and stepped outside. Perry looked at him with raised eyebrows and whispered, "What's wrong?"

Robin explained his momentary lapse and how the rat had saved him from being an awful and possibly dead idiot. All Perry could say was, "Wow, that is some spell, that is really subtle and nasty."

"Yeah, that's what I thought, and I thought since it didn't respond directly to my own spells, maybe it was just me being in there for a certain amount of time that got it started and if I stand outside the room it won't get any messages. I hope so anyway. Look, I'll start again with my exploring and touching spells prior to picking it up, but if you see me take a step to go back in there, grab me and haul me back, okay?"

"You've got it. I'll make sure you don't get near it. How far away can you be and have your spells still be effective?"

"We are about to find out." Again he sent his feather-light spell forward, passing it gently over the box, the top, the sides, staying away from the keyhole. Then he fashioned it into a shovel-shape and gently slide it under the box, stopping there and letting all rest quiet for some time. Not a quiver from the box, and it appeared that outside the room his body didn't set off any reaction. It remained to be seen if all hell would break loose when the spell picked up the box or if, having extracted the box from the room the box would again try inveigling them into touching it. Robin was hoping that the spell might be a function of the room itself.

He again quieted himself and turned his full attention to his intention and need to retrieve the box without harm to it or them. The spell folded gently around the box like a soft blanket, leaving the front with its deadly keyhole free and lifted it a fraction of an inch off the shelf. Here he paused letting everything rest. When absolutely nothing untoward happened, he began to reel it in. The box moved quietly off the shelf, across the room toward the door, with Robin backing away toward the far wall. When it passed through the door without causing trouble, he gently directed it down the hallway back the way they had come. With Perry close behind him, concentrating on their protective spells, they walked as on egg shells following the box as it maintained a steady unwavering progress about eight feet in front of them. It seemed the box thought of itself as still being on the shelf—the height remained the same, and it didn't so much as tip or tilt as they went around corners. Robin's spell, fashioned of intention and need and a lot of intuition, had seduced it into thinking itself safe.

Even going down the stairs to the cellars caused not a tilt or ripple of disquiet. Again the rats provided an escort, also maintaining a careful distance from the floating box. Finally at the cellar door everything paused. Robin took a few minutes to relax as much as he dared without letting the spell falter, and then they again formed their line of box, Robin, and Perry to the rear.

"Have a care when it hits the outside air," murmured Perry. But absolutely nothing happened. The box, wrapped in Robin's 'blanket' was still comfortably unaware of its surroundings. Up the steps they went, and over the flat ground to the bushes that concealed their climbing equipment.

Here was the real test: the box would have to be put into a carrying bag that would be attached to Perry's belt to hang some ten feet down below his feet as they descended the cliff, because there was no way that Robin could maintain the concentration necessary to keep it floating and climb down himself.

The carrying case, an ordinary briefcase large enough for the box, had been worked on by all of them. Every spell they could muster to keep the box quiet and unaware of its position inside the carrier had been applied to the carrier, so that it became in effect a combination of Robin's soft blanket and positioning spell with Kailen's best protective spells on the carrier (much as the fae used to keep the effects of iron away from them, the carrier was designed to withstand any sudden moves or even major explosions from the box). Kate and Maggie applied spells to counteract acids or other poisons and calming and sleep spells to hopefully lull the damn thing into submission. It was the best they could do. Should it break loose anyway and go for the guys, then Perry, who could do a spell and climb at the same time, was to keep their own protective envelope as box-proof as possible. The truth of it all was they had no idea what the box was capable of and had thrown everything they could think of into the mix.

The first hurdle was to lower the box carefully into the carrier, then seal the carrier, at which point all Robin could do was use intention and need to keep it as quiet as possible. And once he started down the cliff face he would have to let go of that, trusting in the spells on and in the carrier to keep the box from reacting. Perry went forward, keeping well away from the floating box, and retrieved the briefcase and opened it. Inside it was foam padded to the dimensions of the box (gathered from the rats who reported to Chauncey), with a little give—better a space too big than too small. Robin floated the box over the case and lowered it carefully, until it was settled into its new resting place still, as far as they could tell, under the illusion it was sitting on its usual shelf. Robin lowered the lid of the briefcase and carefully clipped it closed. Perry

362

and he both activated the variety of spells already in place to seal and protect it and themselves.

"Whew!" Robin was very glad his major part in this was over for now. It had in fact been relatively easy, but that was so dependent upon his keeping both his calm and his concentration, and that was in its own way exhausting. So they sat for a bit discussing how to manage the descent with the least fuss and greatest care.

Then it was buckling up into the harnesses, testing the ropes and carefully roping the carrying case to Perry's belt leaving it to dangle some ten feet below his feet at any given time. As the escarpment was nearly 200 feet high over the river, they hadn't felt it wise to lower it all that way and leave it. Although as Perry said the first time it hit the side of the rock as it dangled below him, "Bloody hell fire, we should have just lowered the thing, at least when it hit the rocks it would have been quite a long way away from us! Merde, that's scary as hell!"

But still nothing happened—the case and the box were silent. No sudden waves of energy came at them or any poisonous gases or any hypnotic spells that told them just to 'let go, let go'. So whatever they'd done, or whatever the box was enchanted to do, bouncing it off the cliff face wasn't setting anything off.

Robin found his fear of climbing down was quite outweighed by his concern over doing his best to help keep the box contented, and therefore the descent wasn't nearly as frightening for him as the ascent had been.

But at the bottom, divesting themselves of their equipment and repacking it in their knapsacks they agreed that this had been an experience such as they hoped never to repeat. It had taken such a long time, with so many unknowns—and the fact that they had got this far without major mishap just made them feel that any second luck could run out.

Robin allowed that fighting in the dojo, even against the masters, or the guy who seemed to have a personal vendetta against him, was miles easier that this bizarre situation, so careful, so tense, so bloody long. Where any second the whole world could have gone boom!—or still might. Perry allowed as how he'd watched a TV series called UXB as a kid and the idea of dealing with unexploded bombs had terrified him. And here he was with something infinitely more tricky, and they hadn't even begun the real work—getting it open safely.

They'd been uncertain whether, providing they got it this far, transporting it by car might be possible or if Robin should take over moving it by magic once more. This was not his favourite idea since they were miles from his house. So he was very relieved when Kate, Kailen and Maggie appeared and the group decision was that, having survived being put in a carrier and lowered down a cliff, a car journey should be a piece of cake…probably. Like everything else they were doing with this wretched box, the maybes, probablies and possiblies far outweighed any certainties at all. They couldn't even vouch for the fact that it contained the spells they needed. Wyvern and Proteus might have something they considered even more important inside. They were working in the dark and would continue to for some time yet.

"Cheer up guys," Kate said. "Maggie says with Samhain coming our powers will be greater and the spaces between worlds thinner. So we just find the counter-spell here or make one by then and we're, err, home and dry— or something. And the dragons will be free and the statues will be an army for us. We'll slaughter them!"

"I would love to do a little slaughtering," said Robin wryly. "That would be a piece of cake compared to this. Err, is there any cake, by the way? We're starving."

Chapter 58

Robin once again took on the task of moving the casket or document box smoothly before him, still encased in the briefcase, into an underground room in the side of a hill where he'd never been before. It was furnished like a cross between a chemistry lab and a meeting room, with extra corners for some sofas and comfy chairs.

"It's where we work with magic we are unsure of, darling," said his mother. "It's protected not just against other spells or those who might harm us, but against all sorts of explosions, getting in or getting out—some of your relatives' chemistry experiments have been epic."

"Uncle Peri?" queried Robin who remembered Kailen's brother being treated by Maggie for burns and who had been deaf in one ear.

"That's right—he had an idea for creating a potion against goblins that got totally out of hand. I don't even think he meant it to explode, but then he was always thinking that the magic would protect him no matter what he mixed together."

"And what did he mix?" asked Perry, staring at some stains on the ceiling.

"We don't know. He couldn't remember, and it burned so fiercely that all traces disappeared," muttered Kailen, clearly not happy to talk about his own kin like this.

"You told me there weren't any goblins!" Kate turned on Robin with her hands shooting blue sparks and her hair standing out with static electricity. She had thought she'd die if anything happened to him while he stole the box, but now that he was safely here with it, her shattered nerves let her down. She was as angry as she had been frightened before. "Just like you told me the moat was safe! I could murder you!"

"I didn't, I didn't tell you those things—I told you I lied about them, and you believed me. Or something. Oh, Kate, Kate, not now, let's not fight now. I've never been so tired or so…so frightened."

And she saw that he was indeed at the end of his tether and near collapse. So the next thing the others saw was her easing him onto a couch and into her arms. "Sorry, so sorry" she murmured. "I was so frightened for you, and then you sort of swanned back with the box as if it was all in a day's work, and I was awed, but I wanted to kick you too for being so 'holier than thou'—so when I heard goblins were real, I just blew."

"Did you see what you did, darling?" said Maggie, coming to stroke Kate's hair and check on her son. "You had so much power it was sparking off your hands and your hair stood on end. We need to work on harnessing that—you could probably blow up a building! No—not this one, it's built specifically to withstand such things."

"Well shall we get started on opening it?" said Kailen. His gaze went from one to the other of them. "Ah, I see, sorry, I haven't been risking my life all day" he said, catching his mate's glare. "So, I'll just shut up now and, err, go away."

"Perry, you and Robin really need a good shower and a soak in our hot tub. Plus a large meal. Okay, don't worry, it's not going anywhere." Maggie was being mother hen again.

"Um—we are *sure* it's not going anywhere?" asked Perry. Getting affirmative nods from the others he relaxed and affirmed that a soak in a hot tub and a lot of food would be the most wonderful things he could think of.

Kailen, who of course hadn't gone away, said, "Then we lock it in here right where it is, and we go back to the house and do something about showers and food and rest. Tonight or tomorrow we'll begin to work on opening the damned thing. All right, Maggie my love?" She nodded approval and they headed out, Maggie and Kailen staying behind a few minutes to make sure physical and magical locks and wards were all in place. Robin called back over his shoulder, "Don't go near it, I think it has an extra added power to make people think they can just touch it safely—I'm sure that would be fatal. Don't touch it!"

§ § §

Late the next morning after Robin and Perry slept in to recover from mental and physical exhaustion, they gathered again in the 'bomb-proof cave' as Robin dubbed it, to contemplate The Box. (It was now officially The Box—its plainness dictating that 'casket' wasn't an appropriate name, and its supreme importance to their cause made capital letters just, well, obvious.) Robin used his skills to unlock the briefcase and gently persuade The Box to exit its shelter and come in for a soft landing on a nearby workspace. It still seemed quite unaware that it had been stolen, carted down a cliff and taken for a ride in a car. Or was it? They couldn't tell, it was something quite beyond their combined experience. Maybe it was lulling them into a false sense of security. Maybe when they got close to opening it, it would suddenly attempt to annihilate the lot of them. It was going to get interesting.

Maggie, ever the organiser, decided it was time to divide and conquer. "What we need are some specialists. And I think we've got what we need right here. Kate, you can make a channel to see and communicate with Chauncey, so what about a channel to see into The Box and interrogate the contents? If we can find out what's inside, we can know if it's worth the trouble to crack it open. Or persuade it, or whatever.

"Perry, you have the most empathetic magic, you can perhaps communicate with The Box itself, soothing and convincing it that we mean no harm. Convincing it, if we find out it holds the spells, to accept an opening spell. A healing mist could provide a short period of time when we put it to sleep so to speak, and maybe then can open it.

"Robin, you can, if necessary, keep it at a safe distance from us, and stop it from doing anything fatal while we try to investigate it. Kailen, you will be prepared to step in and block it by sheer force of will.

"And I will, if Kate can make a channel to the contents, link in with her and examine them to find out what they are. Then Kailen and I will try various opening spells on The Box itself.

"But first, before any of that, we will form a circle of protection, calling on earth, air, fire and water to protect us and The Box and its contents. It's absolutely crucial that The Box feels safe here or we won't get any cooperation and might have it blowing the place up."

Robin said, "Mum, it's a box, well, The Box, but it's not alive, it can't feel all this stuff. You talk about it like we're going to befriend a tiger."

"It's a strongly enchanted, be-spelled Box, capable of not just repelling boarders but of trying to entice them into touching it so it can deliver a fatal blow. I'd say that comes close enough to alive for me. If we knew the enchantments it's under we could perhaps undo them, but we don't, they have no resonances that Kailen or I have encountered before, they are outlandish, even otherworldly. So our best chance, possibly our only chance is to 'befriend' it, lull it into a sense of trust and ask it to drop its guard so we can examine the contents. Failing that, possibly Kate can make a clear enough channel to the contents that we can read them or photograph them or something—so we have a facsimile even if we can't get to the contents themselves."

368

"Well, for my part," said Perry, "I'm fairly sure I'll be somewhat less frightened if I can think of The Box as having the personality of a slightly mad, somewhat sinister, great aunt or uncle, full of spite and malice possibly, but amenable to flattery. I can deal with that concept a lot easier than that of a spell-bound container that could just blow us all to kingdom come."

"Yeah, me too," said Kate, squeezing Robin's hand to show she wasn't exactly contradicting him. "The locks throughout the castle that I had to deal with certainly seemed to have strong, err, personalities, and although that made it a bit difficult at first to 'hurt' them, it got easier as I went along, because every one of them was simply horrid. Maybe The Box is more subtle, and it seems to be basking in comfort at present. But a personality to be dealt with—since we don't know the magic, but we've all dealt with personalities all our lives—it seems to even the odds a bit."

Maggie resumed, "But—sad as I am to say it—we must keep in mind that what is inside may not be the spells we are so eager to find. If it is something else, we are not done for however. Freeing creatures under spells is an area in which I have a lot of training, and making a spell or spells to set the dragons free may be possible without knowing the spell used to trap and paralyse them.

"I don't want to do this unless there is no other choice, because there is always the chance of harming the creature you are trying to free. I would want at the very least to know the general type of spell Ivor and Proteus have used before I start trying to free Chauncey. It has to be quite an impressive one if Chauncey himself, who has had over one hundred years to contemplate it, has been unable to undo it. Although I'm very interested that it seems to wear off every couple of years so that Ivor has to come back to Wyvern Hall to re-do it. There is also the spell he must do to knock Chauncey out so he can't hear or see the enslaving spell being done. I'm intrigued by that. It has certain things in common with a category of spells I know of—those that involve a healing mist for short-term unconsciousness and long-term healing. Not sure Ivor is interested in the healing aspects, although he does of course need to keep Chauncey in good health—so maybe he is using a healing mist. That would explain the unconsciousness and the regaining of strength and movement when the other spell is wearing off. Even a dragon, if kept virtually immobile for many years, would suffer muscle wastage and probably many other problems, even pressure sores. So the more I think of it, healing mists are almost certain to be part of Chauncey's 'treatment'."

Kailen broke in, "Kate, could you ask Chauncey tonight if he has any memory at all of how he felt after coming round from these spells of unconsciousness. Also if he remembers any foreign language Ivor may have been using. If it is Proteus who comes from the same world as the dragons, and he who has the deep hatred of them, then it might be that he came here with the spells that could vanquish them. My sense of this duel being—the Body Buddies—that he and Ivor are is that Ivor is the creator, the sculpture and painter, but also the human paranoid psychopath who acts out, and that Proteus is the Chimaera from a parallel world, the same one the dragons come from, and that he is the one with the most powerful magic. My guess is that he had to join with Ivor in order enact this magic, that for some reason he was incapable of doing it on his own. In which case it may be that the spells are in his language, and Chauncey would recognise it, even understand it, which is why Ivor has to render him unconscious."

"I'll find out as much as he knows," promised Kate. "Meanwhile, do we make a circle of protection and have a go at The Box now?"

370

"Yes," confirmed Maggie. "A protective circle is always used if possible when doing magic. We've got enough people to make a strong circle. I'm Earth with the position at North, Kailen, Air, is East. Robin you have a strong fire element, so you are Fire, compass point South, and Perry you will be Water, to the West. Kate, you and The Box will be in the centre. As our most powerful witch, you will be active in drawing down power and using it to make a channel to see inside The Box."

Before Kate could protest or any of them ask the dozens of questions they had, Kailen bent and floated an oriental rug away revealing a circle incised in the stone floor with a pentagram within it. The compass positions of the four ancient 'elements' were clearly marked around the circle and Robin and Perry took up their places. Maggie came forward with a container of salt which she scattered around the circle, then took her place as Earth. Kailen floated himself into position as Air—Robin gasped, having never seen his father fly or levitate before.

"Kate, come into the centre, please," said Maggie. "And Robin, we need you to float The Box over here and position it near the centre, but not too near any of us. The circle should help to contain its energy, hopefully entirely, and have a calming influence as well."

Music began softly in the background, panpipes, plaintive but soothing. The Box rose off the granite workbench and came slowly to the circle, passing between Robin and where Maggie would have been had she not been gathering up some papers, Robin carefully keeping it centred between them. He lowered it gently to a spot a few feet from Kate.

"Damn glad this is a big circle," muttered Perry. Maggie gave each of them a piece of paper. "Each of you will read this out as we go around the circle. As my power is Earth based in the North, I'll start, then Kailen in the East, then you Robin, finally Perry in the West. Kate, this should form both a dome of protection and you can channel the elemental power we've called to probe The Box. Gently, it must be very gently, with healing included, and ask it to reveal what it contains. Be careful here, as you must be clear that we want to know and see what the contents are, we do not want to experience its powers."

"Oh, merde," said Kate. "That's a huge ask. I'm not at all certain I can make it understand the distinction. Or keep it from just spitting destruction at us, since it's been enchanted to deal in 'shock and awe' with anyone who tries to get inside it."

"If you feel anything but cooperation happening, if you feel threatened by it, back off your probing and tell us. The circle is a powerful protection against things that could go 'bang'. I can promise you that it won't go bang unless you mount a direct frontal assault, and you of course are not going to do that."

"Of course not … I think. What do I do if it seems agreeable?" Kate was feeling decidedly underwhelmed by the expectations that she could handle this. She suddenly felt quite frightened by the responsibility everyone seemed to think she could handle. "Maggie, I'm not trained, not really, the channels I've made, the connections, have been with Chauncey who loves and trusts me, and with you all, not with something the Body Buddies have set up to stop someone like us. I could get this so wrong."

"I don't think so, honey," Maggie responded swiftly. She didn't want Kate's nerves to affect The Box. "You have great powers of empathy, just as Perry does, and you will instinctively know if things get dangerous and you will respond with gentleness and without fear. I believe that you, of all of us, have it in you to simply ask for what we need and get it. There is no malice, avarice or power-hunger in you about this. You will be using your empathy and power to reassure and guide The Box. It may, after all, be labouring under these enchantments, hurt by

372

them—because I'm sure the Body Buddies had no care at all for it when they slapped these on it. Whatever they are, they are dark evil magic, and that can be a painful burden to bear."

"I'm glad I wasn't thinking of that when I beat up those enchanted locks," said Kate with a rueful grin. "I might have felt too sorry for them and not got out."

"Or you might have coaxed them into relaxing and letting you go through," said Perry. "That's what Maggie is saying to try now. Just be yourself as you are with the people you trust and… ask."

That seemed more clear somehow. Forget that The Box was enchanted with powerful, possibly lethal magic, and imagine it as something like Chauncey, someone important to her that needed her help. That's what she'd do—go in asking for cooperation in helping. What could be the harm in that?

Maggie nodded at her as if she'd heard what Kate was thinking, although more likely it was the settled feeling she picked up on.

Robin seemed to get the same vibe. He nodded to her and smiled in a way that seemed to go right through and light her up. "Okay folks, it's circle time." he said.

Maggie stood at the North and started: "I at the North call on Earth, on growth and fertility, the rocks beneath and the mountains above, I at the North call on Earth, as I will so mote it be." Kate felt the power running across the ground and it seemed both to lift and to sustain her. She saw Maggie as a wonderful tree, rooted and growing, restful but full of energy.

Kailen spoke: "I at the East call on Air, wind and storm, breath and flight, I at the North call on Air, soft breeze of night, waves at sea, as I will so mote it be." Kailen's many braids were waving in a wind. Kate could feel a breeze that refreshed her.

Robin stared at the paper in his hand, then looked up and with his hair tipped with golden fire, he spoke: "I at the South call on Fire, creator and destroyer, heat and light, I at the South call on Fire, bringer of energy, as I will so mote it be." Kate was wrapped in his warmth and felt a glow of that energy.

Finally Perry, who seemed to glow with a sheen of liquid: "I at the West call on Water, cleansing and sustaining, providing and maintaining, I of the West call on Water, from stream and river and the sea, as I will so mote it be." Kate felt fear and fatigue wash away, and a sparkling sense of well-being.

She gathered up all the power they offered and gently sent questing tendrils toward The Box. It quivered. She paused, waiting for a response she could understand. There came a small slight whimper, as of a whipped puppy. Kate's immediate reaction was to send out love and consolation, and a sort of promise that such things would not happen if it let her in. The Box moved minimally closer to her. Everyone in the circle held their breath, ready to leap to protect if necessary. The Box let out a soft breath. It could be seen as a black dust, but it dissolved harmlessly in the glow of light surrounding Kate, washed away by droplets of pure water. She opened a channel and sent her message of hope and need.

The Box shuddered with fear. Fear of what would happen to it if it didn't do as it had been enchanted to do. Kate matched this with the equivalent of a dog biscuit. *It's all right, they can't hurt you here. Let me see what you hold, let me free you from this ugly spell, let me cut away the thing that hurts you, it will all be all right.* The Box wanted to let go, wanted to believe. Kate reached out a gentle tendril and stroked it. She could feel the constricting spell like barbed wire trying to choke The Box into defending, but it could feel freedom and kindness so strongly coming from her. The tendril became magical

374

wire cutters, and cut through the spell, letting it fall, ugly but harmless, to the ground, where the power of Earth, Air, Fire and Water immediately rusted it into harmless powder. The Box seemed to shake itself and gasp. The lid opened. And the spirit that had animated The Box rose up and evaporated. As it went it appeared to the five who watched that it was a bird or perhaps a butterfly, something gentle and urgent to escape. And The Box was simply an inanimate document box, open and not enchanted. The papers within ruffled gently with the air stirred by the wings of the being that had been entrapped to defend them.

"You did it! You did it!" Robin was jumping up and down from his point on the circle, but didn't come any nearer. He knew that the circle had to hold to make sure Kate and The Box and the papers stayed safe. "Holy smoke, how? How did you do that?"

Kate looked at him with affection and just a little sadness. "I thought of Poppet when they found her and brought her to me. She was so frightened, and she had barbed wire wrapped around her neck and one paw caught in it, as though she'd tried to free herself and just made it worse. Her neck had dried blood on it and she was crying and she was afraid. I told her I would free her and take care of her, and I cut the wire with wire cutters. She was so scared, but she seemed to understand that and she settled and let me unwrap the wire, even though that started the bleeding again. She let me take care of her and she licked my hand.

"So I used intuition and need with The Box and it seemed to me it was terrified of allowing me to see what it contained, it whimpered. And at that moment, I could see the spell that bound it, like dreadful, rusty, dark barbed wire wrapped all around it. So I cut the wire and the spell just rusted away in seconds. And the response was like relief and even gratitude—and it opened. So whatever animated it before is gone now, and grateful to be free I think. And The Box is just a document box now."

Chapter 59

Maggie from her position at North said, "Kate, it's now for you to have the privilege of taking out the documents and seeing what it is we have exactly."

Kate looked at the open box with the papers or parchments lying there before her. In her mind she said a quiet prayer of thanksgiving and asked once more for permission to approach the box, this time in physical fact. The box had no opinion on the matter: whatever had animated it was gone, freed and, as they used to say in New York, 'outa here'. The box was just a box, nothing magical or animate was going on. So she bent down and carefully lifted out the sheaf of thick parchment pages. A dozen or so pages of closely written script with large capital letters interspersed in a language she didn't know, but thought might be Latin.

"Maggie, I think these are safe to handle," she said. "But I can't just walk out of the circle, can I. We need to do the closing ceremony or whatever it is, right?"

"Just so, Kate, we will all give thanks to the Divine, withdraw our protective spells back into our compass points and I will close the circle by walking anticlockwise around it, releasing each of you from your positions. Then we can examine those parchments." Which is what they did. Then they gathered around the granite work top where Kate placed the documents.

"Latin, it's in Latin!" said Perry. "Oh, thanks be to whatever, I can read this I think."

"That's good, because none of the rest of us can, at least Kailen can up to a point, but his Latin is very old." said Maggie.

"As in nearly prehistoric," said Kailen, "more like Oggish probably."

Perry held up a hand and they were all instantly quiet. "This is the sleep spell. Interesting, it doesn't rhyme in Latin, but does in English. And it's extremely simple.

The moon has awoken with the sleep of the sun.
The light has been broken, the spell has begun.'
You will sleep and remember naught,
As I command so it be wrought,
And now a healing mist begins,
Taking away all that pains.'

"Well, that's rather good I must say, sounds like something I could use."

"Is there a reversal of that spell? He has to bring Chauncey back out of that sleep once he's renewed the main spell." Kate was eager.

"Yes, it's here, and it's also very simple and direct. I think they have it in Latin just to confuse, because it rhymes in English."

In this night and at this hour
I call upon the ancient power.
Beast that was in slumber deep
Back to consciousness you creep
Blessed with forgetting you remain
Under magic thrall again.

"Well, that is simple, and just what I might have used," said Maggie. "Nothing deeply dark and evil about that, except the magic thrall bit. And 'creep' wouldn't be my choice perhaps. But it's exactly what's needed to produce sleep and healing and then awakening, so—except that they tried to make it complicated with Latin—I'll just bet that was Ivor trying to show off—it didn't need to be deep and dark."

378

"But what we need," Kailen broke in, "is the spell that Wyvern uses to revitalise the power spell, the one they use to keep the dragons enslaved."

Perry leafed through the parchments. "I've got it, I think," he said slowly, sounding not excited but bemused. "It's what we speculated on, some language that appears to be outside human experience. Kailen, are you familiar with this?" And he handed the page over.

"Oh, if only…" Kailen said. "Ancient Oggish I could deal with. This is a language and script totally outside my experience."

"That's what we were afraid of…," Robin sounded defeated. "If we can't figure this out then it's all been for nothing."

Kate put her hand on his arm. "No Robin, you're forgetting Chauncey. If this is in Proteus' language then there's every chance that Chauncey will be able to understand it. That's why he had to be put to sleep every time the Body Buddies cast the spell—so he wouldn't recognise it and know or be able to create a counter spell. We have to get this to Chauncey."

"Can you make contact with him now? I know it tires you out, that's why you do it just before you sleep, but could you do it now?" Robin was enthused again.

"I can, at least from my end. He has to be awake and waiting to pick up on his end. But I'm sure he is since I told him what we'd be doing today."

Kate settled herself onto one of the couches. "Could you give me the spell, please, Kailen," she said, holding out her hand. She looked it over, ran her hand over the writing, and suddenly pulled back. Shaking her fingers as if trying to get rid of something stuck to them, her nose wrinkling, she muttered, "Oh, yeech, ugh. Gods, that's really creepy."

"What? What?" Robin was at her side in the instant.

"No, it's okay, it's not dangerous—at least I'm pretty sure not. Not to people or faeries anyway. Just really creepy—like, making my flesh crawl. Whoever wrote this out—and it must have been Proteus—everything about it, about *him*, is just ugly. He hates dragons, and this spell just radiates that. But since he can't kill them he's put all his anger and, and grief—there's grief there too—into this spell. It … reeks, like a skunk would to a human. Touching it was like having to deal with rotten meat or something equally nasty."

"Well, probably it's good that Chauncey will be seeing it filtered through you then," said Robin. "Maybe coming in physical contact with it would make him ill."

Maggie was quick to agree. "Kate, perhaps he can view it through your eyes and not need to have it near him. Possibly there is magic there that works on him if it is in the same space. Anyway, do get him. I'm sure he's been on tenterhooks waiting to find out what has happened."

Kate, holding the parchment gently and keeping her fingers away from the writing, closed her eyes and went about the usual settling that would calm her before opening her channel (or her witch's third eye according to Maggie) to Chauncey. She felt the tendrils seeking him and was answered quickly by a feeling of connection.

Chauncey appeared before her, radiating interest and concern. "Are you all alright?" he rumbled. "No one hurt, everyone have all their extremities? Kate, you do look tired, but I can see you are all there. Please favour me with looking around at your friends so I may see for myself how they are."

Kate did as he asked, thinking, *Isn't that just like him? We may hold the secret of his freedom here, but he thinks first of our welfare. It's part of what makes him the Dragon King, I suppose, and what makes me love him.* As she thought this she was also looking carefully at each of this band of weary but hopeful warriors and making their images as clear as possible for Chauncey.

"Bone weary, I see, but not downcast. You have news for me, you have good news, I can feel it!" Chauncey's horns were glimmering and his hide once more rippled slightly with changing hues of blues and turquoise. Kate loved it when that happened, when his mood was reflected in the rippling colours of his skin and horns.

"We do," said Maggie. "The box did indeed contain the spells used to disable and enslave you. Kate disabled the box with kindness, leaving the spells unharmed..."

Chauncey broke in, "She what? She made the enchanted box give up the spells with kindness? Kate is a genuine wonder worker, but I have never heard of that approach."

"It whimpered," said Kate sadly, "It reminded me of Poppet when she was found bound up in barbed wire, so it hurt when she moved. I just went with my gut and, well, used magic to cut the hurtful spell away and sooth the box. It opened all by itself. I think, I felt, that the spell that the Body Buddies used must be a painful, horrible spell, a spell that—if you're under it—you are full of fear and pain and afraid to do anything but what the spell requires for fear of consequences."

"But it was a box..." offered Chauncey. "Famous for being inanimate, boxes. I would have thought the spell would be a great danger to any of you, but not to the box."

"Remember the locks I tormented to get them to open the day we met?" asked Kate. "They weren't inanimate, they had been animated as part of the spell to keep the doors locked. They were full of spite and anger and some could talk. I don't think you buy those out of a catalogue...I think they must have been made into something with feelings, and be-spelled to stay shut probably with the fear of great pain if they didn't. I'm sorry to say I provided pain enough to get them to open."

"Well, it is true that the spell that holds me here does indeed provide unbearable pain that knocks me flat if I try to move outside of the limited amount needed to operate as a furnace," allowed Chauncey. "But what a nasty bit of extra agony to make even inanimate objects without feelings, into something animate that is tortured into tormenting others."

"The sleep and awakening spells that they use are very similar to what I would use," said Maggie. "They include healing as well, but also are topped off with touches I would never use. They're in Latin, which happily Perry can read. But we think they're only in Latin as an extra layer of protection against someone knowing exactly what they are for, because translated into English they rhyme, as so many Wiccan spells do—mainly because that's easier to remember—whereas they don't in Latin. A reverse of a reverse if you like."

"But what we have that's most important is what we're almost certain is the spell that binds you and enslaves all the dragons," said Kate. "It's in an alphabet and script and a language none of us has ever seen. So we think it must belong to the Chimaera. And I'm sure it does because it gives off a feeling of dire peril and sheer evil that reminds me of the spell on the box itself. Whoever did this spell and wrote it out is a really nasty piece of work. I can feel it."

"Can you show it to me?" queried Chauncey.

"Yes, of course, and with your photographic memory can you store it in your head and translate it for us? Look here it is," and she held up the page, carefully keeping her fingers away from the ink that gave her such powerful feelings of uncleanness and dread.

Chauncey's face came closer in her mind. She could see his great golden eyes scanning the page. Then his entire face grimaced as if he'd smelled something horrible. "This is indeed the spell, even though I have never heard it pronounced over me, this says exactly what would be needed for enslaving me. And frankly, it stinks to high heaven—an uglier way of putting it I couldn't envision. I can translate it into English for you. But once we come up with a good counter-spell, that will have to be translated back into this ugly barbaric language, memorised by one of you and said here to my face for it to work. Spells are usually quite hands-on—you can't bespell a creature through a television, for example, or even hypnotise them, no matter what a horror film might show."

"But what about the fact you found out that by spell-binding you, they renew the enslavement of all the other dragons, then?" asked Robin, ever quick to find the flaws.

"A rather different sort of metaphysical binding is involved there," said Chauncey. "The other dragons are all my blood kin, and dragons, unlike humans or other species on this earth, are blood kin in every sense of the word. You might get the genetic code from a parent that gives you the propensity to a disease, or a talent, and never get the disease or the talent, but might pass it on to one of your children. For this there has to be physicality. But you would never get the same injury as your parent or aunty, say, once you were born and at a distance from them. For us, from our world, it is possible for those malignantly disposed to us to create a way to hurt one and hurt all. A very unfortunate circumstance that wouldn't have been a problem for us had the diabolical Chimaera not managed to make his way into this world in search of us and found a depraved human to be guided by him.

"Kate, I will say good night now, and ponder this document. I am quite sure it is the spell. The language is indeed Chimaera, not something I have ever wanted to speak, but I do know it. It will take some time however to make absolutely sure I translate it into English without losing any part of its magic. You must have the real spell to create a fully functional counter-spell. Every syllable of every word must be as exact as I can make it. Then you will have the right spell to work against.

"And thank you, all of you, from the very bottom of my soul. You have I know endured great peril and pushed yourselves to the limit for this—for me. I am grateful beyond measure."

Chapter 60

"We did it for ourselves, too," Kate said wearily. "Poor Chauncey, he's been through so much, and it must be almost unbearable sometimes to be helpless, but he shouldn't have to think it's all for him. Ashley Manor will be lost or burnt or something if we don't stop them. And the Statues—they want to help, so possibly we can first release them from the boundary that keeps them, as stone warriors, from marching on Wyvern Hall and destroying the Wyvern army, and the moat creatures and even taking the ugly place to bits. They would love that." She leaned her head back against the arm of the sofa, always more tired after making the channels to communicate with the Dragon King.

Perry was lying back in a chair with a cool cloth on his forehead for his headache but he hadn't forgotten the statues either. "We need to look at the rest of these spells—there should be something there that could free the statues. At least allow them to move outside the perimeter boundary Wyvern has enforced on them."

"Yes!" said Kate, "When we go to free Chauncey, it would make all the difference to have them to protect us from the Wyverns and the Things in the Moat. Being stone, they should be able to dispatch anything softer without being hurt themselves. Oh, and how they would love to get their own back on Ivor!"

"Plus that means we don't all have to climb up that horrible cliff," said Robin. "We go in like we own the place!"

Kailen was looking as Kate had never seen him before—tired out. Robin was pacing like a caged panther. Only Maggie was looking anywhere near normal.

"Back to the house, everyone! Kailen, please bring the parchments and the box." Just as when forming the circle, she was in charge.

Maggie shepherded them out of the bunker for doing dangerous magic and back across the field to the house and the kitchen. Here she used domestic magic liberally to create hot drinks that soothed aches and pains, injecting a bit of energy at the same time as calming the mind and spirit. These were followed by plates of food, bowls of soup and cake warm from the oven.

When they'd taken the first edge off their hunger, Perry said, "Why can't we just devise the counter-spell and use Kate's channelling to Chauncey to free him? That would eliminate so much risk—no marching on Wyvern Hall, no battles with the wyvern army or the moat creatures, no chance of getting stuck in there."

Kailen grinned and the irony was detectable in his voice: "And while we're at it, we could be-spell text messages or emails, so whoever opened them would become enslaved or even destroyed. Or we could send spells on magic breezes to do our bidding a continent away."

"Oh," said Perry, "I get it—actually that does happen with computers and phones—opening some texts and emails lets loose a virus that can destroy your data or give a hacker access to all of your accounts and information."

"Which can ruin your life for significant periods," Maggie agreed. "But it wouldn't send up a little puff of poisonous gas or a spell that would hurt, change or kill you directly. If major spells (other than those voodoo ones that work by influencing the victim with knowledge that someone is trying to hurt him, so that his fear acts to do the work) could work at a distance, the amount of damage done would have the world in worse turmoil than it is. For every time it saved a few of us some trouble or danger it

386

would be catastrophic a dozen other times. Almost every mage of every persuasion has tried their hand at making spells like this—how simple to sit at home warm and dry and uninjured and fling serious spells out to work their magic. Thank the goddess no one has managed to do such things."

Kate, who, having gone through the food on offer like a starving pup, and who dearly wanted just to go to bed, nevertheless said, "I've got to get back to Ashley. Anyone could have noticed I'm missing by now. We can't afford for them to raise a hue and cry, not after the fire and all the anxiety. Uncle Hugh will go totally mad if he thinks I'm lost somewhere."

Maggie hugged her, "We've got it covered, Kate. Kailen, Robin and I all worked a protection and forgetting spell over the entire manor. It means they won't think you're gone, and if they look into your room—highly unlikely, we made wards against that, but still if someone does they will think they see you there asleep. Poppet is safe in the kitchen and has been walked by Sykes as usual before bed. No-one will see anything they aren't expecting, and this should hold for at least 48 hours. Perry isn't expected on Monday in any case, so there's no school. Everyone will believe you have come over here to visit us. So we'll all get a good night's sleep here now and can sleep in tomorrow morning as well. Then you can go back. Robin and I'll come with you—I'll be working in the office as usual and you and Robin can take Poppet out. Then we come back here to work on the spells and for you to hopefully get Chauncey's translation of the spell that enslaves the dragons. Do you want the Queen's Room again, sweetheart?"

Kate smiled, thinking of how that extraordinary room had enchanted even Chauncey, but she declined it. "I'd rather have the one just down the way here, with the cosy red and white toile de joie wallpaper and the double bed that has that wonderful mattress—oh and that huge bathtub to soak in. Is that okay?"

"Absolutely. Perry there's a really nice bedroom three doors down from that. Robin your usual room?"

"No Mum, I'm staying next door to Kate's room. And please take the spell off the mobiles. I want to be able to text or talk in case she needs me."

"Okay with me," said Maggie. "Because I know if I said no, you'd do it anyway." Robin grinned and hugged her.

Perry said, "Mind if I take the parchments we haven't gone through yet? I can probably find the spell that keeps the statues from going shopping in Exeter." Which made everyone laugh—much needed after the days they'd had.

Chapter 61

Late the next afternoon Perry came into Maggie's office in the house over the stream, waving one of the parchments. "I think I've got the spell that Ivor used to enclose the statues within Ashley's gardens. Maggie, can you use it to produce a counter-spell?"

Maggie looked up from the ledger she was studying. "Is it in Latin too?"

"Oddly enough, not. He wrote it out in French. Maude told me that their wedding trip was to Paris. Perhaps he was trying to connect it to her in some way— that he wanted to keep her forever. In a horrible way it may be a love token to their union."

> *Chaque pleine lune vous réveillera*
> *Libre de jouer parmi les fleurs.*
> *Profitez de votre nuit à cœur joie,*
> *Mais pas plus loin que les limites que je définis.*
> *A l'aube tu cherches tes plinthes*
> *Calme encore jusqu'à ce que la lune soit pleine.*

Maggie smiled, "That's to the point. Is this what it is in English?"

> *Each full moon you will wake*
> *Free to play among the flowers.*
> *Enjoy your night to heart's content,*
> *But no further than the bounds I set.*
> *With the dawn your plinths you seek*
> *Quiet again until the moon is full.*

"That's it exactly," said Perry.

"Then we need to free them of the perimeter on the full moon," said Maggie. "All that will take is to position them around that boundary, and then we can walk it anticlockwise chanting a spell to destroy it. And I should be able to reverse the part of the spell that takes them back to paralysis at sunrise as well. I will work on that. But first we need to convince them to stay quiet and hidden until Samhain when we will attack Wyvern Hall. Perhaps our bunker for explosive magic will serve for that."

"But, Maggie, once you've freed them to wander at will, what then? After they help us take down Wyvern and free Chauncey, they will be free—and some, maybe a number of them, are mentally ill. Some may have other enemies they'd like to destroy. These are animated stone creatures. They will cause mayhem, not to mention the shock to ordinary people just seeing them."

"Send them to Barcelona?" suggested Robin. "To the Ramblas. They could make good money."

"I don't understand, Robin, why is that a good idea?" Maggie looked perplexed, but Perry was laughing.

"Because the Ramblas is famous for its many mime artists posing as stone statues on plinths, then suddenly moving, or moving if they are given money. They wear costumes cleverly painted to mimic stone." said Perry. "Actually, it is a possibility. As you all keep telling me, people see what they want to see. They might get away with it for ages."

"Oh, what a very clever idea. But not for many of them, they are too unstable," said Maggie sadly. "I think the only proper thing to do is to free those statues who are compos mentis to make their own choices, so long as they understand and abide by certain rules about the ordinary human world. And, for those that have lost their minds, to free their spirits to go to the goddess."

"You mean kill them, don't you Mum?" said Robin.

"I mean set them free," said Maggie firmly. "Ivor killed their bodies long, long ago. Their spirits have been in a stone trap ever since. Some could deal with it, some could not. It is the same as offering a ghost, a spirit trapped on this plane, the opportunity to move on. It is a real kindness, not without its grief and sadness, similar to when we offer a beloved pet or person the opportunity to escape intolerable illness or pain. There is responsibility, but it is not murder."

"But we will give them the choice?" asked Perry. "Each and every one should get to choose. Okay, they cannot be allowed to choose to wander freely in ordinary society. But they can choose to remain within their statues or be 'set free' as you say. Or even, for a few, whose friends vouch for them—because surely what the statues know about each other is very pertinent here—they could have a go at being 'living' statues in a place like Barcelona?"

"And some may decide they prefer to live here in the garden as they have now for over a hundred years, yes" said Maggie. "But we must set a new perimeter boundary if that is the case and restrict their movements to a few times a month. It is too dangerous for them to perambulate every night. No disguising spell would work over the long term to keep Sir Hugh or Sykes from spotting them."

"I think many might appreciate that rest of going back to their plinths and just 'sleeping'," answered Perry. "My conversations with them over these past months seem to indicate that many might choose to be 'set free' entirely, but others have come to enjoy the passing seasons, the rest without pain or stress, and the occasional party gathering at full moon. As angry and bereft as they are at being snatched away from their families and previous lives, they have come to appreciate the life they have now. However, we must gently put that poor eagle trapped in the stone griffin out of its misery."

Kailen had entered the room and been listening with interest. Now he offered a word of caution. "As much as we need their help with the wyvern army and possibly the things in the moat, we must be aware that once they have fought and won that battle it may set off a rage in some of them to keep killing. Rage and power, once indulged in, can be a difficult thing to put down again. If any of them then refuse to be either set free of their stone or bound over to keep the peace as it used to be called, what then? What do we do with them?"

"Maybe it won't come to that," said Maggie. "We aren't going to allow those who are obviously mentally ill to take part in the battle. But if it does affect one of those that are sane and willing, then we must be prepared to step in and separate spirit from stone. That's the only answer I think."

Kailen, coming over to embrace her, said softly, "My dearest one, I fear you are naive, it is those that display insanity that I am sure could make the most ferocious warriors. They have had everything stolen from them, and they will fight. And I want them to fight. We need them."

Robin, listening in, now spoke. "But look, this is cart before the horse—we need to discuss this with them, they know each other after all this time. They can know if someone like 'Plato' who hasn't even spoken for decades would want to fight, could fight. Or if he just wants to be 'let go' to wherever souls go. He isn't deaf, or dumb, he's just withdrawn into himself. We need to ask him. And we need to respect what these people tell us. And then if—after all that—there are any berserkers left after the fighting is done, we can deal with them then. Mum, can we do spells that will set a soul free of the statue if that soul wants to stay in there and raise havoc?"

"Don't know the answer to that, love, but I am sure we are shortly going to have some." Maggie was looking at her beautiful son with real respect. "You're the one with the ability to move things, even to move them gently or give them a good shove. Maybe that would be a way. Or Kate's move with the box: cut the evil, hurtful spell away and let the soul go free. That also has real possibilities. But you're right about them, they must be consulted and chose for themselves insofar as possible. And Kailen, yes, if someone like poor Plato wants to fight, then we let him, and any others. It might be just the medicine they need in this strange world in which we find ourselves. And we will be there to pick up the pieces and help them to whatever new life they choose."

Chapter 62

Perry offered to tell Maude all that they had discussed about the need for the statues to form a combat unit against the wyvern army and possibly the moat dwellers so that Kate, Robin, Maggie, Kailen and Perry could enter Wyvern Hall via the drawbridge to free the dragons.

The next morning therefore found Perry sitting on a bench beside the statue of the beautiful sad harpy. She had told him she valued his visits, and he knew that, once she awoke to his presence, she could hear what he said to her, even though she remained under the enchantment that kept her silent and still.

He chatted about this and that until he could be as sure as possible that she was aware and listening. Then he began "We've decided to leave it entirely to all of you— the statues—to choose those who will fight and those who will not."

He stopped and looked at her to see if there was any sign she heard and understood. Of course there was not, there never was, but usually it didn't matter, as he was just chatting about his day. Now it mattered very much that she took it all in. He had to trust that she was doing just that.

He continued, "The decision as to whether any of you then wish to have your souls freed from the stone to go on to who knows where or stay as statues for some time to come—free at any time to ask for release—is also entirely yours. And if there are some of those with mental disturbances who want to fight—well, then it is up to the rest of you as to whether you think them fit to do so, and up to you also to pass judgment on any that might rebel against the new perimeter once the battle was over and you returned to the garden.

"Insofar as possible, all of you are free to make your own decisions about your individual fates—and also it will be your responsibility, not ours, to pass judgment on any of your fellows who might decide to go rogue. You would do this with the understanding that then those deemed dangerous would have their souls separated from their stone by the witches.

"I've written this all out and printed it for you and will leave it here in a waterproof container for you to read over when you can move at next full moon. Then you need to present this to the others on the night. We'll meet with you a few minutes before so that we can include any modifications you might suggest."

"Maude, I know this will be both a blessing and a curse for each of you. I know most of you have longed to fight this evil. But the aftermath—provided we win of course—the choice of whether to go back to your plinths and your existence as before—except that we can probably offer you more nights of freedom—or to have your souls set free of the stone—I can't imagine that will be an easy choice for most of you. I have no idea what lies beyond life here, if anything at all. In a way it will be another death. Your bodies are long gone and once your souls are released... There is no one who can tell me where you would go, or if there would be any 'you' left at all. I confess I would find that hard to bear in your case, but I don't want to influence you on that, any more than I would have suggested to my grandmother when she was dying and wished for a release that she must stay because I would miss her. I do miss her, but I'm glad she isn't suffering any longer. I would miss you, but equally I do not want you to suffer."

The full moon was only a week away, and Samhain only six days after that. Once the statues had had this crucial meeting and made their decisions, the five who would be freeing the dragons would join the statues in the garden. The statues would show them the limits of their freedom of movement by each going as far as possible before the perimeter spell stopped them, where they would stand marking the outline so that Maggie and Kate could perform the counter spell that would destroy the perimeter. Then all those that wanted to and were deemed fit to fight would take refuge in the bunker for dangerous spells until it was time to head for Wyvern Hall. The others would return as usual to their plinths and the perimeter spell put back in place.

Meanwhile, Chauncey would have translated into careful English the dark spell that held him. The counter-spell would be a rush job for them all, and they could only hope that their spell-craft was up to the job. Then it would be Chauncey's task to turn the counter-spell that would free him back into the Chimaera's language. And after that he would have to help all of them to learn to pronounce it flawlessly in that language, because even a mispronounced syllable could result in failure, or possibly worse, a different spell. Because they would have to stand in front of him and recite the freedom spell for it to be effective. Although there was such a thing as doing magic at a distance (such as using poppets or voodoo dolls) this was not nearly as quick or effective as doing a strong spell on the spot.

Kate had spent the day at Ashley Manor, playing with Poppet, taking a walk with her great-uncle Hugh, generally making her presence felt. Now, having cast her own disguising spell that allowed the Ashley residents to believe she was still there, she arrived back at the house over the stream. Tonight she hoped Chauncey would have the dragon spell translated into English so they could work on a counter-spell.

396

Chapter 63

"I think I've created a good disguising spell," Kate told her friends. "Everyone at Ashley will think I've simply gone to bed early after getting Mrs Sykes to fix me a few sandwiches. I told Uncle Hugh I wanted to watch a box set of old *Friends* series. That is bound to keep him away, he can't really stand that sort of thing. I left him in his study listening to Leonard Cohen records. If anyone should knock on my door, my voice will say I'm in the bath and going to bed shortly. I added a bit of magic that will get them to go away without me having to say it. And everyone will think they saw me going upstairs."

"That will work so long as there isn't another wyvern attack," said Robin.

"Or an ordinary fire, or a hurricane or a sudden subsidence where the manor falls into a huge hole," laughed Kate, pretending to wrestle with him. "For a gorgeous bloke with superpowers you sure as hell worry a lot. We can count on you to find the negative side!"

"Well someone has to have your back. And for a beautiful girl with superpowers you sure can get in a lot of trouble," laughed Robin, getting her in an arm-lock, then leaning forward to kiss her.

Dinner was left-overs, but in the kitchen of a magical house, left-overs seemed able to turn themselves into mouth-watering confections. There still wasn't a magic spell for doing dishes though, although Kate didn't mind when it meant she and Robin could spend a bit of time alone while the adults were out in the garden with drinks.

"Why doesn't Maggie have a magical dishwasher though?" she asked Robin.

"I think it was when I was behaving a bit weird and Kailen decided I needed to go to a normal human school, she re-programmed the house so it was more human-normal and told me I would have to learn these things if I wanted to fit into the world. I didn't want to fit, but I didn't want not to fit either, so I was being difficult. Washing dishes without breaking any was something I had to do to get any free time for awhile."

"Didn't want to fit, but didn't want not to fit either…" Kate repeated. "That's exactly how I felt living with my mother—I hated her house, her friends and the friends she thought I should have. I didn't want to be like them, but I hated being different too. Then I went to my Grandmother Lucinda and everything changed. I would have loved to be like her, I felt like I fit there—but only there with her. All the rest of it, school, 'activities' all that—I still didn't fit. Until I came here. I guess being a powerful magical person means by definition you don't fit in many places."

"Well, we both fit here, and we fit together," said Robin, suiting words to action, as he embraced her. As always, it seemed their bodies melded into an exciting new whole. "Is tonight the night Chauncey delivers the translation of the Dragon Spell?"

"I'm really hoping so. We haven't all that much time, not for creating a counter-spell and all the other spells we need before full moon, let alone before we march on the Hall at Samhain. Oh, did I tell you Chauncey has adopted me?"

"Err, no. How will that work, you get wings and scales and a tail with an arrow head on the end? Horns?" Robin put his hands above her head and wiggled them.

"Oh, stop! No, none of those—although wings would be fun maybe. No, he says I'm as brave and bright as a dragon and he wants to symbolically adopt me because I don't have a father. I didn't say I have a good father, only I never see him, and Uncle Hugh as well. But it's a great honour, and maybe some protection, plus I love him dearly, so I'm very pleased."

"Then I'm pleased for you too," said Robin.

Somewhat later Kate was in her bed, cocoa and biscuits on a tray, and she quieted her mind and made her rainbow channel, the different colours spreading as tendrils through time and space to reach the Dragon King.

It was more difficult than usual to calm herself sufficiently to make the connection and she realised that she was very much counting on Chauncey's skills to create a good translation. Because the problem with magic spells (as with most communication, but with magic there was a real element of danger) being translated back and forth is that things could get garbled and if they did the best you could hope for was that casting the spell would result in a damp squib. More likely you'd be on the receiving end of some sort of really nasty surprise. The wrong word, the wrong intonation, and instead of the rabbit out of the hat you could get a rabid Tasmanian devil set on world domination. There was a lot riding on how well they could all pull this off.

But it had to start with Chauncey, and she had faith in him. With that thought, her mind settled, the 'screen' of her third eye cleared and there he was. She could tell he was pleased—that wonderful squid-like ripple of colour running through his scales was sky blue over turquoise and deep navy—she'd learned that indicated satisfaction. And his horns were glowing as gold as his eyes, which meant he felt really pleased with what he'd done.

"Good evening, Kate," he said (another of his traits was to get more formal when there were important things happening). "I believe I've made a satisfactory translation of this odious spell. Can you take it down as I say it to you? I am going to make some pauses and insert a nonsense word here and there—these will be obvious to you, and you can put them in parentheses. But I don't want to take any chances saying the real thing aloud even in English and in my mental connection to you. Who knows what devils could be released? So I caution you also not to say it aloud, even in English. We must be very careful."

Kate had her tablet ready. "Ok, Chauncey, I'll take extra care. Please go slowly. And can I ask a question about a word if I didn't hear or understand correctly?"

"Certainly, a word out of context is just a word, not a fireball," rumbled Chauncey. "Here it goes then. Ready?"

"Ready!"

I who dwell in the — (hic) —Hall of Gore
Command thee — (hup)—come to my abode.
Abandon all your —(ziz) — hopes and dreams —
Never living... never dying
With this — (hum) — spell I do command
You are woven to the dark — (hic) —and damned
Forever enthralled to my — (hum) —least wish
You will stand — (hup) —or lie or burn,
You will nevermore be free.
As I speak so — (ziz) — it will be.

Kate was nearly giggling by the end of this, Chauncey's nonsense words making the whole thing sound silly and trivial. But then she retyped it leaving them out. And shuddered.

I who dwell in the Hall of Gore
Command thee come to my abode.
Abandon all your hopes and dreams
Never living... never dying
With this spell I do command
You are woven to the dark and damned.
Forever enthralled to my least wish

400

You will stand or lie or burn,
You will nevermore be free.
As I speak so it will be.

"Oh, Chauncey, that's, it's … truly dreadful. What a terrible thing to do. I'm so very sorry. Does this mean that within this there is also the summoning spell? That's how, by saying it over you, they got all the dragons who came to this world to come to Wyvern Hall? Is that The Hall of Gore? Well it is very red, I admit."

"You should have heard it in the original Chimaera language—made my scales stand on end, that did," said Chauncey. "But you'll be learning bits of that soon enough when I've translated your counter-spell."

"Oh, stars! The counter-spell! I have to get this to the others. We have to get working on a really effective counter-spell and the other spells. We are working on spells to release the statues to fight the wyverns and make it safe for us to get into the Hall and to you. We have to sort out what to do with them afterward too.

"Darling Chauncey. This is the most wonderful horrible thing ever — wonderful that we have it, horrible that anyone could do it to you. Can we say goodnight now, and I'll let you know tomorrow how we get on?"

"Of course, Daughter. Don't get too tired, I know creating and holding this channel is tiring for you."

"Not nearly so much as when we started. I'm getting better at it, and it takes less of my energy. Anyway, goodnight, dear Chauncey. You've done wonders." She saw again the happy ripple of colours over his scales as she closed the channel.

Chapter 64

Indeed, Kate was not nearly so tired as she used to get when making the channel to Chauncey. In fact for some days now the ritual of contacting him the last thing before she went to sleep was more for the pleasure of his company as a sort of parental figure to figuratively tuck her in and wish her a good night's sleep and sweet dreams. Now she hurried back to the sitting area adjoining the kitchen where Maggie and Kailen had been discussing the best way to break the magic boundary spell that held the statues within Ashley's gardens. They had just settled upon a simple variation on the usual circle-closing magic they did at the end of a spell-casting session.

"Simple, effective, without any extra hocus-pocus," said Maggie. Kailen embraced her and was murmuring into her hair, "I can always count on you, my beautiful witch, not to complicate things. It's just one of the reasons I love you so. The Fae simply revel in complications, it's one of their major characteristics, and a reason I have estranged myself from them."

"And because they went ballistic when their Prince chose to live with a witch." said Maggie wryly. "I've never been sure whether you left just before they could throw you out. Be that as it may, it certainly makes our lives less stressful that we rarely have to deal with them, and I for one am very grateful."

Kailen just smiled. If he had any regrets at having to abandon the many beauties and excitements of the Faerie Court, he'd never let them show. And in truth, whatever he may have missed he felt was more than made up for by the life he had now. He certainly didn't miss the trickery, treachery and cruelty that existed alongside the extravagant life and delicate beauty the fairies created to amuse themselves.

Kate had paused in the doorway and overheard this last bit. She hadn't been aware that Kailen no longer lived in the Faerie Court, but was relieved. Faeries, even Melior who, as a water sprite was a loner, were not considered trustworthy, and she'd wondered a bit about Kailen, although he had always seemed staunch and reliable. But her other news carried her into the room now.

"Chauncey did it! We've got the major spell. And it not only enslaves the dragons, it is the summoning spell as well. Although I suppose they've all been summoned by now." She waved the tablet. "I've written it as he dictated it to me, with extra nonsense syllables to keep from pronouncing the exact spell because, even translated to English, he feared saying it might activate something. And I've written it without those too— and it's horrible."

"Perhaps better not send it to our computers or phones then," said Maggie. "Recently I've been hearing that certain magic spells can work like hacking — there is some sort of crossover possible."

Kailen added, "Of course, from the time computers were first being hacked we magical beings understood that as somehow related to magic spells, although we had no idea there could ever be crossover. But it appears that when you get a magical being with genius hacking skills, then it was only a matter of time before actual magic could infect a computer. It's in its infancy I think, but we need to be careful about sending spells via wifi now."

"So, Kate honey, let's see the translation, and I'll copy it off by hand." Maggie held out her hand for the tablet. "Don't worry, we won't say it. Oh, he is clever," she continued, having read it over. "Straightforward and no messing around. Makes it easier to do a counter-spell. Here, Kate, have your tablet back. Just don't send this to anyone, okay?"

"I wrote it in a text document, I can't send it by accident, so do I need to erase it?" asked Kate. "Because I'd like to work at a counter-spell too."

"Come on then, sit with us, and we'll have a go," invited Maggie. Soon the three were around the kitchen table, pads of paper in front of Kailen and Maggie, and Kate with a blank text document open. Drinks and snacks were supplied by Robin, who had come in from some late evening ramble, before he too sat down with his tablet and took in the warnings about how to handle the spell.

Between them they worked within the parameters of the binding spell Chauncey had given them, arguing occasionally over the choice of a word. Maggie argued for close rhyming, Kailen wanted to include the words Wyvern Hall, Robin and Kate felt it important to mention the duel being—"But don't you dare think we'll call it the Body Buddies!" snapped Maggie—that had cast the spell. In the end it was a little of everyone's input, which made it more free verse than the rhyming Maggie used, and calling it by the name Chauncey had translated. But they could all agree it had covered the bases.

All Dragons bound, hark to me!
Gather up your hopes and dreams,
No longer enthralled to the dark and damned
Nevermore bound
To the masters of the Hall of Gore
Released forever from their vile command.
Freed to move and fly and feel
You will evermore be free.
As I will, so mote it be.

It was in fact quite a fine spell. Their only slight concern was whether to call Ivor and Proteus 'masters' plural or 'master' singular. Kate said, "I think Chauncey would have the answer to that. And if we are all to learn

404

how to say it in Chimaera then perhaps when we learn it, we will be saying 'As *we* will. I will ask him about that too."

Robin, who wasn't finding learning even French easy, was not best pleased that they would all have to learn exactly how to say the spell in Chimaera. "What the hell for?" was his opinion.

"Because," said Kate patiently, "it might be that we all don't make it to Chauncey's cellar. We all learn it absolutely perfectly so that, even if there's only one of us left who gets there and can speak, they can set Chauncey and the others free."

"Oh, my gods," said Robin brokenly. "I hadn't thought. I really hadn't. I've been living in a sort of superhero film, haven't I? With the statue army defeating the wyverns and us just marching across the drawbridge and down to Chauncey and freeing him, and he and his kin would destroy the Body Buddies. The only blood I imagined was from wyverns."

Maggie hugged him close, "And that's exactly how we're planning it to go, my son. That's how it will go if we get it right. We're doing everything in our power to make sure no one gets hurt. It will almost certainly be the five of us standing there like good school children chanting our memorised spell. And repeating it in English too. But, my lovely boy, we can't be one-hundred percent sure. Since freeing Chauncey is the priority we have to be absolutely certain that happens."

"So," said his father, "we all get to learn a spell in a very obscure and difficult language that will make French or Latin seem like a doddle. It's probably full of horrible gargling and tongue-twisting. But we're in it together."

"All for one and one for all!" smiled Robin, recovering from his emotional wobble.

And Kate hugged him and went off with the counter-spell to send it via her channel to Chauncey, so he could work on the translation.

Chapter 65

Once more on this busy night Kate settled into her bed and, quieting her mind, reached out to Chauncey. He was there, as of course he always was. Looking expectant and hopeful, but with some flashes of worry and fear rippling red and black along his scales and his horns dull. Kate wondered how it was that this occurred, if he could control it, or if it just happened. But that was a question for another evening, tonight it was important to give him the spell that would set him free so that he could translate it into Chimera and then—the most difficult part probably—teach them to say it properly.

She showed him their written counter-spell and watched as he scanned it carefully, seemingly up, down and backward, as he was quiet except for the occasional small puff of smoke and a muttered noise she couldn't make out.

Finally he looked up at her and beamed, his horns gleaming once more. "A most excellent effort, young Kate. A group exercise I take it? I can see signs of all of you in this spell. And I think, as the English say, that you've cracked it. This should work. I will set about translating it."

"There's only one bit we haven't included, since it wasn't part of the spell that enslaved you," said Kate. "The part where you lost your invisibility. They didn't take it from you in the original spell. But all of you are perfectly visible. Is there something we need to do to render you invisible once more?"

"Not your problem, as I understand they say these days," said Chauncey. "Isn't that nice? Finally one thing you don't have to worry about."

"Great—but who can do it?"

"Why, we do of course. Every dragon who is not enchanted can become visible or invisible at will. Our will is at present—except for a few Faerie Dragons—not our own. Once we are free, we can render ourselves invisible in an instant. Although I do rather want to see the expression on that miserable demented demon's face when he sees *me* flying at him, claws outstretched and breathing fire that can melt stone. I will be as visible as an avenging angel descending to punish the damned."

Kate couldn't help grinning to think of how deeply satisfying that would be. Like Chauncey's, it was a wicked grin. But her mind turned quickly to the problem she'd arrived with.

She said, "I've been thinking about us learning to say the spell. Chimaera is a difficult language, hard to pronounce properly. I wish there were some way for us to record you saying the spell so we could all listen to it over and over and practice. But Kailen and Maggie and Perry all say that it is dangerous for us to communicate these things via the internet—that it could be magically hacked."

Chauncey smiled benignly. "It is so good to sit here and be able to solve something for you for once, dear, dear Kate. I happen to have an old-style cassette tape recorder here, part of the collection of useless and useful rubbish I sleep upon. The rats found it somewhere and brought it to me as a gift because I had been wishing I might hear music once more. The only tape in the machine is Queen's Greatest Hits—now what does that remind you of?"

Kate laughed, "*Good Omens* by Terry Pratchett and Neil Gaiman! Where they save the world from the apocalypse. Oh, Chauncey, oh, that is—well, an omen, surely? And we're going to do that too, I just feel it now. But if you record your translation, how will you get it to us?"

408

"With a certain amount of difficulty, my dear daughter," rumbled Chauncey. "But I'm sure it will work. The rats will carry the tape—in relays if necessary—to the outside of the castle and Cora will tell the ravens where to be waiting to pick it up. They will fly it to you. I will have included instructions to Cora that neither rats nor ravens are to mess around with it—that it has to be in pristine condition when it arrives at Maggie's house. Otherwise either of those species could get carried away with taking it apart just for the fun of it."

"Uncle Hugh has a portable cassette recorder—I remember teasing him about it," said Kate with excitement. "Now it turns out he has exactly what we need. I wish I could tell him that!"

"Of course you do. Since you can't, why not tell him you are so grateful he took you in and that you have never been happier," suggested Chauncey. "Tell him that everything about Ashley and your new friends and what he has given you has changed your life for the better." Kate nodded her agreement and understanding.

Then she said, "It's a shame to have to record over Queen's Greatest Hits, but this will give us a way to practice and practice. Chauncey, could you perhaps not just say the spell—uh, I suppose you'll have to put in breaks or nonsense syllables in any case—but carefully pronounce each word or even difficult sounds separately? That way we can practice every bit of it as often as necessary and correct each other."

"I will do that, yes," promised Chauncey.

"And if for any reason it doesn't reach us in working condition, we will have some tapes ready to send back to you for you to record again. Belt and braces as Uncle Hugh would say. And it will be Uncle Hugh who provides the tapes. Only I have to steal them..."

"Don't worry yourself unnecessarily. It should be delivered, intact, tomorrow afternoon. Where exactly should they take it?"

"Do ravens and rats see through the glamour that disguises the cottage as an old bridge? Then they should put it in one of the flowerpots on the front porch. If all they see is an old bridge, there is a large flat rock—only the one—they should put it there. Someone will be watching out for its arrival."

"That's that then. Goodnight, my lovely girl." Chauncey, his eyes and horns gold and his scales glimmering with satisfied colours, held up a golden talon, pressed it to his lips and put it out toward her in a kiss.

Kate felt that kiss, felt it in her soul. This whole exchange, while tiring after a long day, was also so encouraging and left her feeling that she knew now that she was the one who could pull it all together and set this beloved being free.

§ § §

They all went to bed and slept until noon, getting up to eat a big breakfast and gather to learn the spell.

Just as Chauncey promised, the tape was in a flower pot by the front door that afternoon. Kate had asked to borrow Sir Hugh's cassette player, explaining she and Robin had found some tapes they wanted to hear. It was also her moment to let her uncle know just how happy she was at Ashley and how grateful she was to him. She could see it made him simply glow with happiness, and she felt better that she couldn't confide what they were really planning. *If he knew what we will be doing in a few days, he'd be incredibly scared for me, so better he doesn't know. But if it all works, then he will have the security and happiness of knowing that his house and land are safe and that will be the best present we could give him.*

Now their band of five sat around Maggie's kitchen table and listened to Chauncey reciting the spell to release the dragons in both English and Chimaera. He carefully added the nonsense syllables, and they did too for safety's sake. After repeating the Chimaera twice through, he then took it a syllable at a time. The five of them carefully tried to get their tongues and mouths around the harsh, guttural sounds, some of which did seem to require gargling. It was a mess, and a funny one hearing each other mangle the sounds, although in some cases mangled was exactly how it should sound. It was stringing these words together that caused most of them trouble. Luckily Chauncey had also written out both in English and Chimaera exactly how they should go. Perry was by far the best at this new exercise, with Maggie a close second. Kailen, who claimed to know some forty languages, still found making the garbled sounds difficult—the language of the Fae was melodious and this he complained was cacophony.

"I cannot do this," finally spluttered Robin, "It's impossible. I'd rather throw myself in front of one of you guys and save you from a moat monster—that way I'd be useful, if somewhat dead. Because I am not going to be able to recite this spell."

Perry tried to rally him. "Listen, if that wretched villain Wyvern can master these sounds, then you can too Robin. You can't let him beat you at this!"

"I'll bet you anything you like that Wyvern never learnt even a word of Chimaera," responded Robin. "He's got his Body Buddy right there to say it in his very own tongue."

"Maybe that's the problem—our tongues," offered Kate. "We don't know what this Chimaera looks like let alone the shape of his mouth and tongue. I could never make the sounds of a whale or an elephant, not even a close approximation. Maybe we aren't constructed to speak Chimaera."

"That one won't fly, dear girl," said Maggie. "According to what we know the Chimaera has to speak, if he speaks at all, using Wyverns voice box and tongue and mouth. So a human can make these sounds. We just have to practice. A lot."

But, although they laughed a lot, which was a real relief to their spirits, they all took extremely seriously the need to learn the spell absolutely correctly. And with a few time-outs to rest their voices and their minds, eat something and make refreshing drinks, they finally felt they had done their best. They agreed however that since Samhain was still a week away that they would practice daily and repeat the results to each other until it was not just word perfect but second nature as well, because the circumstances under which they would be saying it to free Chen Shi might be very tumultuous.

And the next night was full moon, when they would recruit the statues, and that would keep them busy for the intervening time until Samhain when everything should come together. When by freeing Chen Shi they would free all the dragons and bring down Wyvern's empire and hopefully Wyvern himself.

Chapter 66

Once more it was full moon, this time a week before Samhain. Perry had alerted Maude as to their hopes that the statues would be willing to fight the wyvern army and possibly the creatures in the moat so that their group could get across the bridge and into the castle without injury. Now he was waiting with the others on the path down the long walk between the statues of the two harpies. They heard midnight strike and then the panpipes and the haunting strains of what Perry recognised as being very similar to one of the Chants d'Auvergne called *Baïlèro lèrô* — beautiful and melancholy. Both Maude and Eleanor began to move, carefully at first as if stiff from long weeks of no movement at all, then more fluidly, and it also seemed as though their faces and eyes took on life even though still made of stone.

Perry extended his hand to Maude to help her descend from her plinth, a courtesy she appreciated with a smile while being very careful not to put too much weight on him or crush his hand. Kailen offered the same to Eleanor, and both harpies, with a slight flap of their wings to help them, achieved the ground without difficulty. Maude and Eleanor then put their heads together over the typed explanation that Perry had left for them to read over.

Having read it, Eleanor raised her head and met the eyes of the others. "Thank you," she said simply. "Thank you for giving us the options to choose our own paths both before and after this coming battle. I, for one, will fight—my brother gave me a body that should be very good in a fight."

Maude also thanked them for giving them the options and exclaimed "If only because he came to my bed knowing that a third party would be looking on, I will fight. I will fight because the man I thought I loved was a lie—he did not really exist—and because he could perpetrate such crimes against natural law and bring so much pain to so many who had never harmed him in any way. We will go and rally the others now. I can hear that most have already gathered in the fountain garden."

Eleanor said, "We have this now, we will explain and enlist them."

So Perry, Kailen, Robin, Maggie and Kate took up places against the yew hedge that enclosed the fountain garden and watched as the two harpies—stately and magnificent, with their wings half spread and their heads held high, walked to the centre by the fountain and clapped their wings together making a loud sound followed by Eleanor calling out: "Your attention please! This is the evening we finally get to choose our own destiny. Please listen carefully as my sister tells you the details of what is going to happen, our parts in it, and what our choices are."

She stepped back, and Maude stepped forward holding Perry's type-script. She raised her wings and one hand for silence, but didn't get it because both Shakespeare, aka Tom Jenks, and Falstaff, aka Walter Taylor, came forward looking stormy. Jenks even had his fists clenched.

"You're women, you haven't the right to be telling us what we are going to do, or what is going to happen. If this is going to be some kind of town meeting, we men are the proper ones to run that and then we can vote on the various measures that have be put forward." Walter Taylor had been a member of local government back in the 1860s and he felt if anyone was going to run things it should be him. "Step down now ladies, and let us see that paper and we'll decide how this is going to go."

Maude, however, from listening to Perry pour his heart out over the past four months, knew a lot more about the modern world, knowledge she'd passed on to Eleanor. Plus she was more than ready to stand up to any man, let

414

alone a very fat one who was well behind the times. And Eleanor was right behind her. Instinctively they both spread their wings and lowered their heads, their taloned feet gripped the fountain's edge and they glared as only harpies could glare, Eleanor with her fierce distorted angry face, but also Maude the beautiful suddenly became Maude the fearsome. It didn't hurt either that, as harpies, each of them was nearly twice as tall as any of the other statues, all of which had human form and size.

"I think you'll find that they have the advantage of us, Walter, in size alone and also in weaponry," said Hercules aka Arthur the archaeologist. "I suggest we simply listen and then if you have objections or suggestions you can offer them."

"What exactly gives them the right, that's what I want to know," queried Jenks, not ready to give over just yet.

"A fair question," said Maude. "I stand here as the wife of Ivor Wyvern...." she had to pause as there were gasps and even shouts from the gathered statues. But she continued. "It wasn't something I wanted to make known for obvious and not so obvious reasons. He killed me in a fit of rage, and the betrayal was hard for me to endure. But I know more about him and his villainy than any of you except my sister. She is in fact Ivor Wyvern's blood sister, the woman who raised him after their parents' early deaths. She knows him inside out and he murdered her because of that. And you see before you the forms in which he chose to entomb us. Fate has a strange way of turning the injury he did us into our revenge upon him, as we are incredibly well suited to rending and tearing him and his dark arts to bloody shreds. I challenge anyone here to deny us our paramount right to acquaint you with what we and our friends here (she gestured toward the waiting group by the yew hedge) have learned and the opportunities it gives us to fight him and obtain justice and freedom for ourselves."

"It also might interest you to know," Eleanor couldn't refrain from adding, "that while we have lived a twilight existence for over one hundred and fifty years there have been some changes here. Women won the right to vote in 1918 and there have been two female Prime Ministers. So, gentlemen, I suggest you stand down and *shut up*!"

Maude then proceeded to outline and give details where necessary of the plans that had been made to gain access to Wyvern Hall and reverse the spell that would free the dragons. There was some curiosity about the whole issue of dragons, but everyone seemed to catch on quickly that this would, in and of itself, bring the Wyvern empire crashing down, leaving him destitute, and that the freed dragons could hunt down and destroy Wyvern himself, if in fact he wasn't captured or killed on their mission to free the dragons. A large part of this plan involved setting the statues free of both the boundary that prevented them from leaving the gardens and of the spell that kept them 'asleep' for all but the night of the full moon. Reversing these spells would be done by the witches and the Faerie and with the understanding that the statues, or most of them, would march on Wyvern Hall and attack the wyverns and, if necessary, the creatures in the moat, allowing the flesh and blood group to cross the drawbridge and gain access to the interior where they would free the Dragon King with a spell that would automatically free all the other dragons.

The statues as a whole were in sympathy with the dragons, as they too had been 'turned to stone' and sold. And the poor dragons didn't even get their one night off per month. Most of them declared themselves willing to fight. Only a few declined—including Falstaff/Walter

Taylor, who pleaded age and that, due to his weight, he got breathless.

"And you was going to lead our 'town' meeting? You're a disgrace, you are, wanting to boss the women about...*and* the rest of us, but now you know what's involved you're going to stay at home? I wash me hands of you, Walt Taylor, you great puffed-up coward!" said Tom Jenks. "Besides, you idiot, you don't get breathless, because you don't breathe—none of us do."

One of the women, who, as Venus was wearing very little in the way of clothing, begged off on that score and that she was simply too frightened. "I know I'm made of marble, and don't feel pain and probably couldn't be hurt, but my whole being inside here just cringes from having to fight. I would just stand there, or run away. This body wasn't designed to do battle anyway. I'm sorry, I'm letting everyone down, but I don't feel I can." She was told it was perfectly okay, and right for her to say so now, rather than in the heat of battle.

Maude and Eleanor then asked the assembly to pass judgement as to whether they thought the few who seemed to be insane, like Plato, should at least be asked if they wanted to fight, and if they should be allowed to do so. After some argument, the vote was that each of them should be approached and asked, and if they said yes, should be included in their army. So several of the statues went off to collect Plato and three or four others, who had also ceased talking or interacting. Having found them in various parts of the garden, sitting or wandering, they gently led them back to the central group and explained the situation, with emphasis on having revenge on Ivor Wyvern. Each one in turn was asked if they would want to fight to take revenge on Ivor Wyvern. The several that just stared blankly were gently told it didn't matter a bit, they should just sit by the fountain and look at the fish. But two of them, who had tended to sit rocking back and forth, said loudly that yes, they would fight.

Finally they came to Plato. The human being who inhabited the statue of Plato hadn't spoken a word for as long as anyone could remember. He walked about under the full moon, and seemed to be lost. No one remembered his real name. Still he was able-bodied marble and deserved to be asked. So Arthur aka Hercules did: "Plato, old chap, I know you're in there somewhere. We are finally getting the chance to take revenge on Ivor Wyvern. You remember him—the man who killed our bodies and imprisoned our spirits in these statues? Yes, him. It means we are going into a battle where some of us could possibly get smashed or broken, but more likely we will do the smashing and breaking. Do you want to do this with us? Have the satisfaction of bringing him down?

Everyone was quiet, including Plato. Then…"I will, yes, join you, go into battle, take revenge. I will take this marble body and use it as a weapon and hope I have the satisfaction of seeing this hand reach into his chest and rip out his heart!" And Plato fell silent once more, but the expression on his face was quite different. Whereas before it had looked vacant and haunted, now it almost gleamed with purpose and intention. There was a small ripple of applause and several other statues came over to pat him on the back. He smiled.

Kailen by the yew hedge said *sotto voce,* "I told you some of them would make really good fighters."

Chapter 67

Those that wanted to stay within the garden and not join the fight were asked to stay around the central fountain. The majority, those that would fight, then walked out through the gardens until the invisible barrier stopped them. Here they stood, facing outward, their stone hands resting against the invisible wall of the spell. Maggie and Kailen then went around this barrier anticlockwise sprinkling salt and chanting the spell that ended a circle of protection at the end of a witches' gathering. This proved to be effective, and the periphery that enclosed the statues was no more. With many exclamations of excitement, they stepped forward, no longer trapped.

Eleanor and Maude then came forward, and Maggie and Kate each said the spell they had made that would free them of being forced to return and remain immobile on their plinths. They were followed, in two lines, by the rest, to bow their heads and receive the freedom spell that would allow them to be awake and mobile all year round. There was no sure way of checking the efficacy of this until the hour before dawn, but the 'town meeting' and all the talk between them all had in fact taken many hours, so dawn was not far away.

Indeed, those who had chosen not to fight, were already being magically drawn back to their plinths, the spell that controlled them triggered by the approaching dawn. When he felt this happening, Walt Taylor was suddenly aware that he had revoked his own chance at freedom by refusing to fight. He made a break for it, but the spell was stronger, and although he reached the perimeter where the others had crossed, it threw him back none too gently, and he could be seen trudging back toward his plinth, muttering curses under his breath, but

419

unable to fight Wyvern's original spells without the help of the witches.

Indeed, Robin and Kailen were already reviving the perimeter spell while Perry led Maude and Eleanor and the rest of the statues up the stream toward Maggie's house and to the bunker for unstable or dangerous magic set into the hillside. Here they were to stay, out of sight and out of trouble, until Samhain. To prevent Sir Hugh and the other Ashley folk—particularly Sykes the gardener—from seeing empty plinths in the garden, Maggie and Kailen had prepared a complex spell that showed all of them on their plinths exactly as they always were. This involved a bit of magic that actually reached back into the past to when they were there, and projected it in three dimensions many times per second to each plinth. It was complicated magic that had something in common with holography, but was solid. Once set going however it would just go on and on.

Kate and Maggie then went in search of the great stone griffin and, using a spell Kate had devised to free the soul from the stone, set the confused and suffering soul of the eagle free. This left the griffin statue lying on its side not too far from its usual pillar by the gate into Ashley. How this would be explained, they had no idea, but they had to leave it there as no levitation or impulsion spells they tried would move the stone colossus. Perhaps without its 'soul' the stone itself had just given up. It was considered too tricky to try to include it in the spell within the perimeter, it would have needed too much work to both 'disappear' the fallen statue and create its doppelgänger upon the pillar.

"I wish," said Kailen, 'that we could just have slapped some of those virtual reality headsets on Ashley's residents. So much easier than these very tricky spells."

Indeed, none of them was used to doing so much magic in a short space of time, and they were absolutely exhausted. "I wish," said Robin, "that we could levitate back to the cottage or just appear there, and not have to walk." But as they had to walk, they did, and as they progressed, so they also were taking in that they had actually accomplished all they had set out to do. This added some energy to their flagging brains and bodies and they began to move with more of a spring in their step.

§ § §

The next day Kailen and Robin met with their new army. Meetings with the stone brigade, the statues in the underground bunker, could be raucous. A number of them really wanted their freedom to roam once they'd fought (and won of course). Appealing to their common sense was difficult.

"I've been stuck either on that bloody plinth or strolling around the garden for over one hundred and forty years now. Who are you to tell me I have to choose between that same life, with a few extra evenings to stroll, or no life at all? I always wanted to travel, I did. I was planning to join the army and go to India. I wanted excitement. Tell you what, find a good painter to paint me over like a live human being and clothes to fit me and I'll go travelling—I don't need to eat, I don't breathe, I could be in a carnival or in the army—I bet they'd love a living stone man!" The being that inhabited Apollo was not convinced of the fairness of being returned to a very quiet life.

"Yeah, we're going to do your dirty work, fight the wyverns and the moat creatures so's you all get inside safely, and you think you can tell us we then have to go back quiet as mice to being 'good little statues' … or we can die. And don't go on about us bein' dead already—we ain't. I want to walk down Truro High Street and into me old pub and stand everybody drinks and fight with anyone

421

who picks on me." So spoke Alfred, the Cornish fisherman, inhabiting the statue of Socrates.

"That's just the problem," said Kailen, daring to put a 'we're old pals' arm around the sailor from Cornwall. "You do that and you blow the cover of any number of supernaturals. You think Wyvern did terrible things to you? It's nothing compared to what ordinary folk will do if they discover you aren't a man inside a costume. Dynamite or some other explosive would blow you to pebbles, acid could corrode you away, or you could become target practice for the army on Dartmoor. Even ordinary folk with hammers and chisels could destroy you. And believe me they would. People scare easily. They'd be very scared of you, and they'd destroy you. Then they'd start hunting for others. The iconoclastic massacre of thousands of art works and statues during the English Civil War would be as nothing to what a frightened population could do—every statue in the land would be pulverised, and every magical creature would be hunted down or have its habitat destroyed. Is this what you want? To bring down such destruction on this country, even all the world, in exchange for the few days of so-called 'freedom'— which is all you'd get before ordinary people would dismantle you."

Alfred looked more and more like a philosopher who had bitten off more than he could chew. "I…I hadn't really thought all that much about it. I just thought, yeah, we help 'em do in that Wyvern monster and get them into the castle up yonder and then finally we'ens free to go off and live. I didn't think we'd start a world war!"

"Well, my sea-going friend, you would. I would say go to sea and find an uninhabited island thousands of miles from here, like the Bounty's crew did all those years ago. But in the decades you've been snoozing and dreaming this entire planet has been totally inhabited and overlooked by machines they have put up in the sky that can see anyone anywhere they might go. Nowhere is safe for a bunch of stone people and in any case, from what you say, you wouldn't be satisfied with living somewhere in a group staying away from human habitations. You all want to go off and walk the streets of cities, pick fights in pubs, make a very public spectacle of yourselves? It can't happen. You get some choices, but only a few."

"Dad, what about Barcelona?" Robin was utterly serious.

"We can't trust them," Kailen was stern, and even the two stone men looked nervous.

"What's Barcelona?" asked Shakespeare/Tom Jenks.

"It's a beautiful city in Spain. They've got a tradition of 'living statues'—people who paint their hands and faces to look like stone and dress up in costumes painted to look like stone and stand absolutely still on plinths until someone gives them money, then they move. They dance, or bow, or something, and people take pictures with them. Then these 'living statues' go back to being perfectly still until the next time they get some money. You could do it. If someone touched you, you could say it was a very good costume. But you couldn't just stroll around except at the start and the end of the day, and then you'd have to have somewhere to hide out overnight. It wouldn't be all that much of a life, not like what you've been dreaming of, but at least you could talk to people a bit and walk around different places than the garden. But you mustn't under any circumstances let anyone discover what you really are. And that might be difficult." Robin wasn't sure any longer that this was a good idea after all.

"I could do that," offered Martha the school teacher who was Helen of Troy, "I used to do 'living statues'—that is holding perfectly still. That could be fun for a bit. But not for very long. The life here is easier, my

423

friends—don't think for a minute that being out in the world would be easy. Constant vigilance and every chance of being discovered. And Kailen is right—we'd be run out of town or destroyed. If we go there, or anywhere, we'd need a witch to guard us, or the spells that could release us. I'm inclined to vote we stay right here."

"Could *here* possibly include somewhere to do more than stroll around the garden? Could we have a clubhouse or somewhere we could do things? Sports maybe. Or other games. I know we can't eat or drink, but there's got to be entertainment we could enjoy. I mean, there's got to be more to life than what we've had up 'til now." Neptune was waving his trident around. "Maybe we could re-enact old gladiator games—I could be the one with the net and the trident."

Robin was almost sparking with ideas. "Dad, they *could* have a club house with a sports area. And what about films, television, video games? They could do that. And maybe dances? It just has to be hidden. Like we've hidden the cottage. There are the remains of an old hill fort in the woods not far from the garden. What if they help us construct a large underground club house there? Easy to conceal. And soundproof."

"What are these things you are talking about? Tell-a-vision? Fillems? And games called veed-e-o? Are these something we play with? I used to love music, but we can't play musical instruments that require breathing. We walk, we talk, but we cannot breathe (and we don't need to) or cry (although sometimes that might help). We could perhaps paint or sculpt—ha!—yes the stone sculptures could sculpt things, maybe, if any of us wanted to." Neptune was intrigued.

Hercules, once Arthur Adams, said "I used to be a good bare-fisted boxer, we could stage matches. Or, what I'd really like is access to a library and to find out what's been happening in my field of archaeology."

424

Using his phone to illustrate, Robin was quick to introduce them to the internet, videos on You-Tube and some games. All of them were enthralled. "With all of this at our disposal, we'd hardly need to travel, the world is all here," said Shakespeare aka Tom Jenks.

"All the world's a stage, the men and women only players," quoted Robin.

"Oh, aye. That's what the Fiend Wyvern used to quote to me—what I supposedly wrote. Ha! Stupid bugger he were, for all that he were so rich and thought himself master of the universe."

"Lots of good films and videos of Shakespeare's plays and a whole lot of Marvel Universe films including stuff with a Master of the Universe too," offered Robin. "You'd never run out of stuff to watch. Or games to play."

"There's a problem though," offered Arthur/Hercules. "Our fingers and hands are strong and we have been known to crush things by accident. That tiny object you have that connects to all the world—we'd almost certainly break it by tapping it, or doing that swiping thing you do. Plus I don't think earplugs for listening would work—our ears don't connect to anything, we can hear of course, just as we can speak, and see, but somehow I don't think we do it through these marble ears."

"No problem, not really," enthused Robin. "There should be big keyboards that are reinforced for people who have difficulties like that. I'll bet they've done really strong tablets for chimpanzees and gorillas to use—pretty sure I've seen that on telly. Read something about sheep too—that they can recognise pictures of themselves and their relatives, that must involve computers. If not, well, I bet we could create some. And, Dad, that remark you made about virtual reality headsets—maybe that's just the thing for this lot to go travelling. But if their eyes and ears, the marble ones don't really do the seeing and hearing, maybe not. Still, with computers and telly and games, there's no end to what they can learn or entertain themselves with."

Kailen put his arm around Robin. "Gentlemen and ladies, my son is a goldmine of ideas for your entertainment and your education. If it isn't safe for you to go wandering around the world, satisfying your cravings for a larger life—and it definitely isn't—then it seems there are many ways we can bring the world to you. Not ideal perhaps, but honestly neither is travelling. Here you can live in comfort and have endless resources of education and entertainment. There is still the option for those of you that whenever you decide you have had enough of this life, we release your souls from the stone and set them free."

"And where do souls go? You're magical and immortal, do you know? Me mam always said there was a heaven and a hell, but I don't believe all that no more. There could be comfort in simply not being, but it's also frightening."

Kailen turned to Robin, "As half human you will have to face this death someday. Any thoughts on the matter?"

Robin was pensive. "I like the idea that we get the afterlife we think we will get, whether it is nothing, or pearly gates or just another door to another place. But I have no idea if it is true. I suppose someday I'll find out."

Chapter 68

It was 28 October, three days before Samhain, one of the four great holidays celebrated by witches and many supernaturals. Since the Celtic day began and ended at sunset, Samhain started at dusk on the 31st. It was the night when the edges between realities, between this world and next, between the living and the dead were weakest and crossing over of power, even beings, could occur.

So it would be a few hours before sunset on the 31st, when many of the children of Britain would be out trick or treating, that the five 'squishy ones' as Robin had started to call them, much to everyone else's disgust, would muster the statues and start the hike to Wyvern Hall.

"'Squishy ones' — I mean, really, Robin, we're heroes, warriors, supernaturals, and you want to call us 'Squishy Ones'? I, for one, am not going into battle as 'Squishy Super Girl'!" but Kate was laughing.

Robin wasn't put off. "Octopuses are very, very squishy, and very, very intelligent and you love them, I know you do. There's nothing wrong with squishy, it's something to be proud of. Or we could be the Endoskeletals—that sounds more like a band of superheroes."

"Or a bad Goth band. Well, if it has to be one of those, I'm going for the Endoskeletals," announced Kate.

Now the Endoskeletals were sitting around Maggie's table as so often in the past, plotting out with the collection of lead soldiers Perry had found in the Ashley attics where and when their troops would gather and then strike. Copies of the architectural drawings including the surrounding landscape and the changes to that landscape since Wyvern Hall was built (mainly a lot more trees and undergrowth, quite perfect for sneaking closer without being seen) were spread out on the table, and Perry and Robin were grouping lead soldiers to come toward the gates and the drawbridge from various angles.

At first they had considered that each of them might lead a troop of statues, but quickly abandoned that idea as once the fighting with the wyverns and moat things started they might not be able to group together quickly to make their run across the drawbridge. So Kailen had asked the statues themselves to nominate two leaders, and now Diana aka Roberta, who had in fact been an archer and a gymnast, and Hercules aka Arthur, whose physique spoke of years of sports and war, were also at the table making adjustments to the deployment of their troops. The five Endoskeletals—it was astonishing how that label stuck— were to arrive with Hercules' troops from the woods to the left, and Diana's force would close in from the right. They would be walking toward the setting sun, since Wyvern Hall was set upon the crag where the river bent around, with the front facing the drive coming from the east.

Chauncey, using the talents of Cora and Melior, had instructed the crows once more to attack the two bronze wyverns chained to the gateposts. These bronze wyverns could inflict considerable damage on marble statues, so they hoped the same mobbing by the birds would keep these wyverns out of the actual fight until the Endoskeletals had made it across the drawbridge.

The statues however should be quite effective against the wyvern army that they expected would attack once the alarm was raised. Chauncey had found out where they were barracked from the rats. They lived in a tower of the castle that had no direct access to the rest of the interior, but was simply used as stabling for these beasts and had perches for them and large windows for them to fly in and out. There were around twenty of them. As they had some twenty statues they were fairly evenly matched, unless the moat creatures could come out and function on

428

land. Still, being marble and impervious to pain, gave the statues an advantage. Plus, a number of the statues were actually looking forward to mixing it up with the moat creatures. Having no need to breathe, they intended to jump into the moat with spears and swords and knives and kill as many as possible. Neptune, of course, was leading that group—it seemed only right and proper.

Melior, who needed access to water to remain active, and who could easily be killed by either the wyverns or the moat creatures, had opted out of the attack, choosing instead to remain in her pool. She promised to cast as many spells as she had for their success and hoped they might find Melusine if she was there at all.

As to spells, Maggie had asked Melior to add her power to their combined talents to create a spell that would protect the five Endoskeletals from the fire or direct physical attack by the wyverns. Essentially, they needed a box that would repel both fire and the physical impact of a wyvern, inside which they could move across the meadow and then the drawbridge in safety. Maggie confessed she had never attempted such a thing and they were all uncertain about their abilities to create a strong enough protective shell until Perry remembered what Kate had produced during one of their first lessons in making magic. "Kate, you saw the ocean in your vision in response to the pebbles. And because it was too big to bring to the table, you enclosed it in an aquarium that you then recreated on the table. Can you use that to create a bomb-proof 'container' for us that will move with us across the drawbridge and through the castle?"

"Honestly, I have no idea," replied Kate. "But I tell you what, let's design one and describe its defences and powers, and then I think I could probably make it. But I'll need the rest of you to help, and if it means keeping it in place as we move and if it gets direct hits, then I'll really need the rest of you to help keep it working."

"Are we going to have weapons?" asked Robin eagerly. "I know we have to get to Chauncey and free him, but, honestly, I kind of hate the thought of creeping in under a protection and not getting any chance to hurt those evil creatures."

"Which are much more likely to hurt you," Maggie rapped out. "Yes, if we can creep in like—I know what you're thinking, my son—like cowards and actually *get our job done,* then that's exactly what we will do. None of us are going to be dead heroes if I have anything to say about it."

"Yeah, Mum, okay, I get the point. And of course you have plenty of say, since next to Kate you're the most powerful. Can we do spells or can I use my talent for intention and projection to at least throw something at a wyvern? Will it go through the box of protection from inside? Kate, can we build that feature in?"

Kate, who was hoping like mad that none of them had to engage in anything like hand to hand combat or even be wielding a weapon, shrugged her shoulders. "I haven't a clue, Robin, but I think if we sit down and each make a list of what we want from this and then see how much of it we can incorporate in a protection spell, then we'll find out.

"Oh, for cripes sake, more bloody lists! Mum, Dad, can't we just have some rifles?"

"No!" came from Maggie and Kailen simultaneously.

Kailen said, "Seriously, Robin, we have been gifted with magic, and magic is what we're up against as well. I wouldn't be at all surprised if a rifle bullet would bounce off those wyverns and if we're unlucky enough to actually come up against Ivor and Proteus you can bet they would simply turn the bullet around back toward you. I know you want to fight. You may indeed have your chance inside the Hall where any wyvern that follows us in might have to be killed the old-fashioned way. Meanwhile, I think it will be mainly you and Kate who create and operate our protective shell. She can make it. But you will be moving it with great care so that it totally surrounds us as we gain access to Wyvern Hall. That's a huge job, with our lives in your hands, kid." And no more pleas for hand to hand combat were heard from Robin.

The statues were armed with weapons that they chose for themselves—Diana, since she was an accomplished archer, replaced her marble bow and quiver of arrows with real ones. Hercules discarded his marble club in favour of a metal baseball bat. Plus he had a sword in a scabbard belted around his waist and a kindjal knife in a sheath. He was accomplished with both.

Various other statues were armed with clubs, daggers, swords and even double-headed axes discovered in Ashley's attic. Plus Maggie and Kailen had made a number of magic grenades that would also explode on impact. These were thought to be good weapons against the moat creatures, since they would send devastating shock waves through the water. Although some of the statues were eager to go underwater themselves and kill the moat creatures with spears, knives and swords.

Eleanor and Maude were quite content to look at their formidable talons with a certain amount of respect and even laughter. Ivor had unwittingly given them bodies that were in themselves weapons. They had never used their wings, having before this preferred to keep alive as much of their humanity as possible. Now they tried to take to the air with vigour and determination, but were quite clumsy. But as they were flying and falling, they were joined by a white-tailed eagle.

It was Maude who noticed it was semi-transparent. "Eleanor, look, it's a spirit, a ghost! Maybe it's the eagle that Ivor imprisoned in the griffin."

431

Eleanor stared in wonder as the spirit-eagle demonstrated how they could fly, then stoop downward at amazing speed, only at the last minute to change position so that with talons outstretched they could catch or rend an enemy. It flew upside down to show them how, it flapped upward to catch a thermal and circled in it, and they followed. The beautiful spirit-eagle gave them a master class in flight and fighting. Finally it landed in a huge oak, and they followed, finding that to land successfully on a branch you needed to come up from below and soar until you were just above your chosen perch, then drop.

"It's surely the eagle that was trapped inside the griffin by the gates into Ashley," said Eleanor. "It's come to help us." She extended her arm, and the spirit-eagle moved to sit on her arm, then up onto her shoulder. She couldn't feel it, probably it couldn't feel her, but they sat in perfect harmony on the branch.

Maude was perched on her other side. "I never thought how amazing it might be to fly, or to perch in a tree or to reach for the upper limits of the sky," she said. "I was so determined not to lose myself as a person. But this is beautiful. It gives a whole new dimension to life."

"And a whole new dimension to our ability to fight the wyverns!" Eleanor was absolutely delighted. "Just think, with practice, we will be able to fly as they do, and swoop upon them from above when they are thinking they only have to attack the statues on the ground. We will be a really awful surprise!"

"I can hardly wait!" replied Maude. "Finally, something really worth doing. Sister, we have found our new life."

§ § §

Later that night when she talked to Chauncey, Kate described her wonder and happiness to see the two

432

harpies, until then still caught in the net of Victorian womanhood, flying and laughing and planning their surprise attack on the wyverns with something close to glee. She told him how it was the spirit of the eagle she'd freed from the griffin statue who had taught them how to fly.

"I love them both, you know, but now instead of two Victorian gentlewomen trapped in marble monsters, my friends are infatuated with their harpies and are looking forward to as much bloodshed as possible! Actually, it's hard to get my head around," confessed Kate.

"I know just how they feel—to have wings that work, to have claws that can tear out a heart—to avenge oneself upon those who hurt you. But mainly the wings—I did so love to fly. I am looking forward to doing it again very much. It only seems strange to me that these lovely ladies never took wing before."

"Maude explained that they never thought of themselves as anything but spirits trapped in monstrous bodies. It was important to them to keep their humanity, their identity as human beings, as much as possible. Hence the knitting and reading books. They'd hardly ever even moved their wings. Flying—they wouldn't have believed it possible. But then, even before the eagle, they realised that the 'monsters' they are would be really formidable weapons. Wings, long strong talons, enormous strength—it excited them into beginning to fly, and then the eagle—I almost want to say angel—came and taught them how to do it properly. He hangs out with them now, and they…they are roosting in a large oak tree! Eleanor says they have found out where they belong and what they are meant to do. So they will be really effective against the wyverns."

"I look forward to meeting them." rumbled Chauncey. "Perhaps we can fly together one day soon."

Chapter 69

And then, before it seemed they'd even had time to think straight, it was a few hours before the start of Samhain as the sun sank down behind Wyvern Hall, and the mixed band of rescuers and fighters were hidden in the woods on either side of the drive up to the wyvern-topped pillars and the drawbridge.

All were in what could loosely be called combat gear, camouflage trousers, shirts and caps—even the statues, who didn't want their creamy marble to attract attention too soon. The Endoskeletals also had on stab vests, compliments of a friend of Robin's at the dojo who could get most anything if you didn't ask too many questions.

Kate and Robin had practiced the creation and movement, and even quick repairs, on the box that would contain them. Strong enough to repel fire or physical attack by a wyvern or a moat creature, but breathable, so they wouldn't run out of air, it was also invisible. Maggie and Kailen had been responsible for the invisibility spells and would hold them in place. Kate was responsible for keeping it in one piece and, should a talon, or fang or blast of fire breech it anywhere, she was responsible for doing an instant repair. Robin with his talents for moving objects large and small, was responsible for keeping it moving smoothly around and under them, quick to change direction or speed if necessary. For both of them, this was the most complex and dramatic magic they'd ever attempted. Somewhat to their surprise they discovered it was empowering to do it.

Now, while they waited for the sun to set, when their powers would be strongest, they were snacking on homemade sandwiches and energy drinks. As always when Maggie cooked, there were a few extra ingredients that in this case would add endurance, healing and even fearlessness into the mix.

"I love it that when we say your cooking is magic, we are speaking nothing but the truth," said Kate, giving Maggie a quick hug. "Somehow, this feels like a walk in the park compared to the last time I was here—I'm not particularly frightened—is that part of the secret ingredients?"

Maggie laughed, "There could be a bit of that, but also you're here with friends and we all know, insofar as we can, what we're getting into. And we're in it together. You were alone before."

Perry joined them and also got a hug. "Can we," he asked, "go over the way through the Hall to Chen Shi's cellar once more? I'd feel more at ease if I know I could find it even on my own—even though I know I won't be."

And then the sun slipped down below the horizon and Samhain announced itself with blazes of glory streaking the sky in gold and hot pinks and orange and peach. The moon topped the trees behind them and Venus, the morning and the evening star, became visible in the cloudless sky.

"It's time," said Maggie, her voice carrying reverberations that the trees and the bushes seemed to pick up and whisper *it's time, it's time, it's time.*

They gathered together and the protection and invisibility spell surrounded them. Robin had said it was a real shame that they couldn't just be invisible as well. But he let it go when it was explained that they could easily trip over each other or over their own feet. And they were off, followed by Hercules' troops. From the other side of the drive the rest of the statues, almost invisible in their combat gear and the twilight, joined them and they walked briskly toward the pillars with the wyverns, breaking into a fast trot as they came within closer sight of the drawbridge and the moat. Eleanor and Maude waited in the trees,

436

hidden until they could burst upon the attacking wyverns from above.

And now they heard the sharp screech of a wyvern, alerted probably by those on the pillars, and shortly they saw the first of them shooting up from behind the castle walls and gaining height with powerful flaps of its wings. Then came the others, struggling to gain height and then spreading across the sky. Their battle cry was painful to the ears. And their leader let out a gout of flame that made them scream even louder. They formed into a V-shape, much like a flock of geese, and pointed toward the attackers.

Those who came to rescue Chen Shi had already decided that they would not break formation or try to run faster when this happened. They would wait until the wyverns were almost upon them before Diana loosed an arrow or any of the others a spear. As they got near the gates the crows would fly out and mob the bronze wyverns chained to the pillars as they had done before. And when the flying wyverns were concentrated upon the troops on the ground, the harpies would take wing and come upon them from above.

That was how it was supposed to work. That was how it nearly did work. But there always has to be that awkward moment...

One of the statues, trotting briskly along, tripped over something, probably his own booted foot since they weren't used to wearing shoes, and crashed into the one ahead. Who fell forward against the wall of the spell that protected the Endoskeletals. This startled Kate so that her concentration broke for a moment and this made Robin turn toward her to help her, so that his propulsion of the 'box' also turned and both Perry and Maggie had a face full of the spell wall. There was consternation in the ranks. And at that moment the wyverns dove and hit them with multiple bursts of fire.

They hit a statue who screamed from shock (since it couldn't feel pain) and they hit the protective box, where Kate's loss of concentration had allowed a small tear, and a thin arrow of fire got inside. It simply hit the ground, but scared them all. Kate rallied and repaired the box spell and Robin recovered his sense of direction and, with the two of them now holding hands, they all resumed their quick jog trot to the drawbridge.

Behind them Diana had loosed an arrow at close range into the breast of a wyvern. An arrow with the best of Kalien's spells upon it, it sliced through the protective scales and pierced deep into the wyvern's chest. It screamed, and clawed at the arrow, but only managed to break it off. Unable to fly, it plummeted to the ground where several statues with swords and knives attacked it.

The other wyverns had peeled off after their blast of fire and were regrouped into their V-formation and were just preparing to go into their dive when the two harpies came out of the trees, rapidly gaining height, and, as the eagle had taught them, circled upward. Then, before the wyverns were aware of the danger from above, they dove head first, wings tight to their bodies, only to snap those wings out and flip in the air so their great talons were now pointing down. And with those talons they each scored a wyvern, grasping them around the neck, talons puncturing deeply, and flying off with them. Reaching the trees, they landed and proceeded to tear the wyverns limb from limb.

The Endoskeletals had now reached the point where they had to run between the two bronze wyverns. This was the signal for the crows to descend upon the wyverns' heads, circling, pecking, even landing briefly, so that these wyverns were completely snowed under in black feathers, wings and beaks. They thrashed but, chained to their pillars, were unable to break free. The box spell with its squishy contents was making good progress over the drawbridge. But then a flying wyvern saw the problem with the crows and circled around to be able to aim a gout of fire at them. Perry saw this and screamed, "Crows, fire coming! Fly!" And they did. Only two of them didn't quite make it, one was blasted into a fireball, and the other had its feathers singed so badly it couldn't fly properly and fell into the moat, where something with very big teeth snapped it down. The only other casualty of this fire was the bronze wyvern itself, whose head was partially melted by the blast of fire. It seemed to leave it unable to function. "Scores an own goal" yelled Robin.

The box spell was now under the great wall of the castle, inside the portcullis and momentarily protected from the aerial wyverns. They stopped for a brief breather and to check out the large central space they would now need to get across. For the first time they could also look back at the statues—Neptune's lot had indeed plunged into the moat and splashes were heard and the water was turning red in places…and then in more places. They had to believe that meant the statues armed with spears, knives, even axes, plus Neptune's trident, were making good progress, since the statues didn't bleed.

And they saw the harpies make their second raid on the wyverns, which were in some disarray. Again they rose, circling for height, then dropped and, turning, each grasped a wyvern in her claws. This time another wyvern managed to try to claw Maude, and to stab her with its arrowhead shaped tail, but both were useless against her stone. She let out a shout of pure merciless joy as she turned and made off with the helpless wyvern in her claws. Eleanor was already off among the trees with hers.

Kailen called the Endoskeletals back to the purpose at hand, "Quickly, before they can regroup, we go as fast as possible along the shaded side of the wall, make for the door in the far side, it leads to Maude's garden." And once again they were running, keeping to the shadows. Real darkness would arrive soon, and as much as it might shield them from the wyvern army, they too needed the failing light to get safely inside the castle where they doubted the wyverns would be able to follow. They heard rather than saw the remaining wyverns gathering above the central square, but before they could do more than send some fire their way, fire that simply bounced off their protective box, they had reached the door into Maude's garden and huddled for a moment under the arch. Wyverns were already there, two of them marching around, their long tails dragging through the lovely planting. Maggie had the feeling they'd be flaming the foliage if they weren't concerned about running out of fire. Another was sitting on a turret, waiting for them to come through. So far they didn't seem to have figured out that the Squishes were protected by an invisible exoskeleton. Three statues, two of whom had some of their camouflage gear burned away, joined them, holding knives, spears and double-headed axes.

"We'll clear the way for you if you like," said Plato. His grin was fearsome.

"You're talking!" Kate was surprised and pleased.

"I've got a purpose, I've got a plan, I really want to kill some," grinned Plato, twirling the double-headed axe from hand to hand like an expert.

"Be our guest," said Robin, ushering him past them with a wave of his hand. The three, letting out what Kate imagined could be a banshee cry, it was blood curdling enough, burst out from under the archway and fell upon the two wyverns on the ground. And the spell box moved forward as fast as possible down one of the paths leading to the far door. The wyvern on the turret had just launched itself downward preparing to hit them with the best flame it could produce when it was hit by Eleanor's huge talons, smashed against the castle wall on its way up and out, and was gone before most of them had quite grasped what had happened to it.

440

"By Hecate, she's fast!" cried Maggie. "What a warrior, she'd give Boudicca a run for her money."

There was a human-sounding yell from the garden, and they could see that a wyvern had managed to disarm one of the statues—as in literally remove its arm. But it had also got its teeth stuck into the marble and was trying desperately to dislodge the arm from its mouth. The one-armed statue took the opportunity to plunge a spear deep into the body of the beast, and Plato came up and neatly beheaded it with an overarm swing of his axe.

Maude now dropped down into her garden and landed on the other wyvern, sinking her talons into its neck, allowing Helen of Troy to run it through with her sword. Plato came along behind to behead it as well. With no wyverns left in the garden, the box spell lot could get on with getting inside the castle itself. The lock that had given Kate such problems was still there, still functional— but she hadn't forgotten the WD40, and shortly it was choking and opening.

They'd done it, they were inside, away hopefully from the wyverns and as far as they knew, except for the odd malicious lock, there were no other guards.

Chapter 70

As they moved through the hallways and further down into the cellars, Kate was suddenly shivering. Maggie noticed and called a halt to their progress. She put her arms around Kate saying, "I think you're coming off an adrenalin rush. Here, drink this," and she produced one of her magic green drinks that soothed and energised at the same time.

Kate said in a shaky voice, "I was so focussed and full of energy when we were in the battle at the bridge, now I've just crashed. I'm so sorry."

"Don't be sorry, sweet girl, it's perfectly normal, there's a sense of invincibility that comes in the middle of fighting. But our bodies pay a price when there's a lull. Look, we all feel it." And Kate saw that indeed they did…perhaps not as shaky as she was, but Perry was leaning against the wall, Robin was standing head down, hands on knees, breathing deeply, and even Kailen was leaning on his bronze spear with head bowed. Maggie, whatever her own slump might be, was busy passing out drinks and went to Kailen to softly say spells over him to ward him against the ill effects of the iron in the building.

As they started forward again, Kate whispered to Robin, "Okay, now I'm nervous, it's all quiet and there are no wyverns and I never saw another kind of guard down here, and Chauncey says the rats don't see any either…but I feel like any second everything will explode."

Robin was nodding yes to everything she said, and Perry was also. "It's too damn quiet. It's like everything is poised to go boom. But that's almost certainly just us, we were so keyed up, now we've crashed I suppose."

Even as they shared their nerviness, they were moving on through the corridors and passages that they had memorised with the help of Cora, who flew these halls often. Every T-junction, every turn made them pause and

442

reconnoitre, fearful that there might be a guardian or some trap for the unwary. But just as when Kate had first come this way, there was nothing. The being that wore the shape of Ivor Wyvern apparently still believed that his outer defences were more than good enough. Plus they hoped Ivor and Proteus had no way of knowing that the intruders carried with them the spell that would free Chen Shi and all the dragons.

Finally they could hear the slow puffing and feel the warmth that signalled they were approaching the cellar under the central hall where Chen Shi was waiting. When they came through the final archway and could see him— all of them, except Kate, for the very first time—they stopped and gasped.

Chen Shi was not curled into his beehive shaped furnace configuration, as Kate had first seen him, but standing with his neck extended as far as the spell allowed and his huge head was turned toward them. Shades of blue, green and gold flickered over his scales in patterns that betrayed his excitement and joy at seeing them. Seeing a raven perched on one of his horns let Kate know he had been given the news that they had survived the wyvern army and were on their way to him.

Kate broke free of the group and ran across to greet him. Although they all knew of her special bond with the Dragon King, to see her standing, hugging his front foot, or rather hand, made them understand the full magnitude of what she—and they—had done and were about to do. And the full horror of what Ivor and Proteus had done. Chen Shi was enormous, as big as a sperm whale—and they were here to set him free.

Kate had already dropped her hold on the box spell, and now the rest of them came slowly across the floor. Kailen spoke first. In a passable attempt at Dragon-speak, he swept a bow before Chen Shi and said how honoured he was to finally meet face to face, the first of the Fae to see the Dragon King in over a century.

Chauncey grinned and spoke back in his native tongue. None of the others understood, except Kate, who to her amazement was getting a simultaneous translation inside her head of Chauncey's reply: "My Lord Kailen, it is a pleasure to meet you at last, my daughter Kate has told me so much about you, and about this extraordinary group. I am grateful beyond measure that you have managed through all manner of difficulties to get here today to free me and all dragon kind."

Chauncey turned to include them all and spoke in English. "So, the time for meeting and ceremony is not yet come. First, please, come before me and say this spell so that I can rise up and stretch my wings and stand tall and, finally, be free. Please my friends, now is the moment."

"Now is *not* your moment!" came a furious shout. "Take what is mine, would you? I will *burn* you! Dragon, you are mine! Be still and know who is lord here."

Chauncey, to their horror, became still.

A sphere appeared across the cellar from where Kate, Robin, Maggie, Kailen and Perry were lined up in front of Chen Shi. It was enveloped in flames and rolling slowly across the floor toward them. Inside was a vision of an enraged Ivor Wyvern, seemingly in his study in London.

Kate placed herself between her people and the spectre of Ivor Wyvern, a spectre that morphed as she watched into the shape of Proteus as she'd seen him in the Wyverns' London house months ago when the Muse of History had revealed what she could to the people who wanted above all things to free the dragons.

Lightning crackled from Kate's fingertips and a wind whipped her hair. She began to stalk across the floor toward the advancing sphere, every step seeming to increase her power. She was formidable. Behind her,

444

Chauncey was as erect as the terrible enchantment he suffered under allowed, trying to spread his wings to guard her but unable to do so. His huge face was contorted in a grimace of frustration and rage that he was still bound.

Ivor extended his hand, in it a fire ball, and he impelled it forth toward them. Another instantly appeared in its place. Suddenly it was raining fire, oily liquid fire. Where it touched, people screamed.

But Kate continued to stalk toward the sphere containing the flickering image of Ivor/Proteus. "Your time here is finished," she intoned in a voice barely recognisable as her own. "We have found your spells, we have made the counter-spells. Chen Shi will rise again in vengeance. If you go now perhaps you will survive."

"Huh!" said the spectre of the Enemy. "Little you know, girl. We aren't even here. What can you do to us?"

"This!" said Kate, and her hand loosed a lightning bolt. That...hit the sphere and split it apart. Unfortunately that meant now there were twin spheres enveloped in flames, and they proceeded to circle her.

"Not quite what you expected? We aren't even here, and, look—we reach out and...ahhhh!"

The anguished cry broke from both circling images as another being arrived by Kate's side, her long red hair flashing with power. But it was her hands that were green and glowing with tendrils that flashed forward to slash at the spheres. This green plant did what Kate's lightning had not—penetrated the protective shields and reached inside to grab the two images and tighten around them. Ivor/Proteus' scream became a gasp as he tried to keep breathing.

"Grandmother!" shouted Kate. "You're here! Oh, you're here." And Lucinda's other arm reached out to wrap itself protectively around Kate.

"What have you bound them with, Grandmother?"

"Strangler fig, darling girl. Can crush the strongest tree. Not a native species of course, but needs must when the devil drives, and I've seen quite enough of these devils, so it's time to dispose of them. But that's your job, lovely.   Send them away so you can get on with that counter spell."

"I've tried, but all I did was divide them and make more of them! I'm afraid now to blast them for fear of two becoming twenty or even more!"

"Never underestimate the power of the earth, Granddaughter. Remember a plant or a person grows best in the soil that suits it. Root yourself here in the red earth of Devon, from whence you get your power. Here is your place…here!" She moved one finger and a tendril of root pushed upward through the stone floor of the cellar, splitting the granite and sandstone and onyx as if they were cardboard, opening up a crack that quickly became an earthen floor, the red earth of Devon, with a tangle of roots showing, and some tiny green shoots coming off these roots as they felt light and air once more. "Here, child, is the soil that suits you. Make your stand."

And Kate felt her own feet sending out roots into this newly revealed soil under her feet. Through them she felt the power of the earth rising up her legs and through her body. It was like in some oriental combat film, when the master could not be moved, as if he'd grown into or out of the ground he stood upon.

"Now Kate, now you can send your power with the backing of all the earth behind you." said Lucinda.

Kate, rooting firmly, sent power up from the earth, through her body and out her hands as bolts of lightning. But they only bounced off the shields Lucinda had been able to penetrate with her strangler vine.

"It doesn't work!" she cried desperately, shaking her hands toward her grandmother.

It was Chen Shi who rumbled, "Remember Archimedes—you have your place to stand, now—move them!" And Kate's hands flew up … but instead of fire, she sent a blast of energy so strong that the two spheres, flames extinguished, each containing a bound Ivor/Proteus, were sent bowling away like two dust motes in a breeze. They disappeared down what might have been described as a wormhole, the funnel of a tornado, or possibly into a black hole. Kate didn't care—they were gone. Weren't they?

She turned to Lucinda with the question in her eyes. "Yes, child, they're gone, and for some time to come I think. Just to begin with, they'll need time to extract themselves from that strangler fig—and that one's roots are somewhere in Indonesia! Yes, quite awhile, just for that." Lucinda looked quite pleased with herself. "And you, Kate, heart of my heart, you blew them to kingdom come, so to speak."

"Do you know where?" inquired Kate.

"No child, not a clue, as Robin would say, but far away from here, and I wouldn't be surprised if it were somewhere else in time as well. They won't get back here for a long while, maybe forever. That's the important thing."

"You know about Robin?" Kate was surprised, shocked, pleased … confused. "You've been here all along?"

Lucinda, flame haired and garbed neck to toe in green, with her green hands, smiled kindly and hugged her little girl. "Yes, and no, my little love. Yes and no."

"Will you stay now? Oh, please stay—I've missed you so much. So much." Tears of joy were blurring her vision, but she was also hanging on to Lucinda with both hands, willing her to stay.

"That I cannot do, child. Remember I am dead, and even a witch who can manifest under needful

447

circumstances cannot stay in the living world for long. If you could force it, that would be necromancy, and I think you once renounced that as being totally wrong.

"Because Maggie planned this strike at Samhain, when the walls between worlds, between the living and the dead, are thin… because of that I could get here and help. And now I must go, but if your need of me is as great as this was, then you will call and I will try to come. That is allowed. But wherever I may be I will always be near you as well—quite a nice perk of being deceased I have to say, at least if you're a deceased witch. I'm quite enjoying that aspect of afterlife."

"We all wondered if you were a witch, you know," said Kate, easing her strangle hold on her grandmother. "Why didn't you tell me?"

"Because I wasn't entirely sure myself. I never practiced as a living person. I can see now that I used magic in many ways, but at the time it just felt like natural talents. I wondered sometimes about experiences I had. I foresaw my own death, for example, and that you would come to England alone, and face danger—but not alone. I was comforted when it seemed to me that you would finally have a family who loved and honoured who you are. But I couldn't be sure this 'foreseeing' was real so I didn't tell you. It seems your magic was set free when you came to Devon, but my own became most powerful after my death."

§ § §

But while this tender reunion was going on, behind them there was chaos. Perry had been caught in the rain of fire, like fiery oil that stuck to the skin and burned. It was his screams Kate had heard. But though Maggie rushed to him to apply pain relief spells, he waved Kailen

448

and Robin away, saying, "Our job…free Chen Shi. We got here… Do the spell. Free him!"

Perry lay unconscious, or for all Robin knew, dead. But that was his wish and reminder that all of this was for one purpose—free Chauncey. So he and his father stood, holding onto each other, and recited the spell in Chimaera, each syllable carefully pronounced, just as they'd learned it. Then they repeated it in English.

All Dragons bound, hark to us!
Gather up your hopes and dreams,
No longer enthralled to the dark and damned
Nevermore bound
To the masters of the Hall of Gore
Released forever from their vile command.
Freed to move and fly and feel
You will evermore be free.
As we will, so mote it be.

And Chauncey stepped forward, inhaling and exhaling (without flame) deeply, seeming to increase in size as he stretched himself to his full length. Then extended a gentle foreleg and hand to support Kailen, who was slumping toward the floor. He'd been protected by a number of spells Maggie had laid upon him to shield him from iron, and was further protected by the spell box, but now that Maggie was involved with Perry and the spell box was gone, the effort to say the spell correctly and the iron around him had exhausted him and left him in some distress. Chauncey laid a gold talon gently against Kailen and said something in his own language which calmed him and seemed to give him renewed strength.

With a look at Kate, embraced in her grandmother's green arms, their red hair mingling like twin flames, their tears watering the red earth below, where already green shoots were turning into flowers,

Chauncey turned next to Perry, cradled in Maggie's arms. Perry was unconscious but breathing. Maggie had applied magic liberally to his burns, but there were blackened and raw patches of skin that showed he was still gravely injured.

"May I hold him, please?" rumbled Chauncey. "Kailen needs your skills right now."

Maggie moved gently to deposit Perry's body into the hand of the Dragon King and hurried to her mate. Then they all heard Chen Shi singing in a rich baritone voice, not a dragon's song, but *To Dream the Impossible Dream* from the musical play Man of La Mancha. And they looked to see Chen Shi, King of the Noble Dragons, tenderly cradling Perry, burned and broken on the floor, and crooning the words of Don Quixote, the man who believed that even one man must fight evil and could win.

Kate, recalled from her private world, hurried to Chen Shi and Perry, putting forth healing intentions and spells, and she sat on Chauncey's arm next to Perry's head and stroked his hair, half burned away. But where she stroked, the angry burns retreated. Perry came back to consciousness to see the two heads, the redheaded girl and the enormous dragon, both leaning over him with love and concern in their eyes. "I've dreamed the impossible dream…" he murmured and passed out once more.

Chapter 71

"Oh, Perry," Kate groaned. "Chauncey, is he burnt very badly?"

"It looks worse than it is, Daughter, but it must be very painful. Try some more healing and pain relief spells." So Kate did that.

Robin came over, more than a little awe-struck at the size of the dragon but trying not to show it. "Perry…oh my gods, will he be okay? He looks terrible." Robin was still at some distance from the trio and seemed hesitant to come closer.

Chauncey grinned his terrible grin, but softened it by saying, "Come over Robin, I don't bite and I've declared a moratorium on fire-breathing for a bit. I'm pleased to meet you. We have something in common, you and I."

"I…we do?"

Chauncey inclined his head slightly toward Kate nursing Perry in the circle of his great hand.

Robin understood him perfectly, and smiled. "Yeah, she's awesome isn't she? The girl who can see dragons. Your chosen one. My chosen one too."

Maggie came over with Kailen, buoyed up by her refreshing the wards against iron. The two of them put their arms around their son. "Robin do you think you could lift and move Perry gently all the way back to our house? It would be the least traumatic way to move him if you can do it."

"Yeah, I think I can. Can you help at all? I'd hate to drop him. Actually, I couldn't bear to drop him!" Robin seemed to pale under his tan at the thought.

"We can offer you strengthening spells and encouragement. And we should be able to sit and rest once we're back under the trees. Perry's not in immediate danger, but I want to get him back where I can treat him properly and make sure no infection sets in."

"What about the wyverns?"

"We think most, if not all, are dead. And at least one of the bronze ones is also *hors de combat*."

Chauncey rumbled slightly as if clearing his throat. "If you can lift Perry up, I want more than anything to go outside and fly. If there are wyverns left, even the bronze one, I can protect you all."

Just then running through an archway came two much smaller dragons, wings half spread as they raced toward Chauncey. Words in dragon speak were tumbling out of them. Seeing him with humans, they skidded to a stop some distance away. The words now were obviously questions.

Robin and Kailen had already lifted Perry up and they were moving with Kate and Maggie back away from the Dragon King to give him room to get up. Now he gave a great cry, and Kate called out, "What's the matter?"

"My children, these are my children…!" and great tears rolled down Chauncey's cheeks. Kate stood watching her dragon reach out for his young ones. And the roars of delight that they all gave were deafening in the echoing cellar.

Tears coursed down Kate's cheeks once more too, and she turned to reach out for her grandmother. But Lucinda was no longer there. Maggie came over and held her as they watched father and children embracing. "Your grandmother came when you needed her most. She knows you now have a family that loves you. She couldn't stay any longer. But she'll never be far away." Kate nodded, and wiped her tears away with the back of her hand.

And so it came to be that the five who had freed the dragons made their careful way back out of the castle, Robin balancing his most precious burden yet, his friend Perry, evenly and gently propelling him forward, careful around corners and taking with grace the help Kate and his parents offered. They could hear Chen Shi and his youngsters making their way up and out by larger hallways, and from some of the crashes they heard, probably knocking down walls or through doors if the openings weren't big enough.

When they reached the great central square they saw the Dragon King perched on the tallest of the towers, an edifice that hadn't been intended to take his weight, and was shedding tiles and leaning a bit. They had the privilege of seeing him spread his great and beautiful wings for the first time in over a century and take to the air. His two young ones followed and they flew up and up, until they actually looked quite small against the moonlit sky. Then they were amazed to see more dragons flying up and out, perhaps a dozen or more.

"They must be ones Ivor made into statues or light fixtures," hazarded Kate. "He must have kept some to furnish the Hall."

"We did it," breathed Robin. "We freed them all. All of them. Think of it…all of them."

"You did it, you and Kailen. I was, ah, otherwise engaged." Kate smiled, squeezing his hand and leaning forward to kiss his cheek. She would have bear-hugged him, except that he was conveying Perry. Balanced in thin air, Perry looked like he was comfortably fast asleep in his own bed, so great was Robin's skill.

There were no signs of any wyverns. They continued out through the great portcullis gates and across the drawbridge, now with Chauncey and the other dragons flying above them. The remaining bronze wyvern took one look upward and lowered himself into a crouching ball on his pillar. He wasn't going anywhere. But Chauncey wasn't going to leave it at that—he swooped and with one snap of his great teeth he tore off the wyvern's head, spitting it out into the moat. Then he asked them and the

453

other dragons if there was anyone or anything left in the castle. On being told that no, all the dragons were out and the statues and even the rats had already left the premises, he swept back up into the sky and once he saw that they were safely into the edge of the woodland that would take them back to Maggie's house, he came powering down like a dreadnought and let loose a stream of fire that set the tallest tower of Wyvern Hall ablaze. The smaller dragons followed, each flaming and setting other fires around the towers, including the wyvern barracks. The flames suffused the night sky with light. Even as far away as they were, the Endoskeletals could feel the heat. It looked like hell on earth. It felt like heaven.

§ § §

By the time they reached Maggie's house they had found that all of them, not just Perry, had sustained a few burns. They'd gone unnoticed because of the high emotion going on. But now they all hurt and were exhausted. Maggie had prepared for injuries, hunger and exhaustion days before with lots of food and drinks and salves and bandages. They treated each other. And, although claiming they were too tired to eat, when presented with food, they ate like they were starving.

Maggie and Kate put Perry to bed in a bedroom by Maggie and Kailen's own so they could keep close watch on him. Maggie and Kailen used spells and potions and salves and Kate joined in for a bit because she also seemed blessed with the ability to heal small portions of his burned skin. Maggie kept saying it looked worse than it was, but Kate wasn't sure about that. She had no premonition that he might die but she was scared he might be an invalid or live in pain. Maggie assured her this wasn't so, but she worried nonetheless.

Kailen and Robin went off to check on the statues and found them all, even Plato, ensconced in the underground clubhouse. They were sitting around telling each other tales of their prowess and clearly enjoying themselves. Everyone congratulated Kailen and Robin, and received thanks and the promise of amazing technology to come.

Coming outside once more, they met Eleanor and Maude. "We are going to stay in the trees," Maude said. "We like perching and we like flying. We won't let anyone see us. If necessary we'll go to somewhere without people. But we want to live like birds now. Tell Kate and Maggie we love them. And thank you, and thank Kate—we heard what she and her grandmother did to Ivor. Strangler fig and a black hole. No more than he—or they—deserve."

Shortly thereafter, all the 'squishy ones' were safely tucked up in bed, and in a large oak near the cottage a spirit-eagle and two harpies kept watch over them.

Chapter 72

The freeing of all the enslaved dragons led to the collapse of Wyvern's empire. Even the firm of lawyers whose biggest client he was had gone under. Maggie was quick to tie up loose ends with the lawsuits against Ashley, all of which were abandoned for lack of funds to keep them going. This took most of November, but it was work she was extremely happy to do.

The lawsuits now were from the many people who had bought one of Wyvern's extremely expensive 'furnaces' and also from those who had bought the very expensive and unique wall lamps and the garden gates and the dragon statues that graced halls, pillar, plinths and gardens. Each and every one had seemingly crumbled to a very small pile of rust overnight. Or somehow been stolen—there were a number of broken doors and some walls with large holes in them. The owners were furious, especially those whose central heating depended upon a Wyvern Furnace. Even those with very large household insurance accounts couldn't get financial satisfaction. The circumstances in which a massive furnace could simply disappear leaving only a little rust and occasionally a large hole made the insurers wary of paying up. In any case no one had been able to insure their furnaces or statues or light fixtures for the amount they had once paid. Each was unique, and all were now gone.

§ § §

When Maggie came to Sir Hugh in the first week of December and presented him with a large flat envelope tied with red and green ribbons he was flummoxed. "What in the world is this?" he demanded.

"An early Christmas present, Sir Hugh, from me to you." Maggie was grinning and could barely contain herself from shouting *open it, open it quickly!*

In fact Hugh was already slitting it open with his Swiss army knife. Inside were a sheaf of papers bound together with one sheet loose on top. It said simply: *All lawsuits have been dropped. The Wyvern Estate is no longer making any claims against Sir Hugh Mallory, the Mallory family, or any of the Mallory holdings, including Ashley Manor. Everything is free and clear in the ownership of Sir Hugh Mallory and his family. In contrast, the Wyvern Estate is bankrupt and being dismantled.*

"Maggie, you've done it! By gods, I don't know how, but you've been a miracle worker. I can never thank you enough. The best possible Christmas present. The best I've ever had. Please let an old man hug you." Which he did. When he stepped back, Sir Hugh had the streak of a tear on his cheek. "And invite you to Ashley for Christmas, of course—would've in any case. You and Robin and, err, your partner, the exotic-looking gent. Without you there would have been no Christmas. You have to come!"

"We'd be delighted! Thank you, Sir Hugh. And now, if you don't mind, I'm taking the day off."

"Take all the time you want, dear woman,' and he was moved to take her by the shoulders and kiss her on both cheeks.

§ § §

In the gardens where there were still a few of the 'living' statues (and the very strong spell that made it look like all of them were still there), all were decorated with wreaths or garlands. Kate and Robin also carefully put some wrapped presents hidden behind them. Those that were living it up in their club house could count on being inundated with new video games, films and TV box sets, plus the latest updated equipment, crafted to be extra resilient to stone fingers. There were also stringed instruments for those who played, and heavy-duty exercise equipment and a ring where they could wrestle or box.

The ravens and crows were given plentiful food and a game to play—find the shiny Christmas things that everyone had fun hiding in the grounds. The rats were not forgotten either—lots of treats and new bedding were put out where Mrs Sykes would never find them.

Kate often saw the ghost of the white-tailed eagle. When she went out to meet it, it came and bowed its head against her hand then led her to the tree where Maude and Eleanor were roosting. They were delighted to see her and described how much fun they were having flying over Dartmoor on cloudy nights, so high that the clouds were below them and above them the starry sky. There had been one report from an airliner that it had seen a UFO. But airliners were always seeing UFOs so it was filed and forgotten.

§ § §

And the old customs of Christmas were revived at Ashley Manor. Once more the great staircase was garlanded with evergreen decorated with apples and clove-studded oranges and cinnamon sticks and fairy lights. The huge fireplace glowed with a Yule log more than the length of a man. And a great Norway spruce was set up in the main drawing room. Everyone had been invited to arrive on the 21st to make a house party, and Kate and Robin, Maggie and Kailen (in a suit specially made by Maggie to protect him from the weakening effects of iron) plus Bates, Sykes and Mrs Sykes were all helping to decorate it. Perry, who was recovering well but tired easily, was sitting in an easy chair by the fire with Poppet beside him. Sir Hugh sat in his big easy chair the other side of the fire and supervised. First the lights, then the hand-blown balls, some from all the way back in Sebastian and Elizabeth's time, then the one-of-a-kind ornaments. Kate and Robin had bought some really delightful dragons off of a Goth website which they now hung deep inside the greenery. Cora and about a dozen fairy dragons were also there, masquerading as decorations, showing off their rainbow colours like mad. Finally the ropes of gold and silver tinsel. And last of all, while Bates and Kailen held the ladder steady, Kate climbed up and put the beautiful angel robed in her greens, golds and apricot silks and velvet on the very top where she belonged. Kate had stroked her wings with a gentle finger and said very softly so only the angel could hear: *Now you're back where you belong. Look down upon us and hold us in your hand, protect us with your wings. We've come a long way to be here this day, you and I.*

§ § §

And then it was Christmas Day and all the inhabitants of Ashley gathered for the feast. Because these included Bates and Mr and Mrs Sykes, they served themselves from the sideboard, although Sir Hugh of course carved the turkey, and the goose and the ducks. And the great ribs of beef. Mrs Sykes had had the help of Maggie and Kate to make all the traditional accompaniments, plus Kate had made pumpkin pies as her American contribution.

In Kate's channel there was Chauncey. He had decided to be the new master of Wyvern Hall. Only partially burnt by the blasts of dragon fire, the Hall was mainly still habitable. Chauncey had taken over the ballroom and made his new nest—this time piled high with

459

gold and jewels and fabulous ornaments that he and the other dragons had collected from around the Hall, and made more comfortable by a number of goose down duvets. Kate and Maggie had cooked him and his children a feast, and she could see him with a huge paper hat hooked over one gold horn askew on his head. As he picked his teeth fastidiously with a long gold chopstick, she was thrilled to see that his scales, formerly an almost blue-black, were now the glorious blue green of the evening sky, with gold, orange, purple and green streaks. It was plain that he was radiant with happiness. In the background Christmas music was playing on his new stereo system. Chauncey was alternating old carols in many languages with renditions of *Rudolph* and *So This is Christmas* and *Sleigh Ride*. The smile he gave Kate was all about love.

THE END

ABOUT THE AUTHOR

Nancy Wolff always told stories — that is, she would describe things that happened to her as if it were a story full of interest and plot. But she never had the impulse to write them down. She was a good writer of school papers and theses and later as an advertising copywriter. But until several people urged her to start writing down the stories she told, it had not occurred to her. [Mainly because writing, although satisfying to do well, was definitely 'work' and not 'fun'.] Several months of memoir writing led to the fledgling idea for a novel about a young woman and a dragon... and then something magical happened. She became a channel for the story, which virtually wrote itself, and she discovered what some writers have said: that writing is the most fun you can have alone. So of course she's already started on the sequel to this, her first novel, because these characters now share her head and want to get on with their lives. She writes about magic and what is loosely called fantasy, because her life has been full of miracles, and she thrives best in that atmosphere.

Printed in Great Britain
by Amazon